THE PUR`
Aldebarian Allia

by

New York Times
Bestselling Author
DIANNE DUVALL

www.DianneDuvall.com

TITLES BY DIANNE DUVALL

ALDEBARIAN ALLIANCE

THE LASARAN
"Full of adventure, sizzling passion, romance, and yes kick-ass fighting. This book is simply captivating."
— *Book Dragon*

THE SEGONIAN
One of the Best Audiobooks of 2021
AudioFile Earphones Award for Exceptional Audio
—*Audiofile Magazine*

IMMORTAL GUARDIANS

DARKNESS DAWNS
"A strong start in what looks to be a thrilling and chilling new paranormal series. Fantastic!"
— *RT Book Reviews*

NIGHT REIGNS
"Crackles with energy, originality, and a memorable take-no-prisoners heroine."
— *Publishers Weekly*

PHANTOM SHADOWS
"Done so well that I truly want to live in her world regardless of the threat of vampires!"
— *Smexy Books*

IN STILL DARKNESS
"Readers will appreciate the rich characterizations and the kick-butt action ... as Richart d'Alençon, a 200-year-old Guardian, woos charming Jenna McBride with warmth and passion."
— *Publishers Weekly*

DARKNESS RISES
"A thrilling, action-packed, suspenseful, funny, steamy paranormal romance readers won't be able to put down."
— *Affaire de Coeur Magazine*

NIGHT UNBOUND
"Hello epic kick-ass forbidden love story! Night Unbound is simply A-M-A-Z-I-N-G!"
— *Saints and Sinners Books*

PHANTOM EMBRACE
"Duvall's hauntingly beautiful novella, set in the world of the Immortal Guardians, portrays the deep love between two people who can never touch, with a wonderfully unexpected ending."
— *Publishers Weekly*

SHADOWS STRIKE
"Full of awesome characters, snappy dialogue, exciting action, steamy sex, sneaky shudder-worthy villains and delightful humor."
— *A Voracious Reader*

BLADE OF DARKNESS
"Between the banter, the steamy scenes, and all the twists and turns, I was engrossed from start to finish."
— *Little Shop of Readers*

AWAKEN THE DARKNESS
"Heart-stopping, intense, humorous and powerfully romantic."
— *Reading Between the Wines Book Club*

DEATH OF DARKNESS
"Teeming with passion, humor, action and suspense."
— *Reading Between the Wines Book Club*

BROKEN DAWN

"I loved the chemistry and banter between these two. I swooned and laughed... I loved it all."
— *Caffeinated Reviewer*

CLIFF'S DESCENT

"Sweet, sexy, heartwarming, heartbreaking, and so dang beautiful."
— *Caffeinated Reviewer*

AN IMMORTAL GUARDIANS COMPANION

"If you are an Immortal Guardians fan, pick it up as you will smile and enjoy this fun, fast read."
— *Seeing Spots*

THE GIFTED ONES

A SORCERESS OF HIS OWN

"Full of danger, intrigue and passion... an addicting and exciting new series. I'm hooked!"
— *Reading in Pajamas*

RENDEZVOUS WITH YESTERDAY

"Medieval times, a kick-ass heroine, a protective hero, magic, and a dash of mayhem."
— *The Romance Reviews*

THE PURVELI

ALDEBARIAN ALLIANCE: BOOK 3

New York Times bestselling author Dianne Duvall brings readers the third stand-alone novel in a thrilling new sci-fi romance series full of action, humor, and happily-ever-afters.

Ava has always been different. Born with strong telepathic abilities, she lives a very isolated life until she is offered a job with an obscure network that aids powerful Immortal Guardians in their quest to protect humanity from the psychotic vampires who prey upon them. Suddenly, she doesn't feel so different. For the first time in her life, Ava has found a place where she belongs. She's happy. Life is good. And when her employers invite her to join a group of other *gifted ones* and a handful of Immortal Guardians on a journey to another planet, it becomes absolutely fantastic.

In no time at all, she is speeding across the galaxy aboard a Lasaran warship crewed by *two* amazing alien races. It's the dream of a lifetime... until a vicious attack by a mutual enemy of Lasara and Earth lands her alone in an escape pod with no habitable planet in sight and only one ship within range: one that carries the enemy who wants to know why the bioengineered virus they released on Earth long ago didn't exterminate humanity and leave the planet ripe for their claiming.

Jak'ri doesn't know how long he has been a prisoner aboard the *Cebaun*, but he fears the enemy's twisted experiments will soon lead them to a virus that will eradicate the Purveli people. Despair grips him until a female from Earth is taken captive and reaches out to him telepathically. The gift that Ava said caused her such misery in the past soon becomes his salvation as the two of them form a fast friendship. Determined to distract each other from the horrors of their existence, they immerse themselves in telepathic communion during the day, then seek solace and adventure together in shared dreams. As their friendship deepens into love, the two hatch a daring plot to escape their captors. But the enemy will not let them go without a fight.

Can Ava and Jak'ri stand against so many and emerge victorious?

PROLOGUE

A LEG SWEPT AVA'S feet out from under her a split second before a hand shoved her shoulder. Her back hit a mat that was cushy enough to keep her from getting a concussion when her head struck it but not cushy enough to keep the breath from being knocked out of her. In the next instant, a figure knelt over her, raised an arm, and drove a knife toward her chest.

Fortunately, that blade had dulled edges and halted before making contact.

Eliana grinned down at her. "Gotcha. Your attention strayed."

Ava grimaced. "Yes, it did."

When her friend held a hand out to her, Ava accepted it gratefully and laughed when Eliana yanked her up with enough force to make Ava feel as if she'd just bounced off a trampoline. "Thanks. I shouldn't have let my mind wander. Sorry about that."

Eliana gave her a friendly pat on the back. "Don't worry about it. I doubt that would've happened in a real battle." Her smile turned wry. "You tend to stay focused when someone's trying to kill you." No doubt she spoke from experience, having spent centuries battling insane vampires and—more recently—mercenaries.

"I would hope so."

"And you did well up until then."

"Really?" Ava didn't think Eliana was the type to offer empty compliments.

She smiled. "Absolutely."

"Thanks." Sheathing her practice dagger, Ava grabbed a towel off a nearby bench and wiped her damp face and neck.

Though they'd been training for the better part of an hour, Eliana hadn't even broken a sweat. "So what distracted you?" she asked curiously.

Ava motioned to the other activity that was taking place in the spacious training room. "This did."

For the thousandth time since she'd boarded the *Kandovar*, awe filled her as she glanced around. She still couldn't believe this was her new reality. Five months ago, she'd been working in North Carolina for a company that bore no name and simply referred to itself as the network. Consisting of tens of thousands of humans and *gifted ones*, the network aided powerful Immortal Guardians who spent their nights hunting and slaying psychotic vampires most of humanity didn't even know existed.

Ava hadn't known they existed either until the network had invited her to apply for a position. Born with telepathic abilities, she'd been astonished to learn that she and her mother weren't the only ones out there who were *different*.

Astonished and relieved and excited.

When she'd gone to work at the network, she'd finally met other *gifted ones* like herself, worked for powerful immortal beings who were even more different than she was, and had then been offered the opportunity of a lifetime: to be one of fifteen *gifted ones* and immortals to board the alien battleship *Kandovar* and travel to Lasara, a technologically advanced planet on the opposite side of the galaxy and homeworld of the Immortal Guardian leader's adopted daughter, Ami.

Now they were four months into a trip that would take them thirteen. Ava trained daily with an Immortal Guardian and was friend to four others. To her right, Lasarans—a very long-lived alien species with special gifts of their own and amazing regenerative capabilities—trained as vigorously as Eliana and Ava did. On Ava's left, members of the Yona species trained and looked for all the world as if they were stoically trying to kill each other.

Stoically being the operative word. Their grayish skin wasn't the only thing that clued one in that they weren't from Earth. Yona warriors never exhibited *any* emotion. At all. Ava had thought the huge males were some kind of advanced robots when she'd first encountered them.

"It's trippy, isn't it?"

Lured from her reverie, Ava glanced at Eliana. "What is?"

Her friend nodded toward the other occupants of the gym-like training room. "This. Being on an alien ship, heading for an alien planet, surrounded by not one but *two* alien species."

Ava smiled. "It really is."

"Just think how much trippier it must be for Lisa."

She laughed. "I know, right?" Lisa's history was one of the most unusual Ava had ever heard. And she had heard a *lot* of unusual stories since joining the network.

A *gifted one* like Ava, Lisa had met Lasara's Prince Taelon under terrifying and bizarre circumstances on Earth. Now the two were lifemates (the Lasaran equivalent of married), Lisa was an honest-to-goodness princess, and the two had a beautiful infant daughter who had proven that *gifted ones* and Lasarans were reproductively compatible.

Ava couldn't imagine what it must have been like to go from being a cash-strapped woman in her mid-twenties who was virtually alone in the world and painstakingly working her way through college to being a prominent member of an alien royal family to whom crew members frequently genuflected.

When Eliana's gaze strayed to the open doorway, she straightened. "Speaking of aliens, there's Ganix."

"Who's Ganix?"

"Chief Engineer of the *Kandovar*. Do you mind if we cut our training short today? I want to see if he'll help me talk a pilot into teaching me how to fly one of those sleek black fighter craft. Either that or help me talk Ari'k into sparring with me."

Ari'k was the first Yona Ava had met. He was also a member of the royal guard who protected Lisa, Prince Taelon, and their baby daughter. So Ava and her friends from Earth encountered him a lot.

"You want to spar with Ari'k?" she asked, surprised.

"Hell yes. I'm not a hundred percent convinced he can't feel emotion and I want to see if kicking his ass will spark a response and piss him off."

Ava laughed. "You're so bad."

Eliana grinned unrepentantly. "I know."

"Go ahead. I'm about ready to call it a day anyway."

"Yes! Thanks, Ava." She hurried away.

"Let me know what happens," Ava called after her.

"Will do!" Eliana disappeared through the doorway.

Shaking her head, Ava grabbed a bottle of water and headed for the quarters she and her friends from Earth had been allocated.

Lasaran crew members smiled and nodded to her, offering friendly greetings as she strode down one long corridor, then turned up another. It was nice. Evidently every Lasaran was born with strong telepathic abilities and was taught at an early age to erect mental barriers that would keep others out, so Ava wasn't besieged by their thoughts. Her mind had *never* been this quiet while she was surrounded by other people on Earth. It was wonderful. And liberating. Because for the first time in her life, it made her feel normal.

Members of the *Earthling Contingent* were given lodgings that were clustered together in one area and reminded her of efficiency apartments. Each room boasted a narrow bed, a small table and chair, a cramped bathroom they called a lav, and a kitchen that was more of a nook.

As commander of the *Kandovar*, Prince Taelon had apologized for the meager accommodations. They hadn't exactly been expecting guests. But Ava and the others didn't mind. The *Kandovar* was a warship, not a cruise ship.

Through the open door to Mia's quarters, Ava saw Mia, Natalie, and Michelle chatting as they sipped what she suspected was a very tasty tea Lasarans loved.

All three looked up as she passed.

"Hi, Ava," Natalie called with a smile.

She waved. "Hi."

"Want to join us?" Mia asked.

Ava shook her head and wrinkled her nose. "I'm all sweaty from training with Eliana and need a shower. Maybe afterward?"

"Sure."

The bathroom in her quarters was small enough to make her wonder how Taelon and the other guys on the ship managed to avoid bonking their elbows whenever they showered. The men out here in space tended to be quite tall... and broadly built since most were soldiers packed with muscle. Yet even Ava, who stood at a mere five foot three, felt cramped in the sanishower.

Once clean, she donned a comfortable pair of jeans and a long-sleeved shirt.

Lasaran culture required men and women to wear clothing that covered everything except for their heads and hands. Ava didn't have a problem with abiding by that rule. *Or* the one that forbade men and women of childbearing age from touching if they weren't lifemates. She thought it an acceptable sacrifice to make in exchange for a new home on a Utopian planet. Lasara was free from war and strife. It bore no famine. No hunger. No hate. So *no one* on Lasara would dislike, distrust, or seek to harm Ava or her friends because of their differences. No one would try to kill them or capture them to harness their abilities for their own gain, as had happened so often in the past on Earth.

On Lasara, Ava and her friends would find only peace.

No sooner had the thought struck than alarms began to blare.

She jumped, startled by the loud sound. *What the hell?*

"All crew members to battle stations," a male voice called over the ship-wide speakers. "Repeat—all crew members to battle stations. We are under attack."

Oh shit!

Ava hurried over to her door and opened it.

Her friends filled the open doorways of the other Earth quarters, their eyes wide.

The ship rocked beneath their feet as a muffled explosion carried to their ears.

Ava grabbed the doorframe and held on as more explosions followed.

A blurred form streaked toward them from farther up the corridor, then Eliana skidded to a halt in front of them.

"What's happening?" Ava blurted.

Eliana shook her head. "Grab your go bags. Quickly."

Panic flared on every face, including her own, Ava guessed as she ducked back into her room and grabbed the backpack Eliana and the other Immortal Guardians had encouraged them each to pack in case of emergency.

Eliana was waiting impatiently in the hallway when Ava returned. "The ship is under attack," she announced, face grim.

Attack? Attack from whom?

"I'm going to get you all to the escape pods as a precaution."

Oh crap.

Without further warning, Eliana bent, folded Ava and Natalie over her shoulders, and—unhindered by their weight or that of their packs—raced away with preternatural speed.

Ava's head spun as the world around her tipped upside down and zipped past in a dizzying blur. She grunted when Eliana stopped abruptly.

"Get inside," she ordered as she set them on their feet. Then she darted away again.

Disoriented, Ava glanced around, noted the bank of escape pods, then shared a petrified look with Natalie.

Each headed for a different entrance and climbed inside.

Ava barely had time to set her bag down before Eliana returned in a blur with Mia and Michelle slung over her shoulders.

Another Immortal Guardian shot past, then zipped back toward them.

Simone appeared. The French immortal swept Ava and the others with a quick glance and turned to Eliana. "Where are the rest of the *gifted ones?*"

Though Taelon and his sister Ami had assured Seth—the powerful Immortal Guardian leader—that the ten *gifted ones* from Earth would be welcomed on Lasara, Seth had nevertheless tasked five Immortal Guardians with watching over them and protecting them.

"Their quarters," Eliana said. "I'll go get them. Help these get settled in the pods." She left so quickly she appeared to vanish into thin air.

Simone helped Ava secure her bag and strap herself into the single seat the pod provided.

Out in the hallway, Eliana returned with Sam and Emily, then left again.

"All set?" Simone asked.

Ava nodded, incapable of speech. She was too scared.

Simone patted her shoulder, then left to help the others.

Ava's heart pounded in her chest as the alarm continued to blare and one explosion after another rocked the ship.

"Shield integrity compromised," the ship's computer announced in a pleasant female voice. "Shields at seventy-nine percent."

The scent of smoke carried to Ava's nose.

This couldn't be happening. How the hell could this be happening? They were traveling through a freaking wormhole or *qhov'rum* or whatever they called it! How could someone possibly be attacking them?

Dani, one of the other Immortal Guardians, arrived with Allison and Charlie over her shoulders. Rachel followed with Liz and Madeline.

Michaela—the fifth immortal—skidded to a halt beside them, conducted a quick headcount, then zipped away again.

More booms rocked the ship as Dani, Rachel, and Simone secured everyone else in pods. The hatches began to close.

"I'm going to help Eliana and Michaela evacuate the Lasarans," Simone said.

Rachel nodded. "We will, too."

"Be safe!" Dani called before they sped away.

The pod hatch sealed with a thunk.

More booms shook the ship.

"Shields at fifty-four percent," the computer reported placidly.

Ava clutched the armrests in a white-knuckled grip.

This can't be happening. This can't be happening.

"Shields at thirty-two percent."

Boom. Boom. Boom.

This was an advanced alien warship! It *couldn't* be destroyed! Could it?

"Shields at twenty percent."

Her breath shortened to panicked gasps.

Boom. Boom. Boom. Boom.

"Shields at thirteen percent."

A rumbling sound abruptly arose. Sudden pressure shoved Ava back against her seat as light flickered on and off behind the escape pod's impenetrable crystal window.

Oh shit. They were launching the pods!

A heartbeat later, black space filled the window.

A small gray craft shot past, followed closely by a sleek black fighter.

Light flashed as the black craft fired its weapons.

Two more craft shot past.

Then the bright walls of the *qhov'rum* filled the window, blocking out everything else.

Ava's eyes widened as the pod flew toward it.

Light exploded around her. A screeching, grinding noise filled the pod, so loud it was almost deafening.

Crying out, she covered her ears.

Then quiet fell, broken only by her rapid breathing and the pounding of her pulse in her ears.

Eyes wide, Ava stared through the window at calm black space.

"Evie?" she said, voice hushed. Wasn't that what she'd heard the Lasarans call the computer on the *Kandovar*? They'd mentioned something about naming it after the engineer who had installed it... or maybe designed it... but she couldn't remember if it was the engineer's name or the initials E.V.

"Yes?" the same female voice from the ship's computer responded.

"What just happened?"

"The escape pod breached the walls of the *qhov'rum*."

That's what she'd thought. "What about the other escape pods?"

"Unknown. I detect none within range."

"And the fighter craft?" She'd glimpsed a *lot* of fighter craft engaged in a very surrealistic, *Star Wars*–like battle as the pod had flown toward the *qhov'rum*'s walls. If any of the bad guys had followed her—

"No Lasaran or Gathendien fighter craft are within range."

Her eyes widened. "The gray ones were Gathendien?"

"Affirmative."

Those assholes! "What about the ship? Where's the *Kandovar*?" She wasn't seeing it through the window, and that ship was so gargantuan it was impossible to miss.

"Unknown."

Her fear multiplied. "What do you mean, unknown?"

"The *Kandovar* is not registering on my scans, nor is it responding to my attempts to hail it."

"What does that mean?"

"I am currently unable to locate it."

"You can't locate the ship?" she blurted as panic rose.

"Affirmative."

"Do you know why?"

"Not with certainty."

"Well, can you make a guess?"

"Affirmative. I am capable of fabricating multiple explanations, but will not be able to estimate the accuracy of each without further—"

"Just give me your best guess," Ava snapped, nerves on edge. She needed to know where she was, what was happening.

"Based upon the rapid depletion of the *Kandovar*'s shields, the reduced maneuverability within the *qhov'rum,* the extent of the battle the escape pod passed through, and the large burst of energy I detected just before we lost contact, I believe it likely that the *Kandovar* has been destroyed."

All breath left Ava in a rush. "The whole ship?"

"Affirmative."

All those people...

Had her friends' pods launched the same time hers did? Had the Immortal Guardians even *made it* to pods of their own? They had been helping the Lasarans the last time she'd seen them.

And what of the Lasarans? The Yona?

Tears welled in her eyes. "What's your second-best guess?" The one that *didn't* include the destruction of the *Kandovar.*

"We may be unable to hail the *Kandovar* because the pod is too far beyond its reach."

"How is that possible? We just left it."

"The *qhov'rum* propels craft forward at speeds that even the fastest engines cannot replicate. If the *qhov'rum* remained functional after the pod breached its walls, it has already carried the ship and other craft within it a distance that it would take this pod with its weaker engine many months to traverse."

Ava stared through the window at the vast expanse of space.

When Prince Taelon had given them a tour of the escape pods, he'd told them that each one could sustain life for two months.

Not *many* months. *Two* months.

"Are there any Lasaran or Yona outposts near us?"

"Negative."

"Are any members of the Aldebarian Alliance near us?"

"Negative."

"Are there any habitable planets close enough for us to reach within two months?"

"Negative."

Ava swallowed.

What the hell was she going to do?

CHAPTER ONE

*A*VA SMILED AS THE *wind whipped her hair. She, Eliana, Natalie, Simone, and Michaela had all piled into her sleek black seventies muscle car and now jammed to some oldies as they all but flew down a straight two-lane country road.*

Van Morrison's "Brown Eyed Girl" blasted from the speakers as they all sang along. Ava and Natalie were the only mortals present. The other three were powerful Immortal Guardians. All five bore brown eyes, dark hair that ranged from chestnut to black, and wide smiles.

Since no curves or turns lay ahead, Ava floored the accelerator. She loved this car. Her dad had spent many weekends lovingly restoring it and souping it up while Ava helped him and the two of them bobbed their heads to oldies like the one she listened to now. She'd been so thrilled when he and her mom had given it to her as a high school graduation present. Still in excellent shape, the engine didn't rumble. It purred. The updated stereo system rocked. She even adored the sleek black paint and the heavy-as-hell frame that would pulverize one of today's cars or SUVs and keep her safe in an accident, not that she intended to have one.

Pretty fields and verdant forests raced past on either side of the road. A cheerful sun shone down on them. And instead of the cloying heat of summer, a cool breeze bathed them.

Usually, country drives carried her over bumpy, crappily patched cement or tarmac. This road, however, looked as though it had only recently been paved. Concrete so pale a gray it was almost white possessed nary a pothole or crack, perhaps because so little traffic navigated it. They hadn't seen a single car since they'd begun their drive.

Ava glanced over at Eliana, who kicked back in the passenger seat. Her friend winked as she belted out the lyrics.

Ava grinned. Of all the Immortal Guardians she'd befriended, Eliana was her favorite. Somewhere in the neighborhood of four hundred years old, Eliana was five feet tall to Ava's five-three and had long black hair that whipped around her face in the wind that gusted through the open windows. She was also bold, fun-loving, and could totally kick ass.

Ava, on the other hand, had always been rather shy. Her life, thus far, had been very isolated. Like her mother, she'd been born with telepathic abilities that were difficult to control. The thoughts of others had bombarded her without ceasing. And she hadn't gained control over it until her teen years. So her parents had bought a house in the country with no nearby neighbors and had homeschooled her until she was old enough to understand the danger of responding to other children's thoughts as though they had spoken them. Even taking her to the playground had resulted in unpleasant incidents, so they'd kept her home and done their best to fill the gap of friendship themselves.

Some kids might have resented it, she supposed. To this day, her parents still questioned the actions they'd taken that had deprived her of a "normal" childhood. But Ava loved them for it. Yes, she'd been lonely at times. She'd seen children in movies and on television shows playing together and wished she had friends her age. But in the rare instances in which her mom or dad had taken her out in public, she'd heard the ugliness in the thoughts of the men and women—and even the children—they encountered and had understood.

Even so, she had begged her parents to let her attend high school, where she could meet girls and boys her age.

She hadn't even lasted a year before she'd resumed the homeschooling. Movies and television shows often portrayed some of the vile things girls said and did to each other, how mean they were to new kids and eager to torment and ostracize. But that was nothing compared to their thoughts and the things they wanted to say and do but didn't.

A few of the boys had been friendly. She'd even developed a huge crush on one. But hearing his lustful thoughts for another girl had squashed that.

So Ava hadn't really socialized much in her life until the network that aided Immortal Guardians had offered her a job. The purpose of the network was to help the powerful immortals in every way they possibly could to keep the vampire menace in check. The network also protected other gifted ones *like Ava who had inexplicably been born with advanced DNA that granted them special abilities, intervening when those abilities came to light. She guessed about three-fourths of the employees were human. The rest were other* gifted ones, *so she had finally found a place she fit in.*

She'd made friends. She'd dated. She'd even had a lover or two.

But she envied Eliana her bold, daring spirit. Eliana could befriend anyone. *She overflowed with energy and was always looking for a new adventure. And she really could kick ass. She was a fearsome warrior who had no difficulty holding her own with her male immortal counterparts.*

Needless to say, Ava had been thrilled when Eliana had cheerfully offered to teach her self-defense.

As Ava refocused on the road, a cloud passed overhead, dimming the sun's brilliant rays.

In the blink of an eye, the car, the road, and her companions vanished, replaced by forest, and Ava found herself walking along a dirt path that had been carved out of the abundant foliage by animals. Or maybe dirt bikes. It might even be wide enough for one of those ATV things to navigate. But as she trudged forward, the plants that bordered it grew denser and soon began to encroach upon it.

Frowning, she paused and looked around. "Eliana?" she called. "Natalie?"

No answer came.

Where had everyone gone? How had they gotten separated?

The forest around her grew darker.

Was the sun setting? If so, they would have to hurry if they wanted to reach...

Her frown deepened. Wait. Where had they been going?

Unease rising, Ava resumed walking and picked up her pace. The dirt path narrowed further, the smooth, packed surface becoming pitted and ridged and riddled with rocks that made the going more difficult, forcing her to slow down. The last thing she wanted to do was twist her ankle.

Branches and huge fronds from plants she thought might be tropical but couldn't identify began to reach across the path, slapping her face and arms. But Ava batted them aside and pushed onward, ignoring the sting of cuts they inflicted. The terrain grew rockier, the slope upward sharper. And soon the walk turned into a climb.

Ava's breath shortened as she scrambled up the mountainside, gripping rocks and boulders to aid her progress. Huffing, she carefully planted her feet on two boulders while she leaned against a third. "Eliana!" she shouted.

Only echoes of her own voice replied.

"Simone! Michaela!"

More echoes.

"Eliaaanaaaaaa!" she bellowed as loudly as she could. Immortal Guardians' senses were so sharp that they could hear someone speaking in a normal voice from five miles away. If the three immortals were nearby, they would hear her.

But none responded. Nor did the foliage begin to swish or sway the way it would if the immortal women raced toward her.

Her fear growing, Ava resumed her climb. The muscles in her arms and thighs began to ache. Walking several miles a day on a treadmill had not prepared her for scaling a damn mountain. The ground now rose so sharply that she had to grab the trunks of fledgling trees to help pull herself up.

Breath coming in harsh pants, she reached for another of the bamboo-like saplings. If she could just make it to the top of whatever this was, maybe she could get her bearings and figure out where she was.

As soon as she pulled on it, the sapling jerked out of the soil. Clods of dirt and small rocks peppered Ava as she swayed backward. One foot slipped, then the other. Shrieking, she held on to the other branch for dear life. Both feet scrambled for purchase, thwarted by the cascade of loose dirt and rocks she'd inadvertently liberated.

"Shit!" Absolute terror gripped her as she glanced down.

The slope beneath her looked even steeper now.

Kill-you-if-you-fall steeper.

Her sneaker-clad toe landed on a bare patch of rock and stayed. Whispering a quick prayer, she carefully inched her foot forward until the whole shoe was on solid rock. She slid her other foot over and had to dust some loose earth off before she found purchase. As soon as both seemed stable, she carefully shifted until most of her weight was braced on her feet and plastered herself against the boulder in front of her.

Her whole body trembled. Her breath came in gasps. "Elianaaaaaa!" she shouted again as tears threatened.

Where were they?

The foliage above her rustled.

A large hand clamped around her wrist.

Ava started so violently she nearly tumbled from her perch again. Her head shot up.

Silver eyes glinted in a handsome face surrounded by long black hair.

"Please," she implored. "Help me."

Something flickered in those eyes before they glanced at the branch she clutched. "Release the branch."

She let go of the branch and latched onto his wrist with both hands.

As though she weighed little more than a child, he pulled her upward. The muscles in his arm bunched. Ava tried to gain a foothold wherever she could to aid him as more of those damn green fronds brushed her face and blocked her view of him. For a long moment, they were all she could see, but there was no way in hell she was going to let go of him with one hand long enough to brush them aside.

The rock beneath her feet sloped upward into grass and gnarled tree roots before flattening out enough for her to stand.

Ava's savior turned away and walked ahead of her without protesting her tight grip on him. Then the foliage parted, and they stepped out onto a meadow the size of a three-car driveway.

The male turned to face her.

Ava didn't think. She just acted. Releasing his arm, she surged forward, threw her arms around his waist, and hugged the stuffing out of him. "Thank you," she said shakily. "Thank you so much."

After a moment's pause, strong arms encircled her and cradled her close. One big hand gently stroked her hair as she waited for the tremors that racked her to subside.

For a minute there, she'd thought she was going to die.

As her fear faded, she began to register a few details about the man who held her.

He was tall. His chin hovered somewhere above her head, so he must be well over six feet. The arms wrapped around her were thick with muscle. The chest to which she'd plastered the side of her face was, too.

It was also bare.

Some of her annoying shyness returned. A warm flush crept up her neck to her cheeks as she released him and backed away a step. Then another. And got her first good look at him.

Her eyes widened.

Wow. He was freaking gorgeous. And nearly naked. And...

She stared.

Not human.

His skin bore a silvery tone with a barely discernable pattern that resembled... scales?

Yes. Though they were so faint she had to squint to see them, they definitely looked like scales. But his skin felt soft. It also held a subtle sheen that formed little rainbow streaks when the setting sun stuck it in a certain way, sort of like oil on water did, even though he was dry to the touch.

Her heartbeat picked up. He was incredibly fit with thick biceps, powerful pecs, rippling abs, and muscled thighs, all of which were exposed because the only garment he wore was a pair of shorts that resembled tight swim trunks.

At least, she hoped they were swim trunks. Otherwise she'd caught him in his underwear.

Long black hair brushed his shoulders and fell down his back, shifting with the breeze.

Her tongue tied, Ava took another step backward.

He reached a hand toward her. "Careful."

When he nodded to his right, she followed his gaze and gasped.

The lovely meadow they stood upon ended in a cliff only three or four yards away, one that hung high above an ocean.

Swearing, she hastily moved closer to him and the forest.

She was not *a fan of heights.*

He studied her curiously. "You are Lasaran?" She liked his voice. It emerged in a smooth, deep rumble that made her want to hear it again.

Then his question registered.

Lasaran?

She blinked. Oh. Right. They'd been heading to Lasara. "No. I'm an Earthling." It felt so weird to say that, but both the Lasarans and the Yona she'd met had thought it odd that her people didn't name themselves after their planet.

Was this man a Yona warrior? The Yonas' skin was a much more prominent gray. And it lacked the faint scales. So... maybe not.

His frown deepened. "I don't understand."

"I'm from Earth." *Earth was so far away from members of the Aldebarian Alliance that its sector of space had gone unexplored by anyone other than the damn Gathendiens, who seemed intent on eradicating every race other than themselves and taking over their planets.*

He shook his head. "I can't understand your words."

"Oh." *He definitely wasn't a Yona then. If the difference in his skin left any doubt, the frown he wore didn't. Yona never showed emotion. Ever. But perhaps this man was biracial and only half Yona?*

"Do you speak Purveli?" *he asked.*

She shook her head. She'd never heard of Purvelis. But the Lasarans must have dealings with them, otherwise the translator chip they'd implanted in Ava's head wouldn't enable her to understand him.

Too bad it didn't render her capable of speaking his language, too. Unfortunately, that required a more advanced translator chip, and— after a longer than expected sojourn in space—the Lasarans had lacked any spares.

"Alliance Common?" *he queried. Apparently, her rescuer either didn't have a translator chip or his hadn't been updated to include Earth languages the way the Lasarans' and Yonas' had.*

"Yes," *she said with some relief.* "A little bit." *Technology on Earth was so glitchy that she'd been unwilling to rely completely on the translator chip and had been studying Alliance Common just in case the chip ever failed her.* "Thank you for helping me."

His expression lightening, he offered her a little half bow. "I was happy to do so. You are Lasaran? Is your translator chip malfunctioning?"

So they did malfunction! "No. I'm not Lasaran. I'm from a planet called Earth."

He tilted his head to one side. "Earth?"

"Yes. It's..." *Silently, she cursed her weak grasp of the language. How was she supposed to tell him Earth was on the other side of the galaxy without knowing the word for galaxy?* "It's far, far away," *was the best she could come up with.* "Far away. My friends and I were traveling to Lasara with Prince Taelon and..." *Biting her lip, she looked at the* forest. "I don't know what happened. We got separated and..." She shrugged helplessly. "I don't know. I don't even know where I am or how I came to be here."

His handsome features softened. "You are on Purvel."

She motioned to the beautiful blue ocean. "That's what this planet is called?"

He nodded with a smile. "Yes. And I am Purveli." He extended his arm. "I'm Jak'ri."

Smiling, she clasped his hand and shook it. "I'm Ava. It's nice to meet you, Jak'ri."

He glanced at their hands in surprise.

"Oh." She blushed again. "I'm sorry. I forgot. Members of the Aldebarian Alliance don't shake hands." Releasing him, she clasped his forearm, which was thick enough that her thumb and fingers only stretched halfway around it. "Nice to meet you."

His strong fingers curled around her wrist, so long that they overlapped. "It's good to meet you, Ava." Withdrawing his touch, he gave her a friendly smile. "I must correct you, though. Purvelis are not members of the Aldebarian Alliance."

Unease trickled through her. "You aren't?"

The only nonmembers of the alliance she'd heard mentioned on Prince Taelon's ship were the Akseli and the Gathendiens. The Akseli were a warlike race that seemed to behave like mercenaries, selling out to whoever paid them the most. And the Gathendiens were a ruthless species that used biological warfare to wipe out sentient, humanoid races and claim their planets. They had even tried that crap on Earth by manufacturing the vampiric virus. But they hadn't counted on the virus mutating in gifted ones and turning them into immortals instead of transforming them into psychotic killers the way it did humans.

If Purvel wasn't part of the alliance...

He raised both hands in what must be a universal gesture of peace or a take-it-easy sign. "Be at ease. I wish you no harm. Though we are not part of the alliance, Purvel is not hostile toward any of its members."

"Oh. Then why aren't you part of it?" she asked, doubts lingering.

Lowering his hands, he sent her a wry smile. "We are a solitary people and prefer to keep to ourselves."

Her smile matched his. "I can understand that. I am, too."

"Solitary?" he asked curiously.

"Yes." She had to be. It was the only way she could relax her guard without being bombarded by other people's thoughts.

Ava stilled... and barely kept her eyes from widening once more as she stared up at him.

She couldn't read Jak'ri's thoughts. His mind was blessedly quiet to her.

"If you'd like," he said, "I will help you find your friends. But you should rest a moment first. The climb up here is a strenuous one."

Exhaustion was creeping up on her. "Thank you." She sat cross-legged on the ground.

Jak'ri lowered himself beside her and sat, legs bent, with his arms looped casually around his knees. "I should have known you weren't Lasaran. Lasaran women do not bare their arms."

She glanced down. Soft jeans encased her legs. A colorful shirt—now streaked with dirt—hugged her small breasts and narrow waist, the short sleeves covering only a few inches of her upper arms. Ava grinned. "True." Then she winked, though she had no idea where that little snippet of boldness came from. "Maybe I am Lasaran and just like breaking the rules."

He laughed. "You would be the first then."

"I believe you," she said with a laugh of her own. Lasarans were very big on following rules.

A cool breeze wafted over them, dragging their hair back from their faces. "The view here is beautiful," she murmured.

His smile softened. "Yes. I come up here sometimes to forget my worries."

She arched a brow. "Forget your worries in as little clothing as possible?"

He laughed. "I always end my meditations with a long swim." He waved toward the ocean. "I like to dive off the cliff."

Her eyebrows flew up. "That cliff?"

He nodded.

She shook her head. "I love to swim, but no way would I dive off anything this high. Isn't it dangerous?"

He shrugged. "We are a hardy race. A dive from this distance doesn't hurt us."

Cool. Even if she were equally hardy, however, she doubted she would have the courage to make such a jump.

Another breeze caressed them.

"This is nice," she murmured as peace settled upon her, banishing her worries for a moment.

Again he smiled. "I agree."

Ava felt a little flutter in her belly as she met his gaze. It was a friendly smile, one that bore no hint of flirtation or leering. But it was so charming and appealing that she found it impossible to remain unaffected.

Though her heartbeat picked up, her breathing had returned to normal. "I guess we should start looking for my friends."

"As you wish." Rising, he extended a hand to her.

Ava accepted it and let him pull her to her feet.

As soon as she stood, he released her.

She looked toward the forest. Nerves immediately tightened her stomach into knots as she contemplated descending the steep mountainside. The climb up had terrified her. "Is there another way down we could try?" she asked. "One that isn't so harrowing?" She was pretty sure that last word wouldn't translate correctly but didn't want to say scary.

When he didn't respond, she glanced over at him.

But he was no longer there.

"Jak'ri?" She glanced behind her, then spun in a quick circle.

Panic suffused her when she discovered she was alone.

"Jak'ri?" she called.

What had happened? Where had he gone? How had he gone? She hadn't heard any footsteps.

Her eyes went to the ocean.

Her stomach sank.

Had he jumped off the cliff? She hadn't even heard him move. Hadn't heard the grass rustle beneath his feet or the splash of someone hitting the water. But where the hell else could he have gone?

She crept over to the edge and peered over it. The ocean had to be at least sixty or seventy feet below her. The waters were calm, no rocks disturbing it.

She waited a long moment. "Jak'ri?" she called again, waiting for his head to appear, for him to surface, grin up at her, and wave.

"Warning," a woman said calmly. *"Proximity alert."*

Confused, Ava looked around but saw no one. *"What?"*

"Warning. Proximity alert," the woman repeated, her voice very similar to that of the computer on the Kandovar. *"Warning. Proximity alert."*

An alarm sounded, filling the air around Ava as the soil beneath her feet shifted abruptly. A huge chunk of the cliff jerked, then slid toward the ocean, taking her with it.

Ava jerked awake with a cry.

A red light flashed on and off above her as the alarm she'd heard in her dream continued to blare. Wincing, she sat up and glanced around the escape pod that had been her home for the past two weeks.

"Warning. Proximity alert."

Right. "Alarm off," she said loudly.

The alarm ceased.

"What's happening, Evie?" Ava asked as she tapped the button that would turn her makeshift bed back into a captain's chair of sorts.

"A ship has triggered the escape pod's proximity alert," the computer responded.

Her heart leapt. "A ship?" The alarm had blared with at least half a dozen proximity alerts in the past week. But asteroids had caused all of the others.

"Affirmative."

"What ship? Is it the *Kandovar*?"

Please, let it be the Kandovar, she urged silently. She had been unable to achieve communication with them, so she had no idea what had happened after the Lasaran ship had launched her escape pod for parts unknown. Had they defeated the Gathendiens? Were they okay? Were her friends okay? Had Eliana and the other immortals made it to their own escape pods during the mass exodus? Because the last time Ava had seen them, they'd been racing off to help the Lasaran crew.

"Negative."

"Is it another escape pod?"

"Negative. The ship is far too large to be an escape pod."

"Do you know whose ship it is?"

"Negative."

"Can you tell me if they're friend or foe?"

"Please repeat inquiry."

Right. Sometimes the computer didn't understand Ava's questions unless they were very literal. "Can you tell me if those piloting the ship are friendly or hostile?"

"Negative."

"Can you *guess* if they are likely to be friendly or hostile?"

"This will require speculation based on an analysis of the ship itself rather than of the beings within it, so my response may be inaccurate."

"That's fine. Just do whatever you have to do to make a good guess."

"Analyzing ship specs. Analysis complete. The ship is Gathendien in origin."

"Oh crap." Ava's heart sank.

"Though I am unable to confirm the identities of those within it," the computer continued in her tranquil voice that did nothing to dampen Ava's rising fear, "there is a high probability that they are Gathendien. There is a significantly lower probability that the ship has been seized by pirates."

There were space pirates? Seriously?

"Either way," Evie concluded, "the fact that they shielded their presence until they were so close and have not yet hailed us indicates they have hostile intentions."

"How close are they?" Ava blurted with alarm.

"Close enough to seize the pod."

"What?" she bleated. "They can do that?"

"Affirmative. One of their docking bay doors is rising, so that does appear to be their intention."

"Well, can't we do something to prevent it?"

"Any attempt to elude them will likely fail. But if you order it, I will attempt to evade capture."

"Yes! Yes! Do that! Get us the hell out of here!"

An invisible force abruptly threw her back against the chair.

"Fleeing proximity," Evie announced. "Please fasten your harness to avoid injury."

Ava was already fumbling with the straps and snapping them into place.

"Gathendien ship is in pursuit."

Ava grunted as she was tossed to the left as if the pod had made a sharp turn. Thank goodness these pods could pilot themselves. She would've died from a collision with asteroids days ago otherwise. Another swerve jerked Ava to the right. "What's happening?" All she could see through the windshield was black space.

"I am attempting to avoid the Gathendien ship's acquisition beam while heading for Asteroid Belt 116749."

"Excellent!" Surely it would be easier for a small escape pod to zip through asteroids than it would be for a hulking warship. "Let's lose them in the asteroids!"

"Unlikely," Evie said calmly as the pod swerved again. "Asteroid Belt 116749 is far enough away that we will probably be —"

"Just try, damn it!" Ava gritted.

"Affirmative," the computer replied, unruffled.

The harness dug into Ava's shoulders as she was jerked from side to side. She thought about asking Evie to turn off the artificial gravity but honestly didn't know if that would make things better or worse.

"Asteroid Belt 116749 is now in sight."

"Yes!" Ava cried triumphantly. "We can do this!"

"Unlikely," the ever-unflappable Evie replied. "Though the pod can change direction faster than the Gathendien ship and I have eluded its acquisition beam, the ship is still pursuing us and —"

"Evie," Ava gritted, "you're killing me."

"Negative. Killing you is counter to my programming."

"I don't mean literally!" She grunted as the pod changed directions again. Thank goodness motion sickness never plagued her. "I'm trying to be optimistic!"

"Optimism at this juncture is inadvisable."

"Oh, for crap's sake!"

That must not have computed because Evie ignored it. "Approaching asteroid belt."

"Yes!"

"Plotting a course through asteroid field."

"Thank you."

"Warning. Proximity alert."

"Shit!"

Ava suddenly flew forward in her seat as if the pod had jerked to a halt. All breath left her lungs as she slammed into the harness with enough force that she was surprised it didn't crack her ribs.

Yeah. That was definitely going to leave bruises.

"Warning. Acquisition beam is acquiring pod," Evie said, her voice slowing and deepening as if she were running out of juice.

Every light in the pod abruptly shut off, leaving Ava in complete darkness. The faint hum of the AC or atmospheric generator or whatever provided her with air ceased, leaving behind eerie silence broken only by the pounding of her heart.

Ava's body went weightless. Her long hair floated up around her face as the artificial gravity shut off.

Oh crap. The Gathendiens had caught her.

CHAPTER TWO

*J*AK'RI LOWERED HIMSELF BESIDE *the female on the soft grass. Legs bent, he looped his arms around his knees and studied her surreptitiously from the corner of his eyes.*

He had never met an Earthling before. He'd never even heard of her planet. But the difficulty she had speaking Alliance Common indicated she was—as she had told him—from far, far away.

How had she come to be on Purvel? She said she'd been traveling with Prince Taelon. But he had heard nothing of an impending visit from the Lasaran prince. In fact, the last he'd heard, Prince Taelon was missing and presumed dead. "I should have known you weren't Lasaran," he commented. "Lasaran women do not bare their arms." Hers were slender and delicate with small, faint brown speckles sprinkled across them that intrigued him.

She glanced down. Trousers made from a faded blue fabric encased slender legs and nicely rounded hips. A colorful shirt streaked with dirt and torn in a couple of places hugged breasts that were larger than a Purveli female's and a narrow waist.

She grinned, revealing straight white teeth. "True."

He liked hle. It brightened a pretty face that bore more faint brown sprinkles on her nose and cheeks and almost as many smudges as her shirt, attesting to the arduous climb that had brought her to him.

Then she winked. "Maybe I am *Lasaran and just like breaking the rules."*

He laughed. "You would be the first then." Lasarans had very stringent social rules, one of which required both men and women to wear clothing that covered everything except for their heads and hands.

"I believe you," she said with a laugh of her own.

Lasarans also forbade physical contact of any kind between unmarried men and women of childbearing age. So even as distraught as she had been when he'd found her, hugging him would never have occurred to her.

Jak'ri was glad she wasn't Lasaran. Her presence and her embrace had been a wonderful surprise. He'd liked how small she felt against him and the protective instincts she'd inspired as he'd stroked brown hair that was as soft as murwi *fur.*

A cool breeze wafted over them, dragging the hair back from Ava's face. "The view here is beautiful," she murmured, a wistful smile transforming her from pretty to absolutely beautiful.

Peace and contentment seeped in, replacing the tension that had driven him to seek out his favorite meditation spot. "Yes. I come up here sometimes to forget my worries." Worries that—in this instance— revolved around the heated political debate that continued to rage across the planet over whether or not Purvel should enter the Aldebarian Alliance.

She arched a brow as she cast a glance over him. "Forget your worries in as little clothing as possible?"

He laughed. "I always end my meditations with a long swim." He nodded toward the ocean. "I like to dive off the cliff."

Her eyebrows flew up. "That cliff*?"*

He nodded.

She shook her head. "I love to swim, but I would never dive off anything this high. Isn't it dangerous?"

He shrugged. "We are a hardy race. A dive from this distance doesn't hurt us."

She looked doubtful. Perhaps—despite the similarities in appearance —her race was more fragile than the Lasarans.

She had certainly felt *fragile when he'd held her. The females of his species—even those who didn't match the males in height—were all hardy. Years of long hours spent swimming lent them broad shoulders and muscled arms and chests.*

Another breeze caressed them.

"This is nice," she murmured, some of the tension in her expression easing.

He smiled. "I agree."

She held his gaze for a long moment, then looked away and cleared her throat. "I guess we should start looking for my friends."

While he would prefer to spend more time with her and learn more about her, he could understand her concern for her friends. Her inability to remember how she had come to be on Purvel disturbed him. Had she been in an accident of some kind and suffered a head injury? He hadn't felt any lumps when he'd stroked her hair. And his hand hadn't come away wet with blood. But he should coax her into seeing a healer after they located her friends to ensure she was well.

"As you wish." Rising, Jak'ri extended a hand to her.

As soon as she took it, he gently pulled her to her feet. Uncertain of her people's customs, he released her as soon as she stood.

Ava looked toward the forest.

Wee-wonk! Wee-wonk!

Jak'ri jerked awake as a ship-wide alert blared through the lab.

Agony inundated him, dragging forth a moan.

Wee-wonk! Wee-wonk!

What the *drek*?

Groggy from whatever serum the Gathendien scientists had injected him with, he glanced around with bleary eyes.

Everything was out of focus. His stomach churned. His head pounded.

What had they done to him this time?

The shackles that bound him to the cold metal table clanked as they opened.

"Return him to his cell," a male voice growled.

Rough hands gripped him and yanked him off the table.

As soon as Jak'ri's feet hit the floor, his knees buckled. Had the guards not gripped his arms in crushing holds, he would've collapsed in a heap.

Jak'ri?

He sucked in a breath as a voice sounded in his head. It was that of the woman he'd been dreaming about. The woman from

—

The guards cursed him in Gathendien and dragged him forward.

Jak'ri cursed them back in their own language, earning himself a cuff across the side of his head.

Earth! She'd said she was from Earth.

He swore, wishing the alert hadn't woken him. He hadn't had a moment's peace since the Gathendiens had captured him and Ziv'ri.

Jak'ri?

He stiffened. Forcing strength into his limbs, he gained his feet and looked around swiftly.

He'd heard it again. The Earthling's voice. *Ava's* voice. Was he hallucinating?

Some of the potions these *grunarks* had dosed him with in the past had made him see things that weren't there. He'd even thought his brother a monster with knife-like teeth once and nearly attacked him.

Blinking furiously, he tried to clear his vision and glanced over his shoulder.

Saekro and Kunya, the Gathendien scientists who routinely tortured him, trotted out of the lab.

Two guards "escorted" Jak'ri to his cell. Two more stood sentinel at the lab's entrance.

He faced forward. The only other person present was Ziv'ri. And his brother had been unconscious for two days now. Or more. Jak'ri was never certain how long he'd been unconscious when he awoke.

After opening the door to his cell, the guards shoved him inside.

His legs unable to support him fully, Jak'ri stumbled and fell, scraping his hands and knees on the rough floor.

Swearing, he sank down on his ass and sent the guards an obscene gesture as he watched them leave.

Jak'ri?

He swallowed when Ava's voice echoed inside his head again. His heart beat sluggishly inside his scarred chest. Was she real?

No one had spoken to him telepathically since...

He shook his head. He didn't know how long he and his brother had been held here. But the Gathendiens dosed them with *nahalae* to block their ability to communicate with each other mentally.

Was it beginning to wear off? Or could he possibly be developing a tolerance for it?

Ava? he thought, then held his breath.

Minutes passed.

Ava? he thought louder. But no answer came.

Perhaps he *had* imagined it.

Perhaps he had imagined *her*.

Sadness filled him as he mustered what strength he could and crawled over to the bars that separated him from his brother. "Ziv'ri," he whispered. The bars were far enough apart for him to reach his arm through yet close enough to keep the rest of him in his cell despite the weight he'd lost while at the Gathendiens' mercy. The bars could also be electrified, something the guards delighted in doing when the doctors weren't around to complain about it possibly interfering with their *experiments*.

But the guards seemed distracted today and paid him little heed. Leaving the door open, the *grunarks* clustered together in the hallway outside the lab and murmured over whatever carried to them via their ear comms. So Jak'ri risked it.

Reaching through the bars until his side and face were wedged against them, he managed to snag his brother's wrist and pulled. Pain shot up his arm and across his chest as he dragged Ziv'ri closer until he lay only a hand's span away.

The younger male didn't rouse or make a sound.

"Ziv'ri?" Jak'ri uttered softly. Brushing his brother's long hair back from his face, he pressed a palm to his forehead. Ziv'ri's skin was moist. An alarming heat rose from it, fever induced by whatever new bioengineered virus the Gathendiens tested. "Brother?" he called.

Not even the flicker of an eyelid.

Ziv'ri? he thought.

Still nothing.

Despair filled him.

How much longer could the two of them endure this?

Leaning against the bars, he rested a hand on his brother's shoulder.

They had to find a way to get off this cursed ship. The *nahalae* had prevented them from using their telekinetic abilities to secure their release. But there had to be some other means they could employ.

He closed his eyes. They needed to escape before the Gathendiens succeeded in killing Ziv'ri.

Ava?

And before their experimental concoctions drove Jak'ri insane.

———◆◇◆———

A VA'S HEART RACED IN her chest. Panic quickened her breath. "Evie, are there any weapons on board?"

Silence.

As her eyes adjusted to the darkness, she realized it wasn't complete. Her watch face glowed on her wrist. Thank goodness the Lasarans had replaced its battery with a higher tech one that wouldn't need charging or replacing for at least five years. Tapping the surface of the smart watch, she typed in her access code then scrolled down to activate the flashlight.

The whole pod shook. A thunderous thunk startled a cry from her as Ava gripped the arms of her chair.

The hair floating around her face abruptly fell to her shoulders as weight pushed her down in her seat. Either the artificial gravity of the pod had been restored or she was experiencing whatever gravity the Gathendien ship produced.

Shit. Was she on the Gathendien ship?

Those bastards had tried to wipe out Earth's population with the vampiric virus and had nearly succeeded in doing the same with a different virus on Lasara. What was her best play here?

Unfastening the harness, she slid out of the chair and looked around with the help of her watch's flashlight.

Evie's evasive maneuvers had dumped everything that wasn't secured onto the floor. Wrappers from the nutrition bars and MRE-like meals she'd subsisted on for the past two weeks now littered the small space. So did the shirt and jacket she'd discarded before sleeping.

Ava dropped to her knees beside the go bag wedged against the tiny lav that housed the weird space toilet. Pawing through the bag, she yanked out clothing as she searched for a weapon.

Eliana had helped her pack it with photos and keepsakes she didn't want to lose, spare clothing, extra nutrition bars, and other survival essentials. Ava and the other *gifted ones* hadn't thought they would need the bags. They were, after all, traveling to Lasara aboard a huge warship carrying a full regiment of Lasaran ground forces and fighter pilots as well as countless Yona warriors who would die before forfeiting a battle. But they'd humored the Immortal Guardians and—

There! As soon as Ava spotted leather, she latched onto it and yanked it out. She didn't own anything made of leather so it had to be a weapon Eliana had stuck in there.

Once she saw it, she swore. It was a blade. A dagger. A very sharp, expertly crafted dagger. But Ava had been hoping for one of the... whatever blasters so many of the Lasaran soldiers had carried on their hips. *Tronium* blasters! That was it. *Tronium* blasters.

Like the handguns back home, the alien weapons had seemed simple enough. Just point and shoot. Instead of firing projectiles, however, they fired...

Well, she wasn't sure, actually. It looked like balls of energy that could burn holes through just about anything. And since the weapons had tiny but powerful batteries, running out of ammunition wouldn't be a problem. If she stayed in the pod and sheltered behind the chair, she could pick off Gathendiens one-by-one with a blaster as they tried to enter the pod.

She didn't believe for a moment that she could kill every Gathendien on the ship. But she could sure as hell take some out before they hurt or killed *her*.

She looked at the dagger in its sheath. What the hell could she do with a blade?

Ava drew the sleek weapon. Blades required hand-to-hand combat. They required getting up close and personal, in this instance with aliens who outweighed her by well over a hundred pounds and had been trained in warfare.

Eliana could do a hell of a lot with this dagger. She had preternatural speed and strength. She'd spent the past four hundred years killing vampires with swords and daggers like this one. Blades were her weapons of choice.

Ava, however, had only been training for four months.

She slid the blade back into the sheath. The chances of her managing to take down even *one* of the reptilian warriors were pretty much nil. If worse came to worst, though, she'd sure as hell try.

Bending down, she swiftly tied the sheath to her ankle and pulled her pant leg down over it. Another loud clunk made her jump.

Straightening, she watched the round door to the pod swing open. Bright light blinded her.

Throwing up a hand, she squinted against it.

Something clanked outside. Then a dark figure filled the entrance.

Lowering her hand, she swallowed hard.

While someone her size could easily fit through the pod's entrance, the being she now faced would have to duck to enter.

He didn't though. At least, she *thought* it was a he. He was only visible from the waist up. If Ava had only seen his silhouette, she could've easily mistaken him for a human, Lasaran, or Yona. He had one head, broad shoulders, two arms, and two hands that both aimed blasters at her.

But he wasn't in silhouette. Instead, the light of the docking bay illuminated golden reptilian skin stretched across a heavily muscled chest and rippling abs. The peculiar skin darkened to forest green on his shoulders and thickened so much it resembled the hide of an alligator. Thick dark ridges continued down his bulky arms, fading on the undersides to match the smoother golden yellow of his stomach.

Most of his bald head matched the green ridges on his shoulders and arms. Instead of ears, Ava saw only small holes she assumed allowed him to hear. His skin again smoothed and thinned to a light golden color on his face, which was outfitted with two reddish eyes equipped with slitted pupils, a subtle nose, and thin lips.

"It's female." Unless their women had baritone voices, this Gathendien was definitely male.

A grunt sounded outside. "Lasaran or Earthling?"

Did they linger over the "s" sound or was that merely her imagination?

"Unknown."

In terms of their physical appearance, Lasarans and humans looked the same. There *were* some pretty significant differences between the races, but simply ogling them couldn't identify those. While not even one percent of those on Earth were born with special gifts, *all* Lasarans were strong telepaths. Each Lasaran also boasted at least one additional gift on top of that, and they had incredible regenerative capabilities... so great that they could grow back severed fingers and toes. Even Eliana couldn't do that. And they lived very long lives, sometimes even reaching a thousand years old.

The Gathendien warrior's snake-like eyes didn't stray from her. "Are you Lasaran or Earthling?"

Ava didn't know which answer would benefit her or screw her over more. As she understood it, the Gathendiens had abandoned their quest to exterminate all Lasarans when the Lasaran royal family had unleashed the might of their military upon them and—with the help of their Aldebarian Alliance allies —nearly wiped the Gathendiens off the map. So a Lasaran female would likely not be of much use to them and could result in her imminent death.

On the other hand, if she admitted she was from Earth, they would likely see this as an opportunity to learn why the virus they had infected select humans with thousands of years ago had failed to eradicate the human race.

Somehow she didn't think being a Gathendien lab rat would be a pleasant experience.

"Speak," he snarled.

Ava jumped. Then she straightened her shoulders, clamped her lips together, and tilted her chin up in a show of defiance.

"If she doesn't understand you," the second voice speculated, "she must be Earthling."

"I understand you," she said in Alliance Common.

The burly alien's eyes narrowed. "Out," he ordered.

"I'm fine in here, thank you," she replied evenly, surprised she was able to keep the tremor from her voice. She was so terrified she shook like a leaf.

The alien dove inside.

Yelping, Ava attempted to evade him, but it was a small space and he was *fast*. She drew the dagger as he reached for her. Ducking under his arm, she drove the blade into his back. Or *tried* to. His skin was so damn thick the blade only sank about an inch and a half in and stuck there.

Roaring, he swung around and attacked. Ava employed some of the self-defense techniques Eliana had taught her and ended up scraping some of the skin from her knuckles on his rough hide.

He grabbed her by the throat and lifted her until she balanced precariously on her tiptoes. "Are you Earthling or Lasaran?" he snarled in her face.

Barely able to drag in breaths, she refused to answer.

Turning, he dropped her to her feet and pushed her toward the exit. It was high above her head on the sloping wall. Prince Taelon had told them the door was placed there to keep the pod from flooding in the event of a water landing.

Ava balked at climbing the ladder. She knew she was just putting off the inevitable but feared leaving the brief safety the little pod had afforded her.

The Gathendien grabbed her by the back of the neck and slammed her forehead into one of the rungs.

Agony ricocheted through her head. "Ah!"

"Out!" he growled.

With shaking hands, Ava scaled the ladder and pulled herself up into the opening. Outside, a staircase on wheels that reminded her of a cheap one you might see at an airport back on Earth rested against the pod's exterior. It seemed so primitive and out of place inside the high-tech spaceship that it made her wonder just how down-on-their-luck these assholes were.

Her fear of heights intensified the terror coursing through her as she shakily stretched a foot out to the top step, wishing the damn thing had handrails.

Dozens of Gathendiens, loaded down with weapons, waited below. Every one of them had a long tail that looked strong enough to knock a bear on its ass. And most of those tails bore rings with metal spikes.

Yeah. Even with a *tronium* blaster, she wouldn't have had a hope in hell of killing them all.

"Is she Lasaran or Earthling?"

Her gaze shot to the owner of the second voice—a tall, thin Gathendien garbed in something that resembled a white lab coat without pockets.

"Won't say," the burly bastard said as he clambered out behind her. "And her clothing could be either."

Thank goodness she'd worn a long-sleeved shirt today.

"I need to know!" Lab Lizard snapped.

Ava carefully searched for the next step with her toes, wondering if there was any way she could preserve her dignity while sitting and safely scooting down the steep stairs on her butt.

A heavy hand slammed into her back, giving her a hard shove.

Down she tumbled, crying out as the hard edges of the steps slammed into her arms and back until she hit the floor and rolled to a stop. Pain shot through her arm. "Ah! Shit!" she hissed, gripping it with her free hand. When she looked up, she went still.

She lay at Lab Lizard's feet.

Triumph gleamed in the Gathendien's beady eyes. "That word isn't Lasaran. She must be Earthling."

Ava bit back a moan. Damn her propensity to curse when she was in pain or pissed! He must be fluent in Lasaran if he knew "shit" wasn't part of their language.

Cradling her arm to her chest, she glared up at him. "I learned that term from a Yona," she said in Alliance Common.

His smile faltered as uncertainty entered his ruby gaze.

Ha! The bastard didn't speak Yona. And translators rarely translated curse words. So as far as he was concerned, she could still be either Lasaran or Earthling.

Skinny lips tightening even more, he looked at the asshole who had shoved her as that one stomped down the steps and moved to stand behind her. "Take her to the tertiary lab and secure her in a cell while I report to Commander Striornuk."

The burly Gathendien leaned down and jerked her up.

Ava ground her teeth together to keep from cursing again. Her back felt like someone had beaten her with a baseball bat. Both her forehead and her arm throbbed. And she was fairly certain these guys had barely gotten started.

Holding her by the scruff of the neck like a puppy, the big bastard forced her forward at a fast clip.

The docking bay wasn't as large as the one she'd seen on the *Kandovar*, so they crossed it quickly then headed down a bland corridor. Another warrior fell into step behind them, banishing any plans she might've hatched of getting away from her captor and hiding.

There was one thing she *could* do though.

Letting her head hang as though whipped, Ava began to limp heavily. "Please," she said in Alliance Common, her voice pitifully weak, "could we slow down? I think I hurt my leg when I fell."

Though the guard grumbled, he slowed his pace a little.

Ava peered through the curtain of her hair and tried to commit the path they followed to memory, counting steps, memorizing turns, and scoping out possible places she could lose herself in if she got away.

She stumbled, faking a whimper.

The hand at her neck tightened. "Earthling. Lasaran," he sneered. "Both races are worthless."

The other one grunted. "Too puny to enslave."

Some of her fear turned to fury.

If Eliana were here, she would make both those assholes eat their words. Slowly and painfully.

Ava faked a sniffle and reached up as though wiping away tears. "Please," she begged plaintively. "Don't hurt me."

"I won't have to," Burly answered. "Saekro and Kunya will do that."

The other Gathendien guffawed.

The scent of antiseptic reached her nose moments before they entered a small, state-of-the-art lab that made the rest of the ship look like refuse from a junkyard. Everything was white and pristinely clean here.

Everything except the cell that adjoined it on one side. *That* looked like something out of the freaking Middle Ages, without the squalor. Gray with a rough floor and what looked like iron bars equipped with a gate, it bore no furniture, just a tattered blanket and an opaque sheet of glass the size of a door on the back wall.

The guard halted in front of the gate and passed his wrist over a shiny area on it that was about the size of a credit card.

A beep sounded, then the gate opened.

Okay. Definitely not medieval. Instead of keys, she would need whatever was embedded in the guard's wrist to open the gate.

When he gave her another shove, Ava pretended to stumble even though she'd been expecting it.

The gate clanged shut. The security feature on it chirped.

"What are you going to do to me?" she asked in Alliance Common. Then utilizing the telepathy she'd been born with, she delved into the guard's mind.

Or she *tried* to delve into his mind. Much to her shock and dismay, she couldn't see or hear a thing.

He nodded toward the other side of the cell. "Back up against the far wall and I'll tell you."

She doubted that, but them believing her naïve could aid her, so she backed up until her shoulder blades rested against the bars embedded in the far wall. "What are you going to do to me?" she repeated tremulously.

Grinning, he removed what looked like a short wand from his pocket and touched it to the bars.

Electricity crackled through the air and jolted through her body where she touched the bars. Ava stiffened, teeth clamping together. Every muscle locked, leaving her unable to move as what felt like flames seared her insides.

Laughing, the guard retracted the wand.

Ava slumped to the floor, muscles twitching.

"That and more," he said as the two turned to leave. "We intend to do that and more."

"Welcome to the *Cebaun*," the other said with a raucous laugh just before the lab door slid shut behind them.

Long minutes passed while her heart stuttered in her chest. The smell of singed hair filled her nose. Tears leaked from the corners of her eyes as she lay where she had fallen and studied every inch of her surroundings.

The operating table in the lab filled her with dread. But the pain that racked her body claimed most of her attention. As soon as she was able to move, she rolled onto her stomach and forced her aching body up onto her hands and knees. Then she crawled over to the corner and curled up on the blanket.

Though it was old and coarse, it smelled surprisingly clean and was thankfully free of vermin.

Her eyes on the door through which the guards had departed, she cradled her arm to her chest and warily awaited the scientist's appearance.

CHAPTER THREE

A COOL BREEZE BUFFETED *Jak'ri as he climbed the path to the cliff that overlooked the Runaka Sea. Fatigue pulled at him, slowing his steps and making it harder to find each handhold. Heat flayed him. Thirst left his mouth as dry as the Kameshi Desert.*

Why hadn't he brought some bolosi *with him? He usually did when he hiked. A few swallows of the sweet berry juice could leave him hydrated for hours. And he wanted to spend a little time enjoying the solace here among the plants and trees—the world spread beneath him —before he dove into the sea below.*

The ground at last began to lose its sharp slope. Clambering over the edge, he rose to his full height and continued forward, brushing aside large fronds. Others might grumble about the plants barring their path, but he always liked to think they were instead reaching out to welcome him.

It was a fanciful thought. But he allowed himself the fantasy.

Some of the knots in his shoulders began to loosen as the scent of the ocean tickled his nose. Tension fell away, bringing a smile to his lips as he stepped into the open and left the forest behind him. He even forgot his thirst and the hunger that clawed his belly as he drew in a deep breath and released it in a long sigh.

This was why he came here.

The peace. The quiet. The wide-open space. The feeling that he was all alone in the world.

Rustling sounded to his left.

He looked in that direction, a frown forming.

That had better be an animal. He was not *in the mood to engage in conversation with—*

His eyes widened as the foliage parted and Ava stumbled out, vines and leaves clinging to her as if they didn't want to part with her. Turning around, she carefully extricated herself from their green grasp. "Keep it up," she said, amusement lacing her voice, "and I'm going to think you like me a little."

Once free, she spun to face Jak'ri and the edge of the cliff.

Her pretty face lit with a smile. "Jak'ri! You're here!"

He found it impossible not to smile in return. "I'm here."

Brushing her hands together, she strode toward him. "I can't believe I found this place again." She wore the same clothing he'd seen her in before: blue trousers and a colorful shirt that hugged her slender form as she walked.

And the way she walked...

Feminine and alluring without being overtly sexual, he found it very appealing.

"I can't either," he responded belatedly, trying not to let his gaze linger overlong on her breasts and nicely rounded hips.

Her smile turned hesitant. "Is it... okay that I'm here?"

He tilted his head to one side. "What does okay mean?"

She wrinkled her nose. "Sorry. My Alliance Common isn't what I'd like it to be yet. I was asking if it's all right that I'm here or if you object to my presence." She gestured toward the ocean and the wealth of nature that surrounded them. "I know this is your meditation place. At least, I think that's what you called it."

"It is," he confirmed. "And I welcome your company, Ava. It's good to see you again."

Her smile stretched into a grin. "Truly?"

"Truly. Would you like to sit down?" He felt oddly weary, but didn't want to admit it.

"Yes. Very much."

She sat down facing the ocean, legs crossed.

Jak'ri lowered himself beside her. Bending his knees, he looped his arms around them and clasped his hands. "How did you come to be here?"

Her smile turned wistful. "I don't know. I guess I just couldn't stop thinking about this place. It's so beautiful. So peaceful." She glanced at him. "I feel safe here."

Safe? Was someone or something making her feel unsafe?

She had been lost the last time he'd seen her, hadn't she? She'd been looking for her friends.

He opened his mouth to ask if she'd found them, but she spoke first.

"I also hoped I would see you again."

Whatever he'd meant to ask vanished as something warm unfurled in his chest. "You did?"

"Yes. You make me feel safe, too." She sent him an impish grin. "Or maybe I was just hoping I'd see you without a shirt again."

He laughed.

Pink crept into her cheeks as she covered her face. "I can't believe I just said that."

"I can't either." Lasaran women were not known for their boldness, and he kept forgetting she wasn't Lasaran. "But I'm glad you did."

Laughing, she dropped her hands. "I bet you are."

Jak'ri reached up, gripped the back of his shirt at his nape, and dragged it over his head. Tossing it aside, he made a show of flexing his muscles. "How's that?"

"Very nice," she said with a grin, then assumed a comical look of wide-eyed awe. "Oooooh. So many muscles."

Laughing, he looped his arms around his bent knees again. But he noticed her gaze strayed from his face and wandered down his body.

She tilted her head to one side. "Are those marks on your side scars? Or are they... um... I'm sorry. I don't know the Alliance Common word for tattoos."

"What are tattoos?"

"On Earth, some people use needles to inject ink beneath their skin to make permanent marks or images on it." She motioned to his side over his ribcage where three lines marked his skin. "Yours are raised like our scars often are, but they're so perfectly aligned that I thought maybe your tattoos *were three dimensional to add texture or something."*

"They aren't tattoos," *he told her, testing the word and wondering if she had marked her own body with such images.*

"Oh. Then they're scars?" She bit her lip. "I'm sorry. Was it rude to ask you about them?"

"No. It wasn't rude. And they aren't scars either."

"Oh."

He could tell she wanted to ask but feared offending him. "They're gills."

She stared at him a long moment without blinking. "I'm sorry. I think my translator didn't get that one right. They're what?"

"They're gills."

"Like the kind fish have?"

"Yes." He was going to assume by her stunned expression that her people didn't have them.

Her eyes grew steadily wider. "Gills that let you breathe underwater?"

"Yes."

Her brown eyes began to sparkle. "So you can just stay underwater indefinitely?"

"Yes."

Grinning big, she reached over and gave his shoulder a friendly shove. "No freaking way!"

Chuckling, he managed to keep from toppling over. "I don't know what that means."

"It means I can't believe it! I am so jealous!" she exclaimed, her face bright with delight.

"I'm guessing you don't have gills?"

"No. Can I touch them?" Eyes widening, she covered her mouth. "I did not just say that. I'm so sorry. I'm just new to the whole meeting aliens thing and my excitement and curiosity sometimes make me blurt out things I normally wouldn't."

He assumed a look of bafflement. "So you don't normally ask men if you can touch them?"

Laughing, she gave him another shove. "Oh, shut up. You know what I mean."

He grinned. "I do. And yes, you may touch them." He kept his arms looped around his bent legs so his gills remained unconcealed.

Rising onto her knees, Ava scooted closer and reached toward his side.

Jak'ri found himself holding his breath in anticipation of her touch.

Her fingers brushed his flesh, so light it almost tickled.

"You don't have to be tentative," he told her.

A look of amazement fell over her pretty face as she increased the pressure, sliding her fingers along his flesh and tracing each gill. "They feel like scars."

His skin tingled as she stroked him. "Do you have scars?" he asked, giving in to his own curiosity.

Nodding, she sat on her shapely bottom, drew her knees toward her chest, and reached down to tug one trouser leg up. A network of white scars crisscrossed one ankle.

Jak'ri reached out and touched them. As she'd said, they were raised, the skin between and around them soft beneath his fingers. "How did you get them?"

"I was swimming too close to a reef and a wave crashed over me and drove me down into it. My foot got caught, and I cut my ankle up when I yanked it out."

Cuts deep enough to leave scars like this would've wept enough blood to attract dangerous predators in the oceans of Purvel. Had they done the same wherever this happened? "You swim?"

"Oh yes. I love to swim, so I really envy your ability to breathe underwater." Returning her attention to his gills, she reached out and touched them again. "They look and feel as if they're sealed shut. Do they do that when you're out of the water?"

"Yes." He wondered if she realized his hand was still loosely curled around her ankle. He should probably remove it. But her skin was so soft. And the contact affected him in surprising ways. Her touch on his side did, too, stirring feelings of attraction that had been subverted for so long they seemed foreign.

Foreign but good.

Very good, arousing him enough that his swim shorts would not be able to conceal it if he didn't do something to cool his body down.

"You said you swim." He nodded toward the ocean. "Would you like to see how my gills look in the water?"

"Yes!" she exclaimed, then immediately seemed to change her mind. "Wait." She glanced at the cliff's edge. "Do you mean jump from here?"

"Or dive. Either one."

"Ummmmmm."

"Would jumping from this height damage you?"

"I'm thinking it might. We're pretty high up here." She looked around them. "Is there maybe a place lower down we could jump from?"

"There is. But the path to it is more treacherous than the one to this place."

"How treacherous?"

Several minutes later, he and Ava stood staring across at the alternate diving ledge. It was quite large. Almost as large as the meadow he and Ava had just left. And the only way to reach it was by shimmying across the vertical face of the cliff via handholds and the occasional protruding rock he could brace his feet upon.

"That's pretty treacherous," she stated.

"But it is *a little closer to the ocean than my meditation spot, so the dive—"*

"—or fall—"

"—isn't as great."

Face scrunching up, she motioned to the ledge. "How are we even supposed to reach that?"

"There are handholds enough to get us there."

"I think what you mean to say is there are handholds enough to get you *there. I'm not an experienced rock climber." She peered down at the ocean where it met the land beneath their current perch.*

Jak'ri didn't have to look to know that—unlike the ledge he'd recommended—a beach lay below them here that was littered with rocks and boulders.

"Well, diving from here *is definitely out."*

He smiled. "I can get you to the ledge." He had made the climb many times, occasionally with a pack full of gear on his back.

Doubt shadowed her features. "How? I don't like to admit it, but I'm afraid of heights. So if you think my hands will be steady enough for you to lead me over there—"

"I can carry you on my back."

Ava was silent for a moment. "I appreciate the offer," she said slowly, as though worried she might upset him, "but I'm going to have to say no." She again glanced over at the ledge, then down at the rocks that decorated the beach beneath them. "Yeah. That's gonna be a hard no."

The next thing Jak'ri knew, he was working his way across the rock face with Ava plastered to his bare back. Slender arms wrapped around his neck, legs locked around his waist, she managed to hold on tight without choking him.

"How the hell did I let you talk me into doing this?" she muttered, a tremor of fear in her voice.

He reached way over to tuck his fingers into a tiny crevice. "I don't know that word."

"What word? Hell?"

"Yes."

"Oh. I meant, srul. How the srul did I let you talk me into doing this?" she repeated, this time using an Alliance Common curse word.

He laughed.

It felt good to laugh again. For some reason, it felt as though he hadn't done so in a very long time.

"And where the srul are the rest of my clothes?" she blurted. "I'm only wearing my bra and panties!"

Again he laughed. "You were worried your clothing would weigh you down in the water. You don't remember removing them?" The legs wrapped around him were wonderfully bare. The flat stomach plastered to his back was, too.

"No. I think you dangling me over those rocks down there short-circuited something in my brain."

They had actually progressed far enough now that no rocks lay beneath them, only deep water. But she was probably too nervous to look down. "Perhaps I merely convinced you to remove them because I wanted to see you with your shirt off." He grinned at her over his shoulder.

"Don't look at me! Look at the cliff!" she nearly shouted. But she cracked a smile.

Chuckling, he did as ordered.

Minutes later, he stepped onto the ledge. Turning to face the ocean, he reached back and curled an arm around her. "It's okay," he said, hoping he was using the Earth word correctly. "You can let go now."

Unlocking her ankles, she slowly lowered her legs. Her arms tightened around his neck.

"Without choking me," he rasped.

She loosened her grip. "Sorry. You're so tall that I can't touch the ground with my toes."

He patted her back again. "It's okay. I have you."

She let go.

Jak'ri held on and slowed her descent until her toes touched the dirt.

Ava wrapped her arms around his waist and clung to him.

Though her hold was tight, Jak'ri managed to maneuver around so he could face her.

He tried very hard not to notice the lace that cupped her breasts and allowed tantalizing glimpses of their pink tips. When his body responded to the press of hers, he subtly placed more distance between their hips.

Leaning a little to one side, she peered down at the ocean far below them, then buried her face in his chest. "Seriously, how did you talk me into this?"

He stroked her soft hair. "You talked yourself into it. You wanted to see my gills, remember?"

"Damn my curiosity," she grumbled.

Grinning, Jak'ri shifted them so their sides faced the ocean. "Look."

Turning her head, she looked out over the sea and drew in several deeps breaths that seemed to alleviate some of her anxiety. "How secure is this ledge?"

"According to my father, it has been here for many generations."

The twittering of birds drew her attention. Jak'ri followed her gaze as she looked up.

Bright blue and yellow iswani *sang as they peered down from the nests they'd built into the cliff's face.*

Ava's hold loosened. Then she smiled up at him. "I'm surprised this *isn't your meditation spot. It's just as beautiful here. And far more private."*

When a breeze dragged several hairs across her eyes, he brushed them back and tucked them behind her ear. "This is a little harder to access in the rainy months."

She grinned. "I can see why." Drawing in a deep breath, she blew it out slowly. "Okay. I can do this." She took a cautious step away from him.

When Jak'ri reluctantly released her, she latched onto one of his hands with one of hers.

"Don't let go," she said quickly.

"I won't."

Straightening her shoulders, she stood beside him. And he felt an odd surge of pride as he watched her conquer her fear. "You said there are no rocks beneath us, right?"

"Correct."

"So as long as the wind doesn't blow us into the cliff face, we should be good jumping from here."

He nodded. *"The breeze isn't very strong today. But I usually get a running start before I dive or jump off anyway."*

"A running start. Good to know."

He squeezed her hand. *"I wouldn't encourage you to do this if I thought you could be harmed, Ava."*

Some of the tension left her features as she smiled up at him. *"I know. I trust you."*

Those words hit him right in the chest, making his heart beat faster. *"If you change your mind…"*

"Hell, no. Let's do this." She grinned. *"Before I lose my nerve."*

"As you wish."

"Wait. Can we do it together?"

"Yes."

She tightened her grip on his hand. *"Can I keep holding your hand?"*

He nodded. *"I like you holding my hand."*

She smiled. *"Could we jump instead of diving?"*

"Yes."

"Okay." She faced the ocean once more. *"Let's do this."*

"On the count of three," he said. *"One."*

"I can't believe I'm doing this."

"Two."

She grinned. *"This is crazy!"*

"Three!"

The two of them shot forward, running the few steps to the edge and leaping off.

Ava shrieked as they plummeted down, down, down.

Jak'ri grinned, clinging to her hand as the wind created by their fall yanked their hair up.

Then they hit the ocean's surface.

Water closed over their heads. Bubbles surrounded them, tickling his skin as he and Ava slowed to a halt. He kicked his feet and propelled them both to the surface.

Ava's head popped up beside his. Releasing his hand, she wiped the water from her eyes and slicked her hair back. *"That was awesome!"* she nearly shouted.

Jak'ri laughed as he studied her carefully to gauge how proficient a swimmer she was. Relief filled him when she had no difficulty keeping her head above water. *"It's fun, isn't it?"*

"Yes. I wish we could—" Her eyes widened as she stared at him. Her mouth fell open.

"Ava?" He frowned. "What is it?"

"Your hair. It was black before. But now it's silver."

"Ah." He slicked his thick locks back. "The water changes it." It seemed odd that she would be on Purvel yet know so little about his people.

Reaching out, she caught some of the long silver strands that floated on the surface at his shoulders and rubbed them between her fingers. Then she stared at him again.

Unease flickered through him when she said nothing more. "Do you find it... unattractive?"

Her eyebrows flew up. "What? No. Of course not." Her gaze continued to rove him. "Not at all. I can see now why one of the women I used to work with was always attracted to silver foxes."

He frowned. "What is a fox?"

"It's a small mammal on Earth."

That only confused him more. "Your friend was attracted to animals?"

She laughed. "No. 'Silver fox' is a term women sometimes use to describe older men with gray hair."

"I'm not old," he hastened to mention, unsure why it was so important that she not see him as an elder. "This is just what happens to our hair when it's wet."

"It turns silver?"

He nodded. "It's believed to be a defense mechanism ingrained in our genes. When we swim, predators below us have more difficulty seeing us when they look up into the sunlight."

"Oh. Right. On my planet, it's common for sharks and other marine animals to be paler on their bellies than on their backs." Smiling, she again touched his hair, then drew her fingers across one of his eyebrows, which was also silver. "I like it."

Good. "There is another difference between our species that you may not have noticed."

"There is?" She watched him curiously as he raised a hand and spread his fingers, displaying the webbing between them that reached almost to the first knuckles. Her eyes widened. "No way! You have webbed fingers?"

"And toes."

She flashed another of those enchanting grins. "That is so freaking cool!" She took his hand and drifted closer to study it, her slender legs occasionally bumping his.

Jak'ri smiled. "I don't know what freaking *means."*

Without tearing her gaze away from his fingers, she said, "It's a cleaner version of drekking. *"*

He laughed.

"And cool *in this instance means incredibly interesting."*

He grinned. "I'm glad you like them."

Releasing him, she moved her arms and legs in familiar motions to keep herself afloat. "I bet you can swim fast with those."

"Very fast," he confirmed. Then he arched a brow. "Would you like to see?"

"Yes!"

He turned away from her. "Grab my shoulders."

Her small hands came to rest on his shoulders.

He patted one. "Hold on tight. And when you need to come up for air, just let go."

"Okay."

"Ready?"

She drew in a deep breath. "Mm-hmm."

Jak'ri dove beneath the surface and began to swim. Not wanting her to lose her hold, he took off at a sedate pace, then increased his speed until he was cutting through the water like a morilium *missile.*

Ava impressed him. She was able to hold her breath quite a bit longer than many who lacked gills. He was already circling back toward the cliff when her hands left him. Jak'ri halted immediately and spun to see her kicking her way toward sunlight.

He surfaced beside her a second later.

Grinning, she drew in deep breaths and swiped water from her face. "That was awesome!"

Once again, he found himself smiling, something he did a lot *around her. "I'm glad you enjoyed it."*

"You're so fast!"

He nodded. "You should see the Purvelis with tails. They're even faster."

Her mouth dropped open. "Some of you have tails?"

He grinned. "No. I just wanted to see your reaction."

Laughing, she splashed him.

Jak'ri laughed.

"It's weird," she said, still smiling. "The water isn't stinging my eyes. Usually I have to wear goggles when I swim in the ocean to keep the salt from stinging them. Is this freshwater?"

"No. Our oceans are saltwater."

"Hmm." She seemed puzzled. Then her face lit up. "Ooh. Can I see your gills?"

He nodded. "I'll have to duck underwater. I can't breathe oxygen and water at the same time."

"Okay."

He sank beneath the surface and showed her his gills.

When they surfaced, she smiled. "I am so jealous. I would love to be able to swim for hours without having to come up for air or wear a tank. My friend Eliana can hold her breath for an incredibly long time. I envy her that."

Her brow furrowed suddenly. Smile faltering, she glanced around.

"Ava? Are you unwell?"

"No. I just..." She slowly rotated, her brown eyes squinting as she searched the cliff and the beach in the distance. "I was just thinking about Eliana and..."

"And what?" She seemed somber all of a sudden.

"I don't know where she is," she murmured almost absently.

"You didn't find her?"

She turned back to face him. "Does something seem... off to you?"

"I'm not certain I understand your meaning."

Worry crept into her features, erasing the joy that had lit them moments earlier. "Does something about all of this seem not right to you?"

He frowned. "No."

She glanced down at the water. "Why didn't the water bother my eyes?"

"I don't know."

"When we were underwater and you were swimming so fast, my eyes were wide open, but it didn't feel like any water got in them."

Jak'ri didn't know what to say to that.

He glanced down at the water but could find no explanation. When he looked up again, his breath caught. A large bruise as thick as his thumb now streaked across her forehead from one side to the other. "Ava? What happened to your forehead?"

"What do you mean?"

"It's bruised."

"It is?"

"Yes. Did something strike you when we were swimming?" He had been moving fast, wanting to impress her, but not so fast that he wouldn't see any obstacles in their path. "Or maybe when we jumped from the cliff?" He had seen no wood or anything else floating beneath them before they hit the surface.

"No." She jumped suddenly and looked around wildly. "What was that?"

"What?"

"Didn't you hear that?"

He listened intently. "The birds?"

She shook her head as fear entered her expression. "It was a clunking sound."

He frowned. "No. I didn't hear it. Ava, what happened to your forehead?"

Her bruised brow furrowed as she searched the horizon for... he didn't know what. "He slammed my head into the ladder rung," she uttered distractedly.

Fury filled him. "Who did? Someone here on Purvel?"

Again she shook her head and faced him. Moisture welled in her pretty brown eyes as she moved closer and rested her hands on his shoulders. "Jak'ri... I don't think I'm on Purvel."

Confused, he looked around. To the south, the Runaka Sea stretched as far as the eye could see. To the north lay the cliff from which they'd jumped. And lush forest intermingled with sandy beach to the west.

Meeting her gaze, he cupped her face in one hand. "This is Purvel, Ava. This is my homeworld. I'm certain of it."

She bit her lip. "I want that to be true. I really do."

"It is true," he insisted. "Now tell me who hurt you."

Raising a hand, she touched the bruise on her forehead with trembling fingers.

Jak'ri's concern mounted when the movement revealed an even darker bruise on the pale, speckled skin of her forearm.

He gently grasped her hand and drew it away from her forehead. "What happened here?"

She winced when he turned her arm a little bit so he could inspect the dark purplish mark that marred it. "He pushed me down the stairs."

What the drek? *"Who did?"*

"The Gathendien."

Jak'ri stared at her. "There are no Gathendiens on Purvel, Ava." The Lasarans and their Aldebarian Alliance allies had decimated the Gathendien military and driven whatever remained to the outer reaches of the galaxy a long time ago.

His heart clenched when a tear spilled over her lashes and trailed down one cheek.

Her throat worked in a swallow. "That's why I don't think I'm on Purvel."

Jak'ri just stared at her, uncomprehending.

She motioned to the vast blue ocean beyond the cliff. "I don't think this is real." Another tear slipped down her cheek. "And I really *want this to be real, Jak'ri." Easing forward, she slid her arms around him, pressed her face to his neck, and hugged him tight. "I wish this were real," she said brokenly. "I wish* you *were real."*

Sliding an arm around her, he cradled her close as he kept them afloat. "I am *real, Ava. I'm right here, holding you." He pressed a kiss to her hair. "It'll be all right. I won't let anyone hurt you again."*

Squeezing him tighter, she whispered, "I wish this were real."

And the despair in her sweet voice made him want to weep, too.

A VA NEARLY WEPT WHEN a big hand clamped down on her arm and dragged her out of sleep.

She'd been with Jak'ri again, swimming in a sparkling ocean and wonderfully free of the bars that now enclosed her.

Yanked off her little nest of blankets, she stumbled a couple of steps before she regained her balance and straightened.

One of the Gathendiens had entered her cell and now pulled her toward the open gate.

Ava dug in her heels, suddenly sure she would prefer her crappy cell to whatever awaited her outside it. But the lizard guy had to be seven damn feet tall and weighed at least two hundred and fifty pounds. Maybe three hundred. That thick alligator-like skin was probably as heavy as it was hard to pierce.

All she managed to do, unfortunately, was piss him off.

Snarling over his shoulder, he swept his heavy tail toward her and knocked her off her feet.

Ava hit the hard floor on her side, one arm still held in the lizard's grip. She hissed when the floor scraped the skin of her bruised arm. Seriously, could they have made the damn floor *any* rougher? It was as if they had intentionally applied a maxxed-out sandpaper texture to it to make the cell occupants more miserable *and* cause more pain every time the bastards shoved people inside.

"Don't break anything yet, Mocna," a distracted voice murmured somewhere behind the behemoth. "You can do that later if she fails to cooperate."

Well, if that didn't chill her blood, what would?

Ava scrambled to her feet, thankful for the jeans that kept her from scraping her knees.

Mocna—aka the behemoth—yanked her forward out of the cell and deposited her in front of a tall, skinny Gathendien in a lab coat. The same one who had figured out she was from Earth. Something that resembled an operating table equipped with manacles dominated the space between them.

"Disrobe," the skinny one ordered dispassionately as he tapped the surface of something that looked like an iPad.

"Um. No, thank you," she said, keeping her voice neutral. Peering up at him, she attempted to delve into his thoughts. If she could ascertain his plans, maybe she could thwart them while finding ways to exploit any weaknesses she might discover up there.

But his mind was closed to her.

Fighting a frown, she tried harder.

Nope. Not a thing.

"Disrobe," he repeated.

She redirected her mind-reading efforts at Mocna.

Even *his* mind was closed to her. *Crap*. Did Gathendiens have some kind of natural defense against telepathy?

It would explain how they had managed to trick the Lasarans into believing they wished to be allies.

"I would rather not," she responded finally. "It's a little chilly in here."

"Your comfort is of no concern to me. If you do not remove your clothing, I will have Mocna do it for you."

"Why do you want me to remove my clothing?"

The scientist held up a finger.

Footsteps sounded behind her.

Before Ava could turn around, a large hand fisted the back of her shirt and pulled hard.

Buttons popped and clattered to the floor as the shirt burst open down the front and fled her arms.

When Mocna tried to stuff his fingers down the back of her pants, she yelled, "Okay! Okay! I'll do it!"

The skinny finger lowered.

Mocna's hand left her.

Gritting her teeth, Ava unfastened her jeans and pushed them down over her hips.

"The shoes, too," the scientist intoned.

Her mind working furiously, she toed off her sneakers and stepped out of the pants and socks.

Mocna grabbed them and stomped away.

The scientist set his tablet down.

Ava stood there in her bra and panties, feeling infuriatingly vulnerable, trying to cover as much of her bare skin as possible while she sought some way to keep them from doing whatever they intended to do to her.

"Get on the table."

She shook her head. "If you tell the Lasarans you've found me, they'll give you a generous reward." She had no idea if that was the case. She hadn't learned very much about the political side of their planet during her brief tenure on the *Kandovar*. For all she knew, they could have a "we don't negotiate with terrorists" policy. However, it was worth a try. This lab and all of the unidentifiable high-tech devices it held might be state of the art, but the rest of the ship—at least the parts she'd seen—had looked old, worn, and out of date compared to the *Kandovar*, as if they hadn't poured any funds into its upkeep in years.

On Earth, a hell of a lot of people could be bought off with the right price. If these guys were the same...

"I don't desire financial reward," he sneered seconds before his hand shot out and gripped her by the throat.

Ava barely had time to gasp before he picked her up as if she weighed as little as a feather and slammed her down back first on the operating table.

Holy hell, he was strong! Stronger than a human, that was for sure, even with his skinny build.

Within seconds, manacles locked her arms and ankles to the table. Ava struggled against them, her heart pounding in her chest. "What *do* you want?"

"I want to know why you puny Earthlings are still alive." Picking up his tablet, he tapped it several times.

A buzz sounded as a mechanical arm descended from the ceiling above her. A long needle protruded from one end.

Oh shit.

"My ancestors helped engineer the virus we released on your planet," he muttered. "Your race should have long since perished."

Ava struggled harder. But despite her thin wrists and small hands, could not work free of the manacles.

A cold, wet mist hit her arm. Then the needle pierced it.

Wincing, she watched her blood slither up a tube and into the apparatus in the ceiling.

"You're going to help me remedy my bloodline's mistake," the scientist declared.

No. She wouldn't. She *couldn't*. If he figured out where they'd gone wrong when they'd created the vampiric virus, why it only drove *most* Earthlings infected with it insane instead of *all* of them... If he found a virus that would work on humans and *gifted ones* alike...

He could commit global genocide on Earth.

And the blood he currently siphoned from her carried the key.

How long would it take him to sequence her DNA and determine it was far more complex than other Earthling DNA? How long would it take him to understand how it mutated the virus they'd created and morphed it into something positive? To find a way to counter that? Or to create something even viler that would succeed where their previous effort failed?

That will take time, won't it? she thought desperately.

Hopefully a *long* time. But would it be long enough for her to find a way to get the hell off this ship or... get a message out to someone nearby?

Was there anyone nearby?

Frustration over her physical limitations and her inexperience with combat inundated her. If Eliana were here, she could single-handedly slay every Gathendien on this ship.

Eliana! she called.

How far did telepathic shouts carry out here in space? Was it different from Earth?

Simone!

Hers had not been the only escape pod the *Kandovar* had launched into the unknown.

Michaela!

Immortals tended to have much stronger telepathic abilities. The older the immortal, the farther away they could be and still communicate. Seth and David could be on opposite sides of the planet and still speak to each other telepathically.

Dani!

If even one Immortal Guardian could hear her, the woman would move Heaven and Earth to find Ava and kick the crap out of the assholes who had taken her.

Rachel!

And if any Lasarans should hear her...

Well, she didn't know what they could do for her if they were stuck in an escape pod the way she had been. But maybe they could get a message to Lasara or its allies and send help her way.

Ava hadn't been able to reach anyone while in the pod. Even after four months on the *Kandovar*, she wasn't well versed in the use of their computers. Enabling voice commands in the pod had helped. But no one had responded to any of the messages she'd sent.

She stilled. Or had they?

Had those messages been what led the Gathendiens to her?

Would similar messages lead them to the others?

Would they—as Ava feared—kill any Lasarans they encountered because they had no use for them?

The thought made her want to cry. The Lasarans had been so kind to her. Far kinder than her own people had been back on Earth. The Lasarans hadn't cared that she was different, because they were different, too.

The needle withdrew and rose, disappearing back into the mechanism in the ceiling.

"While the computer analyzes your blood," the scientist murmured, "I will take some samples to examine."

So saying, he picked up a laser scalpel.

Ava swallowed hard. *Elianaaaa!*

If she could just touch upon her friend's mind...

CHAPTER FOUR

A HAND CLAMPED ON Jak'ri's shoulder.

He jerked awake. The abrupt shift from swimming in bright sunlight with Ava to the grim reality of being locked in a cell on the Gathendien ship left him confused.

He glanced down, oddly alarmed to find his arms empty and Ava gone. He'd fallen asleep sitting up with his back to the bars that separated his cell from Ziv'ri's. The hand on his shoulder gave it a reassuring squeeze.

"Be at ease," his brother murmured.

Jak'ri swiveled to face him.

Ziv'ri sat just on the other side of the bars, his features pale and pinched, his silver eyes bright with fever.

Jak'ri shot a quick look toward the adjoining lab. The Gathendien scientists hadn't returned yet, and the guards still huddled in the corridor.

Slipping an arm through the bars, Jak'ri cupped Ziv'ri's face. "Brother," he murmured, relief filling him as he urged him closer until they could press their foreheads together between the bars. "You slept so long I feared they had succeeded this time."

Ziv'ri forced a smile as he patted him on the back. "We're hardier than they think."

Though Jak'ri's people lacked the amazing regenerative capabilities of the Lasarans, Purvelis *did* have incredibly robust immune systems. Though he loved the oceans, rivers, and lakes on his planet, they teemed with naturally occurring bacteria, viruses, and other microorganisms. And every time he transitioned from using his mouth and nose to direct air through his lungs to using his mouth and nose to direct water through his gills so he could remain underwater indefinitely he was exposed to those microorganisms.

Yet they never sickened him or anyone else on Purvel.

Releasing him, Ziv'ri shifted to lean his side against the bars. "But they're getting closer."

Though Gathendiens were primitive and barbaric in their views on other alien races, determined to conquer instead of fostering good will, they were brilliant *drekking* scientists. And the *grunarks* were perilously close to discovering a virus that could wipe out the Purveli race.

"How close?" Jak'ri murmured with concern. His brother's shoulders slumped with weariness. Tremors shook his form even as sweat beaded on his forehead and trailed down his temples.

Ziv'ri sighed. "My fever has reached heights that make it difficult to concentrate. Were there anything in my stomach, I would've lost it many times over. Yet my body is fighting whatever they gave me."

Jak'ri reached for the canteen of liquid the Gathendiens kept his cell stocked with and passed it through the bars. "Drink."

If the guards had their way, Jak'ri and Ziv'ri would either starve to death or die of dehydration. But the scientists knew that—if they wanted to exterminate all Purvelis and take their planet without destroying its resources and infrastructure through war —whatever virus they concocted would have to kill healthy individuals with access to nutritious meals, beneficial liquids, and top-notch medical care.

Which was not to say the *grunarks* didn't withhold food and drink on occasion. If one brother didn't cooperate, the other was starved and given only enough liquid to cheat death. And if that didn't drive them to cooperate, the Gathendiens resorted to torturing them in front of each other.

Ziv'ri took the flask.

Jak'ri's worry grew when his brother's hand shook from the effort it took to raise the small container to his lips. Though Ziv'ri was younger than Jak'ri, he was usually a little thicker with muscle. Their bouts with starvation had left both significantly thinner, but...

Seeing his brother so weakened by illness made a lump lodge itself in Jak'ri's throat. He was supposed to protect his little brother. He was supposed to keep him safe. And look what had happened.

Neither could remember how they had come to be here. When they had awoken, Jak'ri had believed they could free themselves. Purvelis could wield their telepathy like a weapon. If they merely wanted to stun their enemy, they could produce a sound in enemy soldiers' heads that could temporarily deafen them and make them drop to their knees in pain. And if that didn't work, Purvelis could emit a *senshi* that would increase the pressure inside an attacker's skull to such an extent that their eyes, ears, and nose would bleed and they would lose consciousness. If Purvelis persisted, the *senshi* would kill their attackers.

When he and his brother had regained consciousness, the guards had opened Ziv'ri's cell door first. The moment the lock disengaged, Jak'ri had emitted a *senshi*. Ziv'ri had done the same. And triumph had filled them when they felled the guards.

But Saekro and Kunya, the scientists who waited in the lab beyond, had merely winced. They hadn't fallen. They had instead shot his brother with a stunner that instantly dropped Ziv'ri to the floor. While Jak'ri continued to emit a *senshi*, hoping to kill every *drekking* Gathendien on board, Saekro had swiftly propped his brother up and held a laser scalpel to his throat.

"Cease or he dies," he'd said, inexplicably immune to the *senshi*.

It was something neither brother had encountered before.

When Jak'ri hesitated, unwilling to abandon hope that he could defeat them, Saekro cut Ziv'ri deep enough to inspire a grunt of pain.

Jak'ri had emitted an even stronger pulse.

And the *grunark* had cut his brother again.

Terrified they would kill him, Jak'ri had stopped. The shorter scientist—Kunya—had then shot Jak'ri with something that looked like a thorn. Before he could yank it out, the pointy nub melted into his skin. Within seconds, he'd lost the ability to communicate telepathically. And he'd watched in horror while they'd tortured his brother, breaking bones and cutting into him to extract samples while Ziv'ri cried out in pain.

If Jak'ri cooperated, they sedated his brother and forwent breaking bones. If Jak'ri *didn't* cooperate or attempted to rebel in any fashion...

His gut churned as he noted the many scars his brother now bore.

Jak'ri boasted almost as many. But he was the older brother. He was supposed to keep Ziv'ri safe and had sorely failed in that task.

Ziv'ri sighed as he handed the flask back. "Where are our torturers?"

He shrugged. "A ship-wide alarm sounded. They haven't returned since."

"How long ago?"

"I don't know. Hours, I think, but I can't be sure." He nodded at the operating table in the lab. "I was unconscious when the alarm began. And the sedative left me so groggy that I fell asleep shortly after they tossed me in here."

His brother's brow furrowed. "How are you?"

"No illness yet. I don't know if they injected me with something else or merely took more samples." How they loved taking their precious samples. Skin. Muscle. Organ. Jak'ri couldn't decide if they actually learned something from the many bits of flesh they took or simply enjoyed inflicting pain.

Ziv'ri grunted. "I guess we'll know soon enough."

Nodding, Jak'ri settled more comfortably against the bars. "While I slept, I dreamed I was back on Purvel."

A sad smile turned up the corners of his brother's lips. "Did you?"

He nodded. "I climbed to my quiet place."

"The cliff that overlooks the Runaka Sea on the north side?"

"Yes." Feeling as parched as he had in the dream, Jak'ri partook of the nutrient liquid. "I felt so free. No walls closing in on me. Just the sun shining overhead, the ocean stretching before me, and a breeze cooling my skin."

Ziv'ri loosed another sigh, his look turning wistful. "I've forgotten what that feels like."

"The breeze or the freedom?"

"Both."

Jak'ri nodded.

A long moment passed.

"There was a woman there," he added softly.

Ziv'ri arched an eyebrow. "Where? Your meditation spot?"

"Yes."

A hint of amusement entered his brother's silver eyes. "Was it Shek'ra? She used to pester me endlessly, trying to get me to reveal the location of your quiet place."

Jak'ri laughed. "No. And once more I thank you for not giving it to her." Shek'ra had been relentless in her pursuit of Jak'ri. And he'd been attracted to her enough to give in to their shared desire. But he had swiftly come to regret it. Shek'ra talked more than anyone he had ever met. And once they had become intimate, that talk had shifted from flirtation to bloviation that usually revolved around praising herself and spreading nasty gossip about others.

Jak'ri was a quiet sort. He enjoyed peace. And her presence in his life had swiftly denied him that. He also abhorred the spread of negative, unfounded rumors, something that had led to a boyhood friend being ostracized to such an extent that his family had moved to another province. So until Jak'ri had finally convinced Shek'ra that he wanted to end their brief relationship, he had frequently fled to his meditation spot.

"Was it Ray'ku?" Ziv'ri asked curiously.

He shook his head at the mention of another former lover, one who had been far kinder than Shek'ra. "The woman wasn't Purveli."

Now both of his brother's eyebrows rose. "What was she?"

"She looked Lasaran."

Ziv'ri smiled. "Ah. The forbidden."

Jak'ri chuckled. "I said she *looked* Lasaran. But she said she was Earthling."

Ziv'ri's brows drew down in puzzlement. "Earthling?"

"Yes. She said she hailed from a planet called Earth."

"I don't think I've heard of it."

"Nor have I."

"Are you sure you didn't just convince yourself she wasn't Lasaran so you could touch her?"

Jak'ri smiled. "I'm sure."

"But you *did* touch her."

He laughed. "Not in the way you think. I saved her from falling and she embraced me afterward."

"I'm still thinking she was Lasaran."

"She couldn't have been. She spoke a language my translator didn't recognize."

"Truly?"

He nodded.

"Then how did you communicate?"

"Alliance Common. But her grasp of it was that of someone new to the language."

"How odd."

"Yes."

Even Gathendiens, Akseli, and other alien races who weren't part of the Aldebarian Alliance spoke Alliance Common so they could conduct business with those who didn't use translator implants.

Jak'ri glanced around his cell. "It felt so real," he murmured. Even as he said it, he heard Ava say with heartbreaking fervency, *I wish this were real.* "She said she and her friends from Earth were traveling with Prince Taelon to Lasara and had become separated. She couldn't remember how she had come to be on Purvel and was afraid. And..."

"And what?" Ziv'ri prodded.

He met his brother's eyes. "After the ship's alarm woke me, I heard her call my name."

Ziv'ri's fevered gaze sharpened. "*After* you woke?"

"Yes. And it wasn't just once. I heard her call my name three times."

His brother's face sobered. "Are you having hallucinations again?"

"Not visual. Just..."

"Her voice in your head?"

"Yes."

A moment passed. "Did you hear that?"

Jak'ri listened intently. "No. What was it?"

"I tried to speak to you telepathically."

Understanding, Jak'ri shook his head. "The *nahalae* is still blocking our telepathy."

"Then that's concerning."

"Having auditory hallucinations? Most definitely."

Ziv'ri reached through the bars and rested a hand on his arm, his worry palpable.

"I was dreaming about her again when you woke me," Jak'ri admitted softly.

"You were?"

He nodded. "She was injured." He motioned to his forehead. "A dark bruise marred most of her forehead. And when I asked her what had caused it, she said a Gathendien had slammed her head into a ladder rail."

"What the *drek*?"

"She also had a bad bruise on one of her arms and said he pushed her down the stairs."

Ziv'ri stared at him a long moment. "So even in dreams, the Gathendiens are *grunarks*."

Jak'ri forced a smile. "Apparently."

Silence encapsulated them, broken only by his brother's jagged breaths as chills induced by fever shook him.

"What was her name?" Ziv'ri asked many long moments later.

"Ava."

One of the guards entered the lab long enough to grab two nutrition packs and toss them into Jak'ri and Ziv'ri's cells. The brothers gave their empty canteens shoves that sent them skipping across the rough floor and under the gate. The guard retrieved them and dropped them into the decontamination receptacle, then took two new canteens from a cabinet and hurled them at the prisoners.

Jak'ri caught his easily.

Ziv'ri's movements were so sluggish that his canteen hit him in the chest before he could get his hands up to try to catch it.

Snorting a laugh, the guard dimmed the lights and left, sealing the door behind him.

Jak'ri's concern grew as he watched his brother fumble, trying to get the lid off his canteen. Even his grip appeared weaker. "Here." Removing the seal on his own canteen, Jak'ri passed it through the bars.

But Ziv'ri stubbornly shook his head. "I can do it." And he did, the slight effort nearly robbing him of what little strength he had. Hand shaking, he raised the canteen to his lips, drank a few swallows, then lowered it to the floor. A weary sigh left him as he slumped against the bars and closed his eyes.

"You should eat," Jak'ri told him softly.

"I'm not hungry."

"You need the energy it will provide."

Ziv'ri said nothing.

Jak'ri drank from his own canteen, then tore open the nutrient packet. The small cubes inside were chewy, like some of the treats he enjoyed on Purvel. But they lacked flavor. As usual, he grimaced while consuming them. The semi-clear morsels had no taste at all. So it was a bit like chewing on shoe fastenings. The green ones tasted like he imagined a soldier's boot would after two years of hard training and no decontamination. He couldn't decide whether the Gathendiens intentionally made the nutrition cubes unpalatable or if they just enjoyed the taste of mildew and sweat.

Eliana!

Jak'ri sucked in a startled breath and *vuan* near choked on the cube he'd been in the process of forcing down.

On the other side of the bars, Ziv'ri grunted and jerked, his eyes flying open.

Simone!

Jak'ri stared at his brother when the female voice bellowed in his head again. "Did you hear that?" he whispered.

Ziv'ri nodded, eyes wide.

Michaela!

"It's her," Jak'ri said.

"The woman from your dreams?"

Dani!

He nodded. "It's Ava." And she was in distress.

Rachel!

Ziv'ri swallowed. "Are we both hallucinating?"

He shook his head. "I don't think so."

"Then how are we hearing her?"

Elianaaaa!

There was only one way he could think of. "She must be on the ship."

A slew of words he couldn't understand flooded his mind then.

Ziv'ri stared at him. "What language is that?"

"I don't know. Our translators must not include Earth languages."

A handful of Alliance Common curse words began to pop up in the strange diatribe.

The corners of Ziv'ri's lips twitched. "I see she's mastered the more important words in Alliance Common."

Jak'ri nearly smiled. "Apparently."

But their amusement, weak though it was, vanished when images began to accompany the telepathic shouts. Images of a familiar face leaning over them.

"Saekro," Ziv'ri growled.

Visuals of delicate wrists constrained by manacles followed. Of laser scalpels drawing blood and taking samples.

Ava, he called, wishing he could help her.

The cursing continued unabated.

"Try to reach her," he told his brother.

Ziv'ri was quiet for a long moment, then huffed with frustration.

Her words grew weaker. The images she projected lost focus.

Then all was quiet.

The brothers shared a grim look.

Ava had been right. Their shared dream had *not* been real.

But *he* was.

And he would find some way to help her now that he knew she was on this ship.

He would *not* leave her to the Gathendiens' mercy.

*A*VA SHIVERED. THE BREEZE *she had thought so pleasant before now raised gooseflesh on her skin and drove her to fold her arms around herself in an attempt to get warm.*

She staggered, uncertain if the wind upset her balance or the dizziness that made the world around her tilt first one way then the other. Once more, she stood atop the cliff Jak'ri loved so much in the same spot they'd laughed and teased each other. Angry clouds clustered together above her. Though no lightning flashed, she heard thunder aplenty. Everything else—the deep blue ocean and the bright green forest—lay shrouded in dreary fog that lent it a gray cast.

"Jak'ri," she whispered, "where are you?"

Leaves whispered behind her.

Ava spun to face the forest, hope vying with fear.

The large fronds parted and Jak'ri emerged.

As soon as he saw her, he halted. No smile of greeting lit his face. He looked about as grim as she felt.

For a moment, they just stared at each other. Then both moved at the same time, hurrying to close the distance that stretched between them.

Jak'ri opened his arms.

Ava entered them gratefully, wrapping him in a tight hug.

One of his big hands cupped the back of her head as he cradled her close. The other smoothed up and down her back as he pressed a kiss to her hair.

Neither spoke for several minutes. They just stood there, holding each other.

A lump rose in her throat. "I'm not on Purvel," she whispered brokenly.

"No," he responded, his deep voice full of regret. "You aren't."

Moisture welled in her eyes. "I'm on a Gathendien ship."

"Yes. I'm sorry, Ava."

She shook her head. It wasn't his *fault.*

Trying hard to keep from breaking down and ugly crying, she drew back enough to look up at him. His handsome features were more somber than she'd ever seen them, his silver eyes full of concern. "Are you just a figment of my imagination?" If so, from where had he sprung? She had never heard of Purvelis before she'd found him in this dream world and hadn't thought her imagination this skillful.

"No." *A sad smile lifted the corners of his lips.* "I'm real, Ava. I'm on the Gathendien ship, too."

She stared up at him. "What?"

"My brother and I have been the Gathendiens' prisoners for..." *Lips tightening, he looked around as though searching for an answer, then shook his head wearily.* "I don't know how long." *He motioned to his bare chest.* "Long enough for me to no longer look like this."

Brow furrowing, she eased out of his embrace and took a step back. "What do you mean? What do you look like now?"

Spreading his arms wide, he stared down at himself.

As Ava watched, his build went from heavily muscled to whipcord lean. He wasn't stick thin. But his muscles were much more compact, the ribs beneath his gills more prominent. And his silver-tinged skin was marred in many places by scars and fresh cuts.

Or maybe incision sites.

She noticed he also now wore shorts that were a little looser than the swim trunks she'd seen him in previously.

Ava glanced down at herself. Her clothing had changed as well. Instead of jeans and a colorful shirt, she now wore a loose, wraparound shirt that tied on the sides and shorts like his. Her smart watch was missing. And her freckled arms bore fresh wounds where the Gathendiens had taken their damned samples.

She stared at him. "We're both being held captive on their ship?"

"Yes. So is my brother, Ziv'ri."

Understanding dawned as she looked around. "That's why we're here. On Purvel." *She met his gaze.* "Because I was drawn into your dreams."

His look turned uncertain. "In truth, I'm not sure how we're together. Ziv'ri and I are both telepathic, but the Gathendiens have been dosing us with nahalae."

"I don't know what that is."

"It's a plant. When administered in certain doses, it robs us of our ability to communicate telepathically or to read the thoughts of those around us." *He motioned to the forest behind them and the ocean in front of them.* "So I'm not certain how I did this, how I pulled you into my dreams. That shouldn't be possible."

"It's because I'm telepathic, too," *she told him.* "If you're like the Lasarans, you probably have far greater control over your ability than I do. Hearing other people's thoughts isn't voluntary for me. Their *thoughts just bombard me all the time unless I consciously block them, and that tends to take a lot of effort."*

It hadn't when she had been among the Lasarans. Significantly stronger telepaths, Lasarans were taught at an early age how to erect mental barriers to keep other telepaths out, so the only thoughts she'd had to block were those of her friends from Earth.

"When I sleep, I lose that ability," she continued. "So if I'm near other people, I often wind up in their dreams without consciously invading them." She shifted uneasily. "I'm sorry if you find that... intrusive. It isn't something I can control easily and—"

He touched a finger to her lips. "I'm glad you entered my dreams, Ava. Those that I've shared with you have brought me the only happiness I've found on this drekking *ship."*

And he'd been the Gathendiens' prisoner for a long time.

She shook her head. "Is there no hope of rescue then? No hope of escape?"

He sighed. "All of our attempts to secure our freedom have met with failure."

She bit her lip. "Aren't your people looking for you?"

Taking her hand, he led her to a soft patch of grass and sat down.

Ava sank down beside him and offered no objection when he wrapped an arm around her to keep her close. Perhaps he sensed her need for comfort.

"I don't know," he said at last. "I'm sure they've realized we're missing. But they may not know where to look for us. They may think we're still on Purvel." He dragged his free hand through his hair, frustration painting his features. "I don't even know how the Gathendiens captured us. One moment my brother and I were rock climbing not far from Runaka Point. The next we woke up on the ship with no memory of how we had come to be there." He shook his head. "A Gathendien ship should not have been able to enter Purvel's atmosphere without triggering alarms." His brow furrowed. "Our defense network should have become aware of their presence as soon as they entered our solar system. Or even as soon as they neared our solar system. If for some reason we missed it—something that would've required a colossal failure on our part—I'm sure the Aldebarian Alliance would've warned us."

"I thought Purvel wasn't part of the alliance."

"It isn't. But we conduct business with several alliance member nations and maintain positive relations with them."

"Oh."

He stared out over the sea, his brows drawing down. "I can't unravel the mystery of how they did it. My brother can't either."

Maybe some of those alien abduction stories people on Earth mocked had actually been real. They often seemed to involve missing time and having no memory of how the humans came to be on the alien ship or wherever the aliens took them.

Turning his head, he met her gaze. "How did they capture you?"

"My friends and I were traveling on Prince Taelon's ship."

"The last I heard, Prince Taelon was missing and presumed dead."

A faint smile lifted the corners of her lips. "Nope. He's very much alive and bonded to an Earthling."

His features lightened. "One of your friends from Earth?"

She nodded. "Several of us were on our way to Lasara aboard the Kandovar. We passed through one qhov'rum and had just entered a second when an alarm sounded. My friend Eliana stuffed me into an escape pod. The ship started taking heavy fire—"

"The ship was attacked in a qhov'rum?" he blurted and came damn close to gaping.

Ava still wasn't sure exactly what a qhov'rum was. It reminded her of a wormhole, but didn't fold space or whatever a wormhole purportedly did. Instead, it was something constructed by an extremely advanced alien race that provided ships with a safe course free of objects or debris while propelling them forward at speeds even the most technologically advanced ships could not achieve. "Yes."

"I've never heard of such happening before."

"I don't think the Lasarans had either. It was sudden and seemed to take everyone by surprise."

"I'm amazed that there was even enough room to engage in battle."

"There wasn't really. The Kandovar's shields quickly began to fail. My escape pod launched. It burst through the walls of the qhov'rum and..." She swallowed hard, thinking of all the Lasarans she'd met. "Evie—the computer in the pod—thinks the ship exploded."

He stared at her with what could only be construed as utter disbelief. "The Kandovar was destroyed?"

"I think so. Or rather Evie thought so. She lost contact with the ship as soon as we passed through the walls of the qhov'rum. And all of her attempts to hail it since have failed."

He looked about as stunned as she would look if someone had told her a massive asteroid had struck Earth and instantaneously eradicated all life upon it. "Do you know who attacked?"

Fury filled her. "Gathendiens."

A slew of curse words erupted from him. "Why the drek would Gathendiens attack a Lasaran warship? Why would they attack Prince Taelon's warship? It should be one of the hardest in the fleet to defeat!"

"I don't know." She had thought perhaps the Gathendiens were just getting some payback for the Lasarans kicking their asses however many decades ago. But since she'd been captured, that question—the why behind the attack—had really been eating at her. "I'm starting to wonder if..." She closed her eyes and shook her head, not wanting to say it. He'd think her a total narcissist if she did.

"What?" he asked. Touching her chin, he turned her face toward him. "What do you wonder?"

She opened her eyes. "I'm starting to wonder if they attacked the Kandovar because they knew my friends and I were on board."

He frowned. "You think you were their true targets?"

It sounded ridiculous, her and fourteen other women from Earth being more valuable than an alien prince and a shipload of Lasaran and Yona soldiers. And yet she kept circling back to it. "The first thing the Gathendiens asked me when they pried open my escape pod was if I was Lasaran or Earthling."

He frowned. "Then they must have known you were on board the Kandovar when they struck."

"That's what I was thinking. I didn't answer when they asked because I wasn't sure which one would screw me over more."

"That didn't translate."

"I didn't know which one would drek me over more."

"Ah." Thank goodness her propensity to use foul language didn't offend him.

"But they figured out I'm from Earth. And when they did, they looked pleased, as if that's what they had been hoping for."

He tightened his arm around her. "How many of you were there?"

"Earthlings? Fifteen." Tears once more pricked the backs of her eyes as she thought of her friends, wondering where they were, if they had survived, if they were prisoners somewhere like her.

Jak'ri looked out over the ocean, seemingly lost in thought. "They destroyed a Lasaran warship, killing countless Lasarans and Yona, all in an attempt to capture fifteen Earthlings."

"I know. It sounds crazy."

"Have your people had dealings with Gathendiens in the past?"

"No. But we learned recently that the Gathendiens released a virus on our planet thousands of years ago that they expected to kill us all off." Anger rose. "I think that's why they captured me. I think they want to figure out why the virus they created didn't work. And if they do..."

"They will correct their mistake and exterminate all Earthlings."

She nodded miserably.

"They wish to do the same to Purvelis. Even now, my brother sickens with the latest virus they're testing on him."

"We have to stop them."

"Yes."

"But how?"

"I don't know," he murmured, his eyes unfocused. "Can you find me outside of dreams?"

She shook her head. "They keep me locked in a cell."

"I don't mean physically. Can you find me telepathically? I can't send my thoughts to you because of the nahalae. But if you could find your way into my mind, send me your thoughts, and listen for mine, we could communicate while awake and perhaps devise a plan."

"I can do that." She frowned. "Wait. Why can't I read the Gathendiens' minds? I've tried and tried and get nothing."

"They've dosed themselves with the nahalae to make doubly sure we can't read them."

"Oh." Several moments of pensive silence ensued. "Any ideas yet?"

"No." He glanced at her from the corner of his eye. "But I tend to think best when I'm swimming."

Amusement trickled through her, displacing some of the fear and stress. "Do you?"

"Definitely."

She waved at the water. "Well, there happens to be a great big ocean right over there."

"So there is," he said with a sage nod before his expression lightened. "Care to join me?"

Ava started to say yes, then remembered just how far down that ocean was. "Um..."

Jak'ri rose to his feet, and she noted again how much thinner he was. Reaching down, he snagged her hand and drew her up beside him. "Say yes."

Part of her actually wanted to, but... "A jump from this height could injure me," she admitted, almost regretting having to decline despite her fear of heights.

"Not in a dream."

"Oh." Really?

Ava liked holding his hand, the feel of his long fingers woven between hers, his thumb stroking her skin in an absent caress. "Are you sure about that? Because a lot of movies back home postulate that if you're physically injured in dreams, your body will register it as if it were real and you'll wake afflicted with whatever injury you suffered in the dream. So if you die in a dream, you'll die in real life."

"What are movies?"

"Entertainment vids."

"Ah. Those vids were incorrect."

"You seem pretty certain about that."

"I am." He gave her a boyish grin. "Ziv'ri and I used to do the most foolish things in shared dreams. Things we would never even think of attempting outside them. And we were always wonderfully free of injuries when we awoke."

She couldn't help but smile. "How foolish are we talking?"

Chuckling, he shook his head. "Very foolish. Perhaps you can coax me into sharing a few with you."

"Will they make me laugh?"

"Yes."

"Then I'll coax you into sharing more than a few," she said with a grin.

He nodded toward the cliff's edge. "Shall we?"

"Not if you give me time to think about it."

He flashed his teeth in a boyish grin. "One-two-three, jump!" he called and took off running, pulling her after him.

Ava's eyes widened and her heart thudded hard in her chest as she ran alongside him.

Their feet hit the edge at the same time, and together they leapt off.

Jak'ri whooped as they plummeted toward the ocean, the sound so wonderfully carefree and appealing that Ava found herself grinning big even as she shrieked and squeezed the hell out of his hand.

He hit the water a split second before her. Cool liquid closed over their heads. Bubbles surrounded them as if they'd just jumped into a vat of club soda. Then he looped an arm around her waist and propelled them both to the surface.

"That was crazy!" she blurted, unable to stop smiling as she swiped water from her face.

"Crazy but fun?" he quipped, eyes sparkling with amusement. And once more his obsidian hair turned silver.

"Maybe," she hedged. "But not as fun at this." Propelling her upper body out of the water, she planted her hands atop his head and dunked him. As soon as she released him, she began a lazy backstroke.

Jak'ri surfaced with a sputter and a laugh. When his silver eyes found her a few yards away, they acquired a devilish glint. "Oh, you're going to regret that, little Earthling."

Ava shrieked when he dove for her. Rolling onto her stomach, she took off, swimming in earnest. But those webbed fingers and toes gave him amazing *speed.*

Jak'ri's fingers closed around one of her ankles. "Caught you!" She swam harder, getting absolutely nowhere, breaking into giggles as he issued dire threats in a villainous voice.

When was the last time she had honest-to-goodness giggled?

She yelped when he gave her ankle a yank.

Then she was in his arms and he was grinning wickedly at her.

"Think you can get the best of me, do you?" he taunted. Then he tucked his hands under her arms and kicked his feet.

Ava laughed as he tossed her up out of the water. Through the air she flew, landing on her back several yards away. The water again closed over her head. When she surfaced, she quickly bent her head to hide her smile and rubbed her eyes. "Hang on a sec," she mumbled.

Jak'ri immediately stopped laughing and swam toward her. "I'm sorry. Did you get something in your eye?"

"No." She grinned at him. "I just needed to lure you closer." Then she swept her arm through the water in front of him, sending a cascade over his head.

Sputtering, Jak'ri dove for her.

Laughter abounded as they played, even more so when he started sharing tales of his exploits with his brother.

Clunk.

Ava jerked awake. Pain inundated her. Damn it! She really hated to wake up. She and Jak'ri had been romping and playing like children. Having to come back to the reality of this cell and the assholes who'd put her in it sucked.

"Use the lav," the guard grunted. "They want another sample."

"Sick bastards," she muttered. Apparently the high-tech toilet in the tiny lav was full of sensors and who knew what else. When she'd had checkups and physicals back home, she'd occasionally had to pee in a cup. But something about these guys collecting and analyzing everything that came out of her body just skeeved her out. "I don't need to go," she said louder.

"Use the lav or I'll *make* you use it."

Unfortunately, she'd learned the hard way that he was serious when he issued that threat.

Biting back a retort that would end with him tasing her or whatever the hell they called using the shock wand, she approached the lav in her cell. The opaque door slid up, allowing her to enter. When it didn't lower, she glared at the guard. "Close the damn door or Doc Frankenstein won't get his *drekking* sample." They had tentatively agreed—that agreement mostly comprised of her *insisting*—that she would only willingly give them their samples if she could do so in privacy without the guard watching her like some freak with a fetish.

His red, slitted eyes narrowed. Then the door slid shut.

Yeah. She was going to regret that.

After peeing into an antiseptically clean toilet, she returned to her cell and found both researchers waiting for her.

The gleam in the tall, skinny one's creepy eyes chilled her to the bone. "We've found some anomalies in your blood."

The short one smiled. "We need to take more samples."

And she knew those samples wouldn't require her to pee in a cup. They would involve laser scalpels and more pain.

Son of a bitch.

CHAPTER FIVE

J AK'RI CAME AWAKE SLOWLY. His eyes burned as fever flayed him. His stomach churned. His thoughts rambled around sluggishly in his head as dizziness made the cell around him swirl despite his lack of movement.

"Jak'ri?" his brother called softly.

He sat up, then had to brace a hand on the floor to keep from toppling over. "How long did I sleep?"

"A few hours."

Groaning, he crawled over to the bars that separated them and sat near his brother.

"How are you?" Ziv'ri asked, his silver eyes full of concern.

Jak'ri shook his head. "I think they gave me whatever they gave you."

"Because they believe they've succeeded." He lowered his voice to a barely audible whisper. "I've been feigning illness, but in truth am nearly recovered."

"I'm not so sure they *haven't* succeeded. I feel like death is only a day away."

Reaching through the bars, Ziv'ri patted his arm. "It will pass, brother. Just don't let *them* see that."

"Their samples will tell them."

"They only look at our urine now. We can throw them off a little longer if you use your canteen to give me a sample for them. The longer we appear to be sick, the more they'll believe they've found the answer."

He supposed so. If they focused on this one, making subtle alterations, then waiting for results, it would keep them from concocting a new substance that might actually accomplish what this one wouldn't.

"I guess I should empty this then." Jak'ri reached for his canteen and drained the contents. Though the liquid wasn't cold, it nevertheless sent chills racing through him as it met a body burning with fever.

The brothers sat in silence for many long minutes.

Jak'ri's lips twitched. "Do you remember the time I convinced you that if we caught the dorsal fin of a *makura* we could swing ourselves onto its back and ride it like a hovercycle?"

"And then talked me into trying it in the shared dream? Yes."

Jak'ri smiled. "That dream did not end well for us."

Ziv'ri laughed. "Mother was so angry. Father was, too, even though I never told them what happened."

Jak'ri snorted. "You didn't have to. You woke up screaming, and I was desperately trying to quiet you when they ran into our room. That's all they needed to know."

Their parents had glared a warning at him every night at bedtime for a whole Maatira moon cycle. And Jak'ri had felt so guilty that he'd saved all of his treats and given them to Ziv'ri for just as long.

Ziv'ri shook his head with a smile. "What made you think of that?"

It had happened when they were still boys not yet on the cusp of manhood.

Jak'ri glanced toward the lab, relieved to find it empty. The *grunarks* often left them alone for a few days while they waited to see if their latest concoction would kill their captive lab subjects. Even so, he lowered his voice. "I was telling Ava about it."

Ziv'ri's eyebrows shot up. "You saw her in another dream?"

He nodded.

"How is that possible?"

"She's telepathic. But her people have less control over the ability. She said when she sleeps near others, she frequently finds herself drawn into their dreams."

"Not of her volition?"

Again he nodded.

Ziv'ri frowned. "That's…"

"Exactly."

His brother grimaced. "Could you imagine going to sleep and waking up in the erotic dreams of one of our parents?"

"Ugh! I don't even want to imagine them *having* erotic dreams."

Ziv'ri laughed. "If this Earling—"

"*Earth*ling."

"If this Earthling can enter your dreams, then the Gathendiens must not be dosing her."

"Apparently, they don't know she's telepathic."

"Can she emit a *senshi*?"

"No. I'm sure she would've tried it by now. But she attempted to read the Gathendiens' minds and couldn't."

"That confirms our belief that they're also dosing themselves."

"Yes."

They sat in silence, each wrapped in his own thoughts.

"How did you come to tell her the *makura* story?" Ziv'ri asked curiously.

"Some of her people believe that if they suffer an injury or die in dreams, the same will happen to their physical body in life."

"Truly?"

He nodded. "I told her about the *makura* to prove otherwise."

Ziv'ri arched a brow. "Why was that even necessary?"

Jak'ri sent him a sheepish smile. "I was trying to convince her to jump off Runaka Point with me."

Ziv'ri blinked. After a moment, he opened his mouth to reply.

Jak'riiii!

Both brothers winced as the mental shout careened through their heads.

Ziv'ri stared at him, eyes wide. "Was that...?"

Ava? Jak'ri thought.

Yes. A long moan filled his head, transforming into a growl. A slew of words he didn't understand followed.

Ava? Are you all right? What's happening?

They've got me strapped down to a table and are— Another moan followed, accompanied by undecipherable Earth words. *They're taking samples.*

He shared a concerned look with his brother. "Can you hear her?" he whispered.

Ziv'ri nodded. *If you cooperate, they'll sedate you.*

Who was that? she asked.

My brother, Ziv'ri, he told her.

Well, I stopped cooperating when they tried to sedate me, Ziv'ri, she said.

His brother frowned. *If they sedate you, it will spare you a great deal of pain.*

I know that, she bit out. Then she said in a calmer voice, *I'm sorry. I didn't mean to snap. This shit just hurts like hell.*

Ziv'ri met his gaze. "I didn't understand some of that."

"This *bura* hurts like *srul,*" he translated before speaking to Ava. *They offered to sedate you?* They must want to keep her in good health long enough to find a way to kill her people, especially if she was the only one of her kind they'd managed to capture.

Yes. I refused, she said. *No way am I waking up with some freaky lizard baby in my belly.*

Jak'ri stared at his brother. *What kind of experiments do you think they're performing, Ava?* It sounded as though she feared they intended to subject her to some kind of breeding experiment. But producing hybrids didn't interest Gathendiens. Wiping out civilizations so they could claim the planet, its resources, and whatever technology was left behind by the sentient race they destroyed was always their goal.

I don't know, she said. *But a hell of a lot of alien abduction stories told on Earth seem to revolve around aliens impregnating our women and probing men's butts.*

Ziv'ri gaped. *What the* srul *kind of aliens have been visiting your planet?* he demanded, appalled.

Jak'ri nodded.

Tinkling laughter brought smiles to their faces but was swiftly cut off by a groan.

The brothers exchanged a somber look.

Then Ziv'ri spoke. *Jak'ri said he told you about the time he talked me into trying to ride a* makura *in a dream.*

Yes.

Did he also tell you about the time he talked me into hunting a giant tsuberi *to impress a female whose affections I coveted?*

In a dream?

I wish *it had been a dream,* he said with a wry smile and dove into the tale, filling it with wild exaggerations Jak'ri was quick to refute, luring more laughs from her.

But the moans and growls of pain in between made his stomach burn.

Jak'ri began a tale of his own as soon as Ziv'ri finished, carefully hiding the rage that built over his inability to spare her the pain she was suffering.

Oh crap, Ava said, interrupting him mid-sentence. *I think... I think I'm gonna pass out.*

Silence fell.

Ava? he called.

His heart hammered in his chest when no response came. Quietly he seethed, curling his hands into fists. Those *grunarks* were hurting her the way they hurt him. And they would continue to hurt her until they found what they sought. "We have to do something," he gritted.

He saw the same rage reflected in his brother's features. "Agreed."

"They're distracted." Engrossed in tormenting their new victim. "We can use that to our advantage."

Ziv'ri nodded. "If we fail, the repercussions may be deadly this time." The punishment last time had been excruciating.

"They won't kill us. They need us to continue their research."

His brother shook his head. "They need *one* of us to continue their research."

Jak'ri swallowed hard. "Research we can't allow them to complete." Such would mean the destruction of their race.

"Agreed." Ziv'ri again rested a hand on his arm. "I have no desire to abandon this life. Nor do I wish to lose you, brother. But if one of us has to die to stop them..."

"And to save Ava..."

"The sacrifice will be worth it."

AVA HUDDLED ON HER little blanket. She had never in her life hurt as much as she did right now.

Apparently this was the first time the Gathendiens had encountered an Earthling with freckles. And they were determined to discover the cause of them, probably hoping to find some genetic defect they could exploit.

She looked down. Her arms and legs now bore multiple raw, red patches where the bastards had cut out samples to study. Large freckles. Small freckles. Dark freckles. Light freckles. Clusters of freckles. Solo freckles.

They'd even cut out her birthmark, which looked like a dime-sized freckle the color of her favorite milk chocolate on one hip. Each wound was covered by what looked and felt like clear rubber cement.

That had surprised her at first, their desire to keep the tiny craters they'd created from getting infected. She supposed it made a sick kind of sense though. They had to keep her alive long enough to figure out what would kill her, didn't they?

The freckle excavation sites hurt. But they weren't what concerned her.

She glanced over her shoulder. The two Gathendien researchers—Saekro and Kunya she'd learned were their names —huddled together in the lab with their backs to her while they worked their mad scientist magic.

Satisfied that they were suitably distracted, she faced the wall again and surreptitiously drew up the hem of her wraparound shirt. Five cuts now defaced her pale stomach. Each was only the width of a nickel, the skin around it puffy and discolored. They, too, were coated with the strange, clear, rubbery substance. But unlike the others, these looked like something that would result from laparoscopic surgery.

What had those assholes done to her while she'd been unconscious? Had they removed an organ? Human doctors could do that with tiny incisions like these now, so she would think it would be easy peasy for an alien race that clearly had more advanced medical technology to do the same.

Or had they—as she'd feared—put a lizard baby in her belly?

Jak'ri and Ziv'ri seemed certain that was not the Gathendiens' goal. They didn't want to breed with humans. They wanted to kill them all. But she couldn't quite shake the fear.

She lowered her shirt, gritting her teeth as agony washed over her.

Any movement, large or small, hurt like hell.

Resting her head on her bent arm, she closed her eyes and tried to focus on something else. Like getting the hell out of here.

I'm not going to urinate in my canteen. I have to drink out of that.

She smiled when Jak'ri's disgruntled voice came to her. She was too tired to block other people's thoughts. And The Gathendiens all dosed themselves with some herb to keep their minds private. So Jak'ri's and Ziv'ri's were the ones she inadvertently found herself immersed in.

For once, she didn't mind.

I don't know why that would bother you, his brother responded dryly. *After you drank that liquor from Promeii 7, I would think urine would be a vast improvement.*

Though they spoke aloud, their thoughts mirrored their words, enabling her to listen in.

Jak'ri laughed. *It probably would. That* bura *was revolting.*

Yet you still drank it.

And won the wager.

Ziv'ri made a grumbly sound. *I never should've wagered my hovercycle.*

Best cycle I ever owned, Jak'ri crowed.

If it wouldn't hurt so much, Ava would laugh.

Did you tell Ava about that?

She raised her eyebrows, surprised to hear Ziv'ri mention her.

No. I think I'll spare her that one.

Why? Don't want to tarnish your virile image by describing the week afterward that you spent hanging your head in the lav and regurgitating everything you ate?

Jak'ri laughed. *I already tarnished my image when I showed her what I look like now.*

Not a wise move. Even Shek'ra wouldn't want you if she could see you now. You're far too scrawny to attract a female.

Drek *you.*

Low masculine laughter accompanied the siblings' teasing.

What does she look like? Ziv'ri asked.

Ava?

Yes. All you've told me is she looks Lasaran.

A moment passed, and Ava found herself holding her breath as she awaited his answer.

She's beautiful, Jak'ri said, something like affection tingeing his voice.

Warmth filled her, taking a little of the edge off the pain.

Small and delicate like the Lasaran princess.

She was actually three inches taller than Ami, who barely reached five feet. But Jak'ri had been a head taller than her or more, so she supposed anyone a foot shorter would seem small and delicate to him.

She isn't built like our women, he continued. *Her shoulders aren't as broad. And her chest and back aren't as muscled.*

What about her breasts?

You don't need to know about her breasts, Jak'ri chastised him. *But they're perfect, plump and round.*

She didn't think he said that last part out loud, thankfully.

Ava glanced down at her modest bosom. She'd always considered her breasts small by society's standards. Certainly nothing that would stop traffic. But it seemed as though they were actually larger than most Purveli women's.

And Jak'ri liked them, judging by the way his thoughts drifted to memories of her lacy bra cupping her breasts while they swam and played together in the ocean, the pink tips beading when the cool air hit them.

You're thinking about her breasts now, aren't you? Ziv'ri asked.

She grinned. *Yes, he is,* she answered telepathically.

Jak'ri gasped.

Oh ho! Ziv'ri crowed on a laugh. *You've made my brother blush, Ava. I haven't seen his face this red since Mother caught him—*

Do not finish that sentence! Jak'ri ordered.

Ava laughed, then wished she hadn't when agony streaked through her belly. Blinking back tears, she held her breath until the pain eased.

Forgive me, Ava, Jak'ri said, his voice full of chagrin. *I didn't realize you were listening to my thoughts. I meant no disrespect and hope I didn't make you feel uncomfortable.*

You didn't. I shouldn't have been listening without telling you. I'm sorry. I just needed a distraction and didn't feel up to talking.

How are you? he asked, the words heavy with concern.

Not great, she admitted. *I woke up with cuts on my stomach that look like surgical incisions and I'm freaking out, wondering what they did to me.*

Was this the first time you've had those marks?

Yes.

Is the pain considerable?

Yes.

They took samples from some of your organs. They did the same to us when they first brought us here.

How can you be sure? Weren't you unconscious when they did it? She had passed out from the pain.

Yes. But Ziv'ri watched it all from his cell.

I did, Ziv'ri confirmed somberly. *I had to make sure they didn't probe his butt.*

Again Ava laughed, then moaned. *Don't make me laugh.*

Yes. Don't make her laugh, minkon, Jak'ri snapped. *You know how much pain their surgeries cause.*

Ouch! You can't hit me, his brother cried with false affront. *I'm dying!*

If you were dying, Jak'ri said, *the Gathendiens wouldn't be grumbling over your latest blood tests.*

They did *seem to be a little angry,* his brother admitted, then sighed in feigned disappointment. *Well,* srul. *I came this close to making him drink his own urine, Ava.*

She grinned despite the pain. *I'm pretty sure that was never going to happen.*

Ha! See? She knows me better than you do, Jak'ri said.

If she knew you better than I do, she would be visiting me in my dreams instead of visiting you in yours. I'm far more interesting than my brother, Ziv'ri proclaimed. And she could almost see him lifting his chin and looking down his nose in arrogance.

She smiled. *I don't know about that. Jak'ri seems pretty interesting to me.*

Ugh, Ziv'ri said. *How can you preen when you're sitting on the floor of a cell?*

I'm not preening, Jak'ri countered.

Yes, he is. He's preening, Ava. Please pay him no further compliments.

She shook her head. These guys were definitely brothers. *What's a* minkon?

Jak'ri is. Ziv'ri answered promptly.

You're too funny, Jak'ri responded, deadpan. Minkon *is a derogatory term applied to people who aren't very intelligent.*

She thought for a moment, searching for the right Alliance Common word combinations that would mimic Earth sayings. *So, it's the equivalent of... dumbass?*

Both men laughed. *Yes!*

Smiling, she closed her eyes as weariness overcame her.

The two men continued to razz each other, seeming almost to compete to see who could launch the most outrageous accusations or recount the most ridiculous stories.

Tears welled in her eyes as she realized what they were doing.

They were trying to distract her from the pain.

Trying to keep fear and despair from overwhelming her by making her laugh.

Helping her feel less alone.

And it was working, she thought moments before darkness claimed her.

A BREEZE WAFTED OVER *her, tickling her face with her hair and carrying the scent of the ocean.*

Ava lifted her lids to half-mast. Moonlight illuminated the vast ocean before her. The reflection of not one but three moons bobbed on the dark water's surface.

Soft grass provided a little cushion between her body and the hard ground but did little to warm her. Shivering, she curled into a tighter ball, gritting her teeth at the pain in her belly and the burning of the cuts on her arms and legs.

Footsteps crunched behind her, but rolling over to see who it was would be too agonizing.

Someone knelt inches away from her back. A large hand gently cupped her head and stroked her hair. "Ava?" Jak'ri whispered.

Reaching up, she captured his hand, drew it forward, and hugged it to her chest.

His lips brushed her temple. Then he lay down and spooned his big body around hers. "Lift your head a moment," he said softly.

When she did, he slipped his arm beneath it so she could use his biceps as a pillow.

"Better?" he asked.

She nodded, incapable of speaking past the lump in her throat.

Warmth seeped into her as he held her, careful not to touch her stomach.

Tears welled in her eyes and slipped down to dampen his skin and the grass.

"When you awaken, drink from the canteen they provide. It contains a medication that will help you heal faster."

"I'm afraid they'll infect me with something," she forced out, her voice thick with tears.

He gave her hand a reassuring squeeze. "It's too early for that. They need time to study what they've taken from you before they can begin to craft their bioweapons."

She sniffled. "Why would they even care whether I healed or remained in pain?"

"Whatever illness they concoct will have to be strong enough to conquer a healthy body. They can't confirm that if they let you weaken too much."

So they wanted her to be healthy when they killed her.

Great. Just great.

"We'll find a way out of this, Ava. I vow it."

She tried to be optimistic, to cling to hope as they lay there drawing comfort from each other. But with so much misery assailing her, she feared their only escape would be in death.

D AYS PASSED. JAK'RI AND Ziv'ri recovered from whatever illness the Gathendiens had given them. Both also underwent more surgeries that left them weak and—they later learned—horrified Ava.

They hadn't realized until afterward that she had witnessed the surgeries through their thoughts, essentially watching the Gathendiens cut into Jak'ri while Ziv'ri observed and cursed and despaired, then doing the same when it was Ziv'ri's turn.

Jak'ri hadn't wanted her to see that. But he couldn't just shut his eyes to keep her from viewing it. He needed to know what the *srul* those *grunarks* were doing to them. And though he loathed the fear it instilled in her, he thought she had a right to know what lay in store for her.

Thankfully, the Gathendiens had performed no more surgeries on her. Nor had they taken more samples. They had largely left her alone while they studied their samples and processed whatever information those provided.

If Jak'ri made it out of this alive, he vowed to corner a medic on Purvel and ask what the *drek* all of that gouging and cutting could actually reveal. Because part of him couldn't help but wonder if these scientists weren't simply sadists.

Though his days as the Gathendiens' prisoner were miserable, his nights provided blissful escape. Every time he fell asleep now, he met Ava at his favorite contemplation spot: the cliff overlooking Runaka Sea. The first few times, the pain of her physical body followed her into sleep. So they either lay together or sat close with his arm around her and stared out over the water.

The tears that glistened on her cheeks as she battled pain and despair cut him as deeply as the Gathendiens' laser scalpels. His inability to spare her that ate at him. But he hid it and instead distracted her by regaling her with more tales of the outrageous escapades he'd embarked upon with his brother or recounting some of the heroic and fantastic tales from Purveli mythology that had enraptured him when he was younger.

Trusting in him, she took his advice and drank from the canteen the Gathendiens provided. Her wounds began to heal, quickly enough that she repeatedly expressed her amazement over it, so her people must not have developed chemical *silnas* that could accelerate healing yet.

The pain lessened as she healed. And in their shared dreams, they abandoned tales of other adventures and sought new ones of their own. They dove from the cliff. They laughed and teased and swam and played in the water with all the enthusiasm of children. He even began to teach her how to rock climb, caging her body between him and the wall of Runaka Point and guiding her small hands and feet to safe holds.

He felt so close to her. Almost as close as he did to his brother.

How was that possible? How had it happened so quickly?

He'd never developed such a strong friendship with a woman before.

Perhaps he might have if he'd consented to live with any of his past lovers. But he had never cohabitated with the women he'd had relationships with because they'd never understood his occasional need for quiet. For solitude. They had instead taken great offense at it, accusing him of needing time away from them.

And he supposed he had.

Oddly, he didn't feel a need for solitude when he was with Ava in their dreams. Even when he was awake, he began to crave her presence in his mind. He had even, much to his chagrin, fostered a moment of jealousy when his brother vied with him to see who could make her laugh the most until he'd realized that Ziv'ri's interest in her was not as extensive as his.

And his was extensive. Jak'ri found it increasingly difficult to ignore her beautiful breasts and the glide of her slender curves against his when they swam and cavorted in the water. His body had even begun to respond in ways that the cold ocean had difficulty dampening, something that shamed him. They were prisoners of the Gathendiens. She bore the same fears and concerns and pain that he and Ziv'ri did. The last thing she needed was to worry about him pressing her to sate his desire.

He shouldn't even be *feeling* desire.

"I think it's time," Ziv'ri whispered.

Blinking, Jak'ri came back to the present and followed his brother's gaze.

The Gathendien scientists were arguing about something.

Ziv'ri looked at him. "Is Ava listening to our thoughts?"

Ava? Are you with us? Jak'ri called. When no answer came, he shook his head. "I don't think so. I think she's still sleeping."

"Good." He nodded to the scientists. "Something's wrong. Saekro and Kunya found some anomalies in Ava's blood and tissue samples. *Significant* anomalies they weren't expecting. Saekro thinks Kunya *drekked* up the tests. Kunya insists he didn't and keeps postulating that there must have been some bizarre evolutionary jump in her race since their ancestors released a virus on Earth. Saekro thinks Kunya is full of *bura* and is just trying to cover his ass. Either way, it sounds as if they're planning more exploratory surgery for her."

"*Drek* that," Jak'ri hissed furiously. "I don't want them subjecting her to that again."

"I don't either."

"Then we should act."

Ziv'ri nodded. "We're both stronger now that the virus has left our system."

"And they're distracted. So they won't expect it. How do we get Saekro or Kunya to open our gates?"

"Before they began arguing over Ava, I heard them say they're going to try something new on us tomorrow."

And whenever they tried something new, they started with Ziv'ri. The brothers had quickly come to recognize a pattern. After removing Ziv'ri from his cell, they would strap him to a surgical table, inject him with their foul serum, then wait to see if he'd have an allergic reaction that would require them to intervene and resuscitate him. Any virus they created that instantly killed the infected party wouldn't benefit them, after all. They needed their victim to live long enough to spread it.

Lowering his voice to the quietest whisper, Jak'ri said, "We should fast tonight."

Ziv'ri nodded. "Feign eating and hide the cubes."

"And don't drink." Both believed the *nahalae* the Gathendiens dosed them with was in the vitamin injections they received every other day. Their first escape attempt had taken place when the Gathendiens waited three days to dose them with the vitamins. Jak'ri and Ziv'ri had both regained some of their telepathic ability as a result and hit them with a *senshi* that took down multiple guards and came *vuan* close to liberating the brothers. Hence the two-day schedule now.

But they sometimes wondered if there was also some *nahalae* in the nutrient cubes or drinks the Gathendiens supplied. The *grunarks* viciously beat them if they refrained from eating or drinking. The brothers just weren't sure if they reacted thusly because they needed healthy subjects or something else.

"Not emptying the canteen will be harder to hide," Ziv'ri said. "You know they monitor our liquid intake."

"Find a way to smuggle your canteen into the lav and pour it down."

He nodded. "Hopefully by the time the lav sends them an analysis of our latest offerings they'll be dead and we'll be on our way home." He glanced at the lab. "As soon as they tell me to get on the table, we'll both try to emit a *senshi* that will weaken them enough for me to either grab a scalpel or disarm the guard."

"Agreed." Reaching through the bars, Jak'ri rested a hand on Ziv'ri's nape and drew him close enough to press their foreheads together between the bars. "If we fail, know that I love you, brother."

Face grave, Ziv'ri reached through the bars and did the same. "I love you, too."

"Find a way to save Ava."

"I will." His lips twitched. "If we succeed... I want my hovercycle back."

Laughing, Jak'ri blinked back tears and released him.

This had to work.

It *had* to.

CHAPTER SIX

T HE NEXT DAY JAK'RI'S heartbeat quickened when Saekro motioned the guards forward.

This was it.

He glanced at Ziv'ri and saw the same knowledge in his brother's solemn gaze.

As two guards approached the door to Ziv'ri's cell, Jak'ri's stomach knotted. But he let none of his apprehension show. Once more, he wished that the *grunarks* would test their vile concoctions on *him* first instead of Ziv'ri. *He* was the older brother. *He* should be the one risking his life to free the others. *He*... couldn't bear the thought of losing his brother.

The guard waved his wrist over the censor and unlocked the gate.

When panic threatened to rise, Jak'ri channeled it into anger and raw determination. This *had* to work. Not just for their sake, but for Ava's.

The guard grabbed Ziv'ri by the arm and roughly ushered him forward.

Saekro barely spared them a glance, too busy arranging his favorite torture tools on the surgical instrument hover tray.

Kunya stood beside him, his eyes on the data tablet he held. A few taps activated the medical apparatus in the ceiling.

"Get on the table," the guard ordered gruffly.

Jak'ri immediately focused his telepathic energy and emitted the most powerful *senshi* he could produce while drugged, hoping it would be enough. He felt an identical pulse radiate outward from his brother.

The guard gasped. Releasing Ziv'ri, he bent forward and grabbed his head. The guard who'd remained in the open doorway grimaced and folded over.

Yes!

The two scientists winced and swung narrowed eyes on Ziv'ri.

Saekro yanked a laser scalpel from the tray and swung at him.

Ziv'ri threw his hands up to block the strikes that came one after another.

When Kunya reached for the shock rod they always kept handy, Ziv'ri swore and grabbed the hover tray. Dumping the instruments off of it, he raised it and swung it hard.

The metal crashed into Saekro's face, sending him stumbling backward into Kunya and toppling them both to the floor.

Ziv'ri lunged for the shock wand.

Sweat began to bead on Jak'ri's forehead as he struggled to keep the *senshi* going.

A shout erupted in the hallway.

The guards straightened as they fought the *senshi*.

Ziv'ri hit the one closest to him with the shock wand.

The guard jerked several times, then collapsed to the floor. Bending over him, Ziv'ri yanked his weapon out of its holster, aimed at the doorway, and hit the other guard with a blast of energy. The second guard stiffened and dropped to the floor, then lay there twitching like the other one.

The weapon must be set to stun.

Jak'ri's head began to ache with effort.

Ziv'ri's features tightened with strain as he fired a shot toward the scientists who were untangling themselves and trying to regain their feet.

Saekro and Kunya ducked back behind the operating table.

Breathing hard, Ziv'ri grabbed the fallen guard's arm and started to drag him toward Jak'ri's cell.

Jak'ri's heart slammed against his ribcage. Just a little farther and he would be free. They both would be.

Stopping on the other side of the bars, Ziv'ri yanked the guard's arm up toward the gate's censor.

A blast of electricity struck him.

Jak'ri cried out as he watched his brother stiffen and grunt. The *senshi* Ziv'ri was emitting halted abruptly.

Two more guards stepped over the one who lay twitching in the doorway and entered the lab, a stunner locking Ziv'ri in place.

Jak'ri tried to strengthen his own *senshi* to combat them, but the *vuan* drug thwarted his efforts.

"Cease!" Saekro bellowed as he rose on the opposite side of the lab. "Or I will order him killed!"

Hope died as more guards crowded into the hallway.

Jak'ri ended his *senshi*.

The guard stopped stunning Ziv'ri.

Ziv'ri collapsed to the floor and lay still, muscles twitching.

Weakness suffused Jak'ri as he watched him, coupled with despair.

They had failed.

And now his brother would pay the price.

The two new guards stomped forward and yanked Ziv'ri up.

Jak'ri ground his teeth as they forced Ziv'ri onto the table and engaged the manacles on his wrists and ankles. Before turning away, one held Ziv'ri's head still while the other locked a fifth, wider manacle across his forehead.

They only ever put the last in place when they wished him to remain completely still for a scan or when they shocked him.

Jak'ri didn't think they planned to scan his brother.

Blood pooled beneath Ziv'ri's hands on the table. His chest bore an ugly wound as well.

Ziv'ri glanced at Jak'ri from the corner of his eye. "This was all part of the plan, wasn't it?" he joked breathlessly. "You knew they'd come for me first. You knew I'd fail to kick their asses. And you knew they'd punish me as they're about to. This was all your way of getting back at me for putting that *yeorxoki* serpent in your bed when I was only ten summers. Am I correct?"

Though his heart broke for his brother, Jak'ri forced a laugh. "*Srul* yes. Maybe after this I'll finally forgive you."

Ziv'ri smiled. "*Drek* you."

When the guard approached with the shock wand, Saekro held up a hand to halt him. "Wait." He glared at the two Purvelis a long moment. Then a gleam entered his eyes that chilled Jak'ri's blood.

The moment stretched.

Gripping the bars, Jak'ri swallowed hard and met his brother's eyes. Were they going to kill him? Would he really have to stand here impotently and watch these *drekkers* kill Ziv'ri?

Dread overwhelmed him. Would it be swift? Or would they torture Ziv'ri for hours until his body finally succumbed to his injuries? The two of them had known this could happen, that this could be the punishment meted out if their escape attempt failed. But now that the moment was upon them...

He didn't want to lose his brother. His best friend.

He *couldn't*.

Saekro motioned the guard closer and murmured something in his ear.

Grunting, the guard unshackled Ziv'ri, yanked him off the table, and shoved him toward the open gate to his cell.

Ziv'ri stumbled but managed to remain on his feet as the gate closed and the lock activated.

The guard left. The brothers stared at each other.

What did this mean?

Saekro remained where he stood, watching the brothers impassively. But the gleam in his eye remained.

Kunya stood nearby, shifting anxiously from foot to foot, his tail twitching. Apparently he didn't know what it meant either.

Jak'ri? Ava called.

Yes.

What's happening?

Ziv'ri and I tried to escape.

What?

He gave her a brief accounting of what had happened.

Ziv'ri, she said, *are you okay? Did they hurt you?*

Only a few cuts. I expected a swift and harsh punishment like those they've delivered in the past, but they returned me to my cell.

Maybe they're afraid hurting you could affect their experiments?

Perhaps, Ziv'ri said, his voice full of doubt.

Did you feel anything when we emitted the senshi? Jak'ri asked. They had focused all of their efforts on the scientists and the guards, but he worried she might have felt it, too.

No. I didn't feel anything. She would have if he'd been at full strength. *I was sleeping until the guards woke me up. I thought at first they were going to make me force down more of those disgusting nutrient cubes. But they appear to have something else—*

Ava walked into the lab, two guards at her back—*in mind.*

Her eyes widened as they met his then skimmed over to Ziv'ri.

Theirs did, too.

Oh drek. Jak'ri glanced at his brother and saw the same horror he felt reflected in Ziv'ri's face. *No, no, no, no, no.*

"Put her on the table," Saekro ordered.

Her face paling, Ava stopped short and addressed the scientist. "What's going on?" She motioned to the brothers. "Who are *they*? Why am I here?"

One of the guards gave her a hard shove.

Stumbling forward, she scowled and stopped short again. Hands curling into fists, she turned suddenly and punched the guard in the throat.

Caught by surprised, the guard cupped his neck and began to wheeze.

Ava spun and delivered a hard kick to his belly, actually managing to drive him back a step. But the Gathendien recovered quickly and backhanded her, sending her sprawling to the floor.

Before she could do more than raise onto her hands and knees, the *grunark* grabbed her by the waist, lifted her, swiveled, and slammed her down on the operating table.

Ava cried out, her face contorting in pain.

Jak'ri struggled to hold back a roar of fury. She was still sore from their *drekking* surgery. That had to have hurt like *srul.*

Ava clamped her pink lips together and struggled, but she was no match for the Gathendiens as they forced her arms and legs into position and clamped the manacles together.

"*They,*" Saekro said, "are two lab subjects who are willing to sacrifice each other to thwart our efforts." His thin lips turned up in an oily smile. "Let us see if they are as eager to sacrifice you."

Ava's eyes grew so wide when they met his that he could see the whites all the way around her brown irises. *What's happening?*

Ava. His body began to tremble with dread and remorse. *I'm so sorry. I didn't know they were going to do this. I swear to you I didn't.*

Ziv'ri spoke, his hands now tight around the bars of his cell like Jak'ri's. *It never even occurred to us that they might punish you for our offense.*

Though she must know it was futile, she struggled against the manacles. *What are they going to do?*

Saekro took the shock wand and held it above her. Blue light crackled from the tip.

Oh shit. Is that a—?

Saekro touched the wand to her shoulder.

Every muscle locked as electricity burned through her small body.

Jak'ri wanted to growl and snarl and curse the *drekker*, demanding he stop, but worried such would only encourage him.

Saekro raised the wand.

Ava slumped against the table, breath coming in pants, muscles twitching.

Then Saekro touched the wand to her thigh.

Again her muscles locked tight.

I'm so sorry, Jak'ri chanted over and over again. *I'm so sorry, Ava. I'm so sorry. I'm going to kill them for this. I'm going to kill them all.*

Saekro raised the wand.

Ava panted, muscles twitching even more. *Not if I kill them first.*

Saekro touched the wand to her tender, still recovering stomach.

Ava screamed, the agonized sound tearing Jak'ri apart.

"Enough!" he bellowed, unable to stop himself. "Enough!"

Saekro raised the wand.

Ava whimpered as the muscles of her stomach continued to twitch and contract. Tears streamed down her temples and dampened her hair.

Saekro stared at him, then at Ziv'ri, and arched a brow. "Is it?"

"Yes," Ziv'ri growled.

The scientist's expression darkened with a combination of anger and satisfaction. "Try to escape again, refuse to cooperate in any way, and *she* will be punished in your stead. Each offense you commit will exact a greater punishment than the previous." Again he lowered the wand to her stomach.

Blue light flickered. Ava screamed again as her muscles locked.

The *grunark* held it even longer this time.

"*I said enough!*" Jak'ri roared.

Saekro raised the wand and smiled in triumph. "We shall see." He turned to the guard. "Throw her in with the older one. Let them live for a time with what they've wrought."

The guard unclamped the manacles and jerked Ava up. When he tugged her off the table, her knees buckled. Swearing, the big Gathendien looped an arm around her waist and half-carried half-dragged her over to Jak'ri's cell. "Get back," he ordered.

Jak'ri immediately withdrew to the center of his cell, wanting to give the burly *grunark* no reason to harm Ava further.

Once the guard disabled the lock, he opened the gate and tossed Ava inside like a pile of old bedding.

Jak'ri lunged forward and fell to his knees, barely managing to catch her before she hit the ground. The rough texture of the floor scraped his knees. But he didn't care. Holding her close, he watched the guard close the gate and reactivate the lock.

Afterward, the guard tugged his fallen colleague to his feet and helped him return to his post outside the door.

Saekro turned to Kunya. "We won't be able to take more samples from her today. Let us go analyze those we have again and see where you *drekked* up."

Kunya's thin lips tightened with annoyance.

Then the two left, the door sliding shut behind them.

Jak'ri rose onto his bleeding knees and scooted closer to his brother's cell. Sitting on his pallet with his legs crossed, he settled Ava in his lap as gently as he could and held her while her muscles continued to twitch and tears bathed her cheeks.

Ziv'ri sat beside them in his cell. His throat worked in a swallow. His silver eyes glimmered with remorse. Reaching through the bars, he took one of her hands in his.

Jak'ri brushed damp hair back from her face, then pressed a kiss to her forehead. "I'm so sorry, Ava."

Giving her head a little shake, she stared up at him. "S-Sorry I wasn't stronger."

The whispered words hurt him so much she might as well have driven a knife into his chest. *He* had caused this. He and Ziv'ri. Yet she was apologizing because she hadn't been able to overpower a Gathendien thrice her weight? "You were strong enough to nearly make that *grunark* choke to death, which was more than my brother managed to do."

"Hey," Ziv'ri declared with false affront, "I can't help it if I didn't hurt my guard as much as Ava did hers. I'm delicate."

Jak'ri snorted. "Delicate, my ass."

"Based on the number of times I've kicked it, I'd say your ass *is* delicate," his brother said.

Though neither felt like joking, the banter did what they'd hoped.

Ava smiled as she closed her eyes.

Ziv'ri squeezed her hand. "Did Jak'ri tell you about the time he landed us in a fight that pitted the two of us against eight Akseli mercenaries?"

Jak'ri groaned at the memory.

Ava's smile widened. "No."

"Well, it happened on Promeii 7."

"What *doesn't* happen on Promeii 7?" Jak'ri retorted.

Ziv'ri laughed. "True."

As his brother embarked upon his tale, Jak'ri stroked Ava's hair, offering what comfort he could. Her tears ceased. But her face remained pinched with pain even when she smiled over their dubious exploits.

Jak'ri met Ziv'ri's gaze.

Though his brother's voice remained light and was sprinkled with laughter, his eyes burned with rage.

The three of them needed to get the *drek* out of here before those *grunarks* killed them.

But every attempted escape they'd hatched thus far had failed.

How could they attempt another without further endangering Ava?

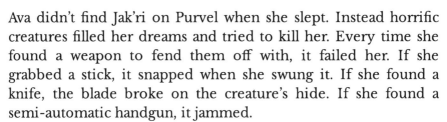

Ava didn't find Jak'ri on Purvel when she slept. Instead horrific creatures filled her dreams and tried to kill her. Every time she found a weapon to fend them off with, it failed her. If she grabbed a stick, it snapped when she swung it. If she found a knife, the blade broke on the creature's hide. If she found a semi-automatic handgun, it jammed.

Pain began to claw at her as consciousness seeped in and dimmed the nightmares. So much pain that she actually thought she'd prefer to keep fighting the damned monsters in her dreams if that would keep the agony at bay.

Alas, she couldn't.

Moaning in protest, she turned her face tighter into the warm blankets.

No. Not warm blankets. A warm chest. Someone held her.

A male voice murmured soothing words as a hand stroked her hair.

Jak'ri.

Sighing, she relaxed against him. Then her eyes flew open.

Wait. Jak'ri was holding her. Not in a dream, but in reality. She blinked, then swore foully and swore some more as the events of the previous day—or what she *assumed* was the previous day—hit her. Those sorry sacks of crap had shocked her repeatedly while they made Jak'ri and Ziv'ri watch. Every time her stomach muscles had contracted it had felt as if someone were driving knives into the partially healed incision sites. Those bastards had tortured her!

And, in effect, they'd tortured Jak'ri and Ziv'ri.

The Purveli brothers' minds had filled with such guilt and remorse.

Ava hadn't held them responsible as they'd feared. She hadn't blamed them. She'd tried so hard to stoically endure the pain and keep them from feeling even worse. But it had just been too much. She wasn't used to it.

Could a person get used it? Could anyone really grow accustomed to suffering that kind of pain?

Her thoughts went to Eliana.

Immortal Guardians did. Eliana had been hunting and fighting psychotic vampires for four hundred years and had sustained so many serious injuries while doing it that the crap these Gathendiens had subjected Ava to probably wouldn't have even fazed her.

I wish I were strong like her, Ava thought.

"You *are* strong," Jak'ri told her softly as he gently stroked her hair.

Sighing, she opened her eyes and found him staring down at her, his handsome face grave.

He sat with his back to the bars of his cell, legs crossed to provide Ava with a lap to sleep upon like a hammock.

Ziv'ri peered over his shoulder through the bars behind him. "Strong like who?"

"Eliana." Every muscle in Ava's body ached as though she had tripled the amount of weight she lifted and had worked out for five hours instead of the usual one yesterday. Even so, she raised a hand and cupped Jak'ri face, smoothing a thumb over his stubbled jaw. She suspected he'd been holding her all night and hadn't yet had what passed for a shower or a bladeless shave here.

She studied him, touched his midnight hair, rested her hand on his neck where it met his strong shoulder and drew her fingers over his barely discernible scales with their silvery hue. "It's strange."

Uncertainty entered his expression. "My scales?"

"No." She rubbed his shoulder. "That you feel as real to me in dreams as you do right now."

He nodded, still stroking her hair. "How are you?"

She tried to think of the Alliance Common word for sore, but couldn't. Besides, she didn't want to whine about how much she hurt when the two of them had been here longer and had suffered far more. "Angry."

His hand on her hair stilled. "At us?"

"No." She jerked a thumb toward the empty lab and winced. "At *those* bastards." Clenching her teeth, she drew in a deep breath, held it, and forced herself to sit up straight.

And there came the pain. She hoped tasing or shocking her in the stomach hadn't messed up the organs that were still healing from whatever the hell they'd done to her.

Jak'ri rested a hand on her back, his brow furrowed with concern.

She forced a smile. "I'm okay." Then she shifted her gaze to Ziv'ri. He looked remarkably similar to Jak'ri with subtle differences in his nose and jawline. If Jak'ri hadn't told her Ziv'ri was younger, she might have thought them fraternal twins.

Ava extended her hand through the bars "Hi, Ziv'ri. It's nice to meet you in person."

He clasped her forearm in what she had come to understand was a common greeting out here in space. "I wish we could've met under more pleasant circumstances."

She took in the scars and many healing wounds that marred his body. "I do, too."

The pressing need to relieve her bladder gradually made itself known, and Ava felt grateful that she hadn't peed her pants while she was being tased. It was a silly thing to worry about, she supposed. But that little humiliation on top of the pain just felt like it would've been too much.

Releasing Ziv'ri, she gripped a bar with one hand and Jak'ri's shoulder with the other and heaved herself to her feet.

Yep. That had felt about as horrible as she'd guessed it would.

Both men rose, extending their hands to offer support.

"I'm okay," she assured them with a tight smile. Heat flooded her cheeks. "I just, uh, need to use the lav."

They nodded, exhibiting none of the embarrassment she felt.

Jak'ri took her elbow. "Do you want me to help you?"

"No, thank you. I'm okay. Really."

Not really. She hadn't been okay since she'd ended up on this ship. But she squared her shoulders, stiffly crossed the cell, and enclosed herself in the bathroom. It was even smaller than the one in the first house she'd rented. A claustrophobic shower took up half of it. Considering how her eyes stung whenever she used the one in her cell, she assumed it was some sort of decontamination shower. These scientists were serious about keeping their subjects clean and moderately healthy for their experiments. The cells their subjects occupied might look like crap, but they were spotless.

On the other side of the lav—close enough that Jak'ri probably bumped his elbows a lot in here—rested a high-tech toilet that apparently analyzed everything they put in it and a sink with a bottle of *wosuur* liquid on the shelf above it. Though the bottle looked like glass, it was unbreakable. She had dropped the one in her cell's bathroom twice and might have thrown it down in anger a time or two as well. All it did was bounce and make a racket.

The Lasarans had used *wosuur* liquid on the *Kandovar*. The liquid dissolved any food particles in the mouth without damaging teeth or gums and was so efficient that it was the equivalent of brushing, flossing, and rinsing with mouthwash combined.

Ava used the facilities, cleaned her hands in the sink, and availed herself of the *wosuur* liquid.

Looking down, she peeled the bottom of her shirt up and examined her stomach.

She'd lost weight since coming here. She'd already been slender before. The network that had employed her and made this whole space voyage possible was very big on helping employees achieve good health. She had heard of other companies that provided their employees with a gym in an attempt to keep the company's health insurance expenses down. But the network that aided the Immortal Guardians instead seemed to genuinely care about its employees, wanting them to be as healthy, happy, and safe as possible.

Once she'd gone to work for them, Ava had taken advantage of everything they offered. Free healthcare. A gym with trainers on hand twenty-four hours a day. Self-defense instruction that was optional at first then became mandatory after mercenaries blitzed the building and the number of vampires—all of whom were swiftly descending into insanity—living several stories beneath them increased. (If only that and the training she had received from Eliana would've enabled her to overpower the damned Gathendiens yesterday.) And three free meals a day.

Thinking of those delicious meals, Ava nearly started salivating.

Thanks to the network, she had been in tip-top shape when she'd left Earth.

Now, however, her ribcage was disturbingly prominent.

She felt a little relieved that the incision sites on her stomach still appeared to be healing. She'd worried that all of that shocking might have sparked bleeding or bruising or something. But whatever the Gathendiens put in her canteen was remarkable in its ability to speed healing. Two places on her abdomen now bore what looked like burn marks. No doubt that was where the bastard had hit her with the shock wand.

She touched one tentatively.

Odd. It *looked* like a burn, but it wasn't as raw as fresh burns usually were.

Sighing, she lowered her shirt. A comb lay on the shelf beside the *wosuur* liquid. Since no mirror graced the wall, she had no idea how her hair looked. But it was probably a tangled mess.

Ava picked up the comb and left the lav.

Both Purveli men stood where she'd left them.

He wasn't exaggerating, Ziv'ri's thoughts floated to her. *She is small.*

Ava dredged up a tired smile as she approached them. "I'm not small. You two are tall."

Jak'ri shot his brother a look.

Ziv'ri eyed her with surprise. "You're not considered small on your planet?"

She shrugged. "I'm five feet three inches. I read somewhere that the average height for women on my planet is five-four. So I guess I'm about average."

Jak'ri tilted his head to one side. "How tall are your men?"

"I think their average height is five feet ten. So most are shorter than you guys."

Ziv'ri tilted his head at the exact same angle as Jak'ri, increasing their likeness. "What are guys?"

"Sorry. I slipped out of Alliance Common and into English there at the end, didn't I? Guys is just an informal term for men or boys."

"Ah."

She smiled up at Jak'ri. "And you guys are *tall*. Are you both above average height or is this the norm for Purvelis?" She had to drop her head back to look up at them and guessed they were both a few inches above six feet.

Jak'ri grinned. "This is the norm for males."

She shook her head, bemused. "I noticed the same with the Yona. Why are so many alien males tall?"

Jak'ri shrugged. "I can't speak for other races, but Purveli youths—both male and female—tend to spend as much time in the water as they do out of it. Sometimes more. Our medics believe that swimming vigorously for long periods of time reduces the load Purvel's gravity places on the body because we are more often than not in a horizontal position instead of vertical, so our bones lengthen more than they would if we were solely land dwellers, allowing for greater height."

"That makes sense. Some scientists on my planet speculate that a child raised in a no- or low-gravity environment would be taller and have weaker bones."

"We don't have weaker bones," Jak'ri said.

Ziv'ri nodded earnestly. "We're also exceptionally attractive."

She laughed, then grimaced and rested a hand on her aching stomach. "And so modest."

Concern flashed in Jak'ri's features as he touched her arm. "Ava?"

"I'm okay. But I think maybe I'd better sit down for a bit."

"Of course." He guided her to the pallet he'd made against the bars.

Ava sank down on it cross-legged.

Jak'ri sat beside her, his knee touching hers.

Ziv'ri seated himself on an identical pallet on the other side of the bars.

"Oh." She held up the comb. "Is it okay if I borrow this? I'm pretty sure my hair is a mess."

"Your hair is beautiful," Jak'ri insisted.

She shook her head. "*Your* hair is beautiful. Mine doesn't change color when it gets wet."

"Yes, it does." Reaching out, he caught a lock of her hair and curled it around his finger. "It turns from brown to black."

Ava stared at him, inexplicably tongue-tied. Her heart rate picked up and butterflies fluttered in her aching belly. "Oh."

He held out his other hand. "Give me the comb."

She didn't hesitate.

Jak'ri began to apply it to her hair, starting at the ends and carefully working through the tangles.

"Why do they even provide you with a comb? I wouldn't think they'd consider that a necessity."

"They grew tired of Ziv'ri's incessant complaints about his tangled locks."

Ziv'ri feigned a glare.

Ava grinned. "Or maybe one of the guards has a boy crush on you."

Jak'ri paused. "What's a boy crush?"

She struggled to find a comparable Alliance Common term. "An infatuation?"

Ziv'ri laughed heartily over the notion of one of the odious reptilian guards desiring his brother while Jak'ri cursed him. He was still grinning when he said, "Tell us how you came to be on the *Kandovar*."

She hesitated.

Jak'ri rested a hand on her shoulder. "I know you worry for your friends. If it distresses you too much to speak of it..."

"No. It isn't that." She sighed. "It's just not going to paint my people in a positive light."

The brothers stared at her.

"I don't know what that means," Jak'ri said.

"It will make you think badly of my people. And I worry it may change the way you see me."

Jak'ri frowned. "We won't judge you by your people's actions."

Ziv'ri nodded. "We'll only judge you according to how brilliant you think we are."

Jak'ri rolled his eyes and resumed untangling her hair.

Ava laughed. "Well... I guess I should start at the beginning. Were you aware of Prince Taelon's sister, Amiriska, disappearing?"

Both nodded.

"She came to our planet several times," Jak'ri said, "to try to coax Purvel into joining the Aldebarian Alliance."

Ziv'ri nodded. "And to negotiate trade deals. She was highly respected by our people."

Jak'ri worked on a particularly stubborn tangle. "Her brothers searched tirelessly for her when she went missing, but could find neither her nor her ship. Their allies couldn't either. Most ultimately assumed her ship crashed on an uninhabited planet, killing all on board."

Ava bit her lip. "That's the thing. Her ship didn't crash. She went to Earth."

Both stared at her with identical looks of surprise.

"She did?" Jak'ri asked.

Ava nodded.

"Why didn't she remain in contact with her family? They've been mourning her loss."

She grimaced. "That's the other thing. She came to Earth against her family's wishes. She wanted to warn Earth that the Gathendiens were headed our way. And she was hoping that—in exchange for technological advancements that would eliminate our dependence on fossil fuels, end all famine and drought on our planet, and enable us to terraform our moon to alleviate overpopulation—Earth would allow some of our women to travel to Lasara and help them with their reproductive issues." The damn Gathendiens had approached the Lasarans as benevolent allies, then released a virus that had rendered almost all Lasaran females infertile.

Those who could still become pregnant had great difficulty carrying babies to term.

Jak'ri finished untangling a lock and paused to stare at her. "Earthlings are reproductively compatible with Lasarans?"

"Yes."

"Then why would Princess Amiriska's family object to such an alliance?"

She grimaced. "Because the Sectas shared their research on Earthlings with them and the Lasarans thought we were too barbaric, violent, and backward as a people. They thought any approach they made would be met with violence."

The brothers shared a look.

Ziv'ri spoke slowly. "What happened when Amiriska arrived at your planet?"

Ava's shoulders slumped. "She was met with violence. Instead of gratefully accepting her help, the dumbasses in power tricked her into trusting them, captured her, destroyed her ship, and spent the next six months doing to her what the Gathendiens are doing to us."

Both men looked appalled.

"Full disclosure, what they did to her as they studied her was actually a lot worse. Lasarans have incredible regenerative capabilities. So the scientists on Earth could basically dissect her without killing her. And did. Over and over and over again—while she was awake, without deadening the pain—until Seth and David found her and rescued her six months later."

A long silence stretched.

"Who are Seth and David?" Jak'ri asked.

She smiled. "They're the good guys. They lead the Immortal Guardians."

As Jak'ri continued combing her hair, she explained that there were actually two kinds of people on Earth: humans and *gifted ones*. *Gifted ones* were born with far more complex DNA, which was why they were compatible with Lasarans. They were also hated, feared, and treated badly because of their differences whenever those differences came to light.

"Why would Earthlings not celebrate those differences?" Jak'ri asked.

"Unfortunately, people on Earth are more likely to distrust, harm, or even kill those with special gifts because they either fear the power it gives them or envy it and resent that they don't have those gifts themselves. In the past, some have even imprisoned *gifted ones* and sought to use their gifts by force to gain wealth and prestige. Today, those in power would capture *gifted ones* if they ever discovered them and dissect the *gifted ones* the way they did Ami in an attempt to find a way to imbue themselves with those special abilities." When a mercenary group had found out about the vampiric virus, they had even tried to use it to build an invincible army they could then hire out to the highest bidder. But the Immortal Guardians stopped them.

She shrugged. "And some people on Earth simply hate anyone who is different from them. So for thousands of years *gifted ones* like me have had to hide our special abilities for safety's sake."

Jak'ri's brow furrowed. "The Aldebarian Alliance would never welcome such a people."

Ziv'ri nodded. "The alliance is made up of many different alien species. Why welcome a people who would scorn other alliance members for their differences?"

"I know. Earth *as a whole* will never be part of the alliance. But one segment of Earth's population—*gifted ones* and Immortal Guardians led by Seth—have fostered relations with the Lasaran royal family. Amiriska ended up falling in love with an Immortal Guardian. And her brother, Taelon, fell in love with a *gifted one* when he came looking for Ami. Both Lasarans are now bonded to Earthlings," she told them, using their word for marriage.

The brothers' jaws dropped.

Ava grinned. "Ami said that was pretty much the same expression her family had when she told them." Then she shrugged. "So Seth agreed to let ten *gifted ones* and five Immortal Guardians travel to Lasara aboard the *Kandovar* as sort of a trial to see how well an alliance with the Lasarans would work."

"This was your first voyage into space?" Ziv'ri asked.

"Yes."

Jak'ri shook his head. "And then the Gathendiens *drekked* everything up."

"Yes." She thought of all the amazing people she'd met on her journey. "I wish I knew what happened to everyone else," Ava said softly. "How many escape pods do you think there were on the *Kandovar*?"

Jak'ri patted her shoulder. "Enough to evacuate everyone on board."

"But the Yona and Lasaran soldiers probably would've just kept fighting until the end, wouldn't they? The computer in my escape pod thought the *Kandovar* was destroyed." Tears welled in her eyes. "Lisa and Taelon have a baby girl. She's only five months old." Had they survived? "Taelon is the commander of the ship. Don't commanders usually refuse to abandon their post? Wouldn't he have stayed until...?"

Jak'ri finished combing her hair and sat close beside her. "I believe the chances are very good that Prince Taelon, his lifemate, and their child survived."

Ava leaned into him, taking comfort.

Ziv'ri nodded. "The first priority of the Yona warriors is to ensure the safety of the royal family. If they believed the danger substantial enough, they would not have allowed one of the first children born into the royal family in fifty years to perish."

That made her feel a little better. But what of the others? Had *any* of them survived?

Had those in escape pods been rescued? Or were they stuck in a Gathendien cell like her?

At this point, Ava wasn't sure she would ever find out.

CHAPTER SEVEN

T HE NEXT DAY, JAK'RI and Ziv'ri spoke softly while Ava slept.

When the door to the lab opened suddenly, three guards entered and headed toward Ziv'ri's cell.

Jak'ri placed a hand on Ava's shoulder and gave it a little shake.

Her eyes flew open and met his.

Something's happening. Sliding an arm beneath her shoulders, he helped her sit up so she wouldn't have to use her stomach muscles and aggravate her wounds.

A guard unlocked the gate to Ziv'ri's cell and motioned for him to come forward. "Saekro ordered us to move you."

Ziv'ri arched a brow and remained where he sat. "What if I don't wish to be moved?" He motioned to the barren cell. "I've grown to appreciate my current, lavish accommodations and am unwilling to settle for less."

The guard scowled. "Move or we'll move you."

"I'd rather stay."

The burly Gathendien entered the cell, the others right behind him.

Ziv'ri rose and faced him, hands curling into fists.

Jak'ri rose, too. What was happening? Why were they moving Ziv'ri? Where were they taking him? Was this another punishment for their attempted escape?

Ava rose beside him.

When the guard reached for Ziv'ri, Ziv'ri ducked his grasp and punched him in the face. The other two guards closed in on him. A brief fight ensued while Jak'ri plastered himself to the bars and did his damnedest to grab a Gathendien and help his brother.

He caught one guard's armor and yanked hard. The Gathendien stumbled and nearly fell but managed to free himself from Jak'ri's grasp. Growling in fury, the guard drew a shock wand and touched it to the bars.

Jak'ri stiffened as electrical current shot through his body. Pain inundated him.

Beside him, Ava cried out and screamed at the guards to stop.

The other two guards continued to wrestle with Ziv'ri.

The guard with the wand lifted it away from the bars.

As soon as he did, Jak'ri collapsed.

Ava dropped to her knees and shoved her hands under his head before it could hit the floor.

Muscles twitching, Jak'ri managed to turn his head just enough to see into the other cell.

The two guards holding Ziv'ri suddenly leapt back. The third guard hit Ziv'ri with the shock wand.

Fury burned in Jak'ri's belly. The guard held the wand to Ziv'ri far longer than he thought a body could take. When he withdrew it, Ziv'ri collapsed. His head struck the floor. His eyes closed. And he went limp, though his muscles continued to twitch intermittently.

Ziv'ri? Ava called.

No response came.

Ziv'ri? she called again with greater urgency.

Grabbing Ziv'ri by the arms, the guards dragged him out of the cell.

They didn't take him to the operating table this time. Instead they took him out into the hallway and closed the door.

Jak'ri swore and forced himself to sit up, waving Ava away when she leaned forward to help him. "You're in enough pain. I'm okay."

Nodding, she bit her lip and sat close.

Jak'ri sighed. "Is Ziv'ri telling you where they're taking him?"

Her face pinched with worry, she shook her head. "He isn't answering when I call him. I think he's unconscious."

A smear of blood stained the floor where Ziv'ri's head had struck it.

Jak'ri hoped he hadn't been seriously injured.

The door to the lab opened again. One of the guards returned and approached their cell. His beady eyes fastened on Ava. "Your turn," he grunted.

Ava sidled closer to Jak'ri, her fear palpable.

Jak'ri dragged himself to his feet, preparing to fight the burly *grunark*.

No, Ava told him telepathically. *Don't fight him. I'll go.*

We don't know what they're going to do, he protested.

You know we can't win against him. If I go willingly, at least I'll be able to tell you where he takes me and if Ziv'ri is there.

"Come," the guard ordered.

Ava rose, wincing as she rested a hand on her stomach.

Jak'ri grabbed her arm to keep her from leaving. "She stays with me."

The Gathendien brandished the shock wand. "No, she doesn't."

When Jak'ri didn't relent, Ava looked up at him. "Please," she whispered. *I don't want anything to happen to you.*

Pulling out of his grasp, she crossed to the guard.

The *grunark* took her by the arm, jerked her out of the cell, and secured the gate. Then he shoved her toward the open gate of Ziv'ri's cell.

Ava's eyes widened when he pushed her inside.

Relief suffused Jak'ri. He wasn't taking her away. He was just putting her in the next cell.

The gate clanked shut behind her.

A hum sounded.

Ava spun around. Clear glass slats rose from the floor between the bars, sealing her inside a clear box. "What's happening?"

Jak'ri sucked in a breath. "*Drek*. Get in the sanishower! Now!" he shouted.

Eyes widening, she raced for the lav, her pretty face contorting from the pain. Just before she reached the door to the lav, liquid began to rain down from the ceiling.

Jak'ri's heart pounded. If that liquid touched her...

Ava cried out. The lav door slid up. More of the liquid rained down inside.

As soon as she entered, the door slid shut and hid her from view.

Ava? he called.

Nothing.

Ava?

He swung around to glower at the guard. "You *drekking grunark!*"

The guard's thin lips turned up in a smug smile.

<hr />

H EART POUNDING, LIMBS SHAKING, Ava ducked into the sanitizing shower. Every millimeter of skin the liquid touched burned and stung as if acid bathed her.

Teeth clenched, she activated the shower and stood beneath the water.

Instant relief.

After a couple of minutes, she peeled her shirt and shorts off and tossed them onto the floor, where they landed with a plop. The shower was so narrow that she couldn't lather up unless she stopped the water, so she turned it off and pressed the button that dispensed foamy soap.

More of that noxious liquid rained down in the rest of the lav for a minute or so, but not in the shower. The toilet hummed.

What the hell was happening?

The rain stopped.

Ava finished soaping up and rinsed off.

She pressed another button and air blasted her from three directions, drying her within seconds.

Smoothing her hair back from her face, she eyed the floor outside the shower warily.

Would the skin on the bottom of her feet start to burn if she stepped out?

Oddly enough, the floor looked dry even though the wind in the shower hadn't brushed it.

Ava tentatively stretched a foot forth and touched the floor with her big toe.

No burning or stinging ensued.

Frowning, she stepped out.

Still no burning. There was an odd scent in the air though. A strong chemical smell arose that made her nose tingle unpleasantly.

Her clothes remained in a sodden heap. Ava picked them up, dropped them in the clothing sanitizer in the wall, and activated it. While it hummed, she examined her wounds. Though they hurt like hell, none bled and no new bruising had formed. Just those burn marks from the damn shock wand.

The sanitizer dinged, indicating her clothes were clean and dry.

Ava donned them in short order and stood staring at the door. *Jak'ri,* she called mentally.

Ava, are you all right? he replied instantly.

Yes. Is it safe to come out?

Yes.

She opened the door.

The glass barriers that had risen between the bars were in the process of lowering.

Jak'ri stood just on the other side, his face dark with fury.

What just happened? she asked.

A muscle leapt in his jaw. *Saekro must have told the guard to decontaminate the cell. He's supposed to either do it before he puts you in there or wait until you're in the shower so the decon fluid won't burn your skin.*

She stepped into the cell.

It looked clean and dry.

In the lab, the guard sent her an evil smile as he tossed a blanket, a canteen, and a nutrient pack through the bars.

She glared at him. "Asshole."

Smirking, he left and closed the door behind him.

Ava grabbed the blanket and rations and headed toward Jak'ri. It only took her a moment to fold the blanket and make a pallet just on the other side of the bars from his.

Still feeling weak from the previous day, she sank onto it and sat cross-legged.

Jak'ri sat facing her. And she mourned the fact that they were separated yet again.

At least she could still see him. And touch him.

He reached through the bars. "Did it burn you? Let me see."

She placed her hands in his and sat quietly while he examined her arms. Her skin bore pink patches where the liquid had irritated it, but they didn't hurt. "I think I made it to the shower in time. It was only on me a second or two before I rinsed it off." She squeezed his hands. "Thank you."

Shaking his head, he met her gaze. "I wish I could get you the *srul* out of here. I'm sorry our escape attempt failed."

She forced a smile. "Don't worry. Our next attempt will succeed."

Drek *yes, it will,* a voice grumbled.

Her eyes widened. *Ziv'ri?* she called.

Yes.

You heard us? Is your telepathy returning?

No, you were broadcasting.

Oh. She looked at Jak'ri. "It's Ziv'ri." *Where are you?* she asked, sharing the telepathic conversation with Jak'ri.

In a cell by the tertiary lab.

Jak'ri's hands tightened on hers as relief swept across his handsome features.

What happened after I lost consciousness? Ziv'ri asked.

Jak'ri winked. *Ava and I escaped on your hovercycle while Saekro probed your butt. We are now on our way to Promeii 7.*

Drek *you,* Ziv'ri responded with a laugh.

Ava laughed, too, glad to hear the brothers bantering again. *They moved me to your cell, Ziv'ri.*

Jak'ri scowled. *And initiated a decontamination without warning her first.*

Ziv'ri loosed a string of words her translator chip refused to define.

Ava smiled. *One of these days you're going to have to tell me what some of those mean. My translator is apparently too shocked or offended to do it.*

The brothers laughed.

And her nerves calmed. For now at least, the three of them were still okay.

It was a sentiment she would soon come to question.

———◆O◆———

T HE NEXT DAY AVA woke to silence from Ziv'ri. She thought at first he was simply sleeping. When she sought his mind, however, she encountered no dreams.

She encountered nothing at all.

"Perhaps they're performing one of their surgeries on him and have rendered him unconscious," Jak'ri suggested with a puckered brow.

But she encountered the same silence the next day. And the next. And the one after that until a week had come and gone.

Saekro and Kunya remained notably absent. The only Gathendiens Ava and Jak'ri saw were the jerks who threw canteens and nutrient cubes at them.

What had happened? Where were they? In the tertiary lab with Ziv'ri?

What had they done to him?

For a moment, she wondered if the Gathendiens had guessed that she, too, was telepathic and dosed her with *nahalae* so she could no longer communicate with the brothers mentally, but Jak'ri's thoughts still came clearly to her. So whatever had happened had taken place on Ziv'ri's end.

The possibilities terrified her.

Can you still hear me? Jak'ri asked. He had done so several times a day ever since Ziv'ri had gone silent.

Yes.

He nodded, face grim as he dropped his gaze to the floor. *Try him again, please?*

Heart breaking, she called, *Ziv'ri? Can you hear me?*

Quiet settled upon them.

Ziv'ri? she tried again. *Please answer. If you do, I promise I'll make Jak'ri give you your hovercycle back.*

Jak'ri nodded, face grim. *I will. If you answer, you can have your precious hovercycle back* and *I'll buy you a new hoverboard. Just let us know you still live, brother.*

Nothing.

Ava fought tears. *Please, Ziv'ri. It's been days since we've heard from you. We're worried about you. Are you okay?*

Minutes ticked past.

Sighing, Jak'ri rubbed his eyes. *I don't know what to do. He would answer us if he could.*

Ava nodded helplessly. Reaching through the bars, she clasped Jak'ri's hand and held it while he eyed their cells with mounting anger and frustration.

The door to the lab slid up.

Saekro and Kunya, entered.

Mocna, the guard from the tertiary lab, followed with two others she didn't recognize.

Ava surreptitiously withdrew her hand, thinking it best to hide the affection she and Jak'ri shared.

Barely looking up from the data pad he held, Saekro motioned to Ava. "Bring me the female."

Jak'ri stiffened and started to rise, but Ava caught his eye and shook her head.

Fighting would gain him nothing but pain.

At least for now.

Nerves jangling, Ava stood up and eyed Mocna warily as he waved his wrist over the sensor to unlock the gate.

Though she thought apparent capitulation might save her some pain, her feet nevertheless refused to carry her forward. She was too worried about what they intended to do with her.

Would they make her disappear the way they had Ziv'ri?

Jak'ri leapt to his feet, alarm crossing his handsome features.

And she swore inwardly. She must have inadvertently broadcast her thoughts again.

Mocna reached in, grabbed her arm, and yanked her forward.

"Get on the table," Saekro ordered.

Kunya reached for the shock wand and held it up, the threat evident.

And yet she still balked. "What are you going to do to me?"

Saekro set his tablet aside and drew a hover tray covered with surgical instruments closer. "We need more samples."

Her stomach clenched.

Saekro arched a hairless reptilian brow. "Cooperate and we'll sedate you so you will feel no pain."

Until she woke.

Do it, Jak'ri urged her. *Let them sedate you.*

Recalling the pain she'd experienced when they took the other samples—agony so excruciating it had driven her into unconsciousness—she nodded and climbed onto the table. Cold manacles instantly clamped around her wrists and ankles.

She glanced at Jak'ri from the corner of her eye. *Would you watch and let me know what they—*

Saekro pressed an autoinjector to her neck.

Ava jumped as she felt a pinprick.

Then darkness claimed her.

———◆○◆———

JAK'RI COULDN'T SLEEP. HE hadn't seen Ziv'ri in over a week. And whatever sedative the Gathendiens had given Ava had sunk her into unconsciousness for an entire day.

At least he *hoped* it was the sedative. He had watched the surgery carefully, noting every sample they took and committing to memory the organ names they put on the labels. It sounded like Earthlings had the same organs Purvelis did except for the gills. So he could guess which ones the Gathendiens might hope would fail when she fell ill with whatever virus they manufactured.

This time, they injected her with what appeared to be a *silna* afterward. They must want her to heal faster so they can begin testing their carefully engineered contagions.

He glanced through the bars.

Ava lay motionless where they'd left her in the center of Ziv'ri's cell. The marks left by the removal of what she called freckles did seem to be healing swiftly. But what if there had been something else mixed in with the *silna*?

She stirred suddenly, then groaned. Brows drawing down, she opened her eyes and squinted up at the ceiling.

"Ava?"

Turning her head, she looked over at him. "Are we alone?"

"Yes."

"I swear I'm going to kill those bastards."

He nodded, hating the distance and the bars that separated them.

Her movements sluggish, she rolled onto her side. The effort it took for her to rise to her feet and shuffle over to him scared the *srul* out of him.

Jak'ri stood and waited impatiently for her to reach him. Once she did, he reached through the bars and helped her sit on the pallet just on the other side.

Sighing, she pulled her legs up until her knees nearly touched her chest and slumped against the bars.

Jak'ri sat close and curled an arm around her. "How's the pain?"

"Not as bad as last time."

"They appeared to give you a *silna* to accelerate the healing and ease the pain."

Bitterness filled her pretty features. "Gee, how thoughtful of them."

Jak'ri could think of no responses to that.

She studied him through bleary brown eyes. "Any sign of Ziv'ri?"

"None." And he now thought the Gathendiens decontaminating his cell and moving Ava into it a bad sign.

Ziv'ri? she called.

Silence.

Ziv'ri? Please answer if you can and let us know you're okay.

"Anything?" Jak'ri asked.

She shook her head.

Several minutes passed.

"I think they might be testing something on me," she murmured.

His stomach sank as he studied her. "Why? Do you feel sick?" Had the injector he'd seen them use on her contained one of their bioweapons instead of a *silna*? Usually the Gathendiens gave him or Ziv'ri a little time to heal from their surgeries before they tested something new on them.

"My head is pounding." She spoke softly, as though every sound made her head hurt more. "And my stomach is queasy."

"*Queasy* didn't translate."

"Upset. My stomach is upset. Churning. Nauseated?"

"Ah." He frowned. "You've been asleep for at least a full day. Perhaps it's from not eating or drinking anything during that time."

"Maybe." She glanced over at the canteen and nutrition packs that lay in the center of her cell.

Can you hear me? he thought.

Yes.

They inject Ziv'ri and I with nahalae *every two days. But we suspect they might also add it to our nutrient beverages, so I'm reluctant to let you drink from my canteen. I don't want to lose our ability to communicate this way.*

She mustered a tired smile. *Or our ability to be together in dreams?*

Yes.

She shook her head. *I'm okay.*

But she didn't look okay. His alarm grew when—instead of rising and walking over to her canteen—she struggled to her hands and knees and crawled toward it.

What the *srul* had they done to her?

With the canteen in one hand and the nutrient packets in the other, she crawled back to the bars and settled against them. Her long hair hung in lank tangles around her face.

Jak'ri gently brushed it back.

"Thank you," she whispered.

When she had trouble opening the canteen, he helped her. He opened a nutrient pack for her as well.

Just the action of carrying the canteen and the cube to her lips seemed to exhaust her. But she drank deeply and took nibbling bites. "This nutrient cube is *not* helping my nausea," she complained with a grimace. "It tastes like sweaty feet. Or rather it tastes like sweaty feet smell."

"An apt description." His tasted the same.

She stopped eating after only one cube. Resting her head against the shoulder he'd pressed to the bars, she closed her eyes. "Talk to me," she implored softly.

"About what?"

She gave a half-hearted shrug. "Tell me another one of your getting-into-mischief-with-Ziv'ri stories."

He thought for a moment. "Did I tell you about the time Ziv'ri convinced me that if I captured and ate enough *tantovian* fish I would acquire their bioluminescence?"

Her lips turned up in a faint smile. "No."

"I should start by mentioning that *tantovians* are fairly small fish. A mature one is about the size of my palm. But they're hard to catch and even harder to handle because they shock you if you touch them."

"How big a shock are we talking?"

"Less than Saekro and Kunya's shock wand, but more than is comfortable. Most ocean predators avoid them."

"And Ziv'ri said you needed to eat how many?"

"He said he ate twelve, but I could probably get by with ten."

"And you believed him?"

"Absolutely. His skin was glowing a lovely luminous blue at the time. And I was young and gullible enough to believe he glowed for the reason he told me and not because he'd gotten his hands on some *kimensu* berries and rubbed their juices all over him."

"You have glowing berries on your homeworld?"

"Yes."

"Purvel is such an awesome planet. I hope I can visit it someday."

"I'll show you all of its best features when you do," he vowed.

"Starting with Runaka Point?"

He smiled. "Starting with Runaka Point."

"I can't wait. Now tell me how many fish you caught."

Jak'ri only made it halfway through the tale before she suddenly sat up and opened her eyes. "Ava?"

Her jaw clenched. She swallowed hard. Then swallowed again. Swearing, she jumped up and clumsily lurched over to the lav. The door slid up. She ducked inside and sank to her knees. The door slid down. Then retching sounds broke the silence.

Jak'ri gripped the bars tightly.

This confirmed it. That hadn't been a *silna* they'd given her. They were testing a new illness they'd concocted.

She emerged from the lav looking more haggard than she had upon entering it. Her feet dragged as she approached him. And this time she lay down on the pallet, facing him, and closed her eyes instead of sitting.

Jak'ri reached through the bars and rested a hand on her forehead. "You've a fever."

She nodded. "At least my stomach feels better."

Not for long, unfortunately. A short time later, she again tripped into the lav and retched.

Her fever rose.

Jak'ri reached through the bars and snagged her canteen. "Try to drink something."

She shook her head. "It'll just come back up again."

"You'll grow dehydrated if you don't." At least, he feared she would. There was still a great deal he didn't know about her people.

Ava must have agreed, though, because she drank several swallows and even tried to eat another nutrient cube.

Shivers shook her then.

Jak'ri unfolded the blanket he slept on and thrust it through the bars to cover her.

Saekro and Kunya returned to the lab and peered through the bars at her. They shared a look.

Saekro motioned the guard forward.

Mocna, a guard Jak'ri knew from the tertiary lab, unlocked the gate to Ava's cell and crossed to her.

When Mocna bent over her, Jak'ri reached through the bars and shoved him away.

"You stay the *drek* away from her!"

Mocna yanked a shock wand from his belt and touched it to the bars before Jak'ri could withdraw.

Electricity shot through him, locking his muscles and burning through him until he feared it would stop his heart.

When Mocna yanked the wand back, Jak'ri sank to his knees. Muscles still twitching, he watched helplessly as Mocna picked

Ava up and transported her to the operating table.

Since she didn't move or evince a hint of consciousness, they didn't bother to shackle her this time.

"W-What did you d-do to her?" Jak'ri gritted.

The Gathendiens ignored him.

Saekro tapped his tablet. The mechanical arm above the table descended with a needle attached to its end. Apparently they wanted another sample of her blood, but Ava was so dehydrated that they had difficulty drawing enough for whatever test they wished to perform.

Grumbling something beneath his breath, Saekro ordered Kunya to give her intravenous fluids. Then he tried the test again.

This time, blood flowed up a tube into the ceiling.

Ava roused as the needle withdrew. Her gaze unfocused, she stared up at Saekro for a long moment, then rolled onto her side and vomited on him.

Saekro lurched backward, his features twisting with disgust while Kunya scuttled a safe distance away.

Jak'ri would've laughed if he hadn't worried they'd retaliate.

Once finished, Ava rolled onto her back again and seemed to lose consciousness.

Yanking off his lab coat, Saekro glared at Ava then addressed the guard. "Put her in with the Purveli. Let *him* clean her up."

Jak'ri tried not to let his relief show. Ava was too weak to care for herself. Her best chance of surviving whatever the *srul* they had dosed her with was if she was in his cell where he could help her.

As he had the last time, Mocna hooked an arm around Ava's waist and carried her like a bag. "Back away," he ordered.

Jak'ri obediently backed away. When Mocna tossed Ava inside with no care for sparing her injury, Jak'ri again dove forward and caught her before she could hit the ground.

Saekro stomped out of the lab with Kunya on his heels. Mocna activated a disinfection bot, withdrew to his post in the hallway, and closed the door.

Jak'ri sat on his heels, knees scuffed and bleeding, and stared down at Ava as the little bot rolled around the operating table, cleaning up the mess. "They're gone," he murmured.

Her eyes opened, bright with fever and—much to his surprise —amusement. Her chapped lips turned up in a weak smile. "I got him good, didn't I?"

He laughed. "Yes, you did. I have no doubt he is now racing for a decontamination shower. And I don't think I've ever seen Kunya move so quickly."

A chuckle rumbled in her chest. "Wanted out of the line of fire. Thank you for making me eat and drink before they took me."

"I admit that wasn't my purpose."

"Yet it worked out so well." She attempted to sit up. "Would you help me to the lav? I want to rinse my mouth out."

"Of course."

Instead of helping her rise, he carried her in there. It was a tight squeeze for the two of them, but they managed. Jak'ri lowered her bare feet to the floor and steadied her while she rinsed her mouth with *wosuur* and splashed cool water on her face. She insisted on walking out on her own and held onto to the bars dividing their cells while Jak'ri pulled the blankets from her cell into his and made a thicker pallet.

Taking her hand, he helped her kneel on the blankets. Then he sat and urged her to lie down with her head in his lap.

Once settled, she sighed and closed her eyes. One of her small hands sought his and clung to it.

Murmuring soothing nonsense, he rested a hand on her warm head and stroked her hair until sleep claimed her.

CHAPTER EIGHT

J AK'RI FOUGHT BACK DESPAIR. Ava had been ill for three days now and showed no signs of recovery. Rather her condition seemed to deteriorate more by the hour. He had thought the first day the worst. She had vomited up everything she put in her mouth, gradually growing so weak that he'd had to carry her into the lav and support her while she lost the small amount of nutrients she managed to consume because she lacked the strength to stand on her own.

Even when there had been nothing left to come up, her stomach had heaved and heaved until she'd said her abdominal muscles ached.

The loss of liquid concerned him the most. She was stricken with a high fever, her face flushing from the heat of it, the light in her eyes dulling. He didn't know if dehydration would kill her people as quickly as it would his but feared the answer as her fever continued to climb.

How much heat could her frail form tolerate?

Ava had gamely told him not to worry that first day. But by the second she was barely coherent, slipping in and out of consciousness.

Jak'ri reached for her canteen and removed the lid. Sliding an arm beneath her shoulders, he elevated her head and chest and sat behind her so she could lean against him. "Ava?" he called softly.

She turned her head into his chest. Her hand moved as though she wanted to curl an arm around him but was too exhausted to do so.

He pressed a hand to her forehead and found it as warm as a stone in the desert that had spent a full day collecting the heat of the sun. "Ava." He touched the canteen to her mouth. "You *must* drink something." He dribbled a little liquid onto her dry, cracked lips.

Her brow furrowed. "Hmm?"

"Try to drink something, *sakara*," he coaxed.

Her eyelashes fluttered, then lifted. She stared up at him a long moment, her brown eyes unfocused. "Jak'ri?"

"Yes." Forcing a smile, he pressed the canteen to her lips again. "Drink for me, *sakara*."

She parted her lips a fraction. Jak'ri dribbled liquid between them, going slowly in case she had any difficulty swallowing. Her throat had been sore the previous day.

She swallowed. Once. Twice. And hope rose that she might be improving.

A few swallows later, however, she coughed, splattering him with the nutrient drink.

Jak'ri hastily set the canteen aside and helped her sit up straighter so she wouldn't choke. He feared for a moment she might vomit again and lose what little liquid she'd consumed, but she managed to bring the coughing under control and sank against him with a weary sigh.

"This sucks," she murmured.

He'd learned enough of her Earth vernacular to understand her meaning. "Yes, it does."

"How long have I been sick?"

"Three days."

He poured some of the liquid from his canteen onto a folded strip of fabric he'd torn from their pallet. Then he drew the damp fabric over her face and down her neck and arms in an attempt to cool her, wishing there was more he could do, struggling to combat the fear that she was dying.

"Have you slept at all?" she asked.

Tears burned the backs of his eyes. Even as miserable as she must be, she thought of *his* well-being. "So much that Ziv'ri would accuse me of being lazy were he here."

Ava mustered a faint smile. "Liar."

"Perhaps," he conceded and cuddled her closer. He had already lost his brother. How could he stand to lose Ava, too?

"I'm dying, aren't I?" she asked softly.

He stubbornly shook his head. "No. You'll recover from this."

"I'm so weak," she breathed. "It's hard to think straight."

He reached for one of the nutrient cubes he hadn't had the appetite to consume. "You should eat something. It'll help you rebuild your strength." Peeling the packaging off one-handed, he touched it to her lips.

Grimacing, Ava turned her face away. "I can't."

"Please, *sakara*. For me."

She stared up at him. And she went so long without blinking that absolute terror gripped him.

"Ava?"

She blinked.

And the relief that flooded him left him shaky inside.

"What does *sakara* mean?" she asked.

"It's a Purveli endearment," he confessed.

One corner of her lips turned up the slightest bit. "I like it."

He forced a smile. "I was afraid you might object, or think me presumptuous."

Her lips curled up even more. "Oh. So it's *that* kind of endearment. The serious kind."

"I'm afraid so."

She raised a trembling hand and caressed his jaw. "*Sakara*. I like it." Her hand started to slip down as strength deserted her.

Jak'ri dropped the nutrient cube on her lap and caught her hand to hold it in place.

"You can call me *sakara*," she said softly. Then her expression sobered. "But you can't fall in love with me."

He pressed a kiss to her palm. "I'm afraid it's too late for that. I believe I fell for you the first time you jumped from Runaka Point with me."

She shook her head. "You're already mourning for your brother." Tears welled in her eyes despite the fever and dehydration. "I don't want you to mourn for me, too."

Jak'ri blinked back tears of his own. "That isn't going to happen. Because you're going to eat and drink and overcome this. You *will* recover, Ava."

She *had* to.

Lowering her hand, he picked up the nutrient cube and again touched it to her lips.

After a moment's hesitation, she took a tiny bite, then took another until she ate the entire cube. And she drank when he pressed the canteen to her lips, her brown gaze clinging to his.

But in what seemed only minutes, she rested a hand on her stomach and gritted, "Lav."

Jak'ri quickly carried her into the lav and supported her while she leaned over and vomited up the little bit she'd just consumed.

He helped her rinse her mouth with *wosuur*, then carried her over to the pallet of blankets and sank down on them with Ava cradled in his lap.

"The damn Gathendiens must be gloating," she grumbled.

Jak'ri ground his teeth and opted not to comment.

"What are they saying?"

He stroked her hair. "They argue a lot. They don't know what the *srul* they're doing."

"If they didn't know what they were doing, I wouldn't be so sick."

"No. They truly don't know what they're doing. They don't understand what's happening to you and keep arguing and slinging accusations at each other."

Her brow furrowed. "Why?"

He hesitated, wanting to tell her the truth but fearing it might make her stop fighting.

"Jak'ri?" she prodded softly. "Tell me."

A long sigh escaped him. "The virus they injected you with.... They think it's working. And they're arguing because they didn't expect it to."

"I don't understand."

"It's the same virus they released on your planet thousands of years ago. The one that failed to exterminate your people." He swallowed hard as a lump rose in his throat. "But they said it's doing exactly what it's supposed to. It's destroying your immune system. They think within a couple of days..." She'd be gone, dead of a simple bacterial or viral infection her body would ordinarily be able to defeat but would no longer have any defense against.

Ava stared up at him, a stunned expression on her features.

"I'm sorry," he whispered, voice hoarse. He'd fought the truth as long as he could, unwilling to admit it because he didn't want to lose her, but telling her... speaking it aloud... merely made it more real. And he thought she deserved to know.

Yet Ava didn't weep. She didn't rail against the unfairness of it all or curse the Gathendiens or express any fear over her—according to the scientists—imminent demise.

Instead, her chapped lips stretched in a slow smile. "Don't be sorry." Though her voice was weak, it now lacked despair and sounded almost... gleeful. "Those stupid bastards have no idea what they've done."

Jak'ri stared down at her, uncomprehending.

Her brown eyes suddenly acquired a strange amber glow.

He sucked in a breath. "Ava?"

Her lids lowered, long eyelashes brushing her cheeks.

Then her frail body went limp as unconsciousness claimed her.

<hr />

*A*VA SCRAMBLED UP THE *trail to Runaka Point. It seemed clearer today, the slope not as steep. Even the vegetation seemed sparser as if the plants didn't want to get in her way or slow her down because they knew how eager she was to reach the top.*

And she was very *eager to reach the top.*

At last the ground evened out, and Ava burst into the open.

A tall, slim figure stood at the edge of the cliff, staring out at a turbulent sea.

She smiled. "Jak'ri."

Gasping, he spun around. His brow lost its pensive furrow as he rushed forward and swept her into his arms. Burying his face in her hair, he squeezed the stuffing out of her. "I thought I wouldn't see you here again," he uttered, his voice hoarse with emotion.

Ava hugged him back, her feet dangling several inches above the ground. "Why would you think that? I love it here."

He shook his head. And for a moment, he seemed too overcome with emotion to speak.

Concern rose. "Jak'ri?"

With palpable reluctance, he lowered her until her bare feet touched the soft grass, then stared down at her.

Her heart clenched at the sorrow that darkened his eyes.

"It's been five days," he whispered.

Surprised, she stared up at him. "Five days since what? Since I wandered into your dreams?" She'd had no idea she had been sick that long.

He nodded, his Adam's apple bobbing. "I thought..."

"Go on," she coaxed softly when he seemed disinclined to continue.

"I thought we wouldn't be together like this anymore." When moisture welled in his eyes, he blinked it back.

"You thought I was dying."

He remained silent.

"You still *think I'm dying."*

More silence, full of despair.

Reaching up, Ava rested a hand on his strong jaw and smoothed her thumb over his cheek. "No, sakara*. I'm not dying. I won't leave you." Rising onto her toes, she brushed a kiss against his lips. "I'll* never *leave you."*

Dipping his head, he captured her lips in a long, hungry kiss tinged with desperation that both aroused her and broke her heart. Then he buried his face in her hair again and held her tight as though he could keep her with him as long as he didn't let go. "Please, don't leave me, Ava," he whispered. "I know it's selfish to want you to stay, but I don't think I can bear to lose you, too."

"I won't leave you," she promised again. "And we're going to make those assholes pay for whatever they did to Ziv'ri. But first I need you to help me with something."

"Anything," he responded fervently.

Drawing back, she stared up at him. "I need you to explain Gathendien weaponry to me. All of it. Every weapon the guards carry. How they work. If they can be used without blowing a hole in the outer hull of the ship and killing us all. Or if I need to adjust the settings.

Which ones are quiet. Which ones are loud. Which ones will kill. Which ones will stun."

"Ava."

"And escape pods. I think I might be able to find my way back to the Lasaran escape pod they found me in, but if I can't... do you know where the Gathendien escape pods are on the ship? I'm sure they must have some."

"Ava," he said again, staring down at her somberly. "I don't think you realize how ill you are. You need to concentrate on fighting the virus they've infected you with. Once you're better, we can—"

Reaching up, she pressed two fingers to his lips. "I need you to trust me, Jak'ri. Or at least humor me." After days of watching her puke her guts up, he probably thought her delirious.

"I trust you, Ava."

"Then give me this," she said, rewarding him with a smile. "Give me this fantasy that we're going to escape."

Hesitance seemed to grip him.

"What is it?" she coaxed gently. "Surely there can be no harm in it."

His expression suggested otherwise. "I was remembering your people's belief about dreams and..." He shook his head. "I found myself suddenly fearing that if you acquire the means to escape here in the dream world..."

She stared up at him. Did he think that would somehow lead to her escaping the mortal body he saw steadily weakening in real life?

Rising onto her toes, she pressed another kiss to his lips. "You aren't going to lose me, Jak'ri. I'm not going anywhere without you, here in the dream world or in reality." She patted his cheek. "Now tell me what I need to know."

Resolution filled his handsome features. "Where do you wish to begin?"

Ava smiled. "Let's start with weapons."

It was a good thing talking endlessly didn't leave one hoarse in a dream, because she proceeded to pepper Jak'ri with questions for what felt like hours. When at last they'd exhausted everything she could think of, she nodded at the ocean. "Swim with me?"

Nodding, he pressed a kiss to the hand he clasped. "Let's jump instead of diving."

Her heart swelled. Jak'ri had held her hand or kept an arm around her the entire time they'd talked as though he was terrified she would disappear if he let go.

And Ava knew she would be just as fearful if their positions were reversed and Jak'ri was the one who appeared to be at death's door.

How had he come to mean so much to her so quickly?

"On the count of three?" she asked.

He nodded. "One. Two. Three."

Together they raced forward, lips stretching into grins, then whooped as they leapt off the cliff and plummeted to the sea.

A VA AWOKE FULL OF energy and thirsty as hell. The floor beneath the pallet she lay on was still annoyingly hard and cold. But Jak'ri's big warm body was spooned up behind her. And like the dream they had just swum and played in, he held her tight as if he hoped the constant contact could somehow keep her alive, keep her with him.

She smiled.

He was such a sweetheart. Even in sleep, he was careful not to touch her stomach. But those wounds didn't ache anymore.

Nothing ached now. Except for her teeth.

Ava cautiously ran her tongue along the edges of her upper teeth.

Her heartbeat quickened as fangs descended over her eyeteeth.

Yes!

She drew in a deep breath and held it.

A plethora of scents bombarded her. Many, many more than before. And the most appealing was that of the man who held her.

She glanced toward the lab. Saekro and Kunya huddled together with their backs to her. Though they muttered to each other in low voices, Ava could easily hear every word the bastards spoke. Jak'ri was right. They thought the virus was killing her and were puzzling over why it hadn't succeeded in killing the rest of the human race. Did some Earthlings harbor a natural immunity to it? Or had the virus—once it had been released on the planet—mutated into something Earthlings' bodies could more easily combat?

Surely the Earthlings, so ignorant and inferior, had not devised a medication that could treat it.

How would the Gathendien emperor react when they told him they'd killed the only Earthling subject they'd managed to acquire from their attack on the *Kandovar*? All they had learned since they'd captured her was that the virus their ancestors had created worked. It destroyed the immune system of those infected with it. Weaker Earthlings like Ava (she snorted silently over that) died. Any who remained *should*—as ancient test subjects had repeatedly confirmed—quickly go insane and slay all others in their thirst for blood, but they couldn't confirm that since Ava was dying.

In other words, they'd screwed up and learned absolutely nothing new.

And they totally wouldn't see her coming.

Jak'ri, she called telepathically.

Stirring, he snuggled closer and sighed.

Jak'ri.

He stiffened.

Don't move and don't speak aloud, she warned him.

Ava? Are you all right? How do you feel?

I'm good. She patted the big hand she'd pressed to her chest in her sleep. *You know all that stuff we talked about last night in our dream?*

Yes.

I'm about to put it to good use.

Ava...

Everything is going to be okay. But I need you to know that what I'm about to do is just an act, okay?

What are you going to do? he asked, dread entering his deep voice.

I'm going to tell you to get your filthy hands off me.

My hands aren't filthy.

I know. And I like having your hands on me.

His hold tightened. And she felt him grow hard against her bottom.

Jak'ri swore. *I wish we had talked about* that *last night instead of weapons.*

Inwardly she laughed though she kept her expression blank. *Don't worry. We'll talk about that plenty once we get off this* drekking *ship. Are you awake now?*

Very.

Excellent. Here we go.

"What the hell?" she blurted, doing her best to sound sluggish.

Both Gathendien scientists spun around.

Angrily shoving Jak'ri's arm off her, Ava rolled away and lunged to her feet. She stumbled a step or two and raised a hand to her head, feigning dizziness.

Jak'ri sat up and stared at her, his arousal made obvious by the shorts he wore.

"Are you fucking kidding me?" she railed drunkenly, adding another stagger. "I'm dying of whatever crap they injected me with and you think it's okay to *grope* me?"

He rose, brow furrowing. "I thought you liked me."

Ava hoped he was a fantastic actor because he sounded genuinely hurt. "Not like *that*! I just felt sorry for you for losing your brother. And I needed someone to take care of me." She turned to face the scientists, wobbling so much she nearly fell over. "Get me out of here. I want to go back to my cell." She glowered over her shoulder. "Where I can sleep without someone grabbing my breasts and poking me in the butt."

Jak'ri stiffened, his hands curling into fists. His expression darkened with anger. "I cared for you while you were ill."

"So now you think I owe you?" Stumbling over to the gate, she grabbed a bar as though to brace herself. "They *tortured* me because *you* tried to escape!" Ava shifted her glare to their captive audience. "Well? What the hell are you waiting for? Get me out of here! I can take care of myself."

Saekro motioned to one of the guards who appeared in the doorway. Both scientists looked relieved that their test subject hadn't yet expired.

Mocna approached the gate.

Ava purposefully didn't look back at Jak'ri.

"Step back," the guard growled.

She obediently moved to one side, weaving on her feet, and hastily reached out to grab another bar and steady herself.

Behind her Jak'ri made a scoffing sound. "You can barely stand up and you think you can take care of yourself?"

"If the alternative is you pawing me, then I'll manage," she snapped.

Mocna disengaged the lock and swung the gate open. "Out," he ordered, then glared over her head at Jak'ri. "You stay where you are, Purveli."

Ava slowly shuffled out of the cell.

Just as she'd hoped, the guard kept his gaze on Jak'ri.

Oh, but Jak'ri wasn't the greatest threat here.

Quick as a blink, she burst into motion. Moving so swiftly she blurred, Ava grabbed the guard's blaster from its holster, shoved it under the armor that protected his soft belly, and fired. Light and energy flared as the straps holding the chest covering in place broke, the armor fell aside, and a scorched hole the size of a baseball appeared in his yellow gut.

While he cried out and fell, she whirled around and shot the second guard in the throat.

Sheesh! The blast nearly severed his head!

He was dead before he even hit the floor.

Adrenaline flooding her, Ava shot the first guard again, this time in the throat to ensure he couldn't call for help. And she did it all so amazingly fast that the Gathendien scientists only had time to gasp before she turned her wrath upon them.

Being an Immortal Guardian was freaking *awesome*!

Ava crossed the lab in a single leap and tackled the scientists. Though both probably outweighed her by one or two hundred pounds, the transformation wrought by the virus had given her far greater strength.

Thor and *Superman* kind of strength.

While Saekro and Kunya floundered on the floor, she rose above them and shot them both in the stomach.

Unlike the guards, they wore no armor and howled in pain.

In another blur of motion, she robbed them of all their devices and—following the instructions Jak'ri had given her in their shared dream—deactivated voice commands on the computer.

Zipping across the room to the doorway, she dragged the second guard inside as easily as she would a pillow and closed the door.

Ava stilled. No more than a minute had passed since she'd shuffled out of the cell.

Elation filled her as she looked at the hulking aliens she'd defeated and grinned.

"Ava?"

She swung toward the cell.

Everything had happened so quickly that Jak'ri still stood where she'd left him, eyes wide, mouth gaping.

Stepping over the guard, she walked toward him. "I'm sorry. You know I was lying when I said I didn't want you grabbing my breasts, right?"

"Yes." He walked toward her, his expression dazed. "If I hadn't been terrified you were going to do something that would result in your being tortured again, I would've made a joke about butt probing."

Laughing, Ava hugged him, the blaster still clutched in one hand.

"How the *drek* did you do that?"

Aware of the scientists, she answered him telepathically. *The virus they injected me with has unintended side effects in some Earthlings.* Releasing him, she stepped back.

Unintended. He looked at the four downed Gathendiens, two dead, the other two moaning. *To use one of your Earth phrases, no shit.*

She grinned. *I really need to clean up my language.*

Did you know your eyes are glowing?

Yes. It's because those dumbasses unknowingly transformed me from a gifted one *into an Immortal Guardian. I'll explain it all later.*

Okay. "Let's get the *srul* out of here," he said aloud and crossed to Saekro and Kunya. "Where's my brother?"

Saekro spewed a slew of what Ava guessed were Gathendien curse words because only one or two translated.

She glanced around. "Here." Handing Jak'ri the blaster, she picked up the shock wand the bastards had repeatedly used on them. As per Jak'ri's instructions in the dream, she brushed a thumb across a circle above the handle and activated it.

Saekro's tail suddenly whipped out and swept Jak'ri's feet out from under him.

Crap! She'd forgotten about their tails.

As soon as Jak'ri disentangled himself and jumped to his feet, Ava touched the wand to the hole in Saekro's belly.

Blue energy crackled as the bastard stiffened, his face contorting with agony.

As soon as Ava lifted the wand, Jak'ri kicked Saekro where a human male's balls would be.

Saekro cried out.

Kunya...

Ava swore. Kunya was either dead or unconscious. His eyes were closed and he didn't so much as twitch.

Returning her attention to Saekro, Ava brandished the wand. "Where's the other Purveli?"

He spat at her, but her new speed enabled her to duck it.

Ava touched the wand to his stomach again.

The Gathendien stiffened and made a garbled sound of pain.

Holding the wand in place, she leaned over him and glared. "It's not as fun when you're on the *receiving* end, is it, asshole?" Straightening, she raised the wand. "Where's Ziv'ri?"

"Dead," the scientist gritted once he got his breath back. "He's dead." And the bastard even managed to curl his lip as he looked at Jak'ri. "Did you think your attempt to escape would go unpunished?"

Jak'ri's face filled with fury. "It *didn't* go unpunished! You punished *her!*" He flung a hand out toward Ava.

Red blood painted Saekro's teeth as his lips stretched in an oily smile. "That wasn't punishment. That was entertainment."

Roaring, Jak'ri yanked the wand from Ava's hand and held it to Saekro's chest, just above his heart. Or where she thought his heart should be.

Saekro stiffened a long moment, then went limp, eyes closing.

When Jak'ri raised the wand, he stood over the bastard, every muscle tense.

Ava reached out and touched his arm. "We'll look for Ziv'ri before we leave, search the ship in case Saekro was lying. Maybe he's just unconscious or in a coma in one of the other labs."

Jak'ri shook his head. "We're sorely outnumbered here, Ava. Do you know how many soldiers are on this ship?"

"It doesn't matter. We can do this. Trust me." She motioned to the high-tech paraphernalia around them. "I know time is tight, but is there any way we can erase or destroy their research? I know they've probably already shared it with the rest of the Gathendiens but—"

"I don't think they have. Saekro and Kunya know that discovering how to eliminate both the Earthling *and* the Purveli races will gain them great favor with the emperor. If they share what they know with other researchers, those scientists might find the answer first."

"And deny them glory and the emperor's reward?"

"Yes."

"Excellent. For once, greed and a lust for power will work in our favor. How do we destroy their research?"

"I can't read Gathendien, so the only thing I know to do is to obliterate everything I've seen them use for their work with this." He held up the blaster.

"Then let's do it."

Again he shook his head and motioned to the scientists. "Shooting *them* may not trigger any alarms, but shooting everything else and damaging the computer systems undoubtedly will."

Fear tried to creep in and shove aside the bravado becoming an immortal had lent her. Ava might have trained in self-defense back at network headquarters on Earth. And she might have sparred with Eliana and her other friends on the *Kandovar*. But the sum total of her actual battle experience entailed having taken out the two Gathendien guards and the scientists.

Sure, she was super strong and fast now. But this ship was big.

Big enough that she didn't think she could take on the entire battalion of soldiers who manned it.

If she and Jak'ri didn't destroy the research, they'd have a much higher chance of getting away.

If they *did* destroy it...

She looked over at him.

Expression sober, Jak'ri said, "Ziv'ri thought they were close to finding a virus that would kill my people. I don't want other Gathendiens getting their hands on that information."

"And I don't want other Gathendiens getting their hands on the tissue samples these assholes took from me and figuring out how to kill my people." Her eyes widened as a new thought dawned. "Wait. Do you know where they keep those? The tissue samples? Or where they keep the blood they took from me?"

Nodding, he crossed to an upper cabinet. It looked like all the others, not so different from kitchen cabinets on Earth that lacked embellishment.

Jak'ri waved a hand across it. A screen appeared on the lower left corner. Though Ava couldn't read the alien text on it, the flashing lines and symbols beneath it seemed pretty self-explanatory.

It was asking for a passcode.

Without hesitating, Jak'ri tapped several symbols.

A hiss sounded as the cabinet opened a fraction. Cold air drifted down from the crack like fog.

"How did you do that?" she asked.

He glanced over his shoulder. "Ziv'ri and I memorized their routines."

"They didn't try to hide the codes from you?"

A bitter smile twisted his lips. "Why hide them from someone who can't escape and will die soon?"

Ava grumbled several choice descriptions of the scientists beneath her breath while Jak'ri tucked his fingers into the crease and pulled.

The cabinet door didn't swing open on hinges. Instead it pulled out like the drawer of a filing cabinet. Rows of transparent containers rested against a glowing white wall. Each contained samples the bastards had taken.

Ava's eyes immediately went to what appeared to be bags of red blood that closely resembled the ones used by hospitals on Earth. "Is that *your* blood or mine?"

"I don't know. We both bleed red. But I believe it's mine and Ziv'ri's."

Ava thought furiously. Immortal Guardians needed regular infusions of blood to maintain their exceptional speed, strength, and greater regenerative capabilities. If they went too long without it, their wounds would cease healing and they would weaken. But she didn't know if Purveli blood was safe to use. Back on the *Kandovar*, Eliana had told her she couldn't infuse herself with Lasaran blood. She could use human, Segonian, or Yona blood, but *not* Lasaran.

Ava wished she could remember why Lasaran blood was off limits. Did it just not provide Immortal Guardians with what they needed? Or did it harm them in some way?

Clearly it wasn't toxic to humans or *gifted ones*, because Prince Taelon and Lisa had a baby together. And Princess Amiriska had married an Immortal Guardian and borne him a child. Yet Eliana had been pretty emphatic that if anything happened to her she should *not* be transfused with Lasaran blood. Ever.

Was Purveli blood equally dangerous?

"Did you see them store my blood in a different cabinet?" she asked.

"No. But I think it likely that they stored your blood and tissue samples in the tertiary lab where they initially collected them. When they performed your second surgery here, they packaged the samples and took them out of the lab."

She dragged her gaze away from the cabinet and met his eyes. "I need that blood, Jak'ri."

"Do you remember how to get back to the other lab?"

"Yes."

"How fast are you now?"

In a blink, she zipped around and came up behind him. "This fast."

Jumping, Jak'ri spun around. His silver eyes widened. Then he nodded. "Okay. Do you remember how to get to the escape pod you arrived in?"

"I'm... not as sure about that."

"It's probably either in the docking bay or the loading bay."

"There were a lot of small ships in the bay I arrived in. Like fighter craft or transports."

"That's the docking bay. You won't be able to get the pod out of there. It'll be too heavily guarded. Did you see any of the Gathendien escape pods on your way to either lab?"

"I don't think so."

He closed his eyes. "Show me what you remember."

Ava projected images into his head, showing him the hangar her escape pod rested in, the path she thought they'd taken to the tertiary lab, then the path that led to the primary lab they stood in now.

Opening his eyes, Jak'ri grabbed several tools embedded in the wall between the countertop and the upper cabinets, then swiftly started arranging them on the operating table. "If this is the ship..." He drew an oval around the tools with his finger. "This is the hangar with your pod in it. This in the primary lab we're in now. This is the tertiary lab that adjoins the first cell they kept you in. And this is the secondary lab they took me to once. There should be escape pods here and here." He pointed to the sides of the ship near the midway point.

"Okay."

"When you get to the tertiary lab, search the cabinets. The one that won't open easily is the one that will contain your samples. If you don't remember the passcode—"

"I'm probably strong enough to force it open."

His lips curled up in one corner. "Yes, you are."

Crossing to a panel on a bare wall with a symbol and alien text on it, he waved a hand across it. A drawer slid out of the wall. "This is an incinerator." He started grabbing the samples from the cabinet and tossing them into the drawer. Ava did the same.

He then added all of the little tablet-like devices the scientists used. "As soon as you close it, everything inside will be reduced to ash and sent to their refuse collection. So keep what you need and destroy the rest. Take Mocna's weapon, because you'll need to destroy the computer in the lav." He must be talking about the one embedded in the toilet that analyzed everything. "From what Ziv'ri and I were able to discern, it stores the data it collects for a full day, then uploads it to the primary lab's computer every night. If they're like the ones used in Purveli med bays, each day's data overwrites the previous day's, which means some of your data may still be stored in the lav in your cell."

"Then we'll destroy it. What about the computer panels in the lab itself?"

"You don't need to worry about those. They're just entrance points for information. All medical research data is stored here in the primary lab's computer banks. Just shoot the one in the lav."

"Okay."

"That might trigger a malfunction alert that could gain some notice from maintenance. So once you've done that, head for the escape pods. You'll know them when you see them because they'll all be lined up in a row."

She frowned. "You keep saying *you* instead of *we*."

He closed the incinerator. A *whoosh* sounded. "I'm not coming with you."

She stared up at him. "What?"

"I'm staying here. Keep me apprised of everything telepathically as you go. If you run into any trouble, I'll start blasting things in here, then run and draw their fire."

"Oh, hell no!" she blurted. "We leave together or we don't leave at all."

"Ava, you have a much higher chance of escaping if I keep them distracted long enough to—"

Closing the distance between them, she rose onto her toes, curled her free hand around the nape of his neck, and pressed a fervent kiss to his lips.

Startled into silence, he stared down at her.

"I'm not going without you, Jak'ri."

"You can move faster without me. *Much* faster."

"I don't care. I won't let you sacrifice yourself for me. We either *escape* together or we *die* together. Those are your two options. Time is ticking. What's it going to be?"

Several seconds passed. Then he looped an arm around her waist, drew her up against him, and kissed her as if he thought there would be no tomorrow.

Her heart leapt. Her pulse quickened.

When at last he broke the heated contact, he pressed his forehead to hers. "We escape together. Just don't die, Ava. Please. And *don't* let them recapture you, whatever it takes." In other words, leave him behind if that was what she had to do to gain her freedom.

She was so falling in love with him. "I won't."

Bending, he retrieved a bag from beneath one of the cabinets.

"What's that?" she asked.

"A medic bag. I saw them take it once to tend some soldiers who bloodied each other up in a fight." Opening another cabinet, he grabbed fistfuls of nutrient cubes and stuffed them into the bag. He did the same with larger packs that reminded her of those juice packs children on Earth sometimes used.

"What's in those?" she asked, helping him.

"The nutrient liquid they put in our canteens." He pointed to another cabinet. "I think they keep our garments in there. Grab a couple."

Ava opened the cabinet he pointed to and grabbed a bunch of folded fabric she hoped would be a change of clothes for them both.

Jak'ri forced the bag closed. "Go wait by the door."

Ava picked up the discarded shock wand and crossed the room. She blew a lock of hair out of her face, then frowned. If they were about to go into battle, the last thing she needed was for her hair to blind her.

Jak'ri entered his cell and headed for the lav.

Zipping into motion, Ava ripped a strip of cloth from the pants of the dead guard at her feet and used it to tie her hair back. Then she palmed a blaster and grabbed the shock wand.

Jak'ri fired his blaster. Through the lav's doorway, she saw the panel above the toilet explode. He did the same with the toilet in the other cell. He caught her eye as he returned to the lab. "That should only alert maintenance that the lav is malfunctioning. But the moment I destroy the computers in here, an alarm will sound on the bridge."

And all hell would break loose. "Okay."

"Ready?" he asked.

Nerves jumping, adrenaline pumping through her veins, Ava nodded. "I'm ready."

CHAPTER NINE

J AK'RI FIRED THE BLASTER multiple times, targeting every panel on which he'd seen the scientists enter data or retrieve information. He fired several more shots into the lower cabinet that housed the primary data storage hub, then turned the blaster on the mechanical apparatus in the ceiling above the operating table, destroying all of it.

The lights began to flicker.

Jogging across the room with the medic bag, he met Ava near the entrance. "Let's go. Read my thoughts and speak to me telepathically whenever necessary."

Okay.

As they approached the lab's exit, the door slid up. Jak'ri tensed and raised his weapon, uncertain whether *they* had triggered the door or if someone else on the brink of entering had.

Poking his head out, he looked up and down the hallway and found it empty. *It's clear*, he thought. Ava slipped past him and started leading the way to the tertiary lab.

She looked so fragile, garbed only in shorts and a wrap-around shirt that gave the scientists easy access to her torso. She'd pulled her mussed hair back at some point and tied it at her nape, revealing a slender neck and narrow shoulders. Her arms and legs were thinner than they were in their shared dreams. The guard's blaster looked huge in her tiny hand, as did the shock wand she clutched in the other hand. And her small feet were bare.

Everything within him demanded he lead so *he* would be the one targeted by the Gathendiens they would encounter. But back in the lab...

He didn't fully comprehend what had happened to her. He only knew she was changed. *Greatly* changed. That alluring, compact little body could now move so quickly he could barely follow the motion with his eyes. In no more than a heartbeat, she had dropped four Gathendiens. And her strength...

He knew the second guard must have been thrice her weight, yet she had dragged him across the floor as effortlessly as she would a threadbare blanket.

As they approached an intersection with another hallway, she stopped suddenly. *Someone's coming. And they're moving quickly.*

Soldiers sent to investigate the alarm, no doubt.

Jak'ri glanced around and saw no alcove in which they could hide. None of the doors they'd passed had opened, so they weren't communal rooms and would require passcodes.

With no other recourse, the two of them hugged the wall.

How many? he asked.

Four, I think.

Able to hear the thuds of approaching boots now, Jak'ri raised his blaster, ready to fire.

His eyes widened when Ava abruptly stepped into the intersection and turned to face whoever raced toward them in the other hallway.

"Hi," she said with a smile and a wave. "How's it going?"

The boots skidded to a halt.

Then her eyes flashed bright amber. She raised her blaster and fired. Shouts burst from the hallway, accompanied by energy bolts. Her figure blurred as she dodged returning fire, then dove out of sight.

Drek! Grunts and cries of pain sounded as Jak'ri ran toward the intersection. Skidding to a halt, he aimed his weapon... and gaped.

Three Gathendiens lay motionless on the floor, blood pooling beneath them, their armor and bodies smoking from blaster fire. A fourth Gathendien bereft of weapons stumbled backward with Ava perched on his shoulders, her legs locked around him.

As Jak'ri watched in astonishment, she grabbed his scaled head and gave it a quick hard twist.

Bone snapped. The Gathendien collapsed.

Ava jumped free before he hit the floor.

Jak'ri stared. Every Gathendien lay dead.

And Ava bore not even a scratch.

"How the *drek* did you do that?"

Even *she* looked a little stunned as she took in the bodies. Her wide eyes met his. "My hands are shaking."

Jak'ri grabbed one of the fallen guard's *osdulium* rifles and looped it over his shoulder. "Let's keep moving." The blaster fire would've alerted anyone nearby to trouble.

Ava confiscated a second O-rifle and retrieved her blaster.

Once more they headed for the tertiary lab, picking up their pace, their bare feet allowing them to move quietly as they darted up one corridor and down the next.

Though shouts sounded distantly behind them, they managed to reach the lab without encountering anyone else.

Ducking inside, they sealed the door.

Jak'ri's eyes went straight to the adjoining cells.

Both were empty. His chest tightened. *Ziv'ri.*

"We'll check the secondary lab," Ava promised as she hurried across the room and started checking the contents of the upper cabinets. "Hopefully, he's there."

Or maybe Saekro had told them the truth and Ziv'ri was dead.

Jak'ri headed into the cell and destroyed the computer in the lav. Then he returned to the lab and helped Ava search for the samples they'd taken from her.

She heaved a big sigh of relief when they found them. Grabbing two cold packages of blood, she shoved them at him. "Put these in the medic bag and don't let anything happen to them."

Surprised that she didn't want to destroy them, Jak'ri did as bidden before turning his attention to the lower cabinets. This lab was set up almost exactly like the primary lab. It was just smaller. So the incinerator should be... He waved a hand across a lower cabinet and it popped open. "Here."

Ava became a blur of motion—a literal *blur* of motion—as she swiftly deposited the remaining samples in the incinerator along with every device she could find.

Jak'ri closed it. A *whoosh* sounded.

She motioned to the walls. "Are you sure nothing in here can store information or were you just trying to protect me and keep me from blasting them?"

He hesitated. "Both?"

She narrowed her eyes.

"I'm *mostly* sure, but I'm basing that on the way *Purveli* ships are often designed."

"Mostly isn't good enough. Shoot everything they might use to enter or store information."

Jak'ri shot every panel and input port. "They'll know we're heading for the secondary lab now."

"I know." She strode toward the door. "But that's the only other place they'd be holding Ziv'ri, and we're not leaving without him." *If he's still alive* went unspoken.

Jak'ri nodded.

As soon as they opened the door, blaster fire hit the frame.

Both ducked back inside.

Ava gave him a quick once-over, as though searching for wounds, then disappeared in a flash.

Battle sounds erupted.

Swearing, Jak'ri dropped the medic bag and blaster, raised the more accurate O-rifle, and ducked into the hallway. Two Gathendiens were already down. Six more fired blindly as a small form barreled through them, seemingly at light speed, knocking them on their asses and firing her blaster. One Gathendien's head snapped back, though Jak'ri hadn't seen what hit him, and the *grunark* shot his own man as he flew backward off his feet.

Jak'ri shot him before he hit the ground, then took out another, hoping fervently that he wouldn't accidentally shoot Ava.

The last man fell. Ava stood in the middle of the pile, breathing hard. Little specks of blood spattered one side of her face. The rest of her body was streaked with it. "Thanks," she said.

Jak'ri nodded. "I was afraid I might shoot you."

"Apparently, I'm fast enough to dodge energy bolts or whatever these weapons fire."

Jak'ri wasn't so sure. One of her arms was liberally coated with blood. So was one of her legs. "Is that blood yours or theirs?" he asked as he started toward her.

She waved a hand as though brushing his concern aside. "I'm okay. Let's keep moving."

Mind whirling, heart racing, Jak'ri tucked his discarded blaster in an outside pocket of the medic bag and slung the bag over his shoulder. Looping the rifle over his other shoulder, he grabbed a second rifle and readied it.

Ava confiscated a long dagger from one of the Gathendiens. When she started toward him, dagger in one hand, blaster in the other, she limped.

He opened his mouth to ask about it, but the ship-wide alarm began to blare.

Wee-wonk! Wee-wonk!

Eyes widening, the two of them took off toward the secondary lab. Abandoning stealth in favor of speed, they ran as quickly as they could.

Or rather as quickly as *he* could. Jak'ri bemoaned the fact that he was slowing her down. Ava was so fast now that even with the limp she could've already been in an escape pod and flying away to freedom if she weren't stuck with him.

You're forgetting that I have no idea how to operate *a Gathendien escape pod,* she said in his head.

Drek. He *had* forgotten that.

When they rounded the corner nearest the secondary lab, his eyes widened.

"Oh shit!" Ava cried.

Jak'ri barely had time to register that ten or twelve Gathendien soldiers waited for them before she shoved him. Hard.

He flew off his feet, fell on his ass, and skidded back down the hallway. The corridor the secondary lab opened onto lit up with energy bolts.

His heart stopped. Ava was nowhere in sight. Had they shot her?

A slew of Earth curses filled his head.

Jak'ri found a smile. *Drek* no, they hadn't. Nor would they.

Leaping up, he raced toward the battle. The rest of the Gathendien ship wasn't as tidy as the lab and provided just enough dust on the floor's surface to enable him to drop into a slide. Energy bolts sailed over his head as he skidded to a halt, body flat against the surface.

Once again, a small blurred form sparked chaos in the center of the group, so Jak'ri focused his O-rifle on the *grunarks* along the edges and fired in quick bursts. *I'm aiming at the outer guards*, he thought, hoping she'd hear him.

Their attention torn between the deadly woman behind them and the Purveli in front of them, quite a few Gathendiens fell beneath his fire. Ava kept them so busy they couldn't take time to aim, so their energy bolts hit the walls, the ceiling, and the floor instead of him.

More bodies fell until only Ava and a lone Gathendien remained, locked in what was clearly a one-sided battle.

Boots pounded on flooring.

More troops approached.

Glancing over his shoulder, Jak'ri scrambled toward the lab.

The last Gathendien fell.

"More are coming," he warned Ava.

The lab door rose at their approach. He raised his rifle. Ava raised her blaster.

But no guards lay in wait for them.

She darted inside.

Jak'ri glanced in long enough to determine Ziv'ri wasn't in either of the cells.

Clenching his teeth, he parked himself in the doorway and watched both ends of the hallway. *I'll stand guard.*

Ziv'ri isn't here, she told him despondently.

I know.

Blaster fire sounded in the lab as Ava destroyed everything she needed to, then returned to his side.

O-rifle ready, Jak'ri moved into the corridor and led the way—he hoped—to the Gathendien escape pods.

They encountered more troops. But every time, Ava's superior speed and strength gave them the upper hand and the two of them emerged victorious.

Jak'ri breathed a sigh of relief when they finally found what they sought. *These are the pods.*

Ava guarded his back as he chose the closest access panel and waved a hand across it to activate it. *Ziv'riiiiii!* she shouted telepathically.

Jak'ri swallowed hard, straining to hear any answer.

Ziv'ri, answer me! Please! We're free! We're escaping! Tell us where you are so you can come with us!

The entrance to the escape pod's dock opened.

Jak'ri grabbed Ava's arm and tried to pull her inside, but she resisted.

Ziv'riiiiii! she called desperately, tears sparkling in her luminous amber eyes. *Pleeeeeeese!*

Jak'ri's eyes burned as he faced the truth. Swallowing the lump of grief that rose in his throat, he forced her to look at him. "Ava. He's gone," he told her hoarsely. "Ziv'ri's gone." Just speaking those words nearly drove him to his knees.

Breath catching on a sob, she bit her lip.

Jak'ri didn't want to believe it either, but if they lingered they would likely die, too, so he forced himself to enter the small, cramped bay and tugged her in after him. After sealing the door, he guided her into the escape pod's open hatch.

Ava stood quietly inside while he entered and closed the hatch behind them.

The pod resembled the ones frequently found on Akseli ships but was larger to allow Gathendiens room to maneuver their thick tails and could accommodate up to four passengers.

Jak'ri studied it carefully. All men and women in the western province of Purvel were required to serve in the military for a minimum of three years. Though a single elected sovereign presided over their intergalactic affairs, his planet was not bereft of war and conflict the way Lasara was. Though he wished it were otherwise, his people *did* battle among themselves on occasion. And the province in which he lived wanted to be prepared for anything.

Jak'ri now thanked that military training for including the study of Akseli mercenary ships—how to fly them, how to destroy them, *and* how to escape them—because this pod was very similar in design. Setting the medic bag and rifles down, he sat in the pilot seat and ran his gaze over the control panel.

There. Triumph filled him. The name of an Akseli manufacturer was etched into one corner. Those Akseli *grunarks* would sell anything to *anyone* for the right price and didn't care who might suffer the consequences. But today that worked in his favor. He might not be able to read Gathendien, but when he activated the control panel, everything lit up in the same pattern as the Akseli pod he'd studied.

Ava moved to stand behind him and placed a shaking hand on his shoulder. "Can you read that?"

"No. But it's an Akseli design, and my military training required me to learn how to navigate both an Akseli fighter craft and an Akseli escape pod." He tapped the unfamiliar symbols in the sequence he remembered.

"Are the Akselis your enemies?"

"They were friends and allies for many generations. Then their planet swung hard toward tyranny, and their ruler's only concern became increasing his own wealth and power at the expense of others. Under his rule, the Akseli now lend their aid to whoever pays the most in wars and have even aided some races in attempted genocide. When the province I was raised in went to war with another on Purvel that thought to steal our water rights, the other province enlisted the help of Akseli mercenaries and escalated the conflict. As a result, Purvel's sovereign banned Akselis from visiting Purvel and added anti-Akseli warfare to our military training to prevent the *grunarks* from successfully interfering in our conflicts again."

The engine hummed as it came online. He patted the seat beside him. "Sit here."

As soon as she did, Jak'ri helped fasten and adjust her harness, then fastened his own.

Blaster fire erupted in the tiny pod bay beyond the hatch.

Jak'ri swore and entered what he hoped was the correct command.

"Launch sequence initiated," a male voice announced in Gathendien.

The pod began to rotate, turning them until the small unbreakable crystal window the pod boasted showed a short passageway in the shape of a tube.

"Here we go," he told Ava.

She took his hand and held it tight.

"Launching," the computer said, "in ten, nine, eight, seven, six, five, four, three, two, one."

A VA HELD HER BREATH as the pod shot down the launch tube, pressing her deeper into her seat. She didn't see space at the end of the tunnel and hoped like hell—

A door at the end of the tube slid up at the last minute to allow them passage. Then the darkness of space surrounded them.

Her heart pounded in her chest. "Did we make it? Are we off the ship?"

"Yes."

"Are they following us?"

Jak'ri studied the control panel. "Not yet. But they will. Computer, enable voice commands."

Silence fell.

"Is it working?" she asked. Reaction began to kick in, driving her hands to shake.

His brow furrowed. "No. But I was speaking Purveli. Perhaps the initial command has to be rendered in Gathendien."

"Do you speak Gathendien?"

"No. Purveli translator chips only enable us to understand *spoken* languages. They don't render us capable of speaking or reading them. But Akselis designed and built this pod, so perhaps the computer will accept the command in their language."

"You speak Akseli?"

He grimaced. "Not well." He stared at the console. "Mathematician can voice commands."

Ava bit her lip. "I don't think you got that right. According to my translator, you said *mathematician can voice commands.*" She didn't know the Alliance Common word for mathematician, so she just used English for that one and hoped he'd get the gist of it.

He swore. "Calculate, enable voice commands."

"Close. That was *calculate enable voice commands.*"

He tried again. "Computer, enable voice commands."

"Voice commands enabled," the computer said in its masculine voice.

Ava smiled and would've high-fived Jak'ri if he were familiar with the gesture.

Relief blanketed his features. "Accept and respond to all voice commands and inquiries issued in Purveli and Alliance Common." He glanced at her. "I want you to be able to communicate with the computer, should it become necessary."

The only reason she would need to communicate with the computer would be if something happened to him.

"All such commands and inquiries will be accepted," the computer responded.

"Map our current trajectory," Jak'ri ordered.

"Mapping trajectory."

Ava looked up at him. "Why would a Gathendien escape pod built by Akselis be able to understand Purveli?"

"Most ship computers are equipped with an understanding of all recorded languages so the commanders or pilots can communicate with anyone they encounter."

"Oh."

A map appeared on one side of the control panel.

Ava willed her body to stop shaking and tried to ignore the throbbing in her arm, thigh, and foot that fear and adrenaline had briefly kept on the back burner.

Jak'ri's eyes widened as he studied the map.

"What is it?" she asked. He looked stunned.

"I can't believe how far we are from Purvel. We knew the Gathendiens wouldn't linger in our solar system after taking us.

Even though we're on the outskirts of Aldebarian Alliance-occupied space and aren't members of the alliance, we're close enough to conduct business with many of its member nations and see a *lot* of import/export traffic."

He shook his head. "The Gathendiens wouldn't have wanted to draw notice from any of those ships. But *this*... We're so far away from the alliance that without the *qhov'rum* you said was damaged in the battle with the *Kandovar* it would take us five and a half Purveli months just to reach Mila 9."

"What's Mila 9?"

"A planet on the farthest reaches of explored space. The Segonians have an outpost there."

"Oh." Though Ava had never met a Segonian, she knew they were members of the Aldebarian Alliance. And their blood was safe for Immortal Guardians to infuse themselves with. There had been a supply on the *Kandovar* that the Lasarans said was left over from the biannual Aldebarian Alliance war games, in which soldiers and ships from all member allies assembled and practiced engaging in battle together for times when they needed to defeat common enemies. Eliana had infused herself with that blood several times to confirm it would be safe for the others once they expended the supply of blood from Earth.

"Can this pod sustain us for five and a half months?" Ava didn't relish the notion of such a long journey in such a small space but would prefer that to death.

"Doubtful," Jak'ri said. "The standard is two months. This pod was designed to support four travelers, though, so we can probably stretch that to four months. Five if we ration. That should take us close enough to hail Mila 9 even with the subpar communications system in this pod. But I think it highly unlikely that we could evade the Gathendiens for that long."

So basically she was back to where she had been before the Gathendiens had captured her: stuck in an escape pod with limited resources and no place to go.

And the same bastards who had captured her last time were going to do their damnedest to capture them again.

"Computer," Jak'ri said, his eyes still on the map, "are there any stations or outposts manned by members of the Aldebarian

Alliance closer to us than Mila 9?"

"Negative," the computer responded.

"Are there any ships that aren't Gathendien or Akseli nearby?"

"Negative."

"Plot a course for Mila 9, maximum speed."

"Plotting course to Mila 9, maximum speed."

"Render control panel in Alliance Common."

"Rendering."

As Ava watched, the symbols on the display transformed from what looked like the gibberish she'd seen on the Gathendien ship to Alliance Common she could only somewhat understand since she was far more adept at *speaking* Alliance Common than reading it.

Jak'ri rapidly typed on a keyboard of sorts that materialized on the screen. "I'm sending a message to Purvel and sending the same to the Segonian outpost on Mila 9. But the communications array on this pod is not nearly as complex or powerful as that on a ship and has limited range. Computer, enable proximity alert."

"Proximity alert enabled. Gathendien warship detected."

"Is it in pursuit?"

"Negative. Warning. Gathendien warship is arming weapons."

"*Drek.*"

"Weapons firing."

Seconds later the pod shook.

Ava grabbed her harness. "Are they trying to blow us up?" she blurted.

He shook his head. "If it were just me, I'd say maybe. But they destroyed a Lasaran battleship with three members of the royal family on board to capture you and your friends. If they intend to claim planets in sectors that remain largely unexplored, they need you to further their research. They're just trying to scare us."

"Well, it's working!"

Again, the pod shook.

"Computer, disable tracking beacon," Jak'ri ordered.

"This escape pod is not equipped with a tracking beacon," the computer informed him.

"Is this escape pod equipped with radar-scrambling technology?"

"Affirmative."

"Enable it."

"Cloaking enabled."

Ava frowned. "This pod has cloaking capabilities?" The Lasaran pod hadn't.

He nodded. "Akselis tend to be as unscrupulous as Gathendiens. Any pods they design and manufacture travel significantly faster than others to enable them to flee the enemies they engender. It doesn't surprise me at all that they also design them to elude detection. Computer, search for habitable planets we can reach before life support fails."

"Searching. Search complete. One planet holds the correct parameters. K-54973 possesses an atmosphere and temperature range suitable for Gathendiens."

"Would it support Akselis?"

"Affirmative."

Jak'ri looked at her. "Then we should both be able to survive there."

She nodded. "Let's go."

"Computer, change course to K-54973. Maintain maximum speed."

"Altering course. Anticipated arrival time is two days, seven hours, and sixteen minutes."

Ava watched Jak'ri type in more commands. "With the greater speed and the radar-scrambling thing, do you think we'll be able to escape any Gathendiens that will come looking for us?"

"That's my hope, particularly since we were headed in a different direction before we activated the radar scrambling. Computer, reject all attempts by exterior factions to override my commands."

"All exterior override attempts will be rejected."

He stared at the portion of the console that reminded her of a radar image.

Ava tried to understand it. "What's happening?"

He pointed. "That's the Gathendien ship." It was pretty hard to miss. "And that's us."

Their little pod looked like a dust mote by comparison.

"What's that?" she asked as little blips lit up a few times.

"They're still firing on our past trajectory. Heading to Mila 9 before we enabled radar scrambling might have bought us a little time. Computer, scan for other craft and alert us if any come into range."

"Affirmative."

Slumping back in his seat, Jak'ri turned to her.

Ava stared at him, clutching the straps of her harness with a tight grip she hoped would hide the way she trembled. She wasn't sure what he saw in her face. Perhaps the fact that she was only a hair away from falling apart as reaction set in? But his brows drew down in concern.

Jak'ri swiftly unfastened his harness, then pried her fingers loose and unfastened hers. "It's okay," he said softly as he lifted her onto his lap.

Wrapping her arms around him, Ava buried her face in his neck as everything seemed to converge upon her at once. The torture they'd both endured. The battles they'd fought. The killing. Coming so close to being killed themselves. Losing Ziv'ri.

The last sparked tears.

Jak'ri hugged her close, rocking her a little. "It's okay." He kissed the top of her head. "It's okay. We made it off the ship. We're free now."

And hopefully would remain free long enough for his messages to generate a search-and-rescue by his people and every freaking member of the Aldebarian Alliance, if they weren't already searching.

"I can't stop shaking," she whispered and wished she were stronger. How had Eliana done this every night for hundreds of years? How had she risked her life engaging in battle with psychotic vampires again and again and again?

"My hands aren't all that steady either," Jak'ri admitted.

She squeezed him tighter. "You're just saying that to make me feel better."

"Not so." Resting his chin atop her mussed hair, he sighed. "When you kept charging into harm's way..." Now *he* squeezed *her* tighter. "Well, to borrow one of your Earth phrases, I was scared shitless."

A weary chuckle escaped her. "I really do need to clean up my language."

"I like your language." He stopped rocking and made a thoughtful sound. "Hmm." His chin left her hair. "Computer," he said, sounding less weary and more alert, "does your language array include Earth English?"

"Affirmative."

"Can you send a linguistic update to my translator that will include Earth English?"

"Affirmative."

"Initiate update. Secta Hanan Translator model one five three three five, personal passcode six seven seven dash one dash eight nine three dash four four nine six eight."

"Initiating update."

Ava looked up at him.

"Update complete."

He arched a brow. "Say something in Earth English."

Loosening her hold, she straightened in his lap. "You're annoyingly attractive and unruffled considering what we just went through." She, on the other hand, probably looked like someone who had just stumbled out of the forest after having been raised by wolves.

He grinned. "I understood that."

"Are we being followed?"

He glanced at the console. "Not yet."

"But you think they'll come looking for us."

Smile dimming, he nodded. "They're probably scrambling their fighters right now. They'll initially follow the course leading to Mila 9. But they'll eventually consider other options and do what we did—look for planets with favorable atmospheres and search those, too."

Ava fervently hoped it would take them a long time to do that.

"Don't forget," he said, most likely noting her morose expression, "this pod was manufactured by the Akselis and was designed more for making a fast escape than for providing shelter in the event one's ship suffers catastrophic engine failure or the like."

"Does this pod have weapons?"

"Affirmative," the computer answered.

Her hopes of surviving grew. "I wish the Lasaran escape pod had been equipped with weapons." Although she doubted whatever limited weaponry a pod might possess could've held off a Gathendien warship. If anything, it might've just pissed them off and prompted them to blow her to tiny bits. "Then again," she added, "if it had, I might not have met you."

Even though most of the time she'd spent with Jak'ri had been in dreams and much of their conversations telepathic, she was beginning to think the pain and horror she'd endured at the hands of the Gathendiens had all been worth it because it had brought the two of them together.

His expression changed as tenderness entered his silver eyes.

He had lost far more than she had at the hands of the Gathendiens. Did her being here with him help? Did he draw comfort from her the way she did from him?

Her heartbeat picked up when he rested his hands on her shoulders. He gave her a reassuring squeeze, then drew those big hands down her arms in a gentle caress.

Ava winced and sucked in a breath as the pain in her arms increased exponentially.

He froze. Alarm replaced the tenderness in his gaze. "Ava? What is it? Are you hurt?"

"It's nothing," she said, trying to be stoic and tough like the action movie heroes who just shrugged or walked it off if they were shot or took a knee to the family jewels. But she had winced, damn it. And now he was looking her up and down as if he feared she might keel over dead in the next instant.

"Why the *srul* didn't you tell me? Since your movements didn't seem to be hindered... except for your limp... I thought the blood coating you was Gathendien."

Looking down, she grimaced. A *lot* of blood coated her. And some of it *was* Gathendien.

Gross.

"Where are you injured? Let me see."

She motioned to her upper arm, where a nauseatingly deep gash marred her freckled skin. "I kept forgetting about the Gathendiens' tails and some of them wore metal spikes on them."

"Where else?" he asked. But he'd already spotted the gash on her thigh and the scorch mark on her other arm where one of those energy bolt things had skimmed her.

Following his gaze to the latter, she grimaced. "Yeah, I might have exaggerated a bit when I said I was fast enough to dodge energy bolts."

"You were limping, too."

"I stepped on one of their damned tail spikes. What about you? Are *you* injured?"

"No," he answered absently as his brows drew down in a deep V. "Let's get these wounds cleaned up and taken care of."

CHAPTER TEN

A T JAK'RI'S UNSPOKEN URGING, Ava stood up and backed away to give him room to rise.

This pod was definitely roomier than the other one she'd been in.

"Why aren't we floating?" she asked as he retrieved the medic bag and opened it. The Lasaran pod had boasted artificial gravity, but she'd assumed that was a luxury.

Gathendiens didn't seem the type to indulge in such. Nor did they look like they could afford it.

"Most pods are equipped with artificial gravity," Jak'ri muttered as he searched the big bag's contents. "Even small floating objects can initiate alarmingly large malfunctions so what was originally considered a luxury in early space travel was soon deemed a necessity." He drew out a canister that reminded her of the WD-40 she always kept on hand at home. "We'll use this to clean the wounds, then I'll apply some bandages."

Glancing down at herself, Ava repressed a shudder. Her shirt and shorts nearly looked tie-dyed they were so stained. "This pod doesn't by any chance have a shower, does it?" she asked hopefully. "Or a cleansing unit?" Whatever they chose to call it. She just wanted to wash the Gathendien filth off.

"No."

When her shoulders slumped, even *that* minor movement hurt.

"But you can use this to get clean." He held up the canister. "And we stowed some clothes from the lab in the medic bag. You can change into those while the pod disinfects what you're wearing."

She glanced at the lav the pod possessed. Even though it had been designed for larger warriors with big thick tails, she still thought getting clean in there without bruising something would be a challenge. And though she had come damn close to getting naked with Jak'ri in their last shared dream, the notion of stripping down to her birthday suit in front of him made her stomach jump. And not necessarily in a good way. She was thinner than she'd been in their dreams. Some might say scrawnier. And she was riddled with marks and scars from the Gathendien's scalpels. So she couldn't help but feel self-conscious. Jak'ri was thinner than he'd been in their dreams and marred with scars, too, but he was still ripped with muscle and freaking hot.

She just looked pathetic.

He motioned over his shoulder. "I can turn my back or step into the lav and close the door to give you privacy."

Her heart melted. Hot *and* sweet. What a great combination. "I'm sorry," she said miserably. "I'm just self-conscious, I guess." She wished she could be bold and fearless like Eliana or Simone. She wished she could be beautiful, too. "I know you've seen me in my underwear in our dreams, but I don't look like that now." And she'd only had two lovers back on Earth, neither of which she'd walked around naked in front of. They'd only ever been naked with each other when they had sex.

She had even felt self-conscious at first over just being braless beneath her shirt in front of Jak'ri and Ziv'ri.

Jak'ri stepped over the bag, the action bringing him within reach.

Ava tilted her head back to look up at him.

"I don't look the way I did in our dreams either." His lips acquired a wry twist. "Except for the one in which I showed you the results of my sojourn in the Gathendien cell." Reaching out, he brushed several stray strands of hair back from her face. "We're the products of the torture and everything else the Gathendiens subjected us to, Ava. If all goes well, we'll make it safely to K-54973, our wounds will heal, and we'll regain our health and strength while we evade capture and await rescue." Amusement lit his silver eyes. "Although I believe I'm the only one in need of increasing my strength. You seem to have more than enough for both of us now."

Some of her nerves calmed as she returned his smile.

Swiveling, he headed for the lav.

Was he giving her the privacy she both wanted and didn't want at the same time?

He entered the lav, pressed something high up on the wall, and pulled out a white towel.

Nope.

Returning to stand in front of her, he held up the canister. "Have you used this before?"

"No."

"I'll show you how, then I'll turn my back." Before she could bolster her nerves and tell him he needn't look away, he draped the towel over his shoulder and motioned to her arms. "Which one hurts less?"

She held out the arm with the cut on it. The burn constantly felt as if something was still searing it.

Jak'ri aimed the canister's nozzle at her forearm where she bore no wounds and sprayed. Cool clear liquid dampened a small circle of skin. As Ava watched, the liquid turned white and swelled into foam that was nearly as dense as shaving cream.

Setting the canister aside, Jak'ri took her hand and held her arm still while he used his other hand to spread the foam until it coated her from her elbow down to her wrist. The foam fizzled, turning pink where blood stained her skin, and reminded her of the way club soda fizzled in her mouth when she drank it. A moment later, it seemed to melt down and turned clear again, leaving her arm damp but clean. No blood remained anywhere the foam had touched her.

Ava stared at her arm a long moment, then drew it closer to her nose and gave it a cautious sniff.

She even smelled clean! "That's amazing. The Lasaran pod only had packaged cleansing cloths." They hadn't looked all that different from the hand wipes one could purchase on Earth, but they had been far more efficient.

"This pod has those as well." Tugging the towel off his shoulder, Jak'ri drew it down her arm to dry it. He nodded toward the canister. "Normally, we only use the *retsa* for first aid purposes, not for bathing. But since most of the blood coating you is Gathendien and we don't know if you're vulnerable to any of their diseases, I'd feel better using the disinfectant."

Crap. She hadn't thought of that. Her transformation had left her invulnerable to any and every illness found on Earth. But Eliana seemed to believe there was something in Lasaran blood that could harm immortals. Who was to say there wasn't something similar in Gathendien blood?

Once her arm was dry, Jak'ri draped the towel over the back of the seat they stood beside and bent to rummage through the medic bag. "Here's a shirt and some shorts. It looks like these are both made to fit someone my size. I'm sorry. I didn't think to look for something closer to your size in the other lab."

"That's okay. I'll make it work."

He set the clothing beside the towel, then bent and drew more fabric from the bag. "There's also a pair of pants," he said, holding them up for her inspection.

They, too, were made for someone Jak'ri's size, and would be *way* too long on her. They also looked like they were meant to fit more loosely than the shorts, so she'd probably have trouble keeping them up.

"I'll stick with the shorts."

Nodding, he returned the pants to the bag. Then he gave her a smile, stepped away, and turned his back.

He was such a good guy.

Ava went to work, peeling the bloodstained shirt and loose shorts off. Her lip curled in disgust. *So* gross.

Without looking back, Jak'ri held out his hand. "Give them to me. I'll put them in the clothing decon unit." Which was what aliens called their magical clothes washer. The Lasaran pod had boasted one, too.

Ava plopped the stained fabric in his hand.

"A little foam can clean a large area," he mentioned as he ducked into the lav to rid himself of her clothing. "So do as I did and spray a small spot, then spread it."

"Okay. Thanks."

He backed out of the lav, careful not to face her. "It'll sting when it touches your wounds, but we need it to disinfect those."

He wasn't exaggerating. The foam stung like rubbing alcohol when she spread it over her cuts and the burns. "Yep," she wheezed. "That stings all right." But she let it sit there longer, even adding a little more. The foam fizzled, turned pink, then dissolved into what looked like water, leaving the wounds nice and clean.

Gritting her teeth as they continued to throb, she hurried through the rest of her peculiar bath. The odd foam left her so clean that when she dried herself off with the towel, she left no bloodstains on it at all. "Can I wash my hair with this stuff?" A quick feel revealed it hadn't escaped the blood splatter. And the stagnant water stench of the Gathendiens seemed to linger in it.

"Yes."

It didn't take much. A little spritz in her palm provided enough foam to coat her scalp and work through her long hair once she untied it. That stuff really went a long way. The can still felt full when she finished.

Once clean and dry, she pulled on the shorts. They reminded her of the stretchy boxer briefs some men wore back home. On Jak'ri they looked great, hugging his muscled butt and thighs whenever he moved. On her they sagged and fell beneath her belly button before settling low on her hips. The shirt was a lot like the one the Gathendiens had given her, just larger. Ava stuck her arms through the short sleeves and pulled it on.

It swallowed her. Instead of crossing in front and tying on the sides, she could wrap this one so far around her that she ended up tying it in the front. And it was so long it nearly hid the shorts.

"I'm dressed," she announced as she rolled up the sleeves.

Jak'ri turned and gave her a quick once over. "Feel better?"

"Definitely."

"Good. Let's tend those wounds." He motioned to the seats.

Ava sat and watched him retrieve first aid paraphernalia from the bag. "I sprayed them all twice, just to be sure."

Nodding, he knelt beside her and inspected the gash on her arm. "I'm surprised this stopped bleeding so quickly."

Ava made a noncommittal sound. She would eventually have to explain what had happened to her, tell him all the ways the Gathendiens' viral concoction had changed her. But she just didn't feel up to it at the moment.

He sprayed his hands with the magic foam and wiped them on her towel. Then he palmed a much smaller canister—one about the size of a tube of lipstick—and aimed it at the cut.

"What's that?"

"*Imaashu.* It's a pain deadener that will also kill any bacteria that may enter the wound." He sprayed it.

Her eyes widened. The throbbing ceased almost immediately. "That's amazing."

Smiling, he covered the cut with a white bandage just long and wide enough to hide the wound. Then he grabbed a third canister and sprayed. A clear substance coated the white fabric, extending an inch or so beyond its edges. Beneath Ava's astonished gaze, the bandage fitted itself to her wound as though suctioned to it and remained there without Jak'ri having to tape it or wrap bandages around and around her arm to hold it in place.

"That is so cool."

Jak'ri moved on to the gash in her leg.

Ava grimaced. It was so deep she didn't look at it too closely, afraid she'd see bone. Those spikes the Gathendiens wore on their tails were as sharp as freaking razor blades. But like the other wound, it no longer bled.

Jak'ri didn't say anything while he ministered to it. The burn on her other arm received the same careful treatment. "Now your foot." Sitting back on his heels, he drew her foot onto his lap and studied it. "This one's still bleeding."

Jogging on it probably hadn't helped.

His brows lowered. "It looks worse than the others."

Worse than her thigh?

That wasn't good.

He sprayed it with the pain suppressor, providing instant relief.

"Best invention ever," she murmured.

He looked up. "What is?"

"That spray."

"You don't have anything like it on Earth?"

Something you could spray on a deep wound and instantly eradicate all the pain? "No."

He carefully bandaged the wound as he had the others.

"Thank you."

He patted her ankle. "How's the pain?"

"Gone." Or mostly gone. Her abdomen still hurt. But she didn't think spraying the pain deadener on the surface would alleviate the pain beneath it where they'd done who knew what to her organs.

"Good. I'm going to give you a *silna* to speed the healing." He placed the canisters back in the medic bag and withdrew something shaped like a small handgun.

Ava eyed it curiously as he searched for something else. "Tell me again: What's a *silna*?"

"It boosts your immune system and enhances your body's ability to repair itself." He found a small vial filled with a clear liquid.

She stopped him before he could insert the vial into the autoinjector thing. "I'm going to pass on that, thank you."

His face lit with surprise. "You don't want it?"

"No."

"Are you sure? It's been tested on multiple alien races and has performed its expected function in every one of them."

"I'm sure. The virus the Gathendiens infected me with has already altered my immune system. I'm afraid to alter it any more."

Lowering the vial, he stared at her. "You think a *silna* might harm you?"

"Yes."

"If the Gathendien virus weakened your immune system, it may slow the healing of your wounds and leave you vulnerable to infection."

The Gathendien virus hadn't weakened her immune system. It had completely obliterated it and replaced it like a symbiotic organism.

"Trust me. I'll be fine without the *silna*."

At last, he nodded. "As you wish. I just want you to be well, Ava."

"I know. And I am. My wounds feel much better. Thank you for tending them."

Nodding, he tucked everything except the canister of foam back in the medic bag. "Would it be all right if I cleaned up a bit?"

"Of course." She hadn't noticed until then that his chest and shorts bore bloodstains and streaks of dirt, too. Her brows drew down. "Are *you* injured?" Why the hell had it taken her so long to ask that?

He glanced down. "No. I think most of this rubbed off on me when I held you. I could wipe it off with a sani-towel but really just want to wash away my stay on the ship."

"I totally understand." She felt much better now that she didn't bear the Gathendien's stink.

Without waiting to see if he'd ask her to, Ava turned her back.

"I don't blame you for looking away," he commented wryly. "I wouldn't want to see me naked either."

Appalled that he would think that, she spun around. "No! That's not why I looked away. You're—"

He grinned at her.

Laughing, she swatted his arm. "Tease."

He shrugged. "I just wanted to see you smile."

She turned away once more.

"I like that I can understand your words better now," he said.

She wrinkled her nose. She'd been speaking English since he'd upgraded his translator. "My Alliance Common isn't great, is it?"

"Not great," he confirmed, no condemnation in his tone, as clothing rustled. "But not bad either. How long have you been studying it?"

"I studied it for three and a half months before the Gathendiens caught me." She heard him spray the foaming liquid and tried not to imagine him rubbing it all over his body. "I was actually on the *Kandovar* for four months, but spent the first couple of weeks oohing and ahhing over all the advanced technology and tripping over the fact that I was traveling through outer space."

"I don't think tripping translated correctly."

"Why? What did your translator say it means?"

"Stumbling."

She laughed. "It does sometimes mean stumbling. But in this sense, it means... marveling, I guess."

"Is Lasaran technology more advanced than that on Earth?"

"It's *much* more advanced. So is Gathendien technology." She glanced around at the pod. "Akseli, too."

Jak'ri shifted behind her, then strode into view as he headed for the lav.

Eyes widening, Ava got a good long look at his bare, muscled ass, then hastily closed her eyes. Heat seeped into her cheeks.

"Apologies," he said as he walked past again. And she almost wished she'd kept her eyes open so she could see *all* of him. "I forgot I'd need a towel."

"No worries," she mumbled.

In no time at all, he was clean and garbed in a pair of pants that fit loosely like sweatpants but were thinner.

As Ava watched him deposit his bloodstained clothes in the clothing sanitizer and hang their towels in the lav, fatigue hit her like a sledgehammer. She wasn't used to battle or moving at exceptionally fast speeds or exerting preternatural strength. Those disgusting nutrient cubes must not provide her with enough carbs or whatever Immortal Guardians needed because her legs suddenly felt like jelly.

She sank down on a seat.

Jak'ri returned and sat beside her to check the console.

"Anything?" she asked.

"No incoming communications and no craft in pursuit yet. Maybe the Gathendiens still think we're heading toward Mila 9."

"I hope so."

Slumping in his seat, he offered her a tired smile and took her hand, twining their fingers together. "I haven't thanked you yet."

"For what?"

"For saving my life." He shook his head. "I never would've made it off that ship if it weren't for you."

"Ditto."

"That didn't translate."

"It means I wouldn't have made it off that ship if it weren't for *you*."

He gave her hand a squeeze. "I'm not so sure about that."

She wanted to say something more, to tell him how sorry she was that Ziv'ri wasn't there with them, that they hadn't been able to save him, but worried that would merely compound the grief he must already be feeling. Until they'd searched the other holding cells, they'd had hope that Ziv'ri was still alive and being kept in a coma or some other state that would prevent her from communicating with him.

Now hope had fled.

Jak'ri glanced at the console once more. "We should probably get some rest while we can. I think initially heading toward Mila 9 will only divert them briefly. Eventually they'll realize we'd never make it that far and start searching for habitable planets nearby."

She nodded.

Jak'ri pressed a button on the side of the bank of seats.

The backs of all four slowly lowered as footrests at the opposite end rose, providing them with a nice-sized bed on which to rest since there were just the two of them.

Jak'ri stretched out on the makeshift bed and extended one arm along the empty space beside him to form a pillow for her.

Ava lay down beside him, curled into his side, and rested a hand on his bare stomach, careful not to touch any of the healing incision sites that might still be tender.

His arm came around her, nestling her close as a deep sigh wafted from him. "We're going to survive this, Ava."

She nodded, trying to muster up some optimism.

"When we do," he continued, "I'm going to take you to Purvel. And on a sunny day, we'll climb to my favorite meditation spot, dive from the cliff, and swim in the Runaka Sea you've only seen in our dreams."

How she hoped that would happen. "I can't wait."

Tucking a finger beneath her chin, he tilted her face up. His silver eyes met hers for a long moment. "I can't either." Then he dipped his head and pressed his lips to hers.

Her heart leapt. Her pulse began to pound. And the simple touch carried so much tenderness that tears threatened once more.

Ending the kiss, he smiled and pressed his lips to her forehead. "Get some rest," he whispered.

She nodded. "You, too."

Relaxing back against the faux bed, he closed his eyes.

Though fatigue clawed at her, Ava remained awake, her mind racing.

Jak'ri slipped into sleep within minutes. Perhaps it was his military training, which she hadn't even realized he'd had until today. Or maybe just the utter exhaustion engendered by being at the mercy of the Gathendiens for weeks or months on end.

Once she was sure he was out for the count, Ava sat up and stared down at him.

His brow was furrowed, as if all his suffering had followed him into dreams.

Tears threatened once more as she fought the urge to run her fingers through his hair and soothe him. She had only known Ziv'ri for a short time and wanted to bawl her eyes out over his loss. How much more anguish must Jak'ri be stoically enduring from losing his brother and best friend? Because Ziv'ri was clearly his best friend.

Blinking the moisture back, she slipped off the reclined seats and crept around to the medic bag. Ava tried not to make a sound as she knelt and stealthily searched the contents for what she needed.

There. Two bags of blood.

Her blood the Gathendiens had drawn before inadvertently triggering her transformation.

Plucking them out, she cradled one in each hand. They were still cold. Odd. The packaging resembled that of the plastic or silicone bags used on Earth. Yet it maintained the correct storage temperature despite having been removed from the chilly compartment at least an hour earlier.

Ava stared at them. If these things could stay cold, perhaps she should only use one and save the other for later. This was all she had.

"Maybe just one," she whispered and glanced at Jak'ri to ensure he still slept. She wouldn't want him to wake up, see her with a bag pressed to her face, and think she was drinking her own blood.

And, too, she might be procrastinating a little.

Or a lot. This was all very new to her.

Just do it already. She'd seen Eliana infuse herself on more than one occasion. She could do it, too.

Drawing in a deep breath, she shifted the bag closer to her face. Fangs slid down over her eyeteeth. And *wow* it felt weird. That was definitely going to take some getting used to.

Ava cautiously touched a finger to the tip of one fang and found it sharp enough to prick her skin. Grunting, she brought a bag to her mouth and sank her teeth in. Within seconds, her fangs began to siphon the blood in and carry it directly to her veins.

She shivered as the cool temperature seeped through her. Then her body seemed to make some sort of adjustment and she was abruptly comfortable again.

Awesome. She'd heard that Immortal Guardians could control their body temperature, but she hadn't realized it was an automatic kind of thing.

In no time at all, her fangs emptied the first bag.

Ava set it aside and waited a moment.

Shouldn't she feel better? She'd assumed it would be kind of a quick thing. She would infuse herself and *bam*, her injuries would instantly begin to heal.

She glanced down at her arms.

But none of the marks the removal of freckles had left appeared to be getting any smaller.

Perhaps the transformation itself had taken so much out of her that she needed more blood initially.

"Okay," she whispered. "Two bags then."

She sank her fangs into the second one, again letting them siphon the blood directly into her veins. And suddenly she didn't feel so exhausted. The pain in her abdomen that had constantly plagued her since the Gathendiens performed their damned surgeries eased. A lot.

When she glanced down at her arms, her eyes widened. The raw spots where freckles had been removed shrank as she watched and metamorphosed into pale pink scars. Had she not been holding a bag of blood to her teeth, her mouth would've fallen open.

She glanced at her bare legs and saw the same thing. Every visible wound closed, shrank and formed pale scars.

The second bag emptied.

Ava set it down, then reached for the hem of her over-large shirt and tugged it up so she could inspect her stomach.

She sucked in a breath. Holding her shirt up with one hand, she smoothed the other over her abdomen. It was completely free of wounds now. No red, enflamed marks. No scars. Just smooth, pale, unmarred skin.

Had the organs she couldn't see healed as well? Because they had stopped aching.

Amazing. No wonder Eliana liked being an immortal so much.

Jak'ri made a sound in his sleep. Jumping, she looked over at him.

His breathing deepened as his eyes moved back and forth behind closed lids.

Rising, Ava gathered the empty blood bags and glanced around.

When she didn't find what she needed, she whispered, "Computer, where is the refuse receptacle?"

A button flashed on the wall near the lav. When Ava pressed it, a compartment opened that resembled the one she'd used on the Lasaran pod.

Ava dropped the empty bags inside and closed it. A hiss sounded as the trash bin turned it to ash that would take up little room.

Feeling better, she returned to the makeshift bed and lay down beside Jak'ri.

Rolling toward her in his sleep, he curled an arm around her.

Smiling, Ava snuggled close, let the world and her worries slip away, and finally welcomed the sweet oblivion of sleep.

Jak'ri stared out over Runaka Sea. The water churned angrily as clouds gathered overhead.

Seated on the grass, his arms looped around bent knees, he tried to pinpoint the source of unrest that filled him and failed. The forest behind him held a dark, ominous feel today. And a sense of danger constantly pricked him.

Why?

Leaves rustled behind him.

Lunging to his feet, Jak'ri swung around to face the trees.

His heart pounded as he clenched his hands into fists.

The foliage parted and Ava emerged. She wore the same blue pants and colorful shirt he'd seen her in before.

She smiled. "Hi, stranger. Fancy meeting you here."

He relaxed as the pensive feeling that had been plaguing him fell away. "I only understood about half of that."

Laughing, she closed the distance between them. "It's something Earthlings say when they run into someone unexpectedly."

Smiling, he shook his head and drew her into a loose embrace. "This is my meditation spot. You always see me here."

"I know. I just didn't want you to get a big head over me following you here so often."

The foliage behind her rustled again. "Too late," a male said just before Ziv'ri stepped into view. He smiled and sent Ava a wink. "His head has been overly large since birth."

She laughed. "As far as I can tell, all of him is large."

Jak'ri grinned and waggled his eyebrows. "And by that she means all of me."

Ziv'ri responded with a comical grimace while Ava blushed an appealing pink.

"What are you doing here?" she asked his brother with a smile.

Ziv'ri shrugged. "I saw Jak'ri brooding up here, knew you'd probably join him, and thought I'd come along and provide you with a superior example of the Purveli male to admire in his stead." So saying, he struck several poses, flexing his muscles, most of which were on display since he only wore his swim shorts.

Jak'ri shook his head in exasperation.

Ava laughed, then assumed a thoughtful expression. "Hmm. I don't know. Jak'ri here has one hell of a fine Purveli form. I don't think anyone can beat that."

Grinning, Jak'ri strutted over to his brother, puffed out his chest, then struck several poses of his own.

Ziv'ri rolled his eyes and gave him a shove.

Ava's pretty face lit with humor as she watched them seemingly vie for her regard.

"All right," Ziv'ri said, "let's just agree that we're evenly matched in appearance. Now let's determine which one of us is the better diver."

Jak'ri glanced at the sea, pleased to find it calm now. Even the clouds overhead had thinned, letting snippets of sunlight peek through. "Since I'm clearly the better diver," he announced with feigned arrogance, "I'll take that challenge."

Smiling, Ava moved to the side. "All right. Let's see 'em, boys. Give me your best dives."

Ziv'ri volunteered to go first and backed up to the trees. After pausing for a dramatic moment, he raced toward the cliff. Hitting the edge with both feet, he pushed off, flew forward, performed a series of twists and flips, then hit the water below with barely a splash.

Ava clapped when he surfaced. "Very nice!" she called. Then she turned to Jak'ri, winked up at him, and whispered, "But I think you can do better."

Grinning, he backed up to the trees. "Srul yes, I can." Then he raced toward the cliff, hit the edge with both feet, pushed off, performed a series of flips and twists on the way down that was even more complicated than his brother's, and hit the water with a splash he was sure was much smaller.

Surfacing, he swam over to Ziv'ri.

Atop the cliff, Ava waved and cheered. "That was beautiful!"

Both grinned.

"My turn!" she called and disappeared.

Ziv'ri glanced at him. "Has she dived from this cliff before?"

Jak'ri nodded. "A few times."

Suddenly, Ava raced into view—clad only in her bra and panties—and sprang from the edge of the cliff.

Their jaws dropped as she sailed overhead, legs straight, toes together, her slender body forming an elegant T as she held her arms out like a bird's wings, flying far, far, far past the two of them. Then she drew both arms over her head and pierced the water with no splash at all.

Both gaped, eyes wide.

Surfacing, she waved in the distance and grinned big. "That settles it," she called. "I'm the best diver."

Jak'ri whooped and swam toward her. He'd never seen her dive like that before. "You were magnificent!" he declared as soon as he reached her.

Grinning, she looped her arms around his neck and gave him an exuberant kiss. "Thank you. That was so much fun! Did you see how far I went this time?"

"I did."

Ziv'ri swam up. "How the srul *did you do that? That was amazing!"*

She shrugged with a grin, content to linger in Jak'ri's arms and let him keep her afloat. "I have no idea. But I want to do it again."

Jak'ri laughed. "I bet you do."

Ziv'ri caught his eye and schooled his expression into one of concern. "This isn't good, brother. She's clearly a better diver than we are. And I think we can both agree that she's also more attractive."

Jak'ri nodded somberly. "Far more attractive."

Ziv'ri shook his head. "We need to find something we're better at. We don't want her to think Purveli males are inferior."

"We certainly don't."

Ava grinned. "Want to race?"

"Srul yes," they agreed simultaneously.

And the competition began, the formerly dark day filling with light and laughter.

———————◆———————

J AK'RI AWOKE WITH A smile, humor striking as he recalled Ava besting him and Ziv'ri at every challenge and the hilarity that had ensued.

Then he opened his eyes, stared up at the ceiling in the escape pod, and reality hit with the force of an energy bolt.

The chuckle that had been rising in his throat as he remembered his brother's antics transformed into a sob.

Sitting up, he braced his elbows on his knees and buried his face in his hands.

Ziv'ri was gone. The *drekking* Gathendiens had killed him. And Jak'ri would never see him, tease him, or swim with him again.

Spearing his fingers into his hair, he clutched it tight and tried to breathe through pain.

Ziv'ri. Brother. He shook his head, not wanting to believe it. *Forgive me.*

A small hand touched his back, smoothing up and down. "Jak'ri?" Ava said softly.

He swallowed past the lump in his throat. "Ziv'ri was with us this time," he whispered brokenly.

"Yes." She sounded as choked up as he did.

Moisture blurring his vision, he glanced over his shoulder and found her sitting close. "How?"

She blinked. Tears rolled down her cheeks as she shook her head. "We were both thinking about him when we fell asleep." Her slender throat worked in a swallow. "Or maybe..."

Maybe he was saying goodbye, he finished for her, unable to say it out loud.

She nodded, more tears welling in her brown eyes, then opened her arms.

A rough sob erupting, Jak'ri drew her into a tight embrace, buried his face in her hair, and gave in to the grief that consumed him.

CHAPTER ELEVEN

T HEY REACHED K-54973 TWO days later.
From space, it reminded Ava a lot of Earth. Blue oceans covered roughly four-fifths of its surface. The rest was dotted with landmasses that varied from verdant green to white in what she guessed were either deserts or snowy regions. Pale, puffy clouds drifted through the sky, blocking some of the view as the pod approached the planet.

Her gaze shifted to one cluster of clouds that was thicker and darker than the others. Every once in a while, portions would brighten as lightning flashed, just like on Earth.

"Long-range sensors have detected three craft," the computer announced suddenly.

Ava and Jak'ri shared a grim look.

"Can you identify them?" Jak'ri asked.

"They are Gathendien fighter craft."

"Are they headed toward us?"

"Unable to determine with certainty. Their current trajectory indicates they are flying in this direction, but it does not intersect directly with this pod."

Ava glanced at him. "So they still may not be able to see us or pick us up on radar?"

He nodded. "Since they didn't find us heading for Mila 9, this is the best place to look for us. Computer, calculate how quickly they'll reach K-54973 at their current speed."

"Calculating. The craft will arrive in thirty-six hours and fourteen minutes."

Sheesh. That was only a day and a half. She looked at Jak'ri. "How many soldiers can a Gathendien fighter craft carry?"

"The smaller ones only carry two. The larger ones can carry eight, possibly ten. But ten would be a tight squeeze."

"How easy will it be for them to find us once we land?"

"That depends on what's down on the planet. Computer, scan K-54973's surface for signs of civilization."

"Scanning surface area currently in view."

A long pause ensued as Jak'ri stared at the console screen.

Images that reminded her of the satellite views of online maps began to flicker across it in such rapid succession that even with the increased speed Ava possessed, trying to look at them all gave her a headache.

"What kind of signs is it searching for?" she asked.

"Dwellings on land or in the sea that could not have been built by animals. Electricity generated by technology constructed by advanced civilizations. Smoke plumes or smoke stains on cliffs that may indicate the presence of civilizations that are less developed or that lack the resources to generate higher tech."

Half an hour later, the images stopped flickering.

"No signs of civilization detected," the computer announced.

Jak'ri nodded. "Perform a life-form scan on K-54973."

"Performing scan. Life-form scan complete."

Ava raised her eyebrows. "That was fast."

Jak'ri smiled. "It's a less intensive search. All the computer does is scan for heat signatures on the surface that indicate life."

The computer spoke before Ava could comment. "K-54973 supports diverse land and water ecosystems that teem with life."

"Are any of its life forms near enough in size to us to emit similar heat signatures?"

"Affirmative. I detect millions of mammals, reptiles, and sea creatures that approximate your size and emit similar heat signatures."

He smiled at Ava. "That's going to make it a lot harder for the Gathendiens to find us."

True. But thinking of the black bears and other large predators back on Earth, she couldn't help but wonder how great a danger those millions of creatures would pose once the two of them landed.

"Computer," Jak'ri ordered, "determine the velocity of K-54973's rotation and determine what area of the planet will face the Gathendien craft when they reach it."

"Calculating." An image of the planet appeared on the console. One continent lit up. "If the Gathendien craft maintain their current course and speed, this landmass will face them when they arrive."

He nodded. "Plot a course for the opposite side of the planet and determine which landmass is most distant from the one currently highlighted."

"Plotting course."

"That's smart," Ava commented.

He smiled. "When they arrive, the Gathendiens will likely perform the same scans we just did. Once they determine there aren't any civilizations with whom we might find safe harbor and realize they can't track us by heat signature, they'll start searching the continents, one by one, looking for signs of a crash or a glimpse of the pod." He nodded at the view through the window. "This is a large planet. That kind of search could take them a long time."

Long enough for his messages to elicit help, she hoped.

A dotted line formed on the map. "Initial course plotted," the computer announced.

Ava had never found her smart watch, but thought only an hour passed before they reached the other side of the planet and the computer determined the most ideal continent for them. It was a little bigger than many of those they'd passed and boasted so many trees it looked like a fluffy carpet from space.

Perhaps it was this planet's version of a rainforest. She saw no meadows or open fields. Only a few small bare patches along some tall cliffs.

"Enable manual controls," Jak'ri said.

"Manual controls enabled," the computer replied.

A panel in front of him slid back, revealing something that vaguely resembled a joystick.

He turned to Ava as he gripped it. "Strap in. Entering a planet's atmosphere in an escape pod can be jarring."

Trepidation struck as she hastily fastened her harness. "We aren't going to burn up, are we?"

"No. I can get us through safely. The difficult part is going to be finding a place to land."

At least he'd said land instead of crash or splash down. She didn't think Earth had mastered the ability to actually land something like this yet. Astronauts always seemed to just splash down in the ocean instead.

Her anxiety rose as the planet grew before them.

Ava trusted Jak'ri. She really did. If he said he could get them safely through the atmosphere, she believed him. But she'd seen so many movies in which shuttles had blown apart and rained down to Earth in balls of fire because they had entered the atmosphere at the wrong speed or angle that her heart nevertheless began to pound when the first vibrations began.

Clinging to her harness with one hand, she clamped the other onto Jak'ri's thigh and hung on for dear life, every muscle tense. The view outside the window blurred. The vibration increased. The medic bag and its contents rattled while she waited for an alarm to start blaring.

Then all was calm.

She blinked.

Cottony clouds slipped past outside the window.

"Are we through?" she asked.

Jak'ri pried her hand from his thigh and brought it to his lips for a kiss. "We're through."

She relaxed. "Sorry. I hope I didn't squeeze you too tight. Space travel is still very new to me."

"No worries," he said with a smile, borrowing her Earth phrase. He lowered her hand to his thigh, gave it a pat, then focused on guiding the pod closer to land.

Night had fallen on this side of the planet. But the light reflected by three moons produced ample illumination for them to see by.

"How many moons does this planet have?" she asked, peering curiously at the world beneath them.

He glanced at the console. "Seven." Tapping the screen, he zoomed in on the continent he intended to land upon. "Computer, show topographical rendering of the landform beneath us."

"Rendering."

The image changed from lush trees to lumpy land bereft of foliage.

"Overlay it."

The topographical map's opacity reduced enough for them to see the trees through it.

Jak'ri pointed to one area she decided to deem the south. "We may be able to find caves in these hills or rock formations that we can shelter in."

Leaning closer, she pointed. "This looks like it might be a small river or stream. So we'd have access to fresh water."

"I'm going to land over here." He motioned to a point some distance away to the north. "I'll try to slip in between the trees and use them for cover, make it harder to detect the pod. Then we can hike over to the..." He paused, looked at her, then swore.

"What?"

"I forgot your foot was injured. We didn't grab any shoes on our way off the ship."

"Well," she said with a smile, "we *were* kind of busy."

But he seemed to be mentally kicking himself for not snagging her some footwear.

"Nothing on that ship would've fit me, Jak'ri. I have small feet even by Earth's standards." Which was why she hated shoe shopping and pretty much lived in sneakers. She could never find anything else she liked in her size.

"I'll land closer to the hills then and—"

"No. The farther away you land, the farther we'll have to walk and climb to find shelter, which means nature will have more time to cover our tracks. This area looks like the rainforests back home, so maybe we'll luck out and it'll rain. If not, maybe those millions of mammals and reptiles the computer detected—all of which are hopefully vegan—will rustle about and muck up any footprints we leave behind before the Gathendiens get here."

"What does vegan mean?"

"They only eat plants."

"Oh. Then yes, I hope they're all vegan, too. But walking that distance will be painful for you and—"

"I'm okay, Jak'ri." She caught and held his gaze. "I can do this." Especially since the wound had at least partially healed after she'd infused herself while he slept.

He rested the long fingers of one hand on her neck just beneath her ear and stroked her cheek with his thumb. Urging her closer, he pressed his soft lips to hers in a sweet kiss that nevertheless made her pulse pick up. "Will you at least let me carry you if your foot starts to hurt more?"

"No. Will you let *me* carry *you* if *your* wounds begin to hurt more?" He did, after all, still bear wounds and scars from the Gathendiens' surgeries.

He smiled. "No. Ziv'ri would mock me if I—" He clamped his lips shut. The little sparkle of light in his eyes died as his expression darkened with grief. Closing his eyes, he sighed and pressed his forehead to hers.

Her heart going out to him, Ava rested a hand on the nape of his neck and stroked him with her thumb.

"I'm sorry," he murmured. "I can't seem to..."

"It's okay," she whispered, offering him what solace she could. "It's okay." They had dreamed about Ziv'ri again last night. It had been so real that both had been crushed upon awakening and realizing anew that he was gone.

Jak'ri had even ordered the computer to search for any other craft that might be near enough for her to pick up the pilot's thoughts. But that slim hope had withered when the computer had detected none.

Something similar had happened after Ava's grandfather had died when she was five years old. Grandpa Vic had been on Ava's mind so much that he'd peopled her dreams for weeks, making it all the harder for her parents to help her understand that he was gone.

Opening his eyes, Jak'ri withdrew and returned his attention to the console.

Blinking back tears, Ava followed his gaze. "So what's our Plan B?"

He guided the pod toward the designated landing area. "Plan B?"

She nodded. "If the Gathendiens do the unexpected and start looking for us here, or if the damn mother ship follows and they send whole squadrons down searching for us, what should we do? I'm faster and stronger now, but I'm guessing there are still limits to how many warriors I can fight at a time. And I doubt your rifles have unlimited fire power."

Brow furrowing, he studied the map. "If Gathendiens descend upon the area in numbers too large for us to handle..." He started to say something, then closed his mouth again without speaking.

"What?"

"Nothing."

"The only way we're going to survive this is if we bounce ideas off each other, Jak'ri."

He must have agreed because he pointed to the western coast of the continent they hovered above.

And how cool was it that this pod could fly and hover without wings or rotors? She would have to ask Jak'ri how it did that once they landed.

"Here's the region we're hoping to seek shelter in," he said. "Most of this coast over here consists of cliffs. Computer, how high are these cliffs?"

The computer offered up a measurement she didn't understand.

"How deep is the water here?" he tapped the screen.

Again the computer offered up measurements she didn't understand.

"And here?"

More meaningless measurements.

She glanced at Jak'ri. "If it isn't in feet, yards, or meters, I have no idea how tall or deep that is."

"These cliffs are almost as high as Runaka Point." And they formed an unbroken wall that took up about three quarters of the coastline on that side.

"Okay. How does that help us beyond giving us a nice high place we can hurl Gathendiens off of?"

He chuckled.

And it was *so* good to see him laugh again.

"I was thinking we might be able to make it to this island over here." He pointed.

Ava studied the map. It was a pretty small island with a hilly— if not mountainous—terrain that would offer far fewer hiding places than the larger continent. "I doubt the Gathendiens would expect us to go there," she said, her mind working furiously.

"Especially since the water at the base of the cliffs is shallow enough to kill anyone who jumps or dives from them. It doesn't get deep enough to be safe until about here. And…" He offered her an apologetic look. "It's a long swim, Ava. Even if—against all odds—we survived the dive, every time you had to come up for air, you'd risk detection."

"Oh." And Jak'ri didn't have to come up for air at all.

She could probably hold her breath for a hell of a lot longer now. But she *would* need to surface periodically. "Let's keep that on the back burner then and hope it doesn't come to that."

He studied her, his brow furrowed. "What?"

"We'll hope Plan A works and keep the island in mind for Plan B."

He opened his mouth to protest, but Ava pressed a finger to his lips.

"If it comes to that, we'll make it work. I can swim faster and hold my breath longer now. And maybe the Gathendiens will take so long to look for us that we'll come up with a Plan C." Because even if she could hold her breath until they were halfway to the damn island, she wasn't sure Jak'ri could dive far enough to avoid the rocks at the base of the cliffs.

He nodded.

She stared at the console. "I don't suppose we can take these lovely, helpful maps with us when we go, can we?"

"Only if we find something to draw them on. If we don't power down the pod and every tech device in the medic bag, the Gathendiens may detect it and locate us faster."

"That's pretty much what I figured."

Jak'ri slowed the pod to a crawl over the forest.

The trees below them were beautiful, many so tall they would dwarf city skyscrapers. Though night dimmed their color, the brilliant moons—coupled with her newly enhanced vision—allowed her to determine that most were various shades of green. A few they passed bore hues of what she thought was either purple or black.

Mountains rose in the distance, the stone a muted purplish-gray color.

Ava wished the crystal window in the pod were larger so she could see more of what lay ahead of them. The console did a better job displaying what lay beneath them, courtesy of what must be incredibly durable cameras situated on the bottom of the pod.

Once more, she wondered how this thing flew. Helicopters back home would've caused the foliage beneath them to thrash and sway. But the trees they passed above only moved with whatever natural breeze worked its way through them. And the pod must not be noisy like a plane or helicopter because no birds startled from the forest as they flew over.

She peered down at the trees. The leaves were *huge*. Some resembled those of the elephant ears her father had grown in their backyard when she was little, but these must be ten feet long and six feet wide.

"What about here?" Jak'ri asked.

The pod paused, hovering above a tiny break in the foliage.

Ava glanced at him, surprised he'd consulted her since she knew absolutely nothing about landing one of these things. "Can the pod fit through there?"

"I've been watching the leaves as they shift with the breeze. They tend to extend quite some distance beyond the branches, so there may be a wide enough gap for us to fit through."

"And if there isn't?"

"This pod is sturdy enough to break some branches on the way down, but that will create a bigger hole."

She nodded. "Here's hoping these things grow like bamboo then and will fill the gap." When he started to guide the pod down, she touched his arm. "Wait."

The pod stilled.

"Computer," she said, "perform a life-form scan below us."

"Performing life-form scan," the computer said. "Life-form scan complete."

The image of the forest below them lit up with red blobs.

Ava stared. "Wow. That's a lot of life forms."

Jak'ri nodded. "What are you looking for?"

"Anything big enough to kill us. It would really suck if we landed safely then ended up getting squashed or eaten by dinosaurs."

He gave her a blank look.

"I'll explain dinosaurs later," she promised. "Computer, only show us life forms that are large enough to pose a danger to us."

The computer didn't alter the image. "Even life forms the size of minuscule insects can potentially pose a—"

"Just show us the big things," she snapped.

Jak'ri nodded, apparently sharing her irritation.

Most of the red blotches vanished.

"Show elevation," Jak'ri muttered, studying the screen as it changed again.

Ava pointed. "Most of these in the trees look like monkeys. Or apes. Simians?" She hoped at least one of those words would make sense to him.

He nodded and drew her attention to the edge of the image. "I think these are the ones we're going to have to watch out for."

Ava stared. The blobs were fairly indistinct but revealed half a dozen creatures that walked on four legs. *Large* creatures that were thick enough to make her think they rarely missed a meal. But that was about all. "I really hope those are elephants."

"Are elephants vegan?"

"Yes."

"Then I do, too. Shall we do this?"

She nodded. "If worse comes to worst and we can't avoid them, maybe we can win them over with nutrient cubes and sic them on the Gathendiens when they arrive."

He smiled. "Sounds like we already have a Plan C."

She laughed.

Jak'ri expertly guided the pod down through the opening in the canopy.

For a moment, those gargantuan leaves blocked their view. Scuffs and squeaks sounded as branches scraped the sides of the pod. She winced and shuddered a little as some of them mimicked the sound of fingernails on chalkboards.

Though the walls of the pod were thick, her preternaturally sharp hearing picked up the snaps and cracks of a few branches breaking. Well, there was no avoiding that. The forest was thick. And they couldn't exactly park on the beach or in a nice meadow strewn with wildflowers. They were trying to lay low here.

Beneath the canopy, absolute darkness reigned.

"Enable night vision," Jak'ri muttered.

The image on the console lit up in shades of gray with blotches of red that she assumed were animals.

Several red images leapt from branch to branch and swung on vines as they headed straight for the pod. The closer they came, the more distinct their appearance grew.

Ava stared in fascination. They looked a bit like lemurs, but with furrier heads.

"Curious little creatures," Jak'ri murmured as he maneuvered the pod down past large branches and hanging vines that were thicker than his biceps.

Ava nodded.

The little cuties followed their progress, leaping down to lower branches and peering through the window at them.

Ava's gaze drifted to the larger forms that remained farther away.

They didn't look like elephants. Now that they were a little closer, the animals looked more like giant freaking panthers. Crap. She really hoped they wouldn't be as curious about the pod as the lemur things.

At last, the pod approached the ground.

"Computer," Jak'ri ordered, "show me what's above us."

Another image appeared on the console, displaying a night-vision view of the canopy above them.

"Expand range," he murmured.

"What are you looking for?" she asked softly.

"I'm trying to determine which trees will shield us best when we set down."

"Ah." They *had* broadened the hole in the canopy a bit, but she was impressed by how few branches they'd broken. Jak'ri was a good pilot.

She looked out the window. Some of the tree trunks near the ground were as wide as the pod. If he could tuck them in close to a couple, she thought they'd be pretty hard to spot from above the forest.

Ava returned her attention to the view the computer provided of the canopy. When several small faces with big eyes abruptly filled the screen and peered back at her, she laughed. "I think they've found the camera."

Jak'ri smiled. "Looks like it. Fortunately, I saw enough before they did."

The pod rattled slightly. Then he released the joystick. "All right. We've landed."

Ava smiled at him. "That was a lot smoother than I expected."

"I had to learn to pilot and land Akseli pods as part of my military training." He grinned. "Fortunately, they started me with simulators because I crashed a lot before I finally grew accustomed to it."

She wrinkled her nose. "I'm glad I didn't have to try to land the Lasaran escape pod. I'm pretty sure it would've gone up in flames before I even finished entering the atmosphere."

Unbuckling his harness, he shook his head. "Most pods are equipped with autopilots that would've guided you safely through the atmosphere."

"Then hurled me at the ground like a ball?"

He paused. "Mmmmaybe?"

Ava laughed. "So now what do we do?"

"Computer, how much time do we have before the sun rises?"

"The sun will breach the horizon in approximately four hours and twelve minutes."

Jak'ri arched his brows. "Want to rest a little before we head out exploring?"

She nodded. "I'd rather not run into those big cats. If they're nocturnal predators, maybe they'll be gone by the time we wake up."

"I hope so. Let's get some sleep."

T HREE HOURS LATER, JAK'RI sighed. Despite his fatigue, sleep eluded him. His mind raced as he lay quietly with Ava snuggled up beside him, deeply ensconced in sleep.

How long would it take his message to reach Mila 9?

Would the Segonians send a rescue crew or merely relay the message to Purvel?

He had referred to Ava as a passenger aboard the Lasaran ship *Kandovar*. Since Segonians were members of the Aldebarian Alliance, he'd thought that might garner a quicker response.

If—as Ava believed—the *Kandovar* was destroyed, alliance members had no doubt already begun a massive search and rescue mission. Might some of them have ventured close enough to render them swift aid?

Considering how far away from alliance occupied space he and Ava were and the inoperability of the *qhov'rum*, he thought it unlikely but hoped he was wrong.

Jak'ri fought the need to tighten his hold on her, not wishing to wake her.

At most, landing here had bought them some time. The question was: how much? He had done what he could to make it harder for the Gathendiens to track them but thought the *grunarks* would find them nevertheless.

Then what would he and Ava do? Swim from continent to continent, island to island, hoping to evade them? Jak'ri could live in the ocean indefinitely and could tolerate cold temperatures. But Ava...

She may look Lasaran, but she didn't have their hardiness or their incredible regenerative capabilities. Back on the ship, the wounds left behind by the Gathendiens' surgeries had been as slow to heal on her as his had been. And he'd seen her shiver at temperatures he found quite comfortable.

What if the ocean water surrounding this continent was too cold for her body to tolerate?

Even if it wasn't and the two of them made it to the island she called Plan B, what then? What if the Gathendiens followed them there? Would he and Ava just head for another island or continent to evade capture? The next closest landmass, according to the map, was days away from Plan B even when swimming at Purveli speeds.

Could Ava's body tolerate being submerged in water that long?

Back when Purvelis and Akselis had been friends and allies, some Purvelis had found Akselian lifemates. Accustomed to living underwater for long stretches, the first Purvelis to bond with Akselis had thought artificial gills would allow their lifemates to reside underwater with them. But they had learned to the detriment of their partners that the water's continuous pressure reduced circulation to Akselis' extremities and weakened their bodies to such an extent that even after spending only a few days in the water, they often couldn't walk for weeks when they emerged. Akselis' skin also began to break down after a few days of constant immersion, spawning open sores and bacterial infections.

Would the same happen to Ava if it took them days to swim to the next island?

What other recourse would they have? Stay and fight?

If the three craft coming after them carried two soldiers each, Jak'ri was confident he and Ava could defeat the *grunarks*. But if they each carried ten, he thought their chances of achieving victory far slimmer. And as he'd pointed out to Ava, the Gathendiens had destroyed the *Kandovar* with three members of the royal family aboard to capture her. He had no doubt that the Gathendien warship from which they'd just escaped would soon follow.

If the two of them—armed with three *osdulium* rifles, two *tronium* blasters, and a couple of daggers—had to battle a warship full of Gathendiens with dozens if not hundreds of O-rifles, blasters, e-grenades, and stun grenades...

Well. The outcome would be grim.

After seeing the increased speed and strength Ava had gained, something he still didn't understand, Jak'ri was certain he would be the first to fall during such a battle. When he did, he feared Ava would do whatever they demanded of her to keep them from torturing or killing him. And he couldn't let that happen. He couldn't let them recapture her.

But as far as he could tell, the only way to avoid that was either to evade the Gathendiens' notice entirely or for him to die so they couldn't use him to bend Ava to their will.

"Proximity alert," the computer said, its voice loud in the silence that had fallen.

Starting, Jak'ri glanced down at Ava.

She didn't so much as sigh. She'd been sleeping more deeply since the Gathendiens had injected her with that virus and appeared not to have heard the abrupt announcement.

Something brushed against the side of the pod. A long *shushing* sound ensued as the body continued to move past, rubbing against the exterior.

A very *large* body.

His heart rate climbed. Was it one of the life forms Ava had hoped were elephants but resembled what she called big cats?

Silence fell.

The long shushing sound began anew.

Was the same animal brushing past them a second time or was there more than one?

"Computer," he whispered, "how many life forms surround us?"

The shushing stopped.

Had the creature heard him? If so, it had incredibly acute senses because the walls of the pod were thick enough that he wouldn't have heard anything taking place outside it if they hadn't rubbed up against it.

"Six life forms linger in close proximity," the computer replied.

And *drek*, the computer didn't whisper.

A rumble arose, so loud he could hear it through the thick walls of the pod.

A chill skittering down his spine, Jak'ri fervently hoped that wasn't a growl.

A thud sounded above.

He glanced at the ceiling.

Had one of those creatures just jumped on top of the pod?

He would've asked the computer to show him what was up there, but he couldn't see the console from the makeshift bed. He *could*, however, see the window. "Activate night-vision mode on window and lower volume of your responses to three," he whispered.

"Activating night vision mode," the computer responded, much softer this time.

And once again, all sound ceased.

The world outside the window brightened with shades of gray, displaying forest.

A furry form slunk past, so big it blocked the view. Then two gleaming eyes peered in at him.

Jak'ri stared. The creature's head was so big he could only see the eyes, nose, and whiskers. The big nostrils flared and fogged up the window as it huffed and sniffed.

The head disappeared, then a huge paw pressed against the window, taking up half the view.

When the window didn't give, the creature peered in at them again.

Jak'ri lay completely still, heart pounding, filled with the certainty that an O-rifle would only anger something that large.

The paw returned, this time scraping the window with claws that looked as long as his forearm.

The crystal window, however, was virtually unbreakable.

Another thud came from above as the pod shook a little, then a third. And he envisioned one of the creatures bouncing on it to see if it would give.

Ava didn't stir.

After a couple more minutes of testing the foreign pod, the creature at the window seemed to lose interest and left. The weight atop the pod disappeared. Four more big furry bodies slunk past.

Quiet fell.

Jak'ri released a long sigh of relief, realizing only then that every muscle had been tense.

Minutes passed. And with each he relaxed a little more.

"If that thing had broken the window, I think I would've peed my pants," Ava said.

Jak'ri jumped, then laughed. "I thought you were asleep."

Tilting her head back, she looked up at him. "I *was* until the computer's loud-ass voice woke me up, saying there were six of those things out there. Sheesh. Can't it take a hint and whisper when *you* whisper?"

He smiled. "It isn't an AI and apparently lacks that programming."

Grunting with displeasure, she sat up. Then she turned brown eyes wide with awe upon him. "Did you see how *huge* that thing was? I was afraid it was going to start batting us around like a toy!"

"If it had gotten its claws into the pod, I think it might have."

"This is so weird," she declared. "I'm super excited about seeing such a cool alien creature. But at the same time, I'm now terrified we'll run into one when we leave the pod. That thing looked feline, and cats back on Earth are notoriously good hunters. And carnivores. And aren't averse to playing with their food before they eat it."

Jak'ri shared her concern. "They appear to be nocturnal hunters, so perhaps we can avoid them by only moving about during the day."

Her brow furrowed. "I hope so. Because cats back home also excel at climbing trees. We'd have to climb pretty damn far to reach branches that wouldn't support them. Computer, how long until sunrise?"

"The sun will breach the horizon in fifty-three minutes," the computer responded, volume still low.

"Fifty-three minutes, huh?" Reaching out, she combed her fingers through Jak'ri's hair.

A rumble of pleasure escaped him. He loved her touch and how frequently she expressed affection for him now that they weren't being watched. His body did, too, responding in ways he thought inappropriate considering her wounds and their situation.

"Have you slept at all?" she asked softly.

He shook his head.

She sent him a sad smile tinged with sympathy as she continued to finger-comb his hair. "Too much on your mind?"

"Too much on my mind," he agreed and sat up with a sigh. "We should get everything together that we plan to take with us."

"Okay."

The medic bag was already full of the supplies they'd brought from the ship. A thorough search of the pod provided them with another bag they filled with cleansing cloth packets, *wosuur*, and as many nutrient cubes as they could fit from the pod's supply.

"I have to admit," Ava said as she grabbed another handful and stuffed them inside, "I'm hoping this planet will yield some yummy fruit that's safe to eat because these cubes are nasty. The Lasaran pod's food supply was much better. It was more like MREs."

Jak'ri added a few canteens. "What are MREs?"

"Meals Ready to Eat. They're basically prepared meals that have been dehydrated and can be stored for a few years without spoiling. All you do is open them, add water, and heat them up. The ones on the Lasaran pod were more compact than Earth MREs. But they were surprisingly tasty."

They found a few more weapons—daggers and blasters enough to accommodate four passengers. Not surprising considering how many enemies the Gathendiens had amassed.

He glanced at her arm. "Before we go, I want to check your wounds, apply fresh dressings, and coat them well. I don't want whatever bacteria thrives on this planet to work its way into them."

She hesitated. "Okay. What about you? How are your incisions?"

He paused and tugged up the shirt he'd snatched from the lab. Tucking his chin, he examined the marks left by the Gathendiens' surgeries and experiments. All still bore a clear coating that would protect them from the elements. "They're good." Setting the bulging bag aside, he motioned to her. "What about you?" Now that it was clean again, she wore the small shirt that fit her form better.

While he waited for her to unfasten it, he opened the medic bag and began drawing out supplies. He frowned.

"What's wrong?" she asked, unmoving.

"The blood is gone." They'd brought two bags of her blood with them, but no amount of rummaging uncovered them.

"I know." Something in her voice made him stop and look at her.

A hesitance entered her expression that hadn't been there a moment earlier.

"What happened to it? I'm sure it was in the bag when we left the ship." Bringing it with them had been important to her.

"I... infused myself with it."

He stared at her blankly. "Do you mean you gave yourself a transfusion?"

"Yes."

"When?"

"While you were sleeping our first night in the pod."

And still he stared. "I wasn't aware you knew how to do that."

"I figured it out," she said with a little grimace.

Reaching out, he took one of her hands. "If you felt you needed a transfusion, why didn't you let me help you?"

"For the same reason that I'm nervous about you checking my wounds."

He frowned, certain he was missing something here. He just couldn't determine what. "I don't understand."

Withdrawing her hand, she began to untie her shirt. "I'm different now."

"Because of the virus?" She'd said it had changed her.

"Yes."

"I know. You're stronger and faster. And sometimes your eyes glow." His frown deepened. "Or were you like that before and I just didn't know it?" She hadn't exhibited those traits in their shared dreams.

She shook her head. "I was a *gifted one*, like I was in the dreams, before they infected me."

"And now?"

"Now I'm an Immortal Guardian."

He shook his head. "I don't know what that means."

She opened her shirt.

Jak'ri's gaze immediately went to her beautiful breasts, pale and plump and wonderfully bare.

Her eyes widened as she yanked her shirt closed again. Her face flushed. "Crap! I forgot I wasn't wearing a bra."

And curse him, his body was already responding to just the brief glimpse he'd received. This was *not* the time for that. "Apologies," he said hastily. "I didn't mean to stare." *She's just so* drekking *perfect*, he thought.

She relaxed a little. "You really think so?" she asked softly.

He swore. "You weren't supposed to hear that."

"I know. But I have less control over what I hear telepathically than you do." A look of surprise crossed her face. "Hey. Is your telepathy returning now that the Gathendiens aren't dosing you?"

He stared at her. "I've been without it for so long that I didn't even think to try it." Especially since she could hear his thoughts without him actively sending them to her.

"Try to read the thoughts I don't send you."

Focusing on her face, he attempted to delve into her mind. Images and thoughts inundated him, so many he had difficulty sorting through them all. Her mind bore none of the barriers Purvelis and Lasarans learned to erect at an early age. He could see everything. Her memories of Earth. The friends with whom she'd embarked upon the voyage to Lasara. Prince Taelon, his lifemate, and their infant daughter. Her time with the Gathendiens. Her time with *him*.

His heart swelled. She was coming to care for him as deeply as he cared for her. And some of his guilt vanished when he realized he wasn't the only one who wanted to physically act upon that growing love.

Then he stumbled upon new fears she harbored.

Fears that eclipsed everything else.

Fears that seemed to center around the ways the Gathendiens' genetically engineered virus had changed her.

And how she had transfused herself with the bags of blood.

"You have fangs?"

CHAPTER TWELVE

A VA WINCED. "YES. DAMN it, how much did you see?"
"More than I intended. You have no natural barriers."
Jak'ri's eyes narrowed, squinting slightly as he stared at her lips
as though hoping to catch a glimpse. "You didn't have fangs in
our dreams."

"I know. I grew them when the virus transformed me." And she
was still coming to grips with just how much she'd changed.

"I don't see them when you speak."

"Because I can't really control them yet so they've only slid
down when I... transfused myself."

"You didn't drink the blood?"

She grimaced. "No. Gross."

He nodded thoughtfully, exhibiting none of the disgust she
felt at the notion of consuming it. Maybe there were aliens out
there who did that sort of thing regularly. "I questioned the
efficacy of ingesting it if you needed a transfusion."

That actually made her crack a small smile. "My new fangs
behave like needles and siphon it directly into my veins."

"Very efficient."

She stared at him, uncertain what to make of his response.

"Why are your eyes glowing?" he asked.

"Because I'm nervous," she admitted. "Being different doesn't
go over well on Earth."

Smiling, he took both of her hands in his. "Ava, this isn't Earth.
Things are different out here. Purvel may not be part of the
Aldebarian Alliance, but we conduct business and interact with
its members often. We wouldn't do that if we disliked anyone

who wasn't Purveli. And there would *be* no Aldebarian Alliance if its member nations actively disliked other alien races because we *all* bear differences. The longer you're out here, the more you'll come to understand that most differences spark curiosity rather than animosity."

"Except with the Gathendiens."

He nodded. "Gathendiens fervently believe that all other alien species are beneath them and unworthy of..."

"Existing?" she supplied.

He smiled wryly. "Yes. But the Gathendiens' determination to conquer the galaxy and claim its riches and resources for themselves has merely reduced their numbers to a fraction of what they once were as they continue to underestimate the capabilities of the enemies they engender. I think that's why you and your friends are so important to them. Your sector of space is largely unexplored and, if you'll forgive me for saying it, less advanced than ours. Now that the Aldebarian Alliance has weakened the Gathendien military so much, your world would be far easier for them to conquer."

"Gathendiens are asshats."

He laughed. "An apt description." He squeezed her hands. "Now tell me more about this virus. I thought you had recovered from it. But your thoughts lead me to believe you still harbor it."

"Doctors on Earth are still trying to understand it. And they're hampered by the fact that it's unlike any other virus on our planet."

"Gathendiens excel at creating such. Even the Lasarans, with all of their advanced technology, didn't fully understand the damage done by the virus the Gathendiens unleashed upon them initially."

"Well, the virus the Gathendiens infected Earthlings with behaves more like a symbiotic organism. The first thing it does is attack and destroy our immune system, which is why some don't survive the transformation."

His eyes widened with alarm.

"Then the virus takes its place."

"Takes what's place?"

"It basically sets itself up as our immune system, providing us with a resistance to all other viruses and illnesses on Earth, healing our wounds far faster, and even making us immune to all known drugs and poisons on Earth. And because—as I mentioned—it behaves like a symbiotic organism, it makes us stronger, faster, and enhances our senses." She shrugged. "If *we* die, *it* dies, so it makes us extremely hard to kill."

He frowned. "I don't understand. If the Gathendiens want to eliminate all Earthlings, why would they make them stronger?"

"We have a few ideas about that. The Gathendiens apparently created this virus thousands of years ago."

He nodded. "That doesn't surprise me. They're one of the oldest races we've encountered, as are the Sectas and the Lasarans. It's one of the reasons Gathendiens believe they're superior."

"Would their medical knowledge that long ago have been equal to their knowledge today?"

He pondered that a moment. "Their medicine would've been more advanced than what you have on Earth, but I think their experimentation with genetic engineering would've still been in its infancy."

"That's pretty much what I was thinking. This virus makes those infected with it so sick initially that some die before they complete the transformation." Smiling, she squeezed his hand. "Thank you for caring for me and keeping me going while I was so sick."

He raised one of her hands to his lips and kissed her palm. "I didn't want to lose you."

Butterflies erupted in her belly.

He kissed the palm of her other hand. "I still don't."

Damn. Jak'ri could make her melt with just a few words and a couple of innocent kisses.

But after everything they'd gone through together, Ava suddenly felt a distinct need for more than that. Releasing his hands, she rose onto her knees, tunneled her fingers through his hair, and drew him close for a kiss.

Jak'ri sucked in a breath, then hummed his approval. Nudging the medic bag aside, he rose to his knees and locked an arm around her waist. Desire rose—swift and unexpected—as he flattened her body against this lean, hard form. He splayed his knees so he didn't loom over her so much, bringing them into better alignment.

Fire burned through her as he slid a hand down her back and cupped her bottom, urging her closer. Now that she was an immortal, her every sense was heightened. And he smelled so good. *Felt* so good. When the hard ridge of his arousal pressed against her...

She moaned and clutched him tighter.

He cupped her breast with the other hand, squeezing and sending a jolt of pleasure through her. "I love your breasts," he murmured.

Since she'd once dated a guy who had mentally wondered if she'd ever thought about getting a boob job, that merely excited her more.

When he drew a thumb across the stiff peak, she gasped.

"K-54973's sun has breached the horizon," the computer announced.

Ava and Jak'ri broke the kiss and growled at the interruption, then looked at each other and laughed.

Ducking his head, he pressed his forehead to hers. "I want you," he admitted softly.

She smiled. "I want you, too."

"But now isn't the time."

She loosed a sigh of regret. "I know. Some lizard-like asshats will reach the planet tomorrow and we need to find a hiding place before then."

Chuckling, he released her with obvious reluctance and sat back on his heels. "I still haven't checked your wounds." He motioned for her to sit back as well and dragged the medic bag close once more. "While I do, explain to me why Gathendiens would think a virus that makes you stronger would annihilate your species."

Ava sat back and watched him remove supplies from the bag. "Well, I was thinking that maybe back then the Gathendiens weren't as concerned about keeping their test subjects healthy while they experimented on them."

"A logical assumption."

"So at least some of the Earthlings they tested it on probably died within a few days of being infected."

"And the others?" He motioned to her stomach.

Cursing herself for blushing again, Ava opened the shirt.

His gaze went to her breasts.

She didn't have to look down to know her nipples were beaded from the desire that still coursed through her.

His eyes met hers. "Perfect," he declared softly, his voice hoarse. Then he examined her abdomen and his eyebrows flew up. "The incisions... They're gone." Reaching out, he drew a big hand across her stomach. And damn her enhanced senses, it merely fed the arousal she was trying to beat back. "There aren't even any scars," he murmured.

She nodded. "The virus healed them." After she'd infused herself.

He dropped his gaze to her thigh. "And this one?"

"That one hurts a little, so it must still be there." She closed her shirt and tied it as he carefully peeled the rubbery bandage off.

"Still here," he confirmed as he examined it. "But smaller than it was."

As he had before, he sprayed the foaming cleanser on the wound, applied the analgesic that numbed the pain and would keep it from getting infected, then topped it with a fresh bandage. He checked the gash on her arm next. Like the other, it hadn't vanished but was smaller. "Why haven't the more recent wounds healed?"

"I think I'm still weak from my transformation."

He sent her a look of astonishment. "*This* is weak?"

She grinned. It felt good to be viewed as someone who was strong.

"What about the test subjects who survived the transformation this virus induces?" he asked as he began to remove the bandage on the bottom of her foot.

"Do you remember me telling you there are two different species of people on Earth, humans and *gifted ones*?" Most humans were blissfully unaware of that.

"Yes."

"There were actually very few *gifted ones* on the planet thousands of years ago. So I'm guessing all of the Earthlings the Gathendiens abducted for their experiments were humans."

"How did that skew the results?"

"The virus causes progressive brain damage in ordinary humans that quickly drives them insane. If the newly transformed humans—or vampires as they're known on Earth— are subjected to torture or unduly harsh living conditions, it accelerates the madness. So whoever survived the Gathendiens' experiments probably went crazy and tore each other apart within a very short time."

Pausing in his work, he stared at her. "Will the virus drive you insane, Ava?"

"No. The advanced DNA *gifted ones* are born with protects us from the more corrosive aspects for the virus, so we get all of the strength, speed, and greater healing abilities without the madness."

"Something the Gathendiens didn't know when they released the virus?"

"Right."

He peeled the bandage off her foot and frowned. "Your greater healing abilities didn't extend to your foot. This one still looks painful and angry."

"Based on what Eliana told me, whatever poses the greatest risk heals first. In this case, healing whatever the Gathendiens did to my organs took precedence." She shifted so she could see the bottom of her foot. "It looks a *little* better."

"But still hurts?"

She grimaced. "Yes. I was just trying not to be a wuss about it."

"Wuss didn't translate." He sprayed the cut with foaming cleanser.

She started to say pansy, but thought that would just confuse him more. "I didn't want to seem weak or whiney."

He snorted. "If you believe *anything* you say or do would make me think you weak, then that virus must have driven you insane after all."

She grinned.

He patted the wound dry with a towel. "It took a lot of bravery to dive into battle with the Gathendiens the way you did back on the ship. And great physical strength to defeat them in hand-to-hand combat. You even broke one's neck. That's not an easy feat."

Her smile faltered. "I've never killed anyone before." She'd probably slain at least half the Gathendien warriors she'd fought back on the ship. Maybe Kunya, too. He and Saekro had both looked pretty dead when she'd left them. "It seems like I should feel some remorse over it, but I don't."

"Of course you don't," Jak'ri responded, no condemnation in his tone. "They were using you with the intent of committing genocide against your people, something they've already attempted once. They very nearly *succeeded* in committing genocide on Lasara. And they were using Ziv'ri and me to find a virus that would eradicate our species as well. I feel no regret for taking the life of someone who has no reverence for any life other than his own."

And they'd killed his beloved brother.

Jak'ri studied her foot. Brow furrowing, he met her gaze. "Though I want to, I don't think I should spray this with the *imaashu*. Pain can sometimes be a good thing, warning us when we're pushing ourselves too far after an injury. I worry that with no soreness, you might forget to tread carefully and could reopen the wound or tear the dressing and allow bacteria in."

"Good point." With no pain, she'd probably walk normally, putting her full weight on the gash too soon.

He held up the analgesic canister and raised his brows. "Perhaps a lesser dose?"

"No. I'll be fine. We can always apply some tonight once we're settled."

Agreeing, he tucked the *imaashu* back in the medic bag.

Ava watched him spread a towel in his lap and prop her foot on it. He was such a nice guy, caring for her wounds so tenderly. It made her feel all warm and fuzzy inside.

"I'm going to spray the whole bottom of your foot with this," he said, picking up the canister of *kesaadi* he'd used to coat her bandages and adhere them without tape. "I'm hoping it will provide some protection for you since you have no shoes."

"Okay."

"Spread your toes."

When she did, he smiled.

"What?"

"Your feet are so small. It's—what's the Earth word?—cute."

She laughed and wiggled her toes at him.

Humor sparkling in his silver eyes, Jak'ri sprayed her foot from toes to heel, then sprayed the other one.

It felt weird, like she had a couple of thick stickers stuck to the bottom of her feet. And her toes felt bulkier. Hopefully, though, it would make walking through the forest barefoot more comfortable. She'd suggest they wrap their feet with bandages but worried they might need those later if the Gathendiens caught up to them.

"You should spray your feet, too," she told him, then grinned. "Your awesomely *big* alien feet."

Laughing, he sprayed his feet. "And yet my feet are still small compared to the paw that pressed against the window earlier."

"I know! That thing was huge! We need to make sure we're somewhere safe before nightfall."

"Agreed. The sooner we leave, the sooner we'll find shelter. Are you ready?"

Ava opted to use the lav one last time and wished the damn Gathendiens weren't chasing them so they could just stay in the pod. She was *not* looking forward to peeing in the bushes and would miss this weird little toilet.

Jak'ri powered down the pod and ensured nothing in the medic bag would emit an electronic signal.

Both of their go bags boasted two sets of handles. The smaller ones were for carrying them by hand. The other set allowed them to wear the bags like backpacks. Jak'ri insisted on donning the heavier one that was full of canteens, nutrient packs, and the like while Ava slipped on the medic bag, the contents of which had been designed to be lightweight and easy to tote into battle.

When Jak'ri manually opened the hatch, nature sounds flooded in. Bird calls. Insects. The scuttling of what sounded like small creatures rustling in the undergrowth.

Jak'ri climbed out first and stood on the lip of the open hatch. "Looks good." He extended a hand down to her.

Ava took it and climbed out beside him.

The canopy above was so thick that everything beneath it was eclipsed by shade and quite dark even though, according to the computer, the sun had risen.

Jak'ri jumped down to the ground, then held up his arms.

She smiled. "I'm stronger now, remember? You don't need to catch me."

He flashed her a grin. "Maybe I was just looking for an excuse to hold you."

"Ooh. Sounds good to me." Ava jumped.

Jak'ri caught her and gently lowered her to her feet, letting her slide down the front of his body.

"Is that a *tronium* blaster in your pocket," she asked impishly, "or are you just happy to see me?"

He laughed. "Both."

Loud hoots erupted above them.

Jumping apart, Ava and Jak'ri raised the O-rifles draped over their shoulders and aimed them up at...

She stared.

The little mammals they'd glimpsed briefly upon their arrival last night leapt from limb to limb as they descended the trees to get a closer look at the newcomers.

"They're so cute," she declared.

About the size of a large housecat, they resembled a cross between a lemur and a kangaroo. Big brown eyes dominated pointy faces surrounded by thick, furry black manes. Their arms, hands, and tails resembled those of lemurs. Their back legs were bigger and more powerful like a kangaroo's. Though their earth-tone base color varied from one to the next, all bore long black and white stripes that began on the tops of their heads and stretched all the way down to the tips of their tails.

And *wow* they were loud, hooting back and forth as they ventured closer.

When the group exhibited curiosity rather than hostility, Jak'ri smiled and lowered his weapon. "Inquisitive, aren't they?"

"Yes." She lowered her weapon, too. "I wish I could keep a couple as pets." These were the first animals Ava had seen since leaving Earth. She hadn't realized how much she missed them.

"Maybe they'll join us on our hike and point out what plants, fruits, and nuts are safe to ingest."

"That would be great. I miss real food." Though she worried that testing alien fruits or berries might make Jak'ri sick. Ava was immune to all known poisons on Earth. Hopefully that immunity would carry over to this planet as well since they bore similar ecosystems. But Jak'ri...

"Look." He pointed to the ground beside them.

When she followed his gaze to the outline of a paw print, her eyes widened. "Holy crap! I can fit both my feet in that!"

"I think whatever left that was a baby," he murmured and pointed again. "Look at that one."

The other one made the first one look small.

"Yeah," she said, stunned. "We definitely need to make sure we're tucked away somewhere safe before nightfall."

Nodding, he took her hand and twined his fingers through hers. "Ready to start our adventure?"

She smiled. "I'm ready."

With their new furry friends leaping, swinging, and hooting above them, they headed away from the pod.

THE INQUISITIVE HOOTING MAMMALS stayed with them as they trekked through the forest toward the hills in which Jak'ri hoped to find shelter. He quickly came to regret not applying the pain suppressor to Ava's foot. Her limp gradually grew more pronounced and her winces more frequent as she tried not to put much weight on it.

Cursing himself, he helped her as much as he could.

Or as much as she'd *let* him. Ava was a proud female, reluctant to exhibit any weakness whatsoever. But Jak'ri didn't think her weak. Even before her baffling transformation he hadn't thought her weak.

Had he wished to protect her?

Of course. That impulse, however, had in no way arisen from a belief that she wasn't strong. He had admired how she'd handled captivity, the way she'd conquered her fears again and again, the sense of humor she hadn't abandoned in favor of despair. He'd been grateful for the reprieves she'd granted him from his own captivity in dreams, treasuring the moments of freedom they'd shared at Runaka Point. And he respected the intelligence she had repeatedly exhibited both back on the ship and here on this alien world.

He studied her from the corner of his eye. She'd pulled her long hair back in what she called a ponytail that slid this way and that across the top of her pack. Little tendrils had escaped and danced around her pretty face as a faint sheen of moisture glistened on her forehead.

Jak'ri's heart thudded in his chest. Since becoming an adult, he had wondered periodically what having a lifemate would be like, if experiencing that depth of emotion and caring would change him in some way.

His parents' union was a loving one, full of laughter, affection, and teasing. Throughout his life, his mother and father had shared a closeness that he'd begun to wonder if he would ever find himself, since past lovers had failed to engender those emotions in him.

But now he knew. Now he understood.

Because he was coming to feel for Ava what Purvelis felt for lifemates.

Ava slowed to a halt.

Jak'ri stopped beside her, his arm tucked through hers and lending support.

Turning to face him, she stared up at him.

He frowned as worry rose. "Are you all right? Do you want to rest a bit?" If her foot pained her too much, perhaps he could convince her to let him carry both bags by hand while she rode on his back.

Her slender throat moved in a swallow. "That isn't how I'd like to ride you," she whispered, her brown eyes acquiring a fascinating amber glow.

As the meaning of her words sank in, desire coursed through him and instantly rendered him hard and aching. "What?" he asked, voice hoarse.

"Did you mean it?" She studied him intently. "Do you really feel for me what your people feel for lifemates?"

As realization dawned, he swore. "You were reading my mind."

"Yes. I'm sorry. It wasn't intentional. When I'm tired or stressed, it's harder to block out other people's thoughts and..." Raising her hands, she cupped his face. "I admit I liked what I heard." She leaned her lithe body into his. "Because I'm falling in love with you, Jak'ri. I have been for a while now. Maybe even since our first shared dream."

He had suspected as much from his perusal of her thoughts earlier, but hearing her confirm it and speak it aloud...

He slid both arms around her, tucking them between her pack and her back. "You're supposed to go to Lasara," he murmured. And yet he wanted desperately to take her back to Purvel with him.

Her slow nod made his heart sink. "I am. But the Lasarans promised to protect us. They told Seth they would keep all of us safe. And I'm thinking—or I'm *hoping*—that their failure to do that may make them more amenable should I... decide to live elsewhere."

"You would consider that?" he asked, hope rising.

Her smile turned wry. "Even though I'm not a fan of camping, I would even consider living here on K-54973 with you if that was the only way we could be together."

His heart pounding, Jak'ri ducked his head and claimed her lips in a fervent kiss that he hoped would convey everything he felt for her.

Looping her arms around his neck, Ava rose onto her toes and kissed him back with a passion that stole his breath.

"Love is what you feel for lifemates?" he asked. She'd used the word once before in much the same way Purvelis did, but he wanted to ensure he didn't misunderstand as he trailed kisses across her cheek to the soft skin of her neck just beneath her ear.

"Yes," she breathed, tunneling her fingers through his hair and sending a shiver through him.

Jak'ri returned his lips to hers.

Do Purvelis kiss with tongues? she asked telepathically, perhaps as unwilling as he was to break the contact.

He paused and drew back to stare at her. "With tongues?"

She nodded.

"No."

"Okay." She leaned in to kiss him again.

"Do Earthlings?" he asked

"Some do. Some don't," she said, a shrug in her voice, then tried to capture his lips again.

But he remained out of reach.

Brow furrowing, she loosed a huff of annoyance that made him smile.

"Do *you* kiss with tongues?" he asked.

She lowered her heels to the ground and stared up at him. "Sometimes."

"It is something you enjoy?"

She hesitated. "With the right person."

"Is it something you think you would enjoy with me?"

The amber glow in her eyes brightened, answering him before she even spoke the words. "Yes. With you, I think I would enjoy it very much." And the husky tone that entered her voice affected him as strongly as a stroke of her hand would.

"Then show me," he murmured.

Rising onto her toes again, she cupped his face. "Just follow my lead." She spoke so softly it was almost a whisper.

He nodded, then dipped his head. Her lips were soft against his, once more inciting desire that paled in comparison to what he felt at the first brush of her tongue against his lips. Jak'ri sucked in a breath, stunned by the shock of need such a simple touch could inspire.

Ava swiftly took advantage of his parted lips and slipped her tongue into his mouth.

Fire shot through him when her tongue stroked his, heating his blood and rendering him rock hard. Groaning, he tentatively followed her example. More heat. More fire. Why the *srul* had he never tried this before?

Moaning, Ava wrapped her arms around him again and crushed him to her with surprising strength. *You taste so good*, she said telepathically.

Even that—her sultry voice in his head while her tongue danced with his and her body rubbed against him—made him burn.

More, he growled.

A heavy weight landed on his pack.

Startled, Jak'ri broke the kiss and staggered backward. What the *drek*?

Ava looked over his shoulder and gaped.

Oh *drek*. What was it?

His hand went to his blaster.

Her face—still flushed with desire—lit with a wide grin as laughter bubbled forth.

Small hands patted his head and tugged at his hair.

"It's one of the lemur things," she said. "One of the *leapers*."

A second one landed on her pack.

When Ava stumbled back a step, Jak'ri hastily reached out to steady her.

"Wow," she proclaimed. "These guys are a lot heavier than they look."

The striped creature sniffed her head experimentally then began examining her ponytail, separating the strands and even putting a few in its mouth.

She smiled. "Maybe they aren't fans of tongue kissing and this is their way of telling us to get a move on."

"Or maybe they heard you mention riding me and decided they wanted rides of their own."

She laughed.

Though he desperately wanted to shoo the little creatures away and see what other passion-related discoveries he could make with Ava, Jak'ri tamped down his need and took her hand. "Shall we continue?"

Her tempting lips pursed thoughtfully as a teasing glint entered her amber eyes. "Continue kissing?"

He grinned. "That would be my first choice. But I think we should continue our journey."

She wrinkled her nose in disappointment.

"Would the journey be more palatable if I promised there would be more kissing at the end of it?"

"*Srul* yes," she answered instantly.

Laughing, Jak'ri stole another kiss then started walking. "The land is sloping up now. I think we'll reach those rock formations soon."

She glanced at the furry creature perched atop his pack. "We may have company if we're lucky enough to find a cave to shelter in."

Jak'ri hoped not. If Ava wasn't too tired by the end of the day, he would *really* like to taste her lovely lips again and explore the ways she wanted to ride him... something he thought would be much more enjoyable without several of these creatures avidly peering at them and plucking at their hair.

The upward slant of the land soon approached a climb. Their furry friends must have decided that lounging atop their packs and being carried forward was preferable to swinging or hopping through the branches above them because they showed no interest in abandoning their perches.

Jak'ri kept a close eye on Ava, worried the extra weight would overburden her. Their time at the hands of the Gathendiens had left neither of them in ideal hiking condition, but she seemed to fare well despite her injured foot.

Some of the soil and detritus beneath their feet gave way to rocks and boulders between which shade-loving plants sprouted. More of their furry friends traveled through the trees above them, hooting back and forth as though carrying on a conversation. Birds twittered. Some screeched.

Ava grimaced. "That's an eerie sound."

Silently, he agreed. It sounded almost like a child's scream. But the creatures on their packs exhibited no alarm so he assumed the bird or whatever creature voiced the odd screeches posed no threat.

Every once in a while, he caught a glimpse of little fuzzy rodents.

"They kind of remind me of chipmunks," Ava commented and shared a telepathic image of a small Earth mammal with him.

One such rodent raced forward and jumped off a boulder. Spreading its paws wide, it exposed long flaps of skin on either side that caught the wind and allowed it to soar across in front of them and land upon the thick trunk of a tree.

"Or not," she added.

The boulders they passed began to exhibit pockets of orange and green moss. The foliage on the ground thickened.

Ava tilted her head suddenly. "I hear running water." She sniffed the air. "I can smell it, too."

Jak'ri couldn't, try though he might.

Minutes passed.

Their passengers abruptly let out a couple of hoots and jumped down.

Ava winced. "Damn, that was loud."

Jak'ri caught her elbow and drew her to a halt as the fuzzy mammals scrambled forward, quickly disappearing from view. He could hear the water now. Faintly. It resembled the happy burbling of a stream rather than the roar of a river. "Water sources attract wildlife. We should proceed with caution."

She stared after the mammals. "Right." Tilting her head back, she drew in a deep breath and held it.

He studied her. "What is it?"

"I'm not smelling any of the big cats."

His eyebrows flew up. "You could smell them when we left the pod?"

She nodded. "My senses are more acute now."

He glanced at the brush into which the mammals had disappeared. "Do you smell anything else?"

Again she inhaled deeply. "Nothing big. Just the *leapers* and a few other scents that make me think they either belong to much smaller animals or are the faded remnants of critters that were here earlier and left."

Nodding, Jak'ri crept forward and peered through the brush. A group of the hooting mammals clustered together beside a wide stream that tumbled its way over a rocky bed. Not far away two colorful birds bathed near the bank while some of the rodents he'd spied earlier sipped the water.

Ava leaned in beside him. "All clear?"

He nodded, assuming that was her way of asking if it was safe to proceed.

As soon as he and Ava stepped into the open, the birds squawked and flapped away. The rodents skittered off to safety, too.

The *leapers*, as Ava called them, just kept carrying handfuls of water to their mouths as they watched the two of them curiously.

Ava lowered her pack to the ground and knelt upstream of them. Plunging her hands into the clear liquid, she smiled. "It's cold, like snowmelt." He worried at first she meant to drink it but relaxed when she merely patted her face and neck with it to cool her heated skin.

Jak'ri joined her and followed her example.

"Feels good, doesn't it?" she asked with a smile.

"Very good."

She drew more of the liquid down her arms. "Do you think it's safe to drink?"

He shook his head. "Not straight from the stream. We know too little about this planet and the bacteria and microorganisms that thrive on it. But the medic bag contains a decontaminant that will render it safe with only a few drops."

"Good. Then all we need now is a fresh food source."

He nodded at the *leapers*. The two smallest ones had wandered over to a bush laden with small, oblong berries. As he and Ava watched, the little ones plucked several of the plump berries and ate them, their paws turning blue with the juices. "Those look promising."

A teasing glint entered her eyes. "I hope you're talking about berries."

He laughed. "Yes. Purvelis subsist primarily on plants and small marine organisms. We don't consume land animals."

Her features lit with curiosity. "Is there a lot of land on your planet? I only ever see Runaka Point in your dreams."

"No. My planet is a lot like this one with far more water than land."

She winked. "Good thing you're such good swimmers then."

He smiled. "Yes." A little voice inside him couldn't help thinking it good that *Ava* was a strong swimmer, too, something that would come in handy if she accompanied him to Purvel.

"How sharp is a Gathendien's sense of smell?" she asked suddenly. "Are they good trackers?"

"No. They tend to rely on *sedapas* when they track their prey."

"What are *sedapas*?"

"Spiked lizards that are about your size. They can scent things from far away with their tongues and are excellent trackers."

Her brow puckered. "Are they dangerous?"

"Oh yes. Their mouths are equipped with multiple rows of teeth they use to viciously tear their prey apart."

"Crap. Did you see any of those on the ship?"

"No. The Gathendiens would've had no reason to bring them to the lab. But they are commonly found in the Gathendiens' company."

"Great."

Sorry to have erased her smile, he touched her arm. "*Sedapas* are often barely tamed. I can't imagine Gathendien soldiers consenting to squeeze into a fighter craft with one for a flight that may take days. So I don't think we'll see any of those unless a shuttle or the ship should follow."

"Okay. Just in case, though, let's walk through the water a ways and hope it'll make them lose our scent."

A good strategy.

Jak'ri withdrew a canteen from his pack and held it out to Ava.

"Thank you."

Once they quenched their thirst, he filled the canteen with cold water from the stream, added a few drops of decontaminant, and tucked it back in the pack. "How are your feet?"

She wiggled her toes. "Good. That rubbery *kesaadi* stuff is working like a charm, keeping branches and rocks from breaking my skin."

He had hoped it would. It was protecting *his* feet well, too. But his bore no injuries.

After donning their packs, they waded into the water and headed upstream.

The current was quite gentle, so they didn't have to strain to walk against it or worry about it sweeping them off their feet.

Drawing in a deep breath, he released it in a contented sigh. The sterile air on ships and pods just couldn't compete with the open air of a forest.

When Ava slipped her hand into his, Jak'ri carried it to his lips for a kiss.

"I know our situation sucks," she said, smiling up at him, "but this is nice."

"Yes, it is." It reminded him of the carefree hours they'd spent together in dreams.

As they continued onward, Ava's limp grew less pronounced. Perhaps the cold water was numbing some of the pain.

"If we do encounter *sedapas*, will they be hard to kill?" she asked.

He considered it for a moment. "Their hide is thick, but you can still damage it with a *tronium* blaster or O-rifle fire."

"And with a blade?"

"Yes. But piercing their hide would require greater strength than piercing ours does." And would require one to get perilously close to the vicious reptiles.

"So strike hard."

"Yes."

As they exited the stream and headed into the forest on the other side, Jak'ri fervently hoped it wouldn't come to that.

CHAPTER THIRTEEN

Ava eyed a crack between two of the boulders that adorned the mountainside they'd begun to climb. "It looks deep," she commented, unsure if Jak'ri's eyes were as good at penetrating darkness as hers. "But I can't see *how* deep because it curves out of sight there at the back."

He nodded. "Think there's a cave at the end of it?"

"Maybe. It's pretty narrow though." She looked him up and down. "Do you think you can fit through there?" His stay with the Gathendiens had definitely robbed him of some of the muscle mass he usually sported in their dreams. But even so, she wasn't certain he could wedge himself between the rough rocks.

"I believe so." He shrugged out of his pack.

Ava followed suit and set the medic bag on the ground.

While she placed her O-rifle atop it and flexed her achy shoulders, he doffed his rifle, palmed a *tronium* blaster, and withdrew a small tube from his bag of supplies.

"Stay vigilant," he advised, then motioned to their furry companions. "The *leapers* should alert you if something dangerous approaches while I'm gone."

Ava grabbed his arm as he started forward. "Wait. Let me do it." When he would've protested, she cut him off. "I'm smaller, faster, and have better night vision. If anything is in there sleeping and wakes up pissed, I'll have a better chance of killing it before it can kill me."

He stared at her for a long moment. And she could see the war that waged inside him. Not because he didn't want to admit she was both faster and stronger than him now. But because his desire to protect her from everything that could possibly hurt her was as fierce as her drive to protect him.

At last, he nodded. "Take a blaster. And keep an eye out for serpents."

Damned if that didn't deepen her feelings for him even more.

Rising onto her toes, she slid her arms around his neck and claimed his lips in a kiss imbued with all of the love and passion he inspired.

Jak'ri crushed her against him, deepening the contact. *Wow* he was a fast learner. His tongue stroked and teased hers until she wanted to climb him like a stripper pole.

Both were breathless when they finally came up for air.

"I really hope that cave is empty," he murmured, voice hoarse with desire.

"*Srul* yes," she agreed, a shiver of excitement tickling its way through her.

He stepped back. "Will your eyes glowing adversely affect your vision?"

Her eyes were glowing? "No." She wished she had a mirror so she could see that. *And* her fangs, which thankfully hadn't descended while they'd kissed.

"Set your blaster to stun."

She blinked. "What?"

"It occurred to me that firing an O-rifle or *tronium* blaster inside the cave could destabilize its structure."

"Oh. Right. Wouldn't want rocks to fall on my head. How do I do that again?"

He showed her how to adjust the blaster so it would stun an opponent instead of firing those cool balls of energy that seemed capable of burning a hole through just about anything.

She eyed the narrow passage. "There shouldn't be anything bigger than me in there. But if I'm wrong about that, will stunning it stop whatever I may encounter?"

"Yes." He shifted his weight, his handsome face pensive. "Perhaps we should both go."

She shook her head. "If I come up against anything I think I can't handle, I'll haul ass back here and you can shoot it. Just be ready with your rifle."

Nodding, he handed her the little tube she'd seen him retrieve earlier.

"What's this?" she asked, studying it.

"It's a light." He took her hand and moved it until she held the tube over her blaster. The tube slipped from her fingers and attached itself to the top of the weapon with a *click*. "If you need it, smooth your thumb over the end in a circular pattern to activate it."

"Will the Gathendiens be able to detect it?" He had powered down everything in the pod to keep the Gathendiens from detecting electronic signals and homing in on their location.

"I don't think so. Not if you only use it in the cave, if there is one. The battery is tiny. And the signal it emits while in use is very faint. Dense rock should block that."

"Okay." Though she was reasonably sure she'd be able to see in the cave without it, thanks to her newly sharpened vision, the light might blind anything that unexpectedly charged toward her.

As Ava had hoped, she was small enough to slip between the boulders. A few yards in, the passage created by the two rocks curved to one side. Pausing, she glanced back.

Jak'ri peered after her, O-rifle in hand, brow creased as one of the little lemur things crept closer to the bag at his feet.

Ava forced a smile before she followed the curve and left his sight.

Raising the blaster, she aimed it into the darkness that enfolded her as she continued forward. The passage soon became tight enough for her to have to turn sideways. Her heartbeat picked up. She had never been troubled by small, enclosed spaces the way some were. But anxiety strung her nerves taut as foreign scents bombarded her. Some were musty, like damp soil. Others bore a bestial aroma that she hoped had been left behind by occupants that had long since abandoned this niche.

The rock walls encasing her widened abruptly. Ava tightened her grip on the blaster as she entered a cave.

An *empty* cave, she noted with relief, that was twice the size of the holding cell she'd been kept in back on the Gathendien ship.

"Cool," she whispered.

There were darker patches near the back that drew her sharp gaze. Just to be sure, she activated the light attached to her blaster when she explored them. One had clearly been used as an outhouse by some animal that apparently preferred not to poop where it slept. She wrinkled her nose. The other was a nook that led nowhere.

Ava? Jak'ri called telepathically.

I'm here, she said as she returned to the main space. *There is a cave. It's empty. And I don't think anything has lived in it for quite some time.* She looked up. *Except for spiders. I'm seeing a lot of webs but haven't spotted whatever spun them yet.*

She turned the flashlight off.

Her eyes widened. *Cool.*

What?

There's something in the walls—a blue rock or maybe ore—that's glowing. Streaks of it now illuminated the cave like string lights.

Was it glowing before?

No. I think it might react to light.

Dragging her gaze away, she headed back through the rocky passage. The forest that had seemed dark before now seemed bright in comparison to the cave.

Jak'ri waited at the entrance with his O-rifle, looking fierce and ready to fight.

Ava shook her head as she emerged from the rocky crevice. "How do you do that?"

His brow furrowed. "Do what?"

She motioned to him. "Come off of months of torture and still look freaking hot."

It took a moment for her words to translate. Or mostly translate, she supposed. Then he grinned. Releasing his weapon, he reached out and brushed her shoulder.

Ava looked down. Cobwebs coated it. She glanced at the other shoulder and found a fairly large, yellow-and-white spider eyeballing her. Yelping, she hastily brushed it off and began to swipe at her hair. "Are there any more?" She didn't fear insects in general. But she had no idea if the colorful alien arachnids were poisonous and would rather not test the limits of her newly acquired regenerative capabilities.

Jak'ri continued to brush at her shoulder and back. "Just one. The rest is empty web."

One of the *leapers* scurried over, grabbed the spiders she and Jak'ri had dislodged, and stuffed them into its mouth.

Ava watched its cheeks plump as it chewed. "I'm hoping that means the spiders aren't poisonous."

Jak'ri grunted, his attention now centered on her hair.

She smiled and closed her eyes as he tugged the tie off her ponytail and slid his fingers through it. Being coated with cobwebs was totally worth it if it meant she could enjoy him finger-combing her hair. "Are there a lot of webs?"

"No."

Opening her eyes, she glanced up at him.

His lips turned up in a half-smile. "I just like your hair. It's so beautiful and soft. And I noticed in the pod that under brighter light it carries hints of red."

Pleasure trickled through her. "It's all still there though, right? I'm pretty sure the little guy who rode on my pack was chewing on it."

"It's all still there," he said on a laugh and glanced toward the dark passage. "Shall we see if I can fit?"

Ava nodded. "If you can't, we'll have to look for another one." And she really did want to be settled before dark.

Though Jak'ri seemed to think himself too skinny, he still had to turn sideways to fit through the passage. And the rocks left streaks of dirt on his chest and back.

Ava followed him inside and watched him explore the cave.

"You're right," he pronounced. "Nothing appears to be using this as a den. I think this would be a good place for us to shelter."

Ava agreed. Getting the packs into the cave ended up being pretty annoying. Both were on the bulky side, and Jak'ri could barely fit as it was. So he pulled them through while Ava pushed them from behind.

Surprisingly, their little furry buddies didn't follow them in.

Maybe they could smell whatever beasts had used this cave in the past and were leery.

The ore that streaked the walls of the cave continued to glow, providing ambient light while she and Jak'ri used their hands and feet to sweep some of the debris left behind by previous occupants to the side so they could have a somewhat smooth place to bed down.

Once done, Jak'ri stared down at the rocky dirt they'd bared, his hands on his hips.

"What's on your mind?" she asked.

"I was thinking about the leaves on those trees outside."

She guessed the ones he referred to: the huge fronds that looked like elephant ears and were about ten feet long and six feet wide. "What about them?"

He glanced over at her. "I was thinking they'd make a far more comfortable bed."

She swallowed as an ember of excitement flared to life in her stomach. Clearly sleep wasn't all he had in mind.

Ava was *so* on board with that. "I'll go climb a tree and cut us some." Her mind fixed on all the ways they could use that leafy bed, she left the cave and strode toward one of the trees.

"Wait." Jak'ri caught up with her just as she reached the trunk, which was so thick you could carve a freaking house out of it. "I'll climb. You catch."

Halting, she smiled up at him. "Catch *you* or the leaf?"

He grinned. "Hopefully, the latter."

How she loved to see him smile. "I can climb it, Jak'ri. I'm stronger and faster now. Remember?"

But he shook his head. "The bark is rough. And you'll have to grip it with your feet. I don't want you to reopen your wound."

Oh. Good point. Her foot throbbed constantly now that the cold from the stream had worn off, and she was kind of dreading looking at the bottom of it. "Okay." He'd spent so much time rock climbing that he would be far more adept at scaling the tree anyway.

Tilting her head back, she stared at the canopy. "It's a long way up," she commented anxiously and cursed the tiny part of herself that was relieved she wouldn't have to make the climb herself.

He shrugged. "Heights don't bother me."

Amusement sifted through her. "Nothing bothers you, Jak'ri. You're a total badass."

He eyed her quizzically. "Is a badass a good thing? My translator isn't clear on that."

Ava smiled. "It's a *very* good thing."

He grinned.

Still, she couldn't help but worry. The lowest leaves were way, way, *way* above them. A fall from that height would definitely kill him.

Touching her elbow, Jak'ri leaned down for a quick kiss. "I'll return safely."

She nodded. "How are you going to cut the leaves?"

He patted a small pouch he'd attached to his O-rifle sling. "I took a laser scalpel from the medic bag." Stepping up to the tree, he eyed the thick, rough bark a moment, then began to climb. "I don't know how heavy the leaves will be, so don't try to catch them when they fall."

"Okay," she replied absently, absorbed with watching his swift ascent.

Damn, he was good. And his confidence—the surety with which he placed his feet and gripped the bark with his fingers—coupled with the flex of muscles revealed by his shirt and pants whenever they stretched taut merely fed her attraction.

Several of the little *leapers* scrambled up after him, hooting and cavorting as if it were a race or some game he played with them.

The rest remained on the ground near Ava.

In astonishingly little time, Jak'ri neared the lowest branch and climbed onto it, inching toward the massive leaves.

He was so far up now she couldn't even estimate how many stories above the ground he must be.

One of the big leaves sagged, then fell toward her, floating down like a discarded parachute.

The *leapers* in the tree hooted louder and gave chase.

Ava stepped back as it hit the ground. Bending, she brushed a hand across its surface and smiled fondly. It even felt like an elephant ear plant, just thicker.

Jak'ri moved to another branch and cut a second leaf.

Ava suspected he didn't want to hack away all the leaves on one branch in case the Gathendiens looked up while hunting them. Nor would he hack away enough to produce a thin patch in the canopy that concealed them.

By the time he started back down the tree, half a dozen leaves covered the ground around her. One of the *leapers* that had been keeping her company wandered over and sprawled atop them.

"Don't get too comfortable," she warned. "That's *our* bed, not yours."

Tension thrummed through her as she turned back to watch Jak'ri's descent. Climbing down always looked more harrowing to her than climbing up did.

When he was near enough to the ground, he jumped the remaining distance and landed in front of her with a grin.

Ava threw her arms around him, glad to have him safely on the ground with her again.

Chuckling, he hugged her close. "I'm well, Ava," he murmured reassuringly. "But when I was near the canopy, I could see the sun sinking toward the horizon. We should hurry and get settled before the nocturnal hunters awaken."

Remembering those huge paw prints, she shuddered. "Right."

I F JAK'RI THOUGHT GETTING the packs into the cave was hard, that was nothing compared to rolling the big leaves up and shoving them through the tight passage. Nevertheless, they succeeded.

Jak'ri smiled. He and Ava worked well together, laughing and teasing instead of growing irritable whenever the task began to frustrate them.

As the already dim light began to fade, they walked some distance away and took turns relieving themselves, then had a quick wash in the stream. He kept a close eye on Ava as she waded into the water. If the barrier he'd coated her feet with had cracked, that gash on her foot would hurt like *srul* when the water touched it.

The barrier must have remained intact, however, because she simply sighed and said the cold felt good.

Jak'ri wished they could linger and soak their weary bodies. But they didn't dare. Those paw prints outside the pod had been terrifyingly large.

The friendly little *leapers* retreated to the trees as he and Ava entered the cave for the night.

The leaves the two of them had arranged as a mattress gave off a scent Ava likened to freshly cut grass that went a long way toward banishing the mustiness of the cave. Jak'ri sat on them and patted the space next to him.

Smiling, Ava sat close beside him as he began to rummage through the pack he'd carried. After a moment, he drew out a *hesku*.

"What's that?" Leaning closer, she peered at it curiously. "It looks like a pancake wrapped in burlap. I love pancakes. You haven't been holding out on me, have you?"

He chuckled. "No." According to his translator, a pancake was a flat pastry of some sort. "Watch." Jak'ri set the flat round object on his palm, then slowly clenched his fist around it, crushing it into a ball.

Light burst forth from it.

Ava gasped and threw a hand up to shield her eyes. "*What?*"

Grinning, he flattened it out once more and set it on the ground in front of them.

"It's so bright!" she exclaimed as she lowered her hand. "What is it?"

"A *hesku*." Jak'ri had been relieved to find several of them among the supplies on the escape pod. If there had been no habitable planets nearby, he and Ava could've conserved the pod's power by shutting off the interior lights and using the *heskus* instead.

Here on the planet, the malleable discs could provide them with more light than a campfire would without emitting smoke or the scent of burning wood, both of which could give away their location.

Ava leaned closer to examine it. "Is it electronic?"

"No. It contains two minerals that produce light when they react to one another. They're separated by a stiff but thin barrier inside the packet that shatters under sufficient pressure and allows them to mingle."

"How long does the light last?"

"Hours. Until morning at least. And we can extend that if we pick it up, shake it, and apply more pressure."

"Is it hot?"

"No."

Ava tentatively touched the tips of her fingers to it. "It isn't warm at all!"

He nodded. "If the temperature in here should drop too much during the night, we can add water. Then the *hesku* will generate heat as a second chemical reaction takes place. Once we do, though, it won't be safe to touch again until it's dry." He patted his thigh. "Let me look at your foot."

Ava shifted so she could prop her foot in his lap.

Jak'ri studied it carefully. "The *kesaadi* coating remains intact. Nothing appears to have pierced it."

"That was a really good idea," she said with a smile. "My feet would be in pretty bad shape if you hadn't thought of that."

Warmed by her praise, Jak'ri dragged the medic bag closer and withdrew a small towel to spread under her foot. Then he sprayed the sole with the *retsa*. When the cleanser swelled into a thick foam, he spread it over her foot and waited for it to melt away like water.

Ava's eyes widened. "That foam removes the rubbery stuff, too?"

Though the bandage remained, the clear *kesaadi* he'd coated the bottom of her foot with to protect it and hold the bandage in place had dissolved. "Yes."

She started to spread her toes, but quickly stopped with a wince.

Jak'ri gently peeled away the bandage. The gash that split the arch of her foot and some of her heel had closed and appeared to be healing well. "It's improving."

"Good."

"But it still hurts?" It looked quite painful to him.

"Yes," she admitted with a sheepish smile.

He sprayed her foot again and gently patted it dry with a sterile medicloth. Once he'd cleaned it to his satisfaction, he spritzed it with the pain-deadening *imaashu*.

Ava sighed, her features smoothing with relief. "That stuff is awesome."

Guilt pierced him. "I'm sorry I didn't apply it before we left the escape pod."

"I'm not," she replied, no condemnation in her tone. "If you had, I wouldn't have limped, and it probably would've gotten a lot worse by the time we found this place."

Jak'ri rested a hand on her slender ankle, his fingers stroking her soft skin. "You experienced enough pain at the hands of the Gathendiens, Ava. I don't want to subject you to more."

But she merely smiled. "You aren't. You're *sparing* me pain by keeping me from doing more damage that would make it take longer to heal."

Nodding, he reached into the medic bag.

He's such a nice guy.

Jak'ri paused. Had Ava sent that thought intentionally?

After retrieving the rest of the necessary supplies, he applied a fresh bandage to her wound and again coated her foot with *kesaadi* to hold it in place.

Honorable and kind.

No. She was inadvertently broadcasting again, he realized as he drew her other foot onto his lap. The *kesaadi* had performed well, keeping the rocks and sticks they'd stepped on from cutting or damaging her smooth skin.

Capable of kicking Gathendien ass, her mental meanderings continued. *And climbing gargantuan trees to provide us with this bed.*

He sprayed her foot with the *retsa* and wiped it with a cloth.

This surprisingly comfortable *bed.*

From the corner of his eye, he saw her gaze sweep over his form with leisurely admiration.

His pulse picked up.

Which I can't wait to use because he is freaking hot. *And passionate. I've never in my life met a man who could turn me on with just a look. And those muscles...*

Though heat coursed through him, he forced himself to concentrate on coating her foot with the *kesaadi* once more.

Damn, I want him.

His ministrations complete, he met her gaze. Heart thudding in his chest, he slid one hand up her shin, curled his fingers around her calf, and drew it back down again in a caress he wanted to take sooooo much higher.

Her breath caught. Then her smile slipped as she sat up straighter. "Wait. You didn't hear what I was just thinking, did you?"

"Yes."

"Damn it."

He smiled, amusement creeping in and taking the edge off the rising desire that demanded he push her back onto the leafy mattress and strip her bare. "I could describe you the same way." *Honorable*, he thought to her as he slid his hand up her lovely leg again. *Kind.* This time he continued past her knee. *Capable of kicking Gathendien ass.* He spread his fingers on her soft thigh, then drew his hand back down again. *Hot. Passionate. And capable of arousing me with just a look.*

An amber glow entered her brown eyes as her lips parted.

His gaze dropped to those lips. The arousal he'd just mentioned intensified as he remembered how it had felt when her tongue stroked his.

Ava's stomach growled, loud enough to drown out his thoughts.

Jak'ri laughed. "Not the response I was hoping for."

She smiled and grimaced at the same time. "Sorry. I think I burn more calories now, and we haven't eaten since breakfast."

Regret filled him as he shook his head. "That was my failure. Apologies. I should've insisted we eat something earlier." Tamping down his desire, he returned the remaining supplies to the medic bag.

But Ava waved his apology away. "Honestly, I didn't even notice we missed lunch. I was too distracted." She motioned to the darkening passage that led from the cave. "This is the first time I've set foot on an alien planet. And even though it bears a general similarity to Earth, there are enough differences to make me want to walk around like this all the time." Widening her eyes, she dropped her jaw until her mouth formed a large O and gaped at the walls around them in exaggerated amazement.

Jak'ri laughed.

"I'm serious," she insisted with a grin. "I saw a butterfly today that was the size of a duck!"

Still smiling, he dragged the other pack closer and dug through it for the nutrient cubes and canteens. "I don't know what a butterfly is. Or a duck. My translator only tells me that one is an insect that often bears colorful wings and the other is some sort of waterfowl."

Removing her feet from his lap, Ava shifted to sit cross-legged facing him and provided him with a more in-depth definition, along with a few telepathic images.

Jak'ri nodded periodically. "We have similar things on Purvel." He placed two canteens and two nutrient packets between them. "Though our insects tend to be fairly small."

She nodded. "When I saw that butterfly, I admit I was a little worried we'd encounter insects on the ground that were equally big. I'm not usually afraid of bugs, but if I encountered a spider the size of that butterfly, I think I would freak out."

He laughed. "As would I."

They tore open the packages and each ate a nutrient cube.

Ava grimaced. "It would be nice if freedom made these things taste a little better."

Jak'ri agreed. "I may try some of those berries tomorrow. These nutrient cubes will only last us so long. We need to find alternate sources of nourishment before they run out." He forced down another swallow. "And including fresh fruit in our diet will provide us with more energy, something I think would benefit you now that you're burning more calories. I saw some fruit that looked promising while I was cutting leaves near the canopy. Tomorrow I'll climb up and cut some so we can see what our curious companions think of it."

"Isn't eating fruit found on an alien planet dangerous?"

He shrugged. "It carries some risk. But I'll be careful when I test it and would worry more about the berries if I hadn't seen the *leapers*, as you call them, consume large amounts with no ill effects. Wild animals tend to learn quickly to distinguish fruits and nuts that are safe to eat from those that are poisonous and can sicken them."

"Or maybe they just have a high tolerance for toxins."

"Possibly. But one thing space exploration and our dealings with member nations of the Aldebarian Alliance has taught us is that planets with nearly identical atmospheres usually sustain life created from the same six essential elemental ingredients that are found in all organisms on Purvel. They may bear some differences in appearance—" he held up one hand and splayed his fingers, displaying the webbing between them "—but their likenesses—the way their bodies function and even their behavior—can be astonishing. Purvel has many mammals similar to the *leapers* and tree-dwelling primates from Earth that you've described that seem to share the same behavior. And those on Purvel—like so many in alliance occupied space—are affected by the same poisons that harm us."

"And bleed red blood?" she said. "I noticed one of the little ones had a cut on its hip."

He nodded. "I've never heard of vertebrates on planets with atmospheres comparable to Purvel's bleeding any other color."

She seemed to ponder that as she finished the nutrient cube. "I saw some nuts we could try."

He'd seen some, too, and had noted the *leapers*' lack of interest in them. "We should cook any nuts we find before trying them. Many nuts on Purvel are bitter and can make you ill if they aren't cooked first."

"Okay." She still seemed weighted with concern though.

He took one of her hands in his. "What troubles you, Ava?"

She sighed. "I'm just worried that anything we try might make you sick."

"Only me?" he asked.

One shoulder lifted in a shrug. "The virus the Gathendiens infected me with renders me immune to all illnesses and poisons."

"On Earth," he pointed out.

Her brow puckered slightly as she stared down at their clasped hands. "True."

When the Gathendiens had thrust her into his cell, he had worried that the viruses the *grunarks* had exposed *him* to would infect her, but they hadn't. "We'll be careful."

She nodded. Lifting her gaze to meet his, she tightened her hold on his hand. "I just don't want to lose you."

The words hit him right in the chest and affected him as strongly as her kisses had.

A heartbeat passed as they stared at each other. Then Jak'ri swept the canteens aside, rose onto his knees, and reached for her.

Of the same mind, Ava was already on her knees and tilting her face up when he locked his arms around her and drew her closer.

She hummed in pleasure when he claimed her lips, her tongue darting out to stoke and tease his as she tunneled her fingers through his hair.

Heat seared him. "I like this tongue kissing," he growled.

"I do, too," she said breathlessly before he captured her full lips once more. Shifting, she rubbed her breasts against him. So different from the chests of Purveli women. So incredibly soft and alluring. Her hips sought his. "Lift me up," she whispered, barely breaking the kiss.

"*Srul* yes." Sliding his hands down her narrow back to clasp her bottom, he lifted her until her breasts rubbed against his chest instead of his upper abdomen. Then he sat back on his heels.

Ava parted her legs, knees sliding to either side of his hips as she scooted forward until the heart of her made contact with his hard shaft.

"Yes," both breathed.

CHAPTER FOURTEEN

A VA TUGGED AT JAK'RI'S shirt. "Take it off."
He swiftly yanked it over his head and tossed it aside.

All those muscles, she thought as she stared at him. Firm. Rippling with every movement. No excess flesh *anywhere*. And that skin...

"I love your skin," she whispered, running her hands across his broad shoulders and down his strong biceps. "Or scales. Is it scales?" Upon close inspection, it looked like scales. But it felt like skin. Soft. With a silvery hue that did the same thing oil in water did... creating flickers of rainbow colors in certain lights or at certain angles.

"Scales," he murmured distractedly as he sought the ties on her shirt and unfastened them.

Ava felt a moment of uncertainty as he parted the fabric and pushed it off her shoulders, leaving her bare from the waist up. She wasn't by any stretch of the imagination what one might call big breasted and had often envied some of her friends' fuller figures. Add to that the weight she'd lost when she was too sick to eat anything during her transformation, her more prominent rib cage, and...

Yeah. She would never qualify as a lingerie model.

But Jak'ri exhibited no disappointment. Instead, he looked enthralled as he studied her pale flesh.

Excitement skittered through her as he rested his big hands on her shoulders.

"You aren't built like our women," he said softly. His words bore no condemnation though. Instead, he seemed... entranced.

"How am I different?" she asked softly.

"Your shoulders aren't as broad. It lends you an air of fragility that I know is alluringly deceptive."

For someone who had envied Eliana her strength and wished to be viewed the same way, that compliment topped any others she had received in her life.

He drew his fingers down over her collarbones, drifting closer to her breasts. "The muscles here on our women are often as developed as ours." Judging by the heated look in his eyes, he didn't mind at all that she had breasts instead of muscular pecs. "And here..."

Her pulse picked up as he cupped her breasts.

"You're rounder here. Softer. Fuller." He squeezed them gently and drew his thumbs across the hard, sensitive peaks.

Ava sucked in a breath as sensation shot through her. "Do that again."

He brushed his thumbs across the tight buds again, toyed with them, and gave one an experimental pinch.

Ava jerked and arched against him.

"You're sensitive here," he murmured.

"Yes."

His lips captured hers once more, tasting and tempting as he explored her breasts and ratcheted up her need. She and Jak'ri had been nearly bare with each other countless times in their dreams as they swam and cavorted in *Runaka Sea*. But they had been out in the open. And the dreams had felt so real that she would never have thought of pursuing her lustful inclinations there for fear of being discovered.

Now, however, they were alone. They were free. And the cave enclosing them might as well have been a honeymoon suite at a secluded resort. So there was no reason for her to hold back.

She moaned.

Jak'ri certainly wasn't holding back. The women of Purvel might not have breasts like hers but he sure as hell knew what to do with them, teasing and tweaking and squeezing until she squirmed against him, her breath shortening.

"Jak'ri," she whispered, tunneling the fingers of one hand through his thick hair while she slid the other down his back and rocked against the thick, hard ridge concealed by his pants. "I want you."

Nodding, he trailed heated kisses down her neck. "I want you, too." One of his big hands left her breast and cupped her ass, grinding her against him. "Are you ready to release your eggs?"

Sensation shot through her. "Hmm?"

"Are you ready to release your eggs so I can fertilize them?" he murmured, clutching her closer.

Her eyes flew open. "Wait. What?"

He leaned back. "I assume you reproduce the same way Purvelis do," he said, dragging his eyes up from her breasts to meet hers. "You release your eggs. Then I fertilize them."

She stared at him, stunned. Release her eggs? Did he mean like a... like a fish?

Her gaze shot to the barely discernible scales that coated his broad chest and handsome face. Did Purvelis not have sex the way humans and Lasarans did?

His lips twitched as his eyes danced with mirth.

Relief filled her. "Oh my gosh!" Laughing, Ava shoved one of his shoulders. "You are *so* bad!"

He laughed. "Apologies. I couldn't resist. My scales seem to fascinate you."

"They do. So do your webbed fingers and toes." She drew a hand down his chest, pausing to toy with his nipple, then continued over his rippling abs until she reached the waistband of his pants.

He sucked in a breath as levity gave way to lust once more.

Emboldened by his reaction, she scooted back a little so she could slip her hand between them to cup his hard length. "Any surprises here I should know about?"

He shook his head. "Not if your men are built like Lasarans."

Good to know. Ava rose onto her knees and backed away from him. "Take them off," she ordered and nodded at his pants.

Jak'ri didn't hesitate.

Ava stared at him as he knelt before her, completely bare. And as he'd promised, there were no surprises. Short hair as black as that on his head surrounded the base of his penis. *One* penis. Two testicles. The former was hard and jutted toward her, the tip more round than the mushroom-shaped crowns of her past lovers'. And while he was certainly big, he wasn't gargantuan.

Ava sighed with relief. She had read a few sci-fi romances that featured heroes who had some freaky appendages she never wanted to encounter in real life.

Jak'ri, on the other hand, was perfect.

He smiled. "So are you."

"Am I broadcasting again?"

"Yes."

Surprisingly, the knowledge didn't bother her. They'd shared their thoughts so often since the Gathendiens had taken her that it seemed completely natural, as if he were a part of her.

And, too, she was distracted because she'd noticed the ridges that adorned his long hard length and wondered how freaking fantastic they were going to feel when he was inside her.

Jak'ri swore. "Take off the shorts."

Ava laughed. He must have heard that thought, too. Cool. The way this was going, she wouldn't have to tell him what she wanted. He'd know it as soon as she thought it.

After ditching the shorts, she waited patiently while Jak'ri's heated gaze roved her bare body. "Any surprises?" she couldn't resist asking.

He slowly shook his head. "You're beautiful. I knew that the first time I met you in our shared dream." He eased closer. So close his erection prodded her stomach. His big hands clasped her hips. "Is your primary pleasure center located on the inside or the outside?"

She stared up at him and saw the reflection of her glowing amber eyes in his. "Outside," she whispered, too turned on to worry about whether that was different from what he was accustomed to.

Without looking away from her glowing eyes, he shifted a hand to her stomach then slid it down. His long, supple fingers slipped into the short curls below.

Ava sucked in a breath when they found her clit. Her pulse picked up as pleasure danced through her. Clamping her hands onto his biceps, she held on as he stroked her again.

"Here?" he asked.

She could only nod her head and arch into his touch. It felt so good. And he proved yet again that he was a quick learner. Or maybe he was just listening to her thoughts and letting them guide his touch because in a very short time she was already close to coming. But she didn't want to. Not yet. Not until he was inside her.

No sooner did she think it than he withdrew his touch.

Ava started to protest but gasped instead when he lifted her and gently laid her back on the makeshift bed. Reaching above her, he grabbed the leaf they'd rolled up for a pillow and placed it under her head. And though her body was on fire and thoughts of making love with him consumed her, her heart melted a little more over him taking the time to ensure she was comfortable when he was probably as eager for more as she was.

Then his lips found hers again, devouring and inflaming. When he settled his hips between her thighs, all thoughts scattered. Nothing else registered. His tongue teasing hers as he palmed her breast and stroked the taut peak.

She moaned. "Yes. More. I want you, Jak'ri. *All* of you."

Reaching between them, he positioned his hard cock at her entrance.

Ava slid her arms around him and flattened them on his back, loving his warmth and the feel of his muscles flexing beneath her fingers. "Do it. Take me."

He pressed forward, his hard length stretching her and stealing her breath. Those ridges did exactly what she'd hoped they would, eliciting another moan. Stopping, Jak'ri withdrew almost to the tip, then thrust again, then again, sinking deeper each time, giving her body time to adjust.

It *had* been a long time, and he *was* a large guy. But by the time he was fully seated, she was clawing his back and arching against him. He felt soooooo good.

And he knew just what she wanted.

Ava didn't think she had ever moaned or gasped or cried out so much during sex. The feel of him driving deep, angling his hips so he ground against her clit with every hard thrust, just kept pushing the pleasure higher and higher. In no time at all she was wound so tight she was panting, her hands sliding down to grip his ass and urge him on as she arched up against him, the pressure building and building until ecstasy finally crashed through her.

Ava bucked against him, her inner muscles clamping down around him and squeezing him tight as the pleasure went on and on until Jak'ri stiffened above her and called her name as he found release.

All strength abandoned her, leaving Ava as limp as a noodle as she struggled to calm her breathing.

Bracing his elbows on either side of her to keep the bulk of his weight off her, Jak'ri burrowed his hands under her back and held her close as he rested his head beside hers on the leaf pillow.

She smiled, loving his scent and the feel of his breath tickling her neck.

He was breathing as hard as she was.

Turning her head, Ava pressed a kiss to his strong jaw. "I forgot to release my eggs," she whispered.

He laughed, his cock jerking inside her and sparking yet another moan.

Any more of that and she would be ready to go again.

"As will I," he said, his deep voice full of amusement as he rolled them to their sides, their bodies still joined.

Ava draped a leg over his hip and smiled at him. He was so damned handsome.

And he meant so much to her.

Jak'ri pressed a kiss to her lips, one so tender and full of emotion that it brought tears to her eyes.

Peace settled upon them as they lay there, feeling no need for words as the night air that wafted into the cave cooled their damp skin. Neither was ready to seek sleep. Rather both craved each other's touch. So they snuggled closer and exchanged leisurely caresses until Jak'ri grew hard inside her once more. His lips sought hers in passionate kisses that again brought need surging to the forefront.

Moaning, Ava urged him onto his back and straddled him.

His hungry eyes fastened on her breasts as he rested his hands on her hips. The muscles in her thighs flexed as she rose, sliding up along his length, then sank down and took him deep.

Now *he* moaned, his grip tightening almost painfully. "More."

Eager to comply, Ava rode him. And the way he looked at her... Just the way he looked at her could make her come.

Reaching up, he cupped her breasts, fondled them, teased the sensitive tips, pinched them.

Pleasure darted through her, arrowing straight to her center. Bracing her hands on his chest, she quickened her pace. The muscles in Jak'ri's abs flexed as he thrust into her. The cords in his neck stood out as she rotated her hips and ground against him.

"Ava," he groaned, then slid a hand down her stomach. Finding her clit with his fingers, he began to stroke her.

Crying out, she came again, her inner walls clamping down around his hard cock in rhythmic pulses until he joined her. His fingers continued to stroke her, drawing the pleasure out until she finally sank, limp and sated, onto his chest.

Breathing hard, Jak'ri wrapped his arms around her and cuddled her close.

Thanks to her heightened senses, Ava could hear his heart slamming against his rib cage with the same speed and force as her own.

Burrowing closer, she wished she had the breath to express the emotion that swelled inside her. She wished she had the words to tell him that she had never in her life felt as close to another person as she did to him.

Burying his nose in her hair, he whispered, "I love you, Ava."

She smiled, eyes drifting closed. "I love you, too."

J AK'RI SMILED AT AVA.

Juice trickled down her chin as she ate the sweet tree fruit with relish.

Several days had passed. Days he would consider idyllic if the Gathendien threat didn't still hover over their heads.

He took another bite of his half of the fruit they shared.

No. Even with the threat hanging over their heads, he thought their time together here idyllic. They spent every night *making love* as Ava called it (a term he liked very much) and simply enjoying each other's company. They spent their days in the fresh air, embracing their new freedom.

This planet had proven to be a safe haven for them thus far. With her extraordinarily sharp hearing, Ava heard everything that ventured close to their little rocky home. Those large mammals that had peered into the escape pod the night of their landing had poked their noses into the passage and given it a sniff on their third night here. But the nocturnal hunters hadn't returned since.

He and Ava had killed spiders and other things she deemed *creepy-crawlies* that ventured into the cave, as well as a snake that had been large enough that Ava had shuddered after they decapitated it. It had taken both of them to drag the massive serpent back out through the passage and leave it what they hoped would be a safe distance away.

He suspected that might've been what attracted the *big cats'* attention, because nothing had remained the next day but red splotches on the soil where they'd left the snake, surrounded by those huge paw prints.

The little *leapers* never ventured inside. They did, however, linger nearby. Ava thought they liked having new neighbors. Jak'ri thought they simply liked the fruit he tossed them.

The berries he'd seen the little creatures consume in large amounts had been sweet when he'd carefully tasted them. They also hadn't made him ill, so he and Ava had been enjoying them. Jak'ri also climbed high into the trees again and cut some of the fruit they currently ate that Ava said were the size of Earth *coconuts* but bore the skin and flavor of something called an *orange*.

To Jak'ri, the odd melons tasted much like the *magani* fruit he loved so much on Purvel. The skin was harder to peel, though, so he had to use one of the daggers Ava had confiscated from the escape pod's weapons stash. The *leapers* had hooted louder than ever and crowded around him as soon as he'd opened one. So he'd climbed back up and retrieved a few extras.

Though he enjoyed his jaunts with Ava, leaving the cave so frequently did raise some concerns. "If we venture out every day, I worry we'll leave too strong a scent trail for the Gathendiens to track," he said before consuming another slice of the tasty fruit.

Swallowing, Ava shook her head. "As long as our little furry friends here continue to hang out with us, we're good." She smiled down at a *leaper* that leaned against her, eagerly devouring another sweet morsel. "These little guys may be cute, but they stink. Even *I* have a hard time picking up our scent when they're around."

He laughed as one of the smaller ones tentatively approached him. They *did* have a rather pungent aroma. "The babies seem to be even more fragrant than the adults." When he offered it a slice, it crept forward, snatched the chunk of fruit from his fingers, and scampered back to its mother.

Ava laughed. "I know. It's so weird." She ate another slice. "Maybe on this planet, the smaller you are the more you smell, because those big ones we caught glimpses of a couple days ago —the ones that looked like gorillas with cheetah fur—didn't have much of a scent at all." And had kept their distance, much to his relief.

Tenderness suffused him as he smiled at her. She looked good. Her wounds were now mere scars and no longer pained her. He thought such injuries healing so rapidly without the benefit of a *silna* remarkable.

It's the virus, she reminded him telepathically.

They slipped in and out of each other's thoughts often, sometimes without intent. Had any other woman inserted herself in his mind to this extent, Jak'ri would've been both disturbed and angry.

But he loved having that connection with Ava.

She winked at him as she took another bite of fruit. *I do, too.*

Every afternoon as the forest began to darken—indicating the sun's descent toward the horizon—they headed for the stream, filled their canteens, washed their clothes as best they could, and bathed. Ava had flushed a pretty pink the first time she'd doffed her meager clothing on the banks. "I can't help it!" she'd said on a laugh. "I've never been naked outside before." But he was the only one around to see her, and he'd thoroughly enjoyed the view.

The lighting was so dim beneath the canopy that dusk left them in almost complete darkness so they performed these tasks fairly early.

They tended to encounter more wildlife at the stream. Nothing that viewed them as prey, fortunately. A four-legged mammal with hooves, bushy dark brown fur, and majestic black antlers had led a small heard of similar mammals to the stream the previous day while he and Ava had been bathing. The beautiful creatures had stood still and stared at them with dark, alert eyes, ears twitching. After a moment, during which he and Ava had murmured to each other over how beautiful they were, the animals had apparently deemed them no threat, drunk from the stream, then ambled away.

After the long months of captivity, Jak'ri relished this time. The fresh air. The delicious fruit. And—most of all—Ava's company.

He cared more for her every day. And not just because they spent each night exploring each other's bodies and losing themselves in the greatest pleasure he had ever experienced.

She grinned. "You're just saying that because I went down on you last night."

He grew hard just thinking about it, her soft lips closing around his length as she sucked him deep. Instead of pouncing on her the way the memory urged him to, however, he arched a brow. "And when I reciprocated, I believe you thoroughly enjoyed it."

Her face flushed as her eyes began to glow. "Hell yes, I did. If I'd moaned or screamed any louder, those giant cat things probably would've come running, thinking I was one of those shaggy deer dying."

He grinned. Their strong telepathic connection had the added benefit of making very clear to him what she enjoyed sexually, including things she was too shy to ask of him.

The latter were his favorites.

Ava laughed. "I bet they are."

The dim light of the forest began to fade. "We should wash and return to the cave soon."

Nodding, she gave her furry friend a last pat and rose.

The *leapers*, already learning their daily pattern, grabbed the bits of fruit he and Ava hadn't finished and scurried away with them.

Jak'ri smiled as he took her hand.

Smiling back, she leaned into his side and hugged his arm.

They had neither seen nor heard any Gathendien craft yet.

No Purveli, Lasaran, or Segonian craft had arrived either.

The second didn't surprise him, considering how far from Aldebarian Alliance–occupied space he and Ava were and the likely instability of the *qhov'rum*.

But the first troubled him. He knew little about Gathendien fighter craft. The ones the escape pod's computer had shown him had not looked Akseli in design. So he had no idea how quietly they ran. Lasaran craft were utterly soundless. Both Purveli and Akseli engines were muted, yet still produced a faint hum he thought Ava would be able to detect with her sharp hearing.

But how quiet were Gathendien fighter craft? He had no memory of the craft the *grunarks* must have used to capture him and Ziv'ri. Had it been noisy enough to warn them, though, he would've thought he and his brother could've evaded them.

As always, thoughts of Ziv'ri drove a spike through his heart. But grief didn't halt his current concerns.

Jak'ri also didn't know how many soldiers the fighter craft could carry. He'd attended the Aldebarian Alliance biannual war games as part of a Purveli delegation invited by Princess Amiriska of Lasara shortly before her disappearance. Select members of the military from each of the six provinces of Purvel had attended together, observing and listening intently as she carefully outlined the many benefits joining the alliance would bring.

"How long were you in the military?" Ava asked, her face lighting with curiosity.

"Three years. The law requires every citizen born on Purvel to serve at least three years in the military when we come of age unless we pursue an advanced education. Then our training is deferred until after we complete our studies. My three-year term was deferred, so I didn't complete my service until shortly after Princess Amiriska disappeared."

"Are women required to serve in the military, too?"

"Yes. Leaders of the six provinces on my planet may disagree on many subjects, but all believe Purvel will be strong enough to fend off enemies without allies as long as we prepare."

Clearly they were wrong, though, he thought with a scowl. Their defense measures were so flawed they hadn't even been able to keep Gathendiens from kidnapping two of their own from right under their noses. Had he and Ziv'ri been taken while they were on Promeii 7, Jak'ri would be more forgiving. A lot of crazy *bura* happened on that little planet. But on Purvel, where entry by alien species was supposed to be carefully monitored?

No. He intended to schedule a meeting with Purvel's sovereign *and* the Planetary Defense Administration as soon as he made it back home.

If he made it home.

His thoughts returned to the war games. He'd seen ships and craft of nearly every size there. So he knew, depending on the planet of origin and the design, that fighter craft could accommodate between one and ten soldiers.

Ava whistled.

The *leapers* spun around and stared at her with wide eyes.

But she paid them little attention. "So when the Gathendiens arrive, we could be facing anywhere from three to thirty soldiers?"

"Yes."

"I'm pretty sure we can kick three Gathendiens' asses," she said, her expression thoughtful. "Or six. Nine. Possibly twelve if we can start picking them off with rifles before they see us. And if I let hubris sway me, fifteen. But thirty?"

Even with her phenomenal speed and strength, he didn't think they could defeat thirty.

"Don't even go there," she ordered with a frown before he could ask the next question that came to mind. "I'm not leaving you. We either fight together or we flee together. Everything else is off the table."

Drek, he hated the idea of slowing her down and endangering her. He should've asked the computer back on the pod how many soldiers were aboard the fighter craft pursuing them. The computer likely would've just told him the capacity of the vehicles. But even that would've helped, giving them a general idea of what to expect. And he cursed himself for not thinking of it.

"I didn't think of it either," Ava murmured.

He wished he could've brought a data pad linked to the pod with them so the pod could keep them apprised of the location of those craft. But on this planet, even that miniscule amount of tech operating would've served as a beacon, letting the Gathendiens know where they were.

Had the three craft been the only ones sent after them?

What if the Gathendiens in those initial craft were being followed by transports carrying more soldiers, or even the warship itself? He had no idea how quietly any of those craft traveled. If neither he nor Ava heard the craft passing overhead, they would have no warning that the enemy was close.

"If their craft make any sound at all, I'll hear them," Ava murmured. "If they don't..." She shrugged. "Once they're on the ground, I'll hear the Gathendien soldiers coming before we run into them. And I'll *scent* them long before that. Those bastards smell worse than the baby *leapers*." She looked at the furry little creatures that scampered ahead of them to the stream. "I'm thinking that even if we're sleeping when the Gathendiens arrive, these little guys will alert us. They hoot a lot when they're excited or nervous."

He nodded, dreading the inevitable confrontation. He'd like to think the Gathendiens would get frustrated and give up the search if they covered the other half the planet first and didn't find them ...

"But they really want to get their hands on an Earthling," Ava said, finishing his thought.

"Yes."

"*And* a Purveli."

He smiled. "Of the two of us, I believe you're the more essential."

Upon reaching the stream, they knelt and plucked the canteens from the bag he carried.

"Maybe we'll luck out," she said. "Maybe the good guys have already received your message and will find us first."

He hoped so. Though he had to admit even *that* sparked anxiety.

She removed the seal on a canteen and began to fill it.

Jak'ri hesitated a long moment. "The Lasaran sovereigns will expect you to travel to Lasara after we're rescued."

Ava stared at the canteen she held just beneath the water's rippling surface. "I know," she said softly, then met his gaze. "But I'm more interested in traveling to Purvel."

Something he wanted very much. Yet he forced himself to speak his fears. "You may change your mind once you're back among your people." She might decide she didn't want any reminders of her suffering. And Jak'ri would be a constant reminder of the captivity and torture she'd endured.

What if she decided she would fare better without him? That she needed to move on and forget what had happened?

"I won't," Ava said. And her words carried not even a *hint* of uncertainty. "That's how I know I'm falling in love with you and not just clinging to you like a drowning man would to a buoy."

"I didn't understand all of that."

She shook her head. "Last night, for the first time, I actually felt a spark of anxiety when I imagined us being rescued."

He frowned. She had?

Her pretty features solemn, she rested a small, wet hand against the side of his face and stroked his cheek with her thumb. "I know it sounds crazy, but I found myself worrying that once we're rescued, you'll go back to Purvel and I'll be taken to Lasara and... that will be it for us. That I'll never see you again."

Everything within him balked at the notion. And he couldn't keep himself from wrapping an arm around her as if such could keep her from leaving.

"I don't want that," she professed softly. "Because I can't imagine not being with you every day, Jak'ri. I can't imagine you not being the first person I speak with when I wake up in the morning or the last person I see before I fall asleep at night." Setting the canteen aside, she leaned in and pressed a gentle kiss to his lips. "You've been in my head often enough these past few days. Don't you know how I feel about you?" She kissed him again. "I love you like an Earth woman loves a husband. Like a Lasaran or a Purveli loves a lifemate."

And that's exactly what he wanted her to be: his lifemate. But how—

"We'll figure it out," she promised softly.

"Together."

The breeze picked up, dragging several strands of hair across her face. A tender smile curled her lips as she nodded. "Together we can do anything."

He arched a brow. "Including start our own colony here on this planet?"

She grinned. "If that's what it takes? Absolutely."

The little *leapers* looked around suddenly, then disappeared into the trees.

Thunder rumbled through the forest.

As one, he and Ava looked up. The canopy above was so dense that they couldn't see the sky. But Jak'ri thought the forest was darkening faster than usual.

"We should hurry," he murmured. "We don't know how harsh the storms are here."

"Agreed."

Having already filled their canteens, they rushed through their baths and washing their clothes. Even so, big drops began to pelt them as they jogged toward the cave. Within minutes, the dry clothing they'd donned was plastered against their skin. The dirt beneath their feet metamorphosed into mud. And rivulets formed in the soil, carrying the water that washed down the rocks toward the stream behind them.

As soon as they reached the cave's entrance, Ava, turned sideways and slid out of sight.

Jak'ri followed, cursing as the rock scraped his arm. Now that he was eating more and in better health, the crevice that allowed them passage into the cave was a tighter fit.

For Ava, too, he noticed. She'd regained some of the weight she'd lost. So by the time they made it inside, her wet shirt bore a streak of dirt across her beautiful breasts. A similar streak adorned her nicely rounded bottom.

Once inside, she turned to him with a wry smile. "If we keep eating the way we have been, you're going to have to shove me through there with a foot on my butt."

He laughed at the image. "And you'll have to pry me out with a stick."

She grinned. Then her smile vanished and her eyes flashed bright amber with fury.

Spinning around, she drew the blade she always strapped to her thigh and sank into a crouch.

Jak'ri dropped the bag and drew his blaster. *What is it?* he asked her telepathically.

I heard a scuttling sound.

His heart pounded in his chest as he listened intently.

There.

He followed her gaze to the southeastern corner. The *hesku* he'd activated the previous night still provided dim enough light to provoke a faint luminescence in the streaks of ore that adorned the walls.

Nevertheless, a few shadows lingered here and there.

Beside him, Ava relaxed. "It's okay. It's three of the *leapers*."

He could see them now as they crept closer. A male, a female, and their young. "Perhaps this storm is going to be a bad one."

Smiling, she knelt and patted the baby on its head. "Or maybe they're greedier than the rest and want more food."

Two more *leapers* peeked into the cave, then cautiously entered, their fur dripping.

Ava laughed. "Nope. It's the storm." She sent him a wry smile. "Looks like we're going to have company tonight."

She barely had time to finish the sentence before the rest of the furry clan tumbled inside.

CHAPTER FIFTEEN

THE STORM RAGED OFF and on all night, bringing with it bright flashes of lightning that lit up the passage and thunderous booms that felt as if they shook the very mountain itself. Although torrential rains fell outside, the cave that served as their home remained dry.

Ava spent many hours calming and crooning to the little *leapers* that huddled together miserably. Jak'ri did, too.

She smiled as she watched him feed one of the babies a piece of fruit. He was such a sweetheart.

Glancing up, he returned her smile and winked.

All was quiet now. Or as quiet as it usually was. With her enhanced hearing, she could hear a *lot*. And what she heard now told her the storm had finally passed.

The *leapers* must have drawn the same conclusion because they headed for the exit and took their leave.

Apparently they weren't big fans of the cave. Ava wasn't sure if the other animals they could smell in here made them nervous or if they just preferred the open space of trees.

She cast Jak'ri an appraising look.

He arched a brow. "Something on your mind, beautiful?"

She loved that he was picking up Earth sayings from her. "Maybe." Scooting closer to him, she leaned in and nuzzled his neck. "Now that the kids are gone..."

Smiling, Jak'ri turned his head and captured her lips.

Pleasure darted through her when he deepened the kiss, his tongue stroking and teasing hers. Turning toward her, he palmed one of her breasts.

Yes. Ava threw a leg over his thighs and straddled him.

Jak'ri continued to stroke her breast as he wrapped his other arm around her and pressed her hips into his, letting her feel his arousal.

A sound reached her ears.

Frowning, she drew back.

Jak'ri trailed heated kisses down her neck, then sought her lips once more.

But Ava turned her face away and listened intently.

"What is it?" he asked, expression solemn.

Fear trickled through her. "I hear a ship."

Eyes widening, Jak'ri surged to his feet, taking Ava with him.

As she dropped her feet to the ground, the sound faded.

"Is it hovering or did it pass by?" he asked.

"It passed by."

"Going in what direction?"

"North."

They stared at each other a moment. And she could hear his heart beating as furiously as her own.

"We need to see who it is," he said. "Rescuers or Gathendiens."

She nodded. "Then we'll decide what to do."

If the craft carried rescuers, the decision would be easy: Get the hell out of Dodge and ask their saviors to ferry them to Purvel. But if instead the Gathendiens had found them swifter than anticipated, she and Jak'ri would have to choose between two paths: "Stay and fight," she murmured, "or Plan B."

They'd yet to devise a Plan C they could agree upon. There only seemed to be one option available to them. If Plan B— swimming to the little island closest to this continent—didn't enable them to evade the Gathendiens, then she saw no other recourse but to try to swim to the next one.

Jak'ri was dead set against it, believing such an endeavor would kill her.

Since he'd told her what happened to the Akseli mates some Purvelis had taken in the past, Ava wasn't exactly thrilled about it either. But what other avenue could they take if they were badly outnumbered?

Ava glanced at Jak'ri and closed her mind to him, hoping he wouldn't notice as he knelt to gather the weapons and ammunition they would take with them. She didn't want him to hear her worries and couldn't seem to quiet them as fears and what-ifs assailed her.

Though she hadn't mentioned it to him, the fantastical strength she had gained during her transformation had begun to wane. And she was pretty sure their battles with the Gathendiens on the ship should have left her with no scars. Eliana's injuries usually healed completely within hours, leaving not a single trace behind. Yet Ava's scars remained.

She took the holstered blaster Jak'ri handed her and buckled it on, wrapping the belt twice around her waist to make it fit.

If the two of them came up against thirty Gathendiens, she would need every ounce of preternatural speed and strength she could muster to defeat them... or to swim to the island she'd dubbed Plan B if the first option ended up being impossible. Immortal Guardians needed regular infusions in order to maintain their speed, strength, and regenerative capabilities. But she had no blood source. And without one, she feared she wouldn't fare well if they eventually had to enact Plan C and swim to an island or continent that was even farther away than the first one.

She feared she wouldn't survive such a swim at all.

While she'd like to think her body could tolerate submersion in water a lot longer than an ordinary human's or *gifted one*'s now that she was immortal, she seemed to be regressing back to having mere mortal strength and resiliency.

She glanced at the pulse that beat beneath the smooth, barely visible scales of Jak'ri's strong neck.

He has blood, a little voice whispered. *Enough for a quick infusion.*

The tips of her fangs descended.

Eyes widening, Ava hastily forced them to recede.

She couldn't transfuse herself with Jak'ri's blood. It was too risky. What if Purveli blood was as a harmful to Immortal Guardians as Lasaran blood?

Was that a gamble she could afford to lose?

Jak'ri glanced over at her. "I know you prefer the blasters and daggers, but I want you to carry an O-rifle, too."

"Okay." Ava took the long weapon he held out to her. "Here's hoping those were the good guys flying over," she said with false levity.

If instead they were Gathendiens and she and Jak'ri failed to kick their asses, Plan B didn't buy them enough time for help to arrive, and they ended up having to go with Plan C...

She might very well end up having to discover if Purveli blood would kill her.

━━━━◆○◆━━━━

A N HOUR LATER, AVA began to suspect she wouldn't live long enough to learn whether or not Purveli blood would kill her.

No. A fall would kill her way before that.

A very *long* fall.

Against her will, she glanced down, then wished she hadn't. Jak'ri didn't want to give whoever landed to the north a scent trail on the ground to follow. So he'd coaxed her into climbing high up in the trees where they now crept from the huge limb of one tree to a limb on the next and the next and so on. Sure, some of the limbs were so freaking big you could drive a riding lawnmower over them. But Ava *really* didn't like heights.

In the dreams with Jak'ri, she had eventually conquered her fear enough to get used to cliff diving because there was a great big beautiful ocean at the base of Runaka Point, waiting to catch her and safely usher her into its cool embrace.

Here there was just dirt. And mud in the lower lying areas.

Somehow, she didn't think that mud was soft enough to break her fall without breaking bones, too.

You're doing very well, Jak'ri told her with a smile.

She shot him a squinty-eyed look. *You aren't nervous at all, are you?*

No. He spread his fingers to reveal the webbing between them, then motioned to his side. *I have webbing like this that's harder to discern on my sides. If I fall, all I have to do is doff my shirt and spread my arms wide, and the webbing will stretch out like a parachute the way it did on those striped rodents we saw our first day here. Such will slow my descent enough that I can land on my feet, unharmed. It's why I like cliff diving so much.*

Ava stared at him.

His lips twitched.

She laughed silently and would've given him a playful shove if they weren't balanced on a damn tree limb. *You're so bad! You almost had me going again!* Then she arched a brow. *But I've seen that big, beautiful body of yours naked often enough to know that's bullshit.*

He grinned unrepentantly. *Did it distract you?*

Not as much as seeing that big, beautiful body of yours naked would, but yes.

Good.

She motioned ahead of them. *They're definitely up ahead somewhere. And I hate to tell you this, but they're Gathendien.*

His brows drew down. *You're sure?*

Yes. She grimaced. *They may not be able to smell us up here. But I can sure as hell smell them down there, and their stench precedes them.*

He pointed. *They're that way?*

Yes.

Then stay here. I'm going to get a little closer and see how many there are.

Two dozen, she said. *Maybe more.* She was still learning how to use her newly heightened senses and hadn't yet managed to calculate precisely how many *leapers* were scuttling toward her when she tried to guess without looking.

When Jak'ri started forward, she took a step after him.

He immediately turned and held up a hand. *Stay here. I'll be back soon.*

I'm coming with you. While Jak'ri didn't think the Gathendiens would be able to catch his scent, she wanted to be there to defend him just in case.

He, on the other hand, had other ideas. *I'm more adept at this than you are, Ava.* He motioned to his bare feet, which gripped the limb firmly.

She wouldn't have thought webbed toes would make much of a difference with that, but he was as stable as a squirrel, his legs lacking the trembling that perpetually afflicted her own at these heights.

I'm not going to engage them, Jak'ri assured her. *I'm just going to do a little reconnaissance.*

She opened her mouth to protest again, uneasy about letting him out of her sight.

Don't worry. We're downwind. And I'm more surefooted than you are up here, he said before she could. *I can move more swiftly through the trees.*

In other words, she would slow him down. Her damnable fear of heights left her pretty shaky as she crept along the tree limbs. Adding preternatural speed on top of that just seemed unwise. *Okay.*

Smiling, he pressed a kiss to her forehead. *Stay vigilant.*

Stay safe.

When he turned to leave, she caught his hand. *I mean it, Jak'ri.* She held his gaze. *Come back to me.*

He brought her hand to his lips. *I'll always come back to you,* sakara.

Ava withheld further protests as she watched him slip away, moving from tree to tree with a confidence she couldn't help but admire. *I wouldn't worry if you didn't smell so damn good,* she commented.

His chuckle filled her head, sparking a smile. *I can't possibly smell better than you,* he returned, his voice deepening almost to a growl. *I love your scent. Especially when you're writhing in my arms. And I lack your enhanced senses.*

She smiled. *You may lack my enhanced senses. But you* do *have a freakish ability to turn me on with just a few words.*

He rewarded her with another chuckle.

Long minutes passed, chock-full of silence that fed her anxiety.

The *leapers* grew bored after a time and wandered away.

When Ava tuned in to his thoughts, she found Jak'ri concentrating on moving swifter through the trees without making a sound.

I don't think you've told me what you do on Purvel now that you're no longer in the military, she said when she could take the quiet no longer.

I'm a sahstin jin.

What's that?

I don't think there's an equivalent on your planet. I'm... an atmospheric scientist. Or rather I specialize in the generation of atmospheres in uninhabitable environments. My people wish to terraform our moons the way the Lasarans terraformed theirs. So I'm working with other scientists to accomplish that.

Damn. He was the full freaking package: hot, funny, brave, honorable, affectionate, *and* incredibly smart. *Wow. How's that going?*

Not as quickly as we'd hoped, he responded wryly. *Most of the oxygen on my planet is produced by* tantiorcea.

That didn't translate.

Floating plants in our oceans.

Oh. Right. I think it's like that on Earth. I remember reading that phytoplankton produce up to eighty percent of Earth's oxygen.

The same is true on Purvel. Our early efforts to bring the ice on our largest moon's surface to a temperature that would allow the tantiorcea *to thrive failed. But we've made some progress since then.*

He went on to describe their successes and failures, the vegetation they'd coaxed into taking root on the moon's surface, the algae colonies they'd managed to grow. It fascinated Ava. *And* saddened her, because his brother had pursued the same profession and had been by Jak'ri's side the whole way. And she could see how painful the prospect of moving forward *without* Ziv'ri was for him.

Jak'ri also expressed his frustration with the governments of Purvel. He, Ziv'ri, and others in their field had petitioned Purvel's sovereign repeatedly, trying to coax him into accepting Lasara's generous offer to aid them in their terraforming efforts, should they decide to join the Aldebarian Alliance. But he refused to do so unless the governments of all six provinces agreed to it. And some of those in power remained determined to go their own way, insisting they would be beholden to the Lasarans if they accepted aid even though Princess Amiriska had made it clear that any help offered would be a gesture of good faith on Lasara's part, one ally aiding another.

Forgive me, he said after falling silent a moment. *I didn't intend to vent my frustration. Did I bore you?*

No. I'm fascinated by it all. And I admit I find myself... I don't know... stunned or maybe embarrassed by how far behind Earth is technologically from all of you out here. Uneasiness slithered through her as she contemplated it.

Tell me, he encouraged, sensing her unrest.

Ava sighed. *I just... don't know what my place would be in your world. I mean, in what way could I possibly contribute to your society? I'm guessing my college degree, which constitutes advanced education on Earth, won't seem advanced at all on Purvel. So what job would I possibly qualify for?*

He went silent for a moment. *Would it surprise you if I expressed the same fears of finding my place in* your *society if I traveled to Earth?*

Jak'ri on Earth? *Oh. No. You do* not *want to travel to Earth*, she told him emphatically. *The slight silver hue to your skin and the scales that are visible if someone looks closely enough make you appear less human than Lasarans. And if* anyone *outside of the Immortal Guardians crew saw you, the dumbasses in power would hear of it and do the same thing to you that they did to Ami. I mean, Princess Amiriska. They would torture you and experiment on you like the Gathendiens did.*

And look for ways to destroy my people?

Yes. They'd do it in the guise of national security, claiming they needed to find a way to defeat your people in case you ever decided to invade Earth.

Purvelis don't invade other planets.

I know. But that's the justification Earth would give for capturing and torturing you.

He was silent for a long moment.

Sorry, she said. *Earth kinda sucks that way.*

Well, you needn't worry about finding a place on Purvel. My people will welcome you and—drek!

Her eyes widened. *What is it?*

Gathendiens. They've already found the escape pod.

Dismay swamped her. They were that close already? *How many are there?*

He went quiet for a moment. *Thirty. And they brought* sedapas.

Those spiked lizard things they use for hunting?

Yes. The grunarks *are already dividing into groups to search for us. And the ground is dry. The storm must not have extended this far north because it looks as if no rain fell here, so they'll have an easier time tracking us.*

Ava thought furiously. *Can you take them out with a* senshi?

No. If I emit a senshi *powerful enough to incapacitate or kill this large a contingent, particularly now that they're scattered, it will be powerful enough to reach* you.

All the way back here?

Yes.

Damn. That was powerful.

Were she at full strength...

No. Even if she *were* at full strength, Ava wasn't sure she could take that kind of damage. A couple of Immortal Guardians had suffered brain trauma once that—according to rumor—had exceeded the regenerative capabilities the virus lent them. Even Seth, the immensely powerful Immortal Guardian leader with his incredible healing gift, had feared he couldn't repair the damage completely because he said brain injuries were more difficult for him to heal.

If Jak'ri's *senshi* incapacitated her, there were no immortal healers around to come to her aid. And she knew there was no way in hell he would leave her behind.

Get to the cave, he urged her.

Ava didn't hesitate. Swiveling, she headed back the way she'd come, not wanting to slow him down. Jak'ri moved so much faster through the trees that he might very well catch up with her before she reached it.

As she picked her way carefully through the broad branches, her mind raced.

How could the two of them defeat thirty Gathendiens and their hunting lizards if they couldn't take advantage of Jak'ri's *senshi*?

We can't, he said. *We could if we had some Z-12s.*

What are those?

E-grenades. But we don't. We only have the O-rifles and tronium blasters.

Are the sedapas *slim enough to make it inside the cave?*

Yes. And, given enough time, the Gathendiens can cut their way in.

Then we'll go with Plan B.

I don't see any other choice.

Ava reached the tree they'd climbed up and slowly started down it.

Her whole body trembled as she felt for toeholds. Whenever she and Jak'ri had climbed the cliffs of Runaka Point, he had caged her between his body and the rock wall, leaving her safe in the knowledge that he'd catch her if she fell.

Now there was nothing to catch her if she fell except the ground.

You can do this, Ava, he told her, nothing but confidence filling his deep voice.

I can do this, she seconded.

Jak'ri fell silent again. She didn't know if he did so to allow her to concentrate or because he needed the quiet to concentrate himself.

Some of the *leapers* returned and clambered around her on the tree trunk.

Ava's fingertips soon grew raw from tucking them into the grooves and gripping the rough bark. The rubbery substance Jak'ri had coated her feet with began to wear away. And by the time the ground grew close, she was sweating.

When at last her feet touched soil, she leaned against the tree, weak with relief. *I did it.*

I knew you could, Jak'ri said, a thread of tension woven through his voice. *Grab your pack and start toward the west coast.*

She straightened. *What?*

Moss grows on the east side of trees here. So just head in the opposite direction. Move as quickly as you can and—

I'm not leaving without you. Ava jogged toward the cave. As soon as she shimmied inside, she grabbed both packs and began the arduous process of getting the damn things back through the slim passage and out into the open.

I'll catch up with you, he said.

Ava made it outside the cave and set the bags down at her feet. *No. Just get your ass here. I'll be waiting for you.*

He muttered several words her translator balked at revealing. But she *did* manage to catch the word *stubborn.*

She smiled over his disgruntled tone. *Yeah, but you still love me, right?*

Yes, he grumbled.

Laughing, she faced the direction of the escape pod and readied her weapons.

Long minutes passed.

A breeze wafted through the forest, rustling the sparse undergrowth and tickling her hair.

When it did, a familiar scent filled her nose: the stench of stagnant water.

Ice filled Ava's veins as she recognized its source.

Gathendiens.

They were getting closer.

J AK'RI RETURNED TO AVA as quickly as he could without risking a fatal fall. He wanted to be angry with her for not going on without him, but... *vuan* it. If he were in her position, he would've done the same thing and insisted on waiting for her.

When he reached the tree they'd scaled earlier, he saw no sign of her.

It took a few minutes for him to make his way safely down to the ground. As soon as his feet touched the soil, Jak'ri ran toward the cave.

Ava stood in front of it, O-rifle at the ready, scowling in the direction of the pod.

She swung around at his approach, her expression lightening when she saw him. "Finally." Leaving the rifle to dangle on its strap, she hurried toward him and hugged him tight. "The Gathendiens' stench is so strong now I'm practically gagging on it."

Alarm struck. "They're that close?"

"I don't know. I'm still learning how to use my new heightened senses, but... Yeah. I think they're close."

He grabbed his pack and thrust his arms through the loops.

Ava did the same with hers.

Then they raced toward the coast.

"If the packs slow us down, we'll have to discard them," he murmured.

"Not the medic pack," she said.

A peek into her thoughts revealed her fear that she might need it to patch up any wounds he received. But—remembering the way she had thrown herself into battle back on the Gathendien ship—he worried *she* would be the one who needed it. *Don't sacrifice yourself for me, Ava*, he told her telepathically. If the Gathendiens were as close as she estimated, the two of them shouldn't speak aloud and give the *sedapas* more to track.

Ditto, she replied.

A moment later, Ava halted.

Jak'ri stopped beside her. *What is it?*

She turned troubled brown eyes up to meet his. *I've lost their scent.*

Readying his O-rifle, Jak'ri warily surveyed the forest around them.

A breeze caught a few strands of her dark hair and dragged them across her face.

Her eyes widened. *Oh shit. The wind has shifted.*

And it would now carry their scent directly to the *sedapas*.

As one, they burst into motion, running in the direction of the coast they still couldn't see.

Hoots erupted from the trees some distance away.

Their eyes met.

The *leapers* had found the new intruders. And *drek*, they sounded close.

Drop the packs! he blurted in her head.

Slowing, they shrugged off the straps.

As Jak'ri's pack hit the ground, a *sedapa* burst from the undergrowth to their right, jaws open wide, exposing three rows of jagged teeth and a forked tongue.

They skidded to a stop.

The *sedapa's* twin tails twitched as it hissed and scampered toward them.

Jak'ri raised his rifle.

Ava moved in a blur. In the brief moment it took her discarded pack to hit the dirt, she circled around and came up behind the beast. Drawing her dagger, she drove it deep into the back of the *sedapa's* neck.

The animal jerked, its mouth snapping shut. Then it collapsed to the ground, twitched a couple of times, and fell still.

Jak'ri gaped at her.

She stared at him, eyes wide. *I didn't know how far ahead of the others it was and thought a quiet kill might benefit us more.* When she tried to withdraw the blade, it didn't budge. Grimacing, she carefully braced a foot on its back between the sharp spikes, and yanked harder. It required so much strength that she stumbled backward and almost fell when the blade finally slipped free of the thick flesh.

Ava had barely regained her footing when her head swung in the direction from which the *sedapa* had come.

Drek, she blurted. *They're here.*

Jak'ri nodded toward the tree beside her. *Get behind the tree. Use it as a shield.*

He backed toward a second tree and did the same.

Another *sedapa* scrambled into view. This one bore a leash and moved so swiftly it nearly dragged the Gathendien clutching the other end behind it.

The creature stopped and hissed when it spied the dead one. Its spikes stiffened and rose as it whipped its head around, forked tongue flicking as it tested the air.

The Gathendien's eyes widened. He dropped the leash.

Jak'ri fired his O-rifle in three quick bursts.

A scorched hole appeared in the center of the Gathendien's chest and pierced his armor, dropping him where he stood.

The *sedapa* didn't even look back. As soon as it saw Jak'ri, it lunged toward him, jaw gaping to expose sharp teeth glistening with poisonous saliva.

An e-blast struck it in the back of the head.

The creature collapsed.

Jak'ri stared at Ava.

The ammunition may be different from Earth's, but it's still just point and shoot. Swinging to the side, she sought cover behind the tree again and readied her O-rifle. *More are coming. Not the whole group. Maybe ten or twelve.*

The racket they'd created firing their weapons, however, would swiftly draw the others.

I have an idea, she said and met his gaze. *Keep them busy and don't let them shoot you.*

His stomach sank. *Ava...*

In the next instant, she bolted away in a blur.

Jak'ri cursed as the *drekking* Gathendiens trotted into view.

Their eyes went immediately to the slain *sedapas* and the dead warrior.

Jak'ri fired his weapon before anger even had time to flash across their features.

Two stumbled backward as the e-blasts caught one in the neck and the other in the head. As those two fell, the other *grunarks* dropped into defensive crouches and raised their weapons to return fire.

Here I come, Ava warned. *I'll go low. You go high. Aim for their heads.*

As soon as she finished issuing the warning, a blur dashed through the Gathendiens' ranks. Blood sprayed. Several yelped as their feet flew up and their backs hit the ground.

Since no e-blasts lit the forest, Ava must be using her blades.

Jak'ri fired at those who remained standing, aiming for their heads and hoping desperately he wouldn't accidentally shoot Ava, who lacked their protective armor.

E-blasts fired by the Gathendiens struck the tree he used as cover so many times that the thick bark began to smoke. Two of the *grunarks* fell beneath Jak'ri's fire. Two more parted and began to walk in opposite directions in a large half circle that would soon make it impossible for him to engage them both.

A small blur of motion swept one off his feet.

Jak'ri's heart lodged itself in his throat as he caught a brief glimpse of Ava. Her face was streaked with blood. The front of her shirt was torn over her abdomen and stained red. And one arm bore a deep gash.

In the next instant, she vanished, striking at the other Gathendiens.

Jak'ri fired at the last one wielding an O-rifle and felled him. Then he took out the one Ava had knocked down before he could fully regain his feet.

The rest of the Gathendiens engaged in a mad attempt to capture the wraithlike bundle of violence in their midst.

Jak'ri managed to shoot a couple more, then swore and held his fire. Ava was no longer going low. She was all over them now, the way she had been back on the ship, striking at their tails one moment and their heads the next. And she was badly outnumbered.

Releasing his rifle, he let it dangle from its sling. He would have to join the fray to help her. Unholstering his *tronium* blaster, he started forward.

A hand touched his shoulder.

Jumping, Jak'ri spun around.

Ava brushed his weapon aside before he could aim it at her. Blood streaked her pretty face as she smiled up at him, her amber eyes bright with glee. "Look what I found." She held up her other hand.

Despite his concern for her, Jak'ri grinned when he saw the round device that rested in her small palm. "I love you so much."

She laughed. "Is this what I think it is?"

He took it from her. "It's a Bex-7 stun grenade." He handed her his blaster. "Keep them busy."

Ava slipped around to the other side of the massive tree trunk and fired multiple times.

The Bex-7 was about the size of his palm and vibrated when Jak'ri activated it. A green circle on its surface lit up and revealed a tiny command screen. Lacking the time to program it, he simply started the timer and tossed it into the Gathendiens' midst.

Take cover, he urged.

A second later, Ava slammed into him and flattened him to the ground behind the tree. "Umph!"

One of the Gathendiens shouted a warning. Then bright light flooded the forest.

Shrieks and thuds and rustling erupted from what seemed like every direction as unseen wildlife flew or stampeded away.

Then more thuds sounded, these just on the other side of the tree.

Jak'ri nudged Ava off of him, leapt to his feet, and peered around their wooden shield.

Every Gathendien was down.

Ava leaned into his side and peered out. "Did it get them all?"

"In this group." He swept her into a hug. "How badly are you injured?"

"Enough to piss me off. But I don't have time to rant about it. The others aren't far behind."

Nodding, he released her. "Let's look for more grenades."

It took them less than a minute to confiscate every one the Gathendiens carried. All were Bex-7 stun grenades. None were Z-12s or other lethal e-grenades, attesting to their determination to take Ava alive.

"And you," she said. "They want you, too."

Jak'ri nodded but still thought her the greater prize.

After depositing the weapons in the outer pockets of their packs, he and Ava once more donned them and took off running toward the coast.

The breeze unfortunately chose not to shift again, so they remained upwind of the rest of the Gathendiens who hunted them.

"I smell the ocean," she said, her breathing a bit ragged.

Jak'ri's was ragged, too. His time locked in that *drekking* cell at the Gathendiens' mercy had weakened him.

Beside him, Ava snorted. "You must have been built like freaking Thor then, because you're still strong as hell."

Jak'ri didn't know what a *thor* was. His translator had no definition for it. But he lacked the time to ask because the undergrowth began to thicken. "We must be getting close." This amount of vegetation indicated exposure to sunlight. So the coast must be—

"I hear waves!" she said, her face lighting with excitement.

Branches tore at them as they fought their way through.

At last, the dense foliage vomited them forth into bright sunlight.

"Finally!" Ava breathed.

Jak'ri nodded. They stood upon a cliff reminiscent of Runaka Point, a vast blue ocean stretching before them as far as they could see. Only one tiny dark spot—far in the distance—disrupted its glassy surface: the island they hoped would provide them refuge.

Ava hissed in a breath and quickly backed toward the forest.

Jak'ri spun around to face her. His eyes widened.

Her pale, freckled skin was now pink everywhere the sun had touched it.

He took a step toward her. "Ava?"

She stared down at her arms. "I forgot. The forest is always so dark that..." She looked up at him. "I just forgot."

"Forgot what?"

"The virus the Gathendiens infected me with causes photosensitivity."

"Sunlight harms you?"

"Yes."

He glanced at the wide stretch of blue that led to the island.

How then could they strike out across the ocean?

"I'll be fine once I'm in the water as long as I swim well beneath the surface," she told him. "Eliana loves to swim and said the water protects her even on the brightest days."

Nodding, he crossed the short distance to the edge and looked down. This cliff was almost as high as Runaka Point. At its base, jagged rocks clustered together as water frothed around them.

"What do you see?" she asked from the safety of the shade.

"Shallow water and rocks."

"How far do we have to jump to avoid them?"

He studied the rocks, which stretched well into the ocean, then turned to face her. "Farther than we're capable." Or farther than *he* was capable. She would have to try to make it without him.

Ava stared at him a long moment, her somber features blood-spattered, her breath still coming in gasps. "We fight together or we flee together," she reminded him.

Then they would both jump. He would rather die down on those rocks than see the Gathendiens take her captive again.

"Do you trust me, Jak'ri?" she asked, her expression earnest.

He crossed to stand before her. "With my life."

She held out her hand. "Then grab my wrist."

Jak'ri curled his fingers around her wrist. It was so small his fingers and thumb overlapped.

"Whatever happens," she said, closing her fingers as much as she could around his thicker wrist and clutching him tightly, "don't let go."

He studied at her. "What are you going to do?"

"Do you remember the dream we had with Ziv'ri? The one we competed in to see who the best diver was?"

He nodded.

"Do you remember how far I went past you both when I dove?"

"Yes." It had been as if she had grown wings and taken flight.

"On the count of three, we're going to run to the edge of this cliff and jump off. But I'm going to jump as far as I dove in that dream." She gave his wrist a squeeze. "And I'm going to take you with me. You just have to hang on tight."

Because she would be dragging his weight.

He swallowed hard. What if it proved to be too much? What if his weight kept her from bypassing the rocks?

Moving closer until her breasts brushed his upper abdomen, she stared up at him. "Jak'ri? I need you to promise me you won't let go."

How could he do that when he knew she'd have a much better chance of making it without him?

"I don't want to make it without you," she whispered, her brown eyes filling with tears. "Promise me you won't let go." Rising onto her toes, she pressed a soft kiss to his lips. "Please. I need you, *sakara*."

He nodded. "I won't let go."

She studied him a moment longer, then shifted to stand beside him. "Okay. Let's do this. On three."

Jak'ri faced the ocean.

"One."

His muscles tensed.

"Two."

He tightened his hold on her fragile wrist.

"Three."

The two of them ran toward the edge and leapt off.

CHAPTER SIXTEEN

AVA CLAMPED HER TEETH together as pain raced up the arm Jak'ri clung to and settled in her shoulder. Jagged rocks stretched below them, so far that icy fear filled her. In the dream, she'd soared impossibly high when she'd pushed off the cliff. She had hoped to do the same here, but the fight with the damn Gathendiens had liberated even more of her blood. The virus had stopped healing her. She could feel her strength draining. And Jak'ri and the packs they'd forgotten to discard pulled her down like a hot air balloon basket filled with too many people.

They made it though. They sailed beyond the rocks and dropped toward the deeper portion of the ocean.

Ava drew in a long breath seconds before she hit the surface.

Cold water closed over her head, the temperature a shock that nearly sucked the air out of her lungs. Then fire erupted in every wound as saltwater burrowed into them. Air bubbles from their splashdown surrounded her for a moment. Her eyes stung. Then Jak'ri floated in front of her, his once-ebony hair now a cloud of silver.

You did it! he thought to her triumphantly as his lips turned up in a grin. *You're amazing, Ava. Are you all right?*

Yes. A lot of stuff ached, but nothing was broken. *Let's see how far we can get before the Gathendiens reach the cliff.*

Nodding, he turned toward the island and began to swim. *Let me know when you need to go up for air.*

I will.

Jak'ri cut through the cool, blue water like a missile.

Once more, she marveled over how quickly he swam. He was so fast! Far faster than even an Olympic gold medalist. But Ava had less difficulty keeping up with him this time despite her waning strength.

Though the sun above was bright, its rays didn't harm her. Eliana had been right. The water protected her. The cold even numbed the instant sunburn she'd gotten.

Ava glanced around as she kept pace with Jak'ri. The water on this planet lacked the pollution that tainted the oceans back home and was as clear as that in a swimming pool. She could see for miles!

And there was soooooo much to see.

Far below them coral bloomed like a flower garden, providing bright splashes of color that boasted every shade of the rainbow. The sand coating the ocean floor was a dark purplish-gray that made the coral seem almost to glow with neon light by comparison. Crustaceans in an equally wide variety of sizes, shapes, and colors scuttled along the sand like cars on a freeway while a captivating array of fish flitted above them.

It was beautiful.

Can you see the island? Jak'ri asked.

She dragged her gaze away from the lovely marine life and peered ahead. *Yes.*

She also saw a shadow headed their way.

Several shadows.

Ava frowned.

We have company, she warned him.

He shot her a look. *Gathendiens?*

She stared at the figures. *No. Large marine life.*

As the creatures swam closer, she began to discern more details. They were about the size of a dolphin, but had the black-and-white coloring of a killer whale and what looked like a narwhal tusk.

A very *long* narwhal tusk.

I hope these guys are friendly, she murmured telepathically.

I do, too. Those tusks look like they can do a lot of damage.

Exactly what I was thinking. Here's hoping they're all friendly and *have full bellies.*

Neither she nor Jak'ri slowed as the creatures approached.

Her heart began to beat faster with trepidation. Even with her waning preternatural speed, she didn't think she could fight worth a crap underwater. If these things were predatory or territorial...

The creatures parted into two groups of four and swam right past them.

Relief suffused Ava... until movement from the corner of her eye drew her attention.

The creatures returned, swimming alongside her now. More swam on the other side of Jak'ri, boxing them in. But they seemed disinclined to harm them.

If anything, they exhibited the same curiosity as the *leapers*.

Ava smiled. She'd always wanted to swim with dolphins. If her lungs weren't burning from holding her breath so long and the Gathendiens weren't hunting them, she would love this.

The creature closest to her darted forward, then slowed until she caught up, then darted forward again. Falling back, it disappeared from her peripheral vision. A moment later she became aware of a presence beneath her and glanced down. The playful dolphin-like creature zigzagged beneath her, seeming almost to say, *Look what I can do*, as another one swam a lazy circle around Jak'ri.

This is so cool, she told him.

He smiled. *They remind me of the* raashini *back home.*

We have something similar on Earth called dolphins.

Thank goodness their new companions weren't like sharks. She and Jak'ri had already battled Gathendiens and two-tailed hunting lizards with spikes and poisonous saliva. She didn't think she was up to battling anything else today.

Nor am I, he admitted with a wry smile.

The dolphin-like creatures remained with them on their swim. Ava held her breath far longer than she normally could. But eventually, she still found herself regretfully announcing, *I need to take a breath.*

Jak'ri halted so quickly she shot past him.

Whoops. Slowing to a stop, she moved her arms to keep her body from floating to the surface while she waited for him to catch up with her.

Go ahead, he urged, his brow furrowing with concern as he approached. *Just break the surface slowly.*

Good thing he warned her. Ava's starved lungs were instead encouraging her to burst above the surface and drag in great gasping breaths, something she probably shouldn't do in case the Gathendiens stood on the cliff with the alien equivalent of binoculars.

Nodding, she moderated her speed as she swam toward the surface and slowed almost to a standstill before cautiously poking her head up out of the water. Her mouth popped open of its own accord and began dragging in air.

The pain in her chest eased even as the skin on her face began to prickle with a sunburn.

That sucked!

Ava glanced toward the cliff and was stunned by the distance she and Jak'ri had covered.

As she stared, the dense foliage at the forest's edge parted abruptly and spewed forth several large bodies preceded by two more *sedapas*.

Crap.

Several of the dolphin-like creatures chose that moment to burst from the water around her, leaping high and splashing as they emitted squeaky calls.

Sputtering, Ava wiped her eyes. Worried her new aquatic companions might attract unwanted attention, she drew in another deep breath and sank beneath the surface while they blocked her from view.

Jak'ri waited close by. *I tried to distract them, but they were determined to join you.*

She nodded.

His brow remained furrowed as he cupped her face in one palm. *Are you all right?*

Yes. The Gathendiens just reached the cliff.

His frown deepened. *Did they see you?*

I don't think so. She motioned to the creatures that continued to cavort on the surface. *These guys were splashing and jumping around enough to block the view.*

Good. Can you keep going?

Absolutely.

He pressed his chilly lips to hers. Then they resumed their swim.

Their new aquatic friends joined them once more, as curious as the little *leapers* had been.

Right about the time Ava's lungs began to burn with the need of another breath, the island rose up before them.

How are you doing? Jak'ri asked.

I'm about ready to take another breath.

Can you make it around that peninsula there? He pointed to a little finger of land that poked out from the island's otherwise round body. Trees and brush covered it, the foliage dipping down to touch the water's surface.

She nodded. That would conceal them well from the Gathendiens if any should look this way.

The water remained deep almost all the way to the shoreline. She and Jak'ri swam around to the other side of the peninsula and surfaced under an umbrella of branches.

Ava drew in more big gasping breaths.

Jak'ri eyed her with concern, his own breathing as even as though he'd just woken from a nap.

"I'm okay," she told him between gasps.

Wrapping an arm around her, he drew her close and kept her head above water so she could relax. Ava leaned against him and rested her head on his shoulder, grateful for the reprieve.

Gathendien blades had caught her several times during their skirmish. And though none of the wounds felt deep enough to threaten her life—barring serious infection she hoped the virus would prevent—they hurt like hell, the saltwater stinging like fire.

As her breathing finally calmed, she closed her eyes.

Fatigue pummeled her.

Jak'ri pressed a kiss to the top of her head. "Can you hold on a little longer?" he asked softly. "I saw something beneath the surface I'd like to check out."

She nodded and tried to look a little less whipped.

Some of the dolphin-like creatures surfaced near them and swam in lazy circles.

Ava motioned to them weakly. "These guys will keep me company."

Jak'ri guided her hands to the branches of a tree that bowed to the water. "Hang onto this. If your friends here scatter suddenly or if you hear or sense anything approaching, call out to me immediately."

"Okay."

He seemed hesitant to leave.

"It's okay. I'll be fine."

He stole another quick kiss. "I'll return quickly."

"Okay."

Seconds later, he disappeared beneath the surface.

Three of their aquatic friends followed him. Two remained with her.

Ava leaned her forehead against a branch, then winced and drew back when the contact sparked pain.

One of the dolphin-like creatures rolled onto its back like an otter. The other followed suit as they chittered to each other and cast her curious looks.

Jak'ri's beloved voice filled her head. *I think this island used to be volcanically active.*

Of course it did.

Ava sighed. *Please tell me it's dormant.* It would be just her luck if the island they sought refuge on ended up erupting and sending rivers of lava chasing after them.

It's dormant, he replied. *I found a tunnel. I'm going to venture inside and see where it leads.*

That sounded dangerous. *What if you get lost?*

I won't. I have an excellent sense of direction. And should it fail me, I can use echolocation to find my way out.

Okay. If you have any trouble, let me know and I'll ride one of these dolphin things to the rescue.

A chuckle filled her head, rumbling its way straight to her heart. *I may fake it just so I can see that.*

She smiled.

Moments passed. *The farther I go, the more convinced I become that this—and the other tunnels that branch off of it—is an extinct lava tube.*

More moments passed.

Yes! he blurted triumphantly.

Yes what? she asked.

There's a subterranean cavern. Half of it is taken up by water. But the other half is dry ground. It's the perfect place for us to evade detection by the Gathendiens.

Excellent!

It's beautiful, too. I can't wait for you to see it. I'm on my way out now.

Tension thrummed through Ava while she waited for him to reappear. She'd heard stories about divers getting lost and running out of oxygen while exploring newly discovered underwater caves.

Not Jak'ri though. He popped up in front of her, teeth flashing in a wide grin.

Ava forced a smile. "Hi there, handsome. What brings *you* here?"

"You," he responded promptly and stole another kiss. "Always you."

Her mood lightened despite the pain and weariness that afflicted her.

His expression softened. "Why don't you hold on to my pack and let me swim us both down there."

She wanted to say no. She really did. But instead, she found herself issuing a tired nod.

As soon as Jak'ri turned away, she released the tree branch and grabbed hold of his pack.

"Ready?" he asked.

"Ready." She drew in a deep breath.

Jak'ri sank below the surface again, taking her with him, and followed the coast a few yards beyond the point at which she had rested. Sure enough, there was a tunnel. The sand leading up to it went from purplish-gray to black as night, the rocky exterior so dark she'd thought it a mere shadow rather than an entrance.

Jak'ri headed inside and began navigating twists and turns with a certainty and dexterity that impressed the hell out of her. He really did have a fantastic sense of direction. She was sure she would've gotten lost if she'd tried to navigate these passages and tunnels by herself.

Light appeared at the end of the tunnel. Ava's burning eyes widened as the tight walls around them abruptly opened up into a large subterranean lake and darkness gave way to light.

Oh wow. It was beautiful. Like the rest of the ocean, the water in here was as clear as that of a well-kept swimming pool. Long, towering strands of a green plant that reminded her of kelp stretched from the sandy bottom almost all the way to the surface, creating a sort of underwater jungle.

Jak'ri skirted its edges and headed for the opposite side of the cavern.

The water grew shallower until Jak'ri lowered his feet to the obsidian sand and stood.

Ava poked her head up out of the water. But Jak'ri had to take several more steps before her toes could touch the bottom. Even when she could stand, she continued to hold onto him while she gaped at their new hideaway.

A tranquil saltwater lake as big as a football field encompassed roughly half the cavern. The black rock that made up the high ceiling and walls was streaked with veins of bioluminescent ore that emitted bright enough light for them to see clearly. And unlike the ore in the cave they'd sheltered in on land, this didn't require an alternate source of light to activate it.

Stalactites abounded in the cavern, producing stunning sculptures, many of which were coated with a pink moss that produced dim light of its own, increasing visibility even more.

"This is amazing," she said with quiet awe.

Beside her, Jak'ri nodded. "The ground over there is dry and looks like it remains so during high tide."

She looked up at him. "I don't think the Gathendiens will find us in here."

He smiled. "I don't either." Taking her hand, he sloshed through the shallows and led her onto dry sand that sparkled like crushed obsidian. "How are your wounds?" His gaze went to her forehead.

Reaching up, Ava gave it a feel and grimaced when she encountered a sizable gash. "Still there. About the same as this one, I guess."

"I'll see to those first. Then I'll go survey the island." When she started to protest, fearing he'd be spotted, he held up a hand. "I'll only explore the side they can't view from the cliff. I want to see if any of the trees here bear the same fruit we've been enjoying on the continent and pick a goodly supply of it so we won't have to venture out for a while."

"If the Gathendiens don't find us dead on the rocks, do you think they'll come here?"

"Probably. But I think their search efforts will be restricted to the island's surface. I don't think they'll find us down here."

"If they do, we'll just hit them all with the stun grenades. They can only enter from the one tunnel."

He smiled. "Which will put them at a distinct disadvantage." Taking her by the shoulders, he turned her to face away from him and relieved her of the medic pack. "Let's see to those wounds."

Ava shook her head. "They'll keep. Get the fruit first. We don't know how soon they'll send someone over here to look for us." And they'd had to leave behind the heavy fruit they'd foraged during their stay in the cave. "How well can those *sedapas* swim?"

"Very well."

She turned to face him with sigh. "It figures."

"But they can't scent us in the water."

"That's something, at least. You want some help with the fruit? I'm pretty proficient at climbing trees now."

He shook his head. "I want you to rest. As soon as I return, I'll tend to your wounds." He shrugged out of his pack and unfastened it. Flipping it upside down, he dumped the contents onto the sand.

There were still quite a few nutrient cubes.

She curled her lip at them.

He grabbed several empty canteens and tucked them back in the bag. "I'll see if there's a fresh water source while I'm up there, too."

"Okay. Just be careful."

"I will." He pressed a kiss to her lips and drew her into a hug. "I'll be quick." Then he waded back into the water and disappeared.

Ava sank to her knees. Everything seemed to hurt more now that she was out of the cold water, which seemed weird considering how much the salt had stung.

She glanced around. Jak'ri was right though. This cavern should keep the Gathendiens from locating them. The problem was... it would also keep potential rescuers from finding them.

So how were they going to get off this planet?

WHEN JAK'RI RETURNED TO the subterranean cavern, he found Ava sitting beside the supplies he'd dumped out of the pack before leaving. She almost looked as if her knees had given way and she'd just slumped down to sit on her feet.

Her chin touched her chest. And she didn't look up when he splashed toward her.

Anxiety gripped him. "Ava?" He touched her shoulder.

She started, then blinked up at him with bleary eyes that glowed amber. "What?"

"Were you sleeping?"

"No." She bit her lip, her brow furrowing as she glanced around. "Maybe." Then her gaze shifted to the objects on his back. "What's that?"

He shrugged out of the pack and showed her the huge leaves he'd rolled up and awkwardly stuffed between the pack and his back. "Our bed."

She produced a weary smile. "I like the sound of that."

When she moved to help him unroll and arrange the leaves, he gently rejected her aid. He didn't like the pallor of her skin, the fatigue that slumped her shoulders, or the pain reflected in her pinched features.

"I'll get more leaves after I see to your wounds," he promised. This makeshift bed boasted fewer layers than the one they'd shared in the other cave, and he wanted her to be comfortable.

She sent him a sweet smile. "This is fine. The sand is softer than the hard ground was in the cave."

Jak'ri took her hand and encouraged her to sit down, noting the way she clamped her lips together and winced with every movement. He reached for the ties of her shirt. "Let me get this off you so I can tend your wounds."

The fact that she didn't help him testified to her fatigue. "And here I was hoping you wanted to get me naked for another reason."

He forced a smile and sent her a playful wink. "There's that, too."

When he parted the sodden material and gently drew it down over her arms, he fought the urge to curse.

"It's not as bad as it looks," she told him softly.

Yes, it was. If the gash some Gathendien *grunark* had carved across her stomach had been any deeper, she would've required surgery to repair internal organs.

More cuts—some deep, some shallow—marred her slender arms.

The shorts she wore were stained red at the waist from the blood that had poured forth from the stomach injury and sported enough blotches of pink despite their long swim that he removed those as well. They hid no more wounds, he was relieved to see. But her thigh once more bore a deep gash. And there was the shallower one on her forehead.

It infuriated him. "I wish we'd found some Z-12s."

"I forgot, what are Z-12s?"

He met her amber gaze. "Grenades that would've left little for the big cat creatures to dine upon."

She blinked. "Yeah. Those would've definitely come in handy."

"Lie back."

The fact that her eyes still glowed and she didn't protest made clear the suffering she battled.

Jak'ri leaned to one side and grabbed the medic bag. Since it was designed for use in a variety of combat situations, its contents remained dry. After retrieving the supplies he needed, he opted to tend her stomach wound first. Unlike the others, it still bled.

Jak'ri sprayed it liberally with the *retsa* and watched the cleanser swell into thick white foam that turned pink before melting away like water.

He patted it dry with a sterile medicloth.

Ava sighed. "That helps. The ocean water stung like fire."

Drek. He hadn't even thought about that. He'd been too focused on whether they would survive the jump. Before he did anything else, he sprayed the deep laceration with *imaashu* to deaden the pain.

Her tense features relaxed even more. "Oh yeah," she breathed as she closed her eyes. "That's the good stuff."

Jak'ri retrieved a tube of *cobruhk* next. Carefully pinching the sides of the gash together, he applied the wound sealant.

The bleeding finally ceased.

Relieved, he topped it with a bandage and adhered it to her skin with the clear *kesaadi* he'd coated the bottom of her feet with. Then he did the same with the cuts on her arms, her thigh, and one on her shoulder near her neck.

That one sent a chill skittering through him. Had the blade that carved it struck two or three fingers to the left, the *grunark* who wielded it might've severed her artery and caused her to bleed out.

The cut on her forehead ended up being shallow. So he just cleaned it and sprayed it with the *imaashu*.

Once the newest injuries were all taken care of, Jak'ri checked the gash that split the arch of her foot.

It was now only a slim scar.

Nevertheless, he cleaned both of her feet and again coated them with the *kesaadi*.

"Thank you," she murmured sleepily.

He pressed a kiss to her forehead, then tucked the supplies back into the medic bag.

"What about you?" she asked. "Any wounds I need to tend?"

He shook his head. "I'm distressingly free of injuries."

She smiled. "You say that like it's a bad thing."

Try though he might, he couldn't find an answering smile. "The fact that you're injured and I'm not makes me feel as though I failed you."

Yet no condemnation darkened her features. Instead, she sat up and leaned in close to press an affectionate kiss to his lips. "I'm pretty sure I didn't kill any of the assholes I fought, honey. I just distracted them. *You*, on the other hand, killed at least half a dozen. *You* reduced their numbers."

He brushed her lips with a light kiss. "According to my translator, honey is a sticky, sweet, golden substance produced by insects on Earth."

Amusement sparkled in her eyes as the amber glow faded to brown. "It's also the English equivalent of the Purveli endearment *sakara*."

He rubbed noses with her. "Shall I call you honey then?"

She grinned. "You can call me anything you want, handsome."

Jak'ri pressed another loving kiss to her lips, then wrapped his arms around her and just held her close, happy they'd survived another skirmish with the Gathendiens, relieved they would have more time together.

She kissed his neck. "Considering how I'd like to *spend* that time with you," she said, having read his thoughts, "I'm thinking you're right." She patted the large leaf beneath her. "We might need a few more of these leaves for a cushier bed."

He laughed. "I'll go get them now."

It took him longer than he'd hoped. The island might be small when compared to the continent they'd left behind, but it was more mountainous, the ground sloping steeply enough that it was more of a climb than a hike. And the trees that bore the leaves he sought were, of course, farther away.

He found some of the berries and fruit they'd been enjoying since they'd landed on K-54973 and filled his pack with them. He'd already picked quite a bit on his first foray but would like to limit their time aboveground as much as he could. And the water in the subterranean cavern was cold enough to keep the fruit fresh longer if they stored it in the medic bag and submerged it.

Surprisingly, the island bore some of the same wildlife they'd seen on the continent: *leapers,* large simians Ava likened to *gorillas* on Earth, and hoofed, antler-bearing mammals. He didn't know if that meant those animals were exceptional swimmers or if the winters here were simply harsh enough to freeze the ocean's surface and allow them passage in the coldest months. Either way, the realization that he and Ava weren't the only significant heat signatures to be found here relieved his mind.

Ava was asleep when he returned and didn't rouse at his approach.

It left him uneasy, as did her pallor.

Jak'ri set the leaves and fruit aside and started unpacking the supply bag he'd lugged through the sea. It, too, he was surprised to discover, was waterproof, no doubt to protect both weaponry and rations from decay. So he filled it with the rest of the fruit and berries he'd collected. Keeping it submerged in the water proved to be a bit of a challenge. He had to use his spare pair of shorts to tie it to the thick stalks of the water plants.

Satisfied with the results, he doffed his shirt and pants and spread them out on the sand to dry. The luminescent ore in the walls and moss on some of the surfaces provided enough light for him to see without a *hesku.* They might need the heat the remaining *heskus* could provide, though, if the temperature dropped.

Jak'ri arranged their weapons—including the stun grenades—so they would be within easy reach. Then he lay beside Ava on his back, his shoulder touching hers. He wanted to roll them both onto their sides and curl his body protectively around hers. But he often wrapped an arm around her waist when he did—either consciously to snuggle her closer or unconsciously in his sleep—and he didn't want to risk putting any pressure on her abdomen. The *imaashu* would prevent her from experiencing pain the contact would ordinarily engender that might alert them if she started bleeding again.

It was a deep wound. He would be consumed with worry if she hadn't repeatedly assured him she was very hard to kill now.

Even so, he feared for her well-being. So he settled for just the simple contact of his shoulder against hers... after ensuring it wouldn't aggravate the cut on her arm.

Sighing, he closed his eyes and wished for the thousandth time that Ziv'ri were still with them.

Tears pricked his closed lids.

I miss you, brother, he mentally broadcast to the cosmos as grief rose. *We both do.* He slid his hand closer to Ava and clasped hers.

Mourning Ziv'ri's loss had been made all the harder by the fact that Jak'ri hadn't seen his brother die. Hadn't been able to claim his body for the traditional Purveli ceremony that marked the passing of his life force from this plane to the next. Hadn't told him goodbye.

Part of him still didn't want to believe it and thought acknowledging his brother's death was a betrayal when he should be out there searching for him instead.

But they *had* searched for him. They'd risked everything to search each of the labs and holding cells on the Gathendien ship before they'd left it. They'd called out to him over and over again for days. And the Gathendiens hadn't dosed Ava with *nahalae*, so she would've heard his responses if Ziv'ri had made any.

Wherever you are, please watch over us, he thought, *as I know you would if you were here.* He swallowed hard. *And join us in our dreams so we can be with you again.*

Opening his eyes, he stared up at the cavern's ceiling and the glowing streaks of ore that painted it. Sleep was slow to settle upon him despite his fatigue. It felt as though hours passed before awareness of their plight, concern for Ava, and the anguish of his brother's loss finally receded, allowing the world to gradually slip away.

Jak'ri!

He jerked awake, his heart pounding in his chest at Ava's terrified cry.

Jak'ri, pleeeeeeese! Answer me!

Bolting upright, he looked around frantically and found the cavern as tranquil as it had been before he'd fallen asleep, the water calm, the quiet broken only by an occasional drop of water falling from one of the stalactites.

His gaze shifted to Ava, who had rolled away from him in her sleep.

Curled up in a tight ball, she emitted a fractured sob.

Jak'riiiiiii!

Scrambling onto his knees, he reached for her, then cursed when he almost clasped her arm over one of her bandages. "Ava." He brushed her dark hair back from her face and revealed pale cheeks that glistened with tears. A faint shudder rippled through her. "Ava," he called louder, giving her shoulder a little shake.

Her breath hitched with another sob. *Jak'riiii!*

Swearing, he slid an arm under her shoulders, turned her toward him, and lifted her upper body so he could cradle her against his chest. *Ava*, he called, telepathically this time, as he gave her another little shake in an attempt to rouse her. When it failed, he peered into her mind… and found himself in a nightmare.

One they both feared may yet come to pass.

Ava was back in the Gathendiens' clutches, on the ship, in a cell. And the guards were dragging her toward the operating table in the lab.

In the dream, she lacked the newfound strength to fight them, her struggles gaining her nothing.

And in the dream, she was alone.

Ava! he shouted.

She jerked in his arms and awoke with a gasp. Her eyes glowed bright amber as she looked around frantically then met his gaze. As soon as reality banished the nightmare and she realized where they were, she threw her arms around him, buried her face in his neck, and wept.

Jak'ri wrapped his arms around her and pressed a kiss to her temple. "It's okay," he whispered soothingly. "It's okay. It was just a dream. We're safe now." He hoped.

When he shifted and sat cross-legged, she pressed closer, curling up into a ball in his lap, her knees practically touching her chest. Jak'ri wrapped his arms around all of her and just held her, murmuring calming words even as he mentally cursed the Gathendiens.

"I was back on the ship," she whispered brokenly. "I dreamed we were both back on the ship. And they took you away." Her breath hiccupped with another sob. "They took you away like they did Ziv'ri. And I couldn't hear you anymore. I kept calling you and calling you. But you didn't answer. I thought..."

She'd thought the Gathendiens had killed him the way they had Ziv'ri, leaving her all alone.

The grief that had swamped him hours earlier returned with a vengeance, bringing a lump to his throat.

Jak'ri buried his face in her hair and rocked her slightly. "I'm here, *sakara*," he murmured, his voice hoarse. "I won't leave you."

Her shudders began to subside, her grip on him becoming a little less desperate. "We fight together. We flee together. Or we die together," she said.

He nodded. "We fight together. We flee together. Or we die together."

At last, her tense muscles began to loosen as she relaxed against him.

"We *won't* let them take us," he vowed.

Ava leaned back a little and looked up at him. Her brown eyes still bore an amber glow as she cupped his face in her hands. "I love you, Jak'ri."

Dipping his head, he brushed his lips against hers in a tender caress. "I love you, too. More with every breath I take."

The amber light in her eyes brightened as she drew him down for another kiss, this one deeper, hotter, and pulse-poundingly arousing. "Make me forget," she pleaded, between teasing strokes of her tongue. "Make me forget everything but us and the way I feel when I'm in your arms."

For a moment, he did, giving in to the fire she ignited and plundering her sweet mouth. Both of them were still wonderfully bare, no clothing impeding the heated explorations of his hands. And he *loved* the feel of her, the dichotomy of so much strength being packed into such a small, seemingly fragile form.

Her soft skin, ornamented with those cute spots she called *freckles*, called to him.

Jak'ri vowed he would kiss every one of them. Then his fingers brushed the *kesaadi* that held one of her bandages in place.

Swearing, he drew back.

"What?" she asked, lowering her lips to his neck.

"You're injured."

She shook her head. "It doesn't hurt."

"That's the *imaashu* masking the pain," he told her, trying to stay strong and do the right thing.

"*This*," she said as she took one of his hands and brought it to her breast, "is the right thing."

And curse him, he couldn't prevent himself from cupping the plump, pale mound and drawing a thumb over the taut peak.

Gasping, she squirmed against him, rubbing her hip against his hard shaft.

He groaned, his resolve weakening.

Those bright amber eyes met his. "We don't know how long we have before they find us."

"*If* they find us."

"A month. A week. A day. An hour."

"Or forever."

"You don't believe that any more than I do."

No, he didn't. The Gathendiens now knew with certainty that he and Ava had landed on this planet. The ship they'd escaped was most likely on its way here, *if* it hadn't already arrived. So even if the two of them managed to slay every Gathendien that had already come looking for them, the *grunarks* aboard the warship would just send more.

She shook her head. "I don't want to squander the time we have together. I want to live each moment as if it's our last."

Because it very well could be.

Dipping his head, he captured her lips in a desperate kiss. "Just tell me if I hurt you," he whispered.

Nodding, she clutched him tight as he eased her back over one arm so he could lower his lips to her breast. She moaned, burying her fingers in his hair.

Jak'ri stroked and sucked and teased the sensitive tip with his tongue while the fingers of his free hand played with the other. "You're so beautiful," he murmured, entranced by the taste of her, the feel of her, the passion she exhibited as she moved against him.

He slid one hand down to her bottom to lock her against him, then rose onto his knees, turned, and gently laid her on her back.

As soon as he pulled back a bit, she parted her thighs to make room for him. But Jak'ri didn't thrust his hard length inside her. Instead, he trailed his lips down over her lightly muscled abs, pressed a gentle kiss to the bandage on her stomach, and continued on to the dark curls below.

She sucked in a breath when he drew his warm, wet tongue over the little nub that gave her such pleasure. A low moan followed when he repeated the gesture.

Burying her hands in his hair, Ava fisted it and urged him on as he licked and flicked and sucked and stroked, increasing her pleasure until she arched up against him, wanting more.

"Jak'ri," she moaned. "*Sakara.*"

And what that Purveli endearment did to him.

He slid a hand up to cup her breast and teased the taut peak, matching the rhythm of his tongue. Slipping the other hand between them, he eased two fingers inside her, nearly groaning at the feel of her, so warm and wet and tight.

Her breath came in gasps as she writhed beneath him. "So good," she panted. "More."

He thrust his fingers deep, pinched the hard tip of her breast, and applied more pressure with his tongue.

Ava stiffened, threw her head back, and called his name. Jak'ri groaned as her inner muscles clamped down around his fingers, wishing his hard shaft was buried deep inside her instead of his fingers.

"Let me up," she whispered as the pleasure faded.

He instantly withdrew his touch. "Did I hurt you?"

Shaking her head, she rose onto her knees, pushed him onto his back, and straddled him. "No. I just wanted to do this."

Heat seared him when she reached down between them, curled her fingers around his hard length, and guided him to her entrance.

Jak'ri groaned as she sank down on him, seating him deep, those warm, wet walls squeezing him as he stretched her. "Ava." Her name escaped his lips, guttural and full of need.

She moaned. "You're so big."

He clamped his hands onto her hips and ground against her. "You're so tight."

Lips parting on a gasp, she met his gaze and began to move.

The muscles of her thighs flexed as she rose, sliding along his shaft, then plunging down again.

Now *he* was the one who demanded, "More."

The sensual smile she sent him merely heightened his need, as did the motion of her breasts as she rode him. Jak'ri palmed them both, stroking and squeezing.

Head falling back, she moaned and raked his chest lightly with her nails. When she curled her fingers in the hair there and tugged, he thrust up against her. Pleasure rose, higher and higher, urging them on. She rotated her hips, altering the angle hers met his. Jak'ri picked up the pace, driving her onward, struggling to hold back his release until she found ecstasy again.

Sliding a hand down her stomach, he bypassed the bandage and teased her curls with his fingers.

"Jak'ri," she moaned.

He stroked her pleasure center as he thrust up to meet her, again and again, the pressure building and building until she cried out. Her inner muscles clamped down around his hard shaft, squeezing and releasing—so *drekking* good—until he joined her, spilling his heat inside her.

As the ripples of pleasure gradually subsided, she sank limply onto his chest.

Worry about the wound on her stomach resurfaced.

Jak'ri rolled them onto their sides, bodies still joined.

He started to put a little space between them so he could check her bandage but stopped when she tilted her head back. What he saw in her glowing amber gaze made everything else dissipate into nothingness.

"I really do love you," she said softly, the tenderness in her pretty features utterly entrancing him.

"I love you, Ava." The words seemed appallingly inadequate, only expressing a fraction of what he felt for her. But she seemed to understand.

Smiling, she pressed a light kiss to his lips, then snuggled against him.

I don't want to squander whatever time we have together, she'd said. *I want to live each moment as if it's our last.*

As sleep crept up on him once more, Jak'ri vowed to do just that.

CHAPTER SEVENTEEN

"KEEP LOOKING. THEY *must* be here."

Ava jerked awake. Fear sliced through her, chilling her blood. That voice… It had been Gathendien.

And it hadn't been part of the nightmare that had gripped her, the third since they'd sought refuge beneath the compact island.

She sat up, her hands beginning to shake as she looked for Jak'ri.

He stood a few feet away with his back to her, his toes inches from the edge of the water, staring intently toward the cavern's underwater entrance.

Distant voices filled her sluggish mind, those of multiple Gathendiens.

They had to be close for her to pick up on them so clearly.

"Jak'ri," she whispered.

He glanced at her over his shoulder, his face grim. "They're searching the island. I heard them coming when I went out to fetch fresh water."

"Did they see you?"

He shook his head. "I never left the ocean and hid among the trees that brush the water's surface."

"How many are there?"

"Eight by my count. More linger on the continent, searching the water at the base of the cliffs."

Motion down by his hip drew her attention.

He clasped a Bex-7 stun grenade in one hand, turning it over and over while he cast frequent glances at the opposite side of the lake.

"What about here? Are they searching the water along the island's coast?" They might find the passage to the cave if they did.

"Not yet. So far they've remained on land. Some are reluctant to go in the water because a large sea creature slew two of their number closer to the continent."

Crap. She and Jak'ri hadn't encountered anything larger than the friendly dolphin-like creatures on their way here. "Maybe you shouldn't venture out anymore." What if one of those things attacked *him*?

He shook his head. "I can protect myself from such. A *senshi* usually poses no danger to marine life. But in water, it's easier for me to focus it on an individual. When we do, it can harm and deter large predators."

"Oh." Falling silent, she tried to tune in to the Gathendiens' thoughts. "I don't think they brought enough *nahalae* with them. I can read some of their minds."

He nodded. "As can I."

She sifted through them, one soldier at a time.

As she did, some of her anxiety lessened. They had no idea that a cavern and underwater passages lay beneath the island. And most of the Gathendiens considered searching the small landmass an exercise in futility, certain their former prisoners had met their deaths on the rocks at the base of the cliffs. Only a couple of them believed she and Jak'ri might have made it here and hoped to find them, worried that their emperor would execute them all if they lost both a Purveli and an Earthling test subject.

It didn't occur to Ava until then to question how she could understand them so well. *Or* Jak'ri.

She frowned. When the Lasarans had attempted to implant translator chips like hers in the brains of the Immortal Guardians, the symbiotic virus her friends housed had rejected it and expelled it like shrapnel.

Yet hers remained.

Did the virus view it as a part of her because it had already been present before she became infected?

Hmm. That was a puzzle she would have to solve later.

When Ava rose, a bout of dizziness struck. Though mild, it was enough to make her freeze in place until it faded.

Damn it. She was weakening. The Immortal Guardians who had traveled with her aboard the *Kandovar* had all transfused themselves regularly and had suffered few wounds. So she really had no idea how swift a decline she should expect.

Her sunburn had faded to a light tan, the prickling in her skin now gone. The worst of her wounds—the ones on her stomach and her thigh—had healed only enough to keep them from bleeding unless she exerted herself... as she did whenever she and Jak'ri made love. Unfortunately, that seemed to be the extent of it. Every cut she'd incurred during their last battle with the Gathendiens remained. None had faded to faint pink scars or disappeared the way her previous wounds had. And all still hurt unless Jak'ri sprayed them with the *imaashu*.

When he'd seen the blood on her bandages after they'd made love their first night here, he had suggested they abstain to give her time to heal. But she'd nixed that idea quickly, using her hands and mouth to convince him otherwise.

And, too, she suspected he felt the same desperate need she did to cram as much living and loving as they could into their time together because they didn't know when it might end.

Or *how* it might end.

"How long have they been here?" she asked him.

"A few hours."

Her eyebrows flew up. "Really?" And she hadn't heard them until now?

He nodded. "You were sleeping deeply." Though the statement was simple and straightforward, she heard the concern that lay behind it.

Had he noticed she was weakening?

Ava sent him a smile and a wink. "You must have worn me out."

His expression warmed as he returned her smile with one full of affection.

As he swung away to keep an eye on the cavern's entrance, she grabbed one of the large hollowed-out fruit rinds they'd been using as bowls. This one contained a bottle of *wosuur* for cleaning their teeth, a canteen, and a few other supplies.

Nooks and crannies abounded at the back of the cavern. Jak'ri had chosen the largest and turned it into a latrine of sorts for them, digging a deep hole in the sand with an alien tool she couldn't remember the name of that had been among the supplies he'd packed. Though she would definitely prefer the sleek lavs on the ship and weird toilets in the pods, she had to admit this was better than peeing in the bushes and hoping none of the vegetation would give her a rash like poison ivy would. And the dark sand she scooped into the hole each time she used it worked as well as kitty litter.

Once she completed her morning ablutions, she joined him by the lake.

Wrapping an arm around her, Jak'ri pulled her up against his side and dropped a kiss on her forehead. He frowned, then kissed her forehead again.

"What?" she asked, curling an arm around his waist.

He pressed his cheek to her forehead. "You feel warm."

Yep. She was a little feverish today. Instead of mentioning that, however, she sent him a wry smile. "Probably because I still blush every time I use our makeshift lav while you're here. If you feel my cheeks, I'm sure they're warm, too."

He chuckled. "They do look a little pink."

They stood quietly, holding each other and listening to the mental mutterings of the bastards above them.

Ava nibbled her lower lip.

She thought the fever worrisome. It was something new that hadn't plagued her when she'd been injured before. But what could she do about it? She was still unwilling to risk infusing herself with Jak'ri's blood unless it became absolutely necessary... as it likely would if the Gathendiens found this cave and she needed a sudden influx of strength to fight them off.

Otherwise...

She wouldn't *die* if she didn't infuse herself. She would simply continue to weaken until she slipped into that odd stasis Immortal Guardians did sometimes. While vampires would die if they suffered immense blood loss, immortals—with their enhanced DNA—instead drifted into a peculiar state of hibernation like that of a tardigrade, their heart rate and breathing reduced to such an extent that emergency room doctors would declare them dead. Then they slept until a new blood source came along.

It was a scary prospect, one that nevertheless appealed to Ava more than possibly dying if Jak'ri's blood wasn't compatible with the virus.

Hopefully, it wouldn't come to either option.

If it did though, she'd have to warn Jak'ri so he wouldn't mistake her stillness and lack of response for death.

"They're leaving," he murmured suddenly.

She blinked, having been so lost in her thoughts that she hadn't noticed. "All of them?"

He nodded. "The sun is setting. They need to get back to the continent before the others activate a perimeter shield to hold off the owners of those large paw prints we found outside the escape pod." His lips quirked up. "Apparently the big cats, as you call them, feasted upon the Gathendiens we slew on our way here."

She faked a shudder. "As bad as those guys smell, I would think they'd taste even worse."

He laughed.

"Did you find anything in their minds about the Gathendien warship?"

"They've lost contact with it."

Surprise coursed through her, as did hope. "They have?"

"Yes."

"Why?"

"They don't know. But they expect it to follow them here."

And there went the hope. She frowned. "Could us shooting the computers in the labs have caused them to lose contact?"

He shook his head. "I wouldn't think those would be deeply linked with their communications array."

"Hmm. That's a puzzle then."

"Exactly."

She smiled up at him. "It's a nice thought though, isn't it? Us taking out their communications array while we escaped?"

Smiling, he dropped a kiss on her lips. "Very nice."

They listened as the Gathendiens piled into whatever craft had brought them to the island. Ava took pleasure in every disgruntled thought that passed through their pea brains. They were getting frustrated. And nervous. Some feared the repercussions they would face if they returned to the warship empty-handed.

"Is it mean of me to hope they'll get their asses kicked by their higher-ups?" she asked.

He snorted. "*Srul* no. I hope they'll all be executed."

Some of them were already grumbling, wondering how much longer they would have to keep searching. They had considered themselves fortunate when they'd been sent to comb the island but expected to have to take their turns in the cold water on the morrow, hoping to find whatever remained of her and Jak'ri's corpses.

Or maybe just *her* corpse. Most of them believed she'd died on the rocks and that Jak'ri had survived the dive and was probably halfway across the planet by now.

"Seriously?" she demanded with a bit of pique. "I kicked a lot of ass on board that damn ship, then again in the forest, and they automatically think I died and you lived? That's some misogynistic bullshit."

He grinned. "Maybe they're just *hoping* you died so the *rest* of them won't get their asses kicked."

She laughed. "I like that explanation much better."

The Gathendiens must have felt confident they'd performed a thorough enough search because they didn't return to the island the next day. Or the one after that. Nevertheless, Ava felt uneasy about Jak'ri venturing out of the cavern again.

He wouldn't let her accompany him when he did, insisting she stay safe and dry. He'd noticed the fever. The weakness. The sluggishness that clung to her long after she woke.

He asked again if he could give her a *silna* to speed her healing, concerned that she might be suffering some kind of bacterial infection from the ocean water that had infiltrated her wounds. But she refused, afraid the *silna* might eradicate the virus.

If the virus died, she would have no immune system. So she'd take her chances without the *silna*.

Since she only had two shirts, Ava had to wash one every day.

Jak'ri offered to do it for her, but she refused. There was no reason she couldn't do it herself. Besides, when he was topside, there was little else for her to do.

The oversized shirt that had been cut and torn in multiple places during the most recent battle was already looking so frayed and ragged that she set it aside. That only left her with the one that fit her a little better.

Shrugging it off, she pursed her lips. If she and Jak'ri were alone on the planet, she would just remain topless while she cleaned the shirt and let it dry. They'd been naked around each often enough now that she no longer felt self-conscious. But the damn Gathendiens were still loitering on the cliff. And if the bastards surprised them with a return trip and actually discovered the cave, she didn't want to be caught with her pants down or—in this instance—her shirt off.

Jak'ri must not either, because they both now slept in their clothes.

Ava rummaged through the medic bag in hopes of finding something useful. The best she could come up with was a roll of bandages she wrapped horizontally across her breasts, then up over her shoulders several times until she had formed an improvised sports bra.

"It'll have to do," she muttered and knelt beside the lake to wash her shirt and spare shorts. She would prefer to soak the fabric in some nice, fragrant laundry detergent or drop it in one of those sleek clothing decon units. Alas, neither was at hand, so seawater and sand had to do the job.

Once she twisted it and squeezed as much water out as she could, she held it up for inspection. "Meh." It looked a little on the grimy side, but at least it didn't stink. If their troubles with the Gathendiens had ended, she'd just spray their clothes with that awesome *retsa* stuff and let it clean the fabric the way it cleaned her wounds.

But their troubles seemed far from over.

After spreading the shirt on a rock to dry, she rose.

The cavern whirled around her.

Swearing, Ava staggered to one side and had to brace her feet to keep from toppling over. She threw out her arms as if she were standing on the deck of a ship that listed this way and that, which was pretty much how she felt.

After several seconds, the dizziness ebbed.

She glanced toward the water, glad that Jak'ri hadn't been here to witness that. He cautiously ventured out twice a day to monitor the Gathendiens' actions and to listen for possible rescuers, telepathically scouring every mind within range in hopes that one might be Purveli. Or Segonian. Or Lasaran.

Sometimes he did the same at night but remained in the water in case any large nocturnal predators roamed the island. He hadn't encountered any yet, but better to be safe than sorry.

As if her thoughts had summoned him, his form appeared in the lake, arrowing toward her with powerful strokes. He rose from the water, chest bare, pants clinging to his powerful thighs, all visible hair silver.

Ava loved watching his hair dry, seeing the strands slowly darken until they were black once more. "Hi, handsome."

His gaze dropped to her chest.

Spreading her arms, she showed off her improvised bra top. "What do you think? It's a sports bra."

As he stopped before her, one side of his mouth turned up in a sheepish smile. "Is it wrong that my first thought was, *Is it removable?*"

She laughed. "No. And you can remove it anytime you want. I just didn't want to walk around topless while my shirt dries in case we end up having unexpected visitors."

He slipped a pack that bulged with fresh fruit and freshly filled canteens off his shoulder. "I don't think that's going to happen. The Gathendiens are still searching the mainland's shore. Most still think we're dead." He winced. "Or that you're dead and I've swum far away, losing myself among the marine life."

"Jerks," she grumbled.

"Agreed."

"Have they had any contact with the warship?"

"No. Still nothing."

That was excellent news.

Moving closer, she rested her hands on his chest. "So you're saying we may have quite a bit of free time on our hands?"

He dipped his head and rubbed noses with her. "Yes."

"Oh my," she breathed as he curled an arm around her and drew her up against his body, still cool from the water. "However shall we occupy ourselves?"

Smiling, he teased her lips with a light brush of his. "I believe I have an idea or two."

———◆◇◆———

J AK'RI HURRIED THROUGH THE forest, eager to return to Ava.

They had been sheltering in the subterranean cavern for almost a week now. The dizziness Ava suffered was worsening. She still felt overly warm. Her movements grew more sluggish by the hour, as though fatigue constantly strove to drag her down. And even the bright amber light that used to flare to life in her pretty brown eyes had dimmed to almost nothing.

It was as if all the life was slowly being drained from her.

And it scared the *srul* out of him. Jak'ri didn't know what to do. He'd checked her injuries again, concerned that one might have become infected. And though they weren't healing the way the one on her foot had, none appeared to be worse or inflamed.

He didn't understand what was happening, why she wasn't getting better.

Some of the island *leapers* followed him through the forest, swinging or jumping from branch to branch. The ones here had dimmer stripes than those on the mainland. They were also larger and had softer hoots of a much deeper tone that didn't reverberate throughout the forest.

He took little comfort in their companionship, though. He hadn't wanted to come out today, hadn't wanted to leave Ava. But afflicted as she was with fever, she needed to consume more fresh water to stave off dehydration. And he kept hoping a constant supply of fresh fruit would benefit her.

His feet sank into soft, dark sand seconds before the trees parted and blue ocean stretched before him. Jak'ri paused only long enough to ensure no silent craft hovered within view, then splashed forward and dove beneath the surface.

Fear for Ava continued to plague him as he swam along the shore toward the peninsula.

A shadow approached him from the dark ocean. Then another.

The playful creatures that reminded him of *raashini* and Ava of *dolphins* soon joined him. They often found him during his excursions, perhaps still intrigued by the newcomers.

When the passage that led to the cave came into view, Jak'ri didn't slow. He'd traveled it so many times now that he'd memorized the path and knew without concentrating which turns he needed to take to avoid the dead ends. The *raashini*-like creatures never followed him inside. Sometimes he wished they would, just to provide Ava with a diversion.

A dim glow grew ahead of him. He picked up speed, eager to get back to her, and had almost reached the cavern when something brushed his mind.

Startled, Jak'ri halted and swung around to face the way he'd come.

What was that?

Though fleeting, it had almost felt like a faint *senshi*.

He frowned. Was one of the *raashini*-like creatures trying to communicate with him? They had bounced some mild *senshis* off him the first time he'd encountered them. But they hadn't repeated it since.

Until now.

Were they trying to tell him something?

He felt another faint pulse.

His frown deepened. Had one of them attempted to follow him into the winding passage and become lost?

He glanced over his shoulder at the mouth of the cavern in which Ava waited, then swore and headed back toward the ocean. As much as he wanted to swiftly return to her, he couldn't let this go without investigating it. What if one of the *raashini*-like creatures had followed him and gotten caught on something?

Some of the passage's offshoots contained plants like those in the cavern that could tangle one up.

Or what if the *drekking* Gathendiens had acquired an underwater exploration vehicle?

He would much rather untangle the former than deal with the latter but encountered no marine life.

When he reached the mouth of the passage, he slowed and cautiously peered out into the vast ocean.

Nothing out of the ordinary caught his eye.

Frowning, he slowly ventured out.

Still nothing.

Even the *raashini*-like creatures were no longer in sight.

Worry niggling him, he dared to swim as far as the tip of the peninsula and peered around it, careful to remain far enough beneath the surface to prevent any Gathendiens from spotting his silver hair if they flew over in a craft.

When he did, he felt... something.

Not a *senshi*. A presence.

One that widened his eyes and drove his heart to batter his rib cage.

It couldn't be.

Ziv'ri? he called telepathically.

Yes! his brother instantly replied.

Had Jak'ri been standing, his knees would've buckled.

I'm coming, Jak'ri, Ziv'ri said. *Where are you?*

Are the Gathendiens with you? he asked, wondering how this could be.

No. I'll explain it when I reach you. Show me the way.

Jak'ri mentally broadcast the way, then spun and shot toward the passage. He didn't know how this was possible, what had happened, but Ziv'ri was alive. His brother was alive!

Jak'ri had never navigated the winding passage to the cave so quickly. *Ava*, he called mentally as he entered the cavern.

She didn't respond.

As soon as the water was shallow enough for him to stand, he breached the surface and jogged toward the shore.

Ava lay on their leafy bed, eyes closed.

"Ava," he called aloud, dropping the bag of fruit he still carried over his shoulder.

She jerked awake. Sitting up, she watched him hurry toward her. As she did, her big brown eyes filled with tears. "I was dreaming. Ziv'ri was alive and was coming to join us."

Jak'ri sank to his knees in front of her and cupped her pretty face in his palms. "It wasn't a dream, *sakara*. He's here, on the planet." Moisture welled in his eyes. "I was returning to you when I felt a mild *senshi*. I went back out to investigate and..." He smiled. "He's here. Ziv'ri's here."

Her eyes widened as her breath caught. "He's alive?" Excitement lit her feverish features. "He's really alive?"

Jak'ri nodded. "He's on the way to the cavern right now."

Releasing a happy cry, she threw her arms around his neck.

He rose, helping her to her feet and hugging her tight.

Jak'ri? Ziv'ri called.

Ava gasped.

Parting, they spun to face the water.

As soon as Jak'ri saw his brother's pale form gliding toward them beneath the surface, he ran for the shore, splashing through the shallows. Two forms broke the surface, but Jak'ri had eyes only for his brother.

Wading forward, he yanked him into a tight hug. "I thought you dead," he uttered, barely able to speak past the lump in his throat. "They said they killed you, and I could no longer sense you. Ava couldn't either."

Ziv'ri banded his arms around him in a crushing embrace, nearly squeezing the breath out of him. "They lied," he replied, his voice hoarse with emotion.

Splashing sounded beside them.

Jak'ri looked over his brother's shoulder.

A woman who was even smaller than Ava stood beside them, her body practically bare. A small band of fabric that resembled a tinier version of Ava's improvised *sports bra* hugged her breasts while an even smaller strip of fabric covered the juncture of her thighs. A sharp dagger was tucked into a strap on her hip. Aside from that, all she wore was a harness that looped over her shoulders and held what appeared to be two swords on her back.

She cast him a curious glance.

Then Ava slammed into her.

The woman's brown eyes widened as she lost her footing, fell backward out of Ava's embrace, and sank beneath the surface.

Ava stumbled, but managed to remain on her feet. A look of dismay sweeping across her features, she scrambled to help the woman, who came up sputtering. "Sorry!" Ava cried. "I'm sorry, Eliana. I'm just so happy to see you."

Jak'ri loosened his hold on his brother. This was Eliana?

"Ava." Relief washed over the woman's features seconds before Ava threw her arms around her. Eliana's eyes began to glow with amber light as her lips trembled and she hugged Ava as tightly as Jak'ri had hugged Ziv'ri.

A grunt of pain escaped Ava.

Releasing Ziv'ri, Jak'ri quickly stretched a hand toward the women. "Careful," he warned softly. "She's injured."

Alarm entered Eliana's gaze as she hastily released Ava and stepped back.

She's hurt? Ziv'ri asked telepathically, his brow furrowing as he noted the cuts on Ava's forehead and stomach. *How badly?*

"I'm okay," Ava said. But her smile faltered as she staggered suddenly.

Emitting a cry, Eliana reached for her.

But Ava turned to Jak'ri and reached for *him*.

Jak'ri quickly grasped her hands and drew her close, looping an arm around her waist. *Ava?*

"Oh crap," she muttered. "I'm *not* okay. I'm think I'm gonna..." Her eyes rolled back as her knees buckled.

Jak'ri quickly lifted her into his arms.

"Ava?" Eliana called.

"She's unconscious." He carried her out of the water and over to the bed.

Ziv'ri and Eliana followed on his heels, their concern palpable.

Kneeling, he carefully laid Ava on the large leaves.

"What's wrong with her?" Eliana asked. "What happened?"

"The Gathendiens happened," he said, unable to hide the fury and bitterness that consumed him.

Eliana knelt beside him as Ziv'ri hovered close.

"I managed to grab one of the Gathendiens' med kits when we escaped," Jak'ri told them. "I tended her wounds as well as I could. And she seemed to improve for a time." Resting a hand on her forehead, he tenderly brushed her hair back. "But she was injured again when more Gathendiens attacked us and has weakened since we came here."

Eliana looked up at Ziv'ri. "Go to Dagon. The fighting should be over by the time you reach him. Tell him Ava needs immediate medical attention and see if they can land the shuttle on the island."

Nodding, Ziv'ri sent Jak'ri a look of concern, then turned and dove into the water.

Jak'ri grabbed one of the hollowed-out fruit rinds they used as a bowl and moved toward the bag he'd dropped earlier. It only took a second to retrieve a canteen and fill the bowl with some of the fresh water he'd collected.

"Ava?" Eliana spoke softly.

As Jak'ri walked back toward her, she rested a hand where his had been and smoothed a thumb across Ava's forehead, careful to avoid the cut that marred it.

"She's been tired and sluggish for a few days now." He knelt on the other side of Ava and dipped a cloth in the water. After squeezing out the excess, he draped it across Ava's forehead. This was the first time she'd lost consciousness. It scared the *srul* out of him.

Ava's friend extended her hand. "I'm Eliana."

He clasped her forearm. "I'm Jak'ri. Ava has mentioned you often. She said you were the one who enabled her to escape the *Kandovar* before it was destroyed, that you put her in the escape pod."

"Yes." Releasing him, she took Ava's hand. "I'm sorry it took me so long to find her." She looked tormented, as though she considered it a failure on her part that she hadn't arrived sooner with whatever reinforcements she'd brought. She mustered a faint smile. "To find *both* of you. But I was lost myself for a while."

He nodded, wondering what she'd had to endure to get here and how she'd come to be with Ziv'ri. "She feared you hadn't survived."

"I nearly didn't."

He resumed stroking Ava's hair. "What of the others? The other women from Earth? Ava has been very worried about them."

Eliana's throat worked with a swallow. "So far only one other has been found. She's safe on Lasara. We're still searching for the rest."

The news would cause Ava great sorrow.

Silence fell between them. Jak'ri wanted to ply Eliana with questions: How had she come to be here? How had she joined forces with Ziv'ri? How had Ziv'ri escaped the Gathendiens' clutches? And what forces had carried them here?

But concern for Ava kept him silent as he hoped those forces—whoever they might be—could help her.

Sensing Ziv'ri's approach, he glanced toward the lake.

Water splashed as his brother strode out of the water. He was even thinner than he'd been back on the Gathendien ship and bore new scars. But despite that, he looked good. His eyes were alert. He didn't breathe hard from his swim. And he walked with his shoulders back instead of slumping wearily.

"The transport was already hovering above the island when I left the cavern," he announced.

Transport?

A large form encased in exo-armor rose up behind Ziv'ri. Water sluiced off it and obscured the wearer's face until the helmet's visor slid up.

Relief filled Jak'ri.

A Segonian. One with a somewhat familiar face, though he couldn't produce a name.

"Dagon." Rising, Eliana hurried past Ziv'ri and threw herself into the man's armor-clad arms.

Right. Commander Dagon. Jak'ri had only seen him once or twice from a distance when he'd attended the Aldebarian Alliance war games.

Dagon embraced Eliana with a familiarity that bespoke a close relationship. "You're all right?"

She nodded. "You?"

"I'm well. Ziv'ri said Ava requires medical attention."

Again she nodded, worry pinching her pale features. "She's injured and lost consciousness right after we arrived."

The Segonian commander patted her back as more exo-armor-clad forms emerged from the water behind him. "The *Ranasura* arrived just as the battle ended. It's positioned above the island now."

The *Ranasura*? Jak'ri rose, but remained close to Ava as he turned to face his brother. *How the* srul *did you end up on a Segonian warship?*

Ziv'ri shook his head. *Though I know it sounds absurd, the Gathendiens put me on it. They wanted me to commandeer it and seize the other Earth female.* When Jak'ri just stared at him blankly, Ziv'ri smiled. *I'll tell you all after we help Ava.*

One of the armor-clad warriors behind Commander Dagon raised his helmet's visor.

Eliana greeted him with relief. "Adaos."

"Dagon said you require a medic."

"Ava does. She's right over there." She pointed.

The Segonian strode past her, issuing orders with the manner of one accustomed to being in command. His eyes met Jak'ri's as they both knelt beside Ava's pale form. "Chief Medical Officer Adaos of the *Ranasura*."

"Jak'ri A'daar of Purvel."

"How long as she been unconscious?"

"Since shortly after Eliana and Ziv'ri arrived." Jak'ri stuck close to Ava, refusing to relinquish her hand when the medic retrieved a handheld scanner and proceeded to pass it over her still form. "This is the first time she's lost consciousness," he murmured. "But dizziness has been afflicting her of late and she's been growing weaker every day since she was injured by the Gathendiens."

Eliana and Dagon murmured to each other near the lake, but Jak'ri's attention remained fixed on Ava and Chief Medical Officer Adaos.

Another medic came forward and knelt beside Adaos. Reaching into his bag, he withdrew a hover gurney that was only the width and length of a large data tablet. Holding it just above the sand, he pressed a corner. The board extended until it was long and wide enough to carry a Segonian warrior, then hovered in the air.

Adaos studied the scanner as results flickered across its screen.

Ziv'ri sank to his knees beside Jak'ri and rested a hand on his shoulder. *Is it her wounds?* he asked telepathically.

It was so good to hear his brother's voice in his head again. *I don't know,* Jak'ri admitted. *I tended them as well as I could, and they don't look inflamed, but... clearly something is wrong.*

The silence stretched.

"Can you help her?" Jak'ri asked when he could take it no longer.

Adaos met his gaze and offered him a kind smile. "Yes. She will recover swiftly once we get her to the *Ranasura's* med bay."

Ziv'ri gave his shoulder a squeeze. *You can trust him. He's the reason I'm alive today.*

Jak'ri met his brother's silver gaze. And at last, the tension that knotted his shoulders began to ease.

Beyond him, Commander Dagon—who had removed his helmet at some point—pressed a kiss to Eliana's dark, wet hair and rested his chin atop her head. "We'll take good care of her, *milessia*," he vowed softly.

Eliana leaned against him. "Thank you."

CHAPTER EIGHTEEN

AVA SIGHED AS CONSCIOUSNESS crept up on her. Thank goodness. She'd been having yet another monstrous nightmare in which the Gathendiens had her at their mercy. In this one, she'd been strapped to a damn operating table again and they'd been cutting her open without administering any sedatives or painkillers. Jak'ri had been manacled to the table beside her, undergoing the same. And Ziv'ri...

Moisture welled in her eyes.

Ziv'ri's corpse had lain atop a table beyond his brother.

But it had been a dream, she reminded herself. Just another nightmare. One of many that had dogged her ever since she and Jak'ri had fought the Gathendiens in the forest. She didn't know why she was having them. She and Jak'ri were safe now. The Gathendiens would never find them here in the cavern. They—

She opened her eyes.

A jolt of absolute terror shook her as she sucked in a breath.

She wasn't in the cavern with its dark sands and pretty glowing walls.

She lay on an operating table in a stark white lab.

"No," she murmured.

Instead of the scent of the ocean, the air carried an antiseptic smell. And where dark rocks with luminescent streaks should lie above her, advanced medical technology instead clung to the ceiling.

Horror suffused her. She was back on the ship. The Gathendiens must have found them and...

She was back on the fucking ship!

Despair inundated her. "No." Her voice rose with each denial. "No, no, *no!*"

A tall figure abruptly loomed over her.

Starting, she threw up her hands to defend herself.

"Ava," a voice said. A deep voice she knew and loved.

"Jak'ri?" She blinked against the bright overhead lights.

"Yes." His handsome face swam above her, full of concern, as he took her hands and carried them to his lips. "It's okay," he murmured soothingly. "You're okay."

Sitting up, she shook her head. "How did they find us?" Throwing her arms around him, she buried her face in his chest. "How did the Gathendiens get us back on their ship?"

"They didn't," a second voice said.

Ava gasped. Releasing Jak'ri, she gaped up at the man who moved to stand beside him. "Ziv'ri?"

He grinned. "Surprised to see me?"

"Yes!" Legs dangling over the side of the bed, she drew him into a hug. He was so thin! Even more so than the last time she'd seen him on the Gathendien ship. "How is this possible? We thought you died!"

"I almost did," he admitted as he returned her embrace. "But I *couldn't.* If I did, Jak'ri would get to keep my hovercycle."

A laugh escaped her despite the grim circumstances. She was *so* glad to see him again. Leaning back, she swept the tears from her cheeks and stared at them both. "What happened? How did the Gathendiens recapture us?"

"They didn't," Jak'ri said, his manner surprisingly relaxed as he shifted closer and curled an arm around her.

Ziv'ri nodded. "We're on a Segonian warship. *The Ranasura.*"

Hope rose. The Segonians were allies of the Lasarans! "We are?" She looked up at Jak'ri. "Did they receive your distress call?"

"No. Ziv'ri snuck onto their ship."

She shook her head, completely baffled. "How?" The last time they'd seen him, the Gathendiens had been dragging Ziv'ri away.

"The, uh..." His brow furrowed. "What was that Earth term you used that I liked so much?" He thought a moment, then his features lightened. "Ah, yes. The dumbass Gathendiens sent me."

She stared at him. "What?"

"They learned another Earth female was aboard the *Ranasura* and forced me to infiltrate the ship."

"How could they force you to infiltrate a ship?"

Jak'ri pressed a kiss to her temple. "They monitored his progress and told him that every hour he delayed enacting the plan they would inflict more pain upon us. If he failed, they'd kill us both... slowly and painfully."

Fury rose. "Those total assholes!"

Ziv'ri grinned. "It's okay. It didn't go the way they thought it would."

The door to the large room they were in slid up.

"Wait. Where are we?" Ava asked, still trying to catch up. "Is this a lab?"

Her eyes widened when Eliana strode inside.

"Nope." Her friend grinned. "You're in the *Ranasura's* med bay."

Releasing a cry of happiness, Ava leapt off the bed and hurled herself at her friend.

Eliana caught her and hugged her so tightly she nearly cut off Ava's breath.

Whatever pants Ava was wearing dropped to her ankles. She swore. "Please tell me this isn't one of those hospital gowns that shows your bare ass in back."

Eliana laughed. "I said the same thing when that happened to me. It isn't." She stepped back. "And it's actually not a gown. It's a shirt I cut the sleeves off. Segonians are *drekking* tall."

Ava glanced down. She did indeed appear to be wearing a large shirt that fell almost to her knees. And the man who stepped through the doorway behind Eliana was definitely tall. Standing well over six feet, he had broad shoulders, a muscular build, and skin that bore enough of a bronze hue to identify him as someone not from Earth.

He was also handsome as hell.

But not as handsome as Jak'ri, she thought as she glanced at the Purveli brothers.

He smiled, likely picking up her thoughts, and strolled over to join them, Ziv'ri at his side.

Feeling weird standing there with oversized pants pooled around her ankles, she stepped out of them and surreptitiously kicked them aside.

Eliana jerked a thumb over her shoulder. "This is Dagon. He's Commander of the *Ranasura.*"

"It's nice to meet you," Ava said.

Commander Dagon performed a slight bow. "Good to meet you, Ava."

Eliana leaned forward as though imparting a confidence and whispered loudly enough for everyone in the room to hear, "I'm totally smitten with him."

Commander Dagon grinned.

Ava did, too. Her friend did indeed look smitten... and very happy as she leaned into the imposing man's side and curled an arm around him.

Ava motioned to the Purveli men who now stood protectively on either side of her. "Have you met Jak'ri and Ziv'ri?"

Eliana nodded. "They insisted on watching over you while you slept." She sent Jak'ri a sweet smile. "I don't think Jak'ri has left your side for more than a minute. He must be exhausted."

Ava studied them all. Eliana made it sound like Ava had slept for quite a while. "How long was I out?"

"A couple of days," she said.

Ava's jaw dropped. She looked up at Jak'ri. "I was?"

Nodding, he rested a hand on her back and gave it a caress. *She said such is normal, that the virus causes those infected with it to sleep deeply while they heal. But I admit I began to fear you wouldn't awaken.*

And the dark shadows she now noticed beneath his silvery eyes testified to his fatigue.

Sorry to have worried him, Ava leaned into his side.

"How do you feel?" Eliana asked, her expression sobering.

Ava shrugged. "Okay." Surprise coursed through her as it dawned on her she really did. Glancing down, she inspected her arms and discovered that all of her wounds were gone. Every cut. Every bruise. Every gash. So was the annoying weakness and dizziness that had bedeviled her in recent days. "Actually, I feel *better* than okay. I feel pretty great." She sent Ava a wry smile. "Especially now that I know I'm not back on the Gathendien ship."

Eliana waved a hand. "You don't have to worry about those guys anymore. We kicked their asses and took their ship."

Ava stared at her.

Dagon smiled. "It might be more accurate to say Eliana did most of the ass kicking while my men and I sat back and wagered over the outcome."

Eliana laughed. "Don't listen to him. He's being modest. Dagon and the guys kicked *plenty* of ass."

One corner of the commander's lips turned up. "Only because we were hoping that if we won your favor, you'd share some of your hoard of *jarumi* nuggets with us."

Eliana snapped her fingers. "That reminds me." She spun toward him. "Did you bring them?"

Dagon held up a bag.

"Yes!" Grabbing it, Eliana turned and held it out to her. "You *have* to try these, Ava. They're called *jarumi* nuggets, and they taste like nacho-cheese-flavored corn chips with some fancy alien spices. I'm totally addicted to them."

Motion at the back of the room drew everyone's attention.

A tall Segonian in a pale gray uniform entered, his focus on a data tablet he held. Glancing up, he stopped short. His eyebrows rose as he noted the small gathering. Then his gaze went to Eliana and his brows drew down in a frown.

Eyes widening, she hid the bag behind her back.

The man's eyes narrowed. "You weren't offering my patient *jarumi* nuggets, were you, Eliana?"

"No," she denied quickly.

He arched an imperious eyebrow.

Grimacing, she stopped hiding the bag. "Yes. I can't help it, Adaos. Med Bay food sucks."

He sighed as if the complaint weren't a new one.

Low murmurs of agreement sounded down the hallway from which he'd just exited.

Adaos swung toward it with a scowl.

Ava laughed.

So did everyone else present.

Leaning toward her, Eliana winked. "You're going to love it here."

———◆◇◆———

J AK'RI SAT ON ONE of the benches that ran along the walls of a large circular training room, Ziv'ri at his side. Segonian warriors crowded the rest of the seating area, all thoroughly entranced by the sparring that took place in the center of the room.

Jak'ri found himself entranced as well.

Commander Dagon entered and crossed to sit beside him.

Both were silent for several long moments as they watched the action.

"Amazing, aren't they?" Dagon commented with a smile.

Jak'ri nodded, his gaze never straying. "Yes, they are."

Eliana was training Ava, helping her explore and learn to wield the dramatically increased speed and strength she'd gained. Right now, they fought each other with wooden staffs, their movements so quick they blurred. Though the tops of their heads didn't even reach the chins of the men around them and both of the Earthlings combined weighed less than every warrior present, it was clear to all that either woman could easily pick up one of the warriors and hurl him across the room.

Whooshes filled the air as the women swung their staffs. Loud *clacks* followed when they made contact. Ava swam in and out of focus as she slowed, then sped up again.

Jak'ri smiled, a warm feeling unfurling in his chest and radiating outward.

She bloomed with good health now. As Ava battled her friend, her cheeks grew pink from exertion. Her eyes filled with excitement, once more shining with that arresting amber glow whenever emotion gripped her. And a smile seemed to perpetually light her beautiful face.

How he loved her.

"Has there been any word on the other missing Earthlings?" Ziv'ri asked.

Dagon sighed. "Regretfully, no."

It was the only dark spot that marred their days. Ava had been given private quarters down the hallway from Eliana and had insisted, cheeks flushing ever so slightly, that Jak'ri be allowed to share them with her. Ziv'ri had opted to bunk in the soldiers' barracks, having grown comfortable with the crew and made some friends during his longer sojourn on the ship. Both brothers trained daily with Segonian soldiers and were slowly rebuilding the muscle mass they'd lost.

To his great relief, Ava had already returned to a healthy weight.

The three of them ate well. They slept well... when Jak'ri wasn't making vigorous love with Ava. They laughed and teased.

They were happy... except for their concern for her still-missing friends.

"The life support in the Lasaran escape pods will run out soon," Ziv'ri commented.

If they didn't find the women before then...

"Such is our fear," Dagon murmured. "But every member nation of the Aldebarian Alliance is searching for them. And some who aren't members as well."

"You speak of Purvel?" Jak'ri asked. He and his brother had been fervently petitioning the ruler of Purvel to reconsider his stance on joining the alliance *and* on strengthening their planet's security.

The fact that Gathendiens had snatched two Purveli citizens right from the planet's surface without the Planetary Defense Administration's notice—*and* their intention to create a bioweapon they could release on Purvel—had been a sharp wake-up call. The Purveli sovereign was closer than ever to agreeing to an alliance and had sent two ships to aid in the search for the *Kandovar*'s survivors.

Dagon nodded. "We appreciate the aid from Purvel. The Akseli rebel, Janwar, is also helping."

Jak'ri's eyebrows flew up. "In truth?" Janwar was a rather notorious Akseli pirate who routinely flaunted the alliance's rules and had infuriated the leader of his own planet greatly enough to have a sizable bounty placed on his head.

None had yet been mad enough to pursue that bounty, of course. Janwar had a reputation for being ruthless when dealing with his enemies.

Again, Dagon nodded. "Apparently he has developed strong ties with Prince Taelon."

Ziv'ri grunted. "How did he manage that?"

Jak'ri wondered the same. Whereas the Lasarans were sticklers for rules, Janwar loved to break them.

"He located Prince Taelon's missing sister."

Jak'ri shared a look of surprise with Ziv'ri. "*Janwar* is the one who located Princess Amiriska?"

"Yes." Dagon's lips curled up in a wry smile. "Apparently the man excels at gathering information."

Since he operated outside the law, Jak'ri supposed that gave him a distinct advantage.

"He also safely conveyed Prince Taelon, his Earthling lifemate Lisa, and their baby to Lasara."

That Jak'ri had already known because he had been present when Ava spoke to Lisa via the *Ranasura's* holocomm system the first time.

His attention returned to the center of the room when Eliana called, "Halt."

The small, blurred forms stilled.

Both women wore black pants and black sleeveless shirts that revealed pale, lightly muscled skin.

"That was excellent," Eliana praised.

Ava beamed. "Really?"

"Absolutely. You nearly knocked me off my feet twice." She smiled. "Why don't we stop there? We can pick it up again tomorrow."

"Okay. Thanks." Ava gave her friend a hug, returned the staff to the rack, and headed toward Jak'ri. "How was I?" she asked as she stopped before him.

He smiled. "Utterly fierce."

Grinning, she gave him a quick kiss.

Ziv'ri rose to provide her with a place to sit.

But she waved him back down and sat on Jak'ri's lap. "I'm all sweaty. Do you mind?"

Jak'ri grinned. "Not at all." *Your sweaty skin has been melded to mine on numerous pleasurable occasions,* he murmured telepathically, calling to mind the many times they'd lost themselves in ardently exploring each other's bodies.

Flushing, she leaned against him. *Flirt.*

In the center of the room, Eliana twirled her staff and addressed the room. "Okay," she said with a grin, "whose ass am I going to kick today?"

Almost every warrior present threw a hand up to volunteer.

Laughing, she pointed. "Looks like it's your turn, Maarev."

A burly warrior strode forward, catching the staff another tossed to him.

"How fast do you think I can knock you off your feet today, big guy?" she taunted with a friendly smile.

He grinned. "Not as fast as I can knock you off yours."

In the next instant, the fighting began. Eliana bore that same fantastical speed that amazed him so much in Ava. Jak'ri expected her to conquer the other warrior within seconds. But the Segonian surprised him by activating his full-body camouflage.

In a flash, he disappeared, blending seamlessly in with the background. His staff dropped to the floor.

Vuan, Jak'ri wished he had access to that technology. No one was sure how the Segonians managed to do that, so it gave them one *srul* of an advantage in battle.

Eliana abandoned her staff, too, and stood poised for action, her expression alert.

Loud calls burst from the small crowd, some favoring Eliana, some favoring Maarev.

Jak'ri didn't know how Ava's friend could possibly defeat an opponent she couldn't see and—

Eliana spun suddenly and struck out with a kick.

A thud sounded. Then Maarev reappeared, sprawled on the floor on the opposite side of the room.

Jak'ri gaped.

Eliana grinned. "That's for sitting next to me after you ate *mamitwa* last night."

Laughter erupted.

Ava looked at Dagon. "They all love her, don't they?"

He smiled. "Every one of them."

Shaking her head with a smile, she patted Jak'ri's hands and rose. "I'm thirsty. Want to come with me to get a drink?"

"Of course."

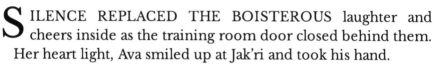

S ILENCE REPLACED THE BOISTEROUS laughter and cheers inside as the training room door closed behind them.

Her heart light, Ava smiled up at Jak'ri and took his hand.

He looked good. Healthy. Rested. Relaxed. And so incredibly handsome.

Butterflies fluttered in her belly as she led him toward their quarters.

"Don't you want to go to the mess hall?" he asked.

"No. Our room will do. Once I quench my thirst, I could use a shower." Leaning closer, she said in a loud whisper, "And if you play your cards right, you can join me."

A chuckle rumbled up from his chest as his lips stretched in a grin.

Damn, she loved him.

As soon as they entered their room and closed the door, Ava dropped his hand and opened her mouth to deliver the news she'd withheld until they were alone.

"Greetings, Ava," the ship's computer said in a calm, female voice. "You have one new message from—"

"Not now, CC," she blurted, her eyes meeting Jak'ri's.

He smiled. "Eager for that shower, are you?" Resting his hands on her hips, he drew her closer. "I admit I am, too. It's been far too long."

She laughed. "We just made love this morning."

Bending his head, he nuzzled her neck. "Exactly. *Far* too long."

Tingles flared to life at the touch of his lips and raced to the rest of her body. But Ava tamped them down. "There's something I want to tell you."

Raising his head, he stared down at her. He must have sensed the import of her news, because all sensual playfulness left his expression. "What is it?"

Ava rested her hands on his chest. "Lisa and Taelon arranged for me to speak with Queen Adironsia and King Dasheon." She had never spoken to royalty before, so she'd been beset by nerves when she'd addressed the Lasaran monarchs this morning.

Dread entered his beloved features. "Do they wish the Segonians to convey you to Lasara?"

"That's what I wanted to talk to them about. I told them I had agreed to travel to Lasara to see if I could find a lifemate among the Lasaran men and help them repopulate their planet after the Gathendiens' bioweapon had reduced their numbers, but that I hadn't anticipated being kidnapped by Gathendiens or"—she smiled up at him—"falling wildly in love with you."

She heard his heartbeat pick up, felt it pound beneath her fingertips. "I told them, with all due respect, that I can no longer envision myself being happy with anyone but you and asked them to please relieve me of my obligations."

His throat worked in a swallow. "What did they say?"

"They apologized for failing to ensure my safety and for everything I've endured. They told me I would always have a home on Lasara." She slid her arms around him and locked them at the base of his spine. "But if my heart is with you, they wish us an eternity of happiness together and will provide me with whatever I need to start a life with you on Purvel."

A long sigh slipped from him as he dipped his chin and pressed his forehead to hers. "*Will* you start a life with me on Purvel, Ava?"

She smiled. "Purvel. Lasara. K-54973. Even Promeii 7. I'll start a life with you anywhere, Jak'ri."

He huffed a laugh. "*Not* on Promeii 7. That planet is insane."

She smiled. "So I've heard." Then uncertainty rose. "They also told me that—now that the Gathendiens have inadvertently transformed me into an Immortal Guardian—there are measures we can take to prevent you from aging. Measures the Sectas can provide us with that would enable us to always be together."

"Truly?"

She nodded.

He tilted his head to one side. "Though the Sectas often seem a cold, clinical race, I *have* heard that they highly value love."

Ava plucked at the fabric of his shirt. "Is that... something you think might interest you?"

"Living forever with you?"

"Yes." Becoming an Immortal Guardian would lose pretty much all of its appeal if she had to watch Jak'ri grow old and die.

He pressed his lips to her forehead. "I can think of nothing that would interest me more."

Relief suffused her as she relaxed against him.

"Do you think I'll fit in on Purvel?" she asked, though that question didn't trouble her as much now that she'd watched Eliana interact with Dagon and his crew.

Jak'ri smiled. "My family and my people will love you as much as the Segonians love Eliana."

She grinned. "The Segonians love Eliana a *lot*."

He chuckled. "Yes, they do." Then his lips found hers in a tender kiss. "And I love you, *sakara*."

Her heart swelled. "I love you, too."

He kissed her again, longer and deeper this time. "Be my lifemate so I can once more view the future with joy."

She nodded. "I'll be your lifemate, *sakara*. And you'll be mine. Together we can do anything."

"And be happy while we do it," he murmured before capturing her lips in a heated exploration that soon left her desperate for more. "Now about that shower..."

She laughed.

FROM THE AUTHOR

THANK YOU FOR READING *The Purveli*. I hope you enjoyed Ava and Jak'ri's story. It was such a pleasure to write. For those who are new to the Aldebarian Alliance series, you can learn more about what happened to Ziv'ri and get to know Eliana in *The Segonian*. You can also see what Eliana's life was like before she embarked upon her space adventure and witness the mischief she got into with her hurting partner, Nick, in *Broken Dawn*, a stand-alone novel in my Immortal Guardians series.

If you enjoyed this book, please consider rating or reviewing it at an online retailer of your choice. I appreciate your support so much and am always thrilled when I see that one of my books made a reader happy. Ratings and reviews are also an excellent way to recommend an author's books, create word of mouth, and help other readers find new favorites.

Want to find out what happens next in the Aldebarian Alliance series? Keep reading for a sneak peek into *THE AKSELI* (Aldebarian Alliance: Book 4).

SNEAK PEEK—THE AKSELI

Aldebarian Alliance: Book 4

J ANWAR STARED AT THE endless array of stars that
stretched before them. Quiet reigned on the bridge of the
Tangata, a ship so technologically advanced that no other
currently in existence could match it. An absolute beauty, it
boasted engines that made Aldebarian Alliance ships appear to
plod along like ancient *navoxi* pulling wagonloads of *alavinin* ore
in comparison.

A good thing, since Janwar and his crew were pirates and often
benefited from their ability to outmaneuver the law-abiding
folk.

He glanced around.

His crew was oddly quiet tonight. Did they share the same
peculiar feeling of unrest that had been plaguing him of late?

He frowned, unable to pinpoint the source of it.

"I miss Lisa," Soval announced. The hulking Kilessian warrior
slumped in his seat, face more somber than usual.

"And Abby," Elchan, the Segonian in their midst, added.

The rest nodded.

Janwar smiled, thinking of Lasaran Prince Taelon and the Earth
female he'd taken as his lifemate. Janwar actually considered
Taelon a friend, as implausible as that seemed to others. Lasarans
were well known for being stringent rule-followers. So for a
Lasaran Prince to befriend a consummate lawbreaker like
Janwar...

He grinned. Both men rather enjoyed the bafflement their
friendship inspired. When Srok'a had recently been stricken
with a vision that compelled them to race to the outer reaches of

explored space, Janwar had been shocked to discover that Prince Taelon's ship had been attacked and destroyed.

Fortunately, Taelon's Yona guard had shoved him and his new family into a royal transport and launched it in time to save their lives. Then Janwar had swept in and rescued them.

He'd enjoyed Lisa's company in the month it had taken them to ferry the royal couple to Lasara. No other woman had stepped foot on their ship since its creation. And he had to admit her tinkling laughter had breathed new life into it. The Earthling had not experienced the lofty upbringing Prince Taelon had. Quite the opposite, actually. And she was delightfully uncomfortable with being treated like royalty, something that had amused his hardened, cynical crew and swiftly won them over.

None of them, of course, had been able to resist the plump-cheeked grins and high-pitched giggles of Abby, Taelon and Lisa's infant daughter.

"Hopefully our usual methods of investigation will enable us to locate some of her friends," Janwar commented.

At last count, only three of the fifteen women from Earth who'd been aboard the *Kandovar* had been rescued. The rest, some presumed, were either dead or soon would be when the provisions in their escape pods ran out. Taelon had disclosed in their latest communication that one of the rescued women—Ava, he believed her name was—had been captured by the Gathendiens and tortured, confirming their suspicions that the Gathendiens had risked everything and attacked the *Kandovar* solely to get their hands on the Earthlings.

Apparently, they believed the Earth women were the key to discovering why a bioengineered virus the Gathendiens released on Earth long ago hadn't succeeded in eradicating all Earthlings and leaving the planet and all its resources ripe for claiming.

"*Grunarks*," he grumbled.

His cousin Krigara glanced over at him. "Who?"

"The Gathendiens."

All nodded.

Janwar looked at Srok'a. "How much longer?"

His navigations officer studied his screen. "We should be able to see them without radar within minutes."

Good. Most pirates' strengths lay in their numbers, the weaponry they accumulated, and their complete lack of a moral compass.

Janwar and his small crew's strength, however, lay in the intelligence they gathered and how they chose to use it.

A primary source of his intel had located a Gathendien warship that had gone undetected by the Aldebarian Alliance's various fleets, which—lacking the *Tangata's* astonishingly powerful engines—still struggled to reach these distances without the benefit of the damaged *qhov'rum*.

The Gathendien ship was close enough to the wreckage of the *Kandovar* to draw suspicion and spark speculation that it had either taken part in the attack or was searching for survivors to either slay or capture.

Janwar leaned forward in his seat as a spec appeared among the stars visible beyond the large, indestructible crystal window that stretched before them. "There it is," he murmured.

"In all its *drekking* glory," Krigara muttered. "I don't know how they manage to travel such distances in those boxes of *bura*."

Janwar nodded. The Gathendien ship that gradually grew in size as they approached it looked as if a boy not quite old enough to grow a beard had constructed it out of spare parts scavenged from a refuse heap. Even the color—a dark, putrid yellow that reminded him of vomit—lacked appeal.

"Any indication they know we're coming?" he asked.

"None," Srok'a's scarred brother Kova mumbled.

Any other answer would've shocked Janwar. His ship's cloaking ability was unmatched, so ships only saw the *Tangata* coming if he *wanted* them to see it coming.

In very little time, the Gathendien battleship filled the window.

"Perform a life-form scan and see how many are on board," he ordered.

Elchan studied his console. "Looks like they have a full contingent aboard."

Janwar rubbed his hands together with glee. "This should be fun then."

Every face lit with a smile of anticipation. All loved a good battle. It got the blood flowing and distracted them from the loneliness their status as rebels and outcasts sometimes spawned.

"That's odd," Elchan said, brow puckering.

Janwar glanced at him. "What is?"

"I think the life-form scanner may be malfunctioning."

"Why?"

Elchan looked up from his console. "The Gathendiens' numbers appear to be dwindling."

Janwar stared at him. "What?"

"Their numbers are dwindling." Elchan again consulted his screen, then pointed at it. "There! It just did it again. Two more disappeared. And a third."

Krigara crossed to stand beside Elchan and studied the screen. His eyebrows shot up. "It's true. The lights indicating life forms are vanishing, one or two at a time." He nudged Elchan. "Run a diagnostic."

Silence reigned.

After a moment, Elchan shook his head. "Nothing. The scan appears to be performing as intended."

"It can't be," Soval grumbled.

Janwar regarded the Gathendien warship with suspicion.

"Could they have obtained some sort of new cloaking mechanism?" Elchan asked hesitantly.

Srok'a scowled. "To borrow one of Lisa's phrases, what kind of backward-ass cloaking mechanism cloaks the life forms but not the ship?"

"Good point," Kova added. "The ship is still visible."

Krigara motioned to Elchan's screen. "But according to the scan, it will soon be bereft of life."

Janwar's eyes narrowed. "It's a trick. They must know we're here."

"How?" Krigara countered. "We have the best cloaking system in the galaxy."

Which wasn't an exaggeration. "The life forms didn't start disappearing until we came within shooting range of them. They *must* know we're here." It was odd, though, that they would conceal their life forms—and in such a ragged fashion—instead of the ship itself. Perhaps they hoped anyone approaching would think it a ghost ship bereft of life and become complacent? Or maybe they hoped other vessels would see the life forms disappearing one by one and fear contagion? Gathendiens did, after all, make a habit of genetically engineering deadly viruses in their labs.

"What do you want to do?" his cousin asked.

"Get close enough to board them," Janwar ordered.

Before Kova could navigate them closer, Elchan shook his head. "I don't think that's a good idea."

"Why?"

"Because I'm detecting heat signatures that weren't there a minute ago."

"More life forms?" Their bizarre cloaking device must be failing.

"No."

"What *kind* of heat signatures?"

"The kind that usually accompany explosions."

Silence.

What the *srul* was happening on that ship?

"Maybe their cloaking array is malfunctioning?" Srok'a suggested, his tone revealing his doubt.

But Elchan shook his head again. "Not unless by *malfunctioning* you mean blowing them all up, because—if my scanner is correct—Gathendiens are dropping like *tikluns*." The fuzzy mammals on Segonia were known for keeling over as though dead anytime something startled them.

Janwar refused to let the rather amusing image of Gathendiens doing the same thing distract him. "Whatever is happening, we need the information those *grunarks* can provide." Time was running out for the survivors of the *Kandovar's* destruction. "Kova, pull up beside them and extend the docking tube. Soval, run a full diagnostic on all systems. If our life-form scan is malfunctioning, I want to know what else might be, too."

Soval refocused on his console and went to work.

Kova began to ease the *Tangata* closer to the Gathendien ship.

"Wait," Srok'a said.

Janwar sighed. "Now what?"

"One of the docking bay doors is rising."

"Then it *is* a trap." Janwar relaxed back in his seat, happy to be back on normal footing. "Arm weapons. Reinforce shields and cloaking."

"Weapons armed," Soval announced.

"Shields and cloaking at full power," Elchan said.

Janwar turned to his cousin. "Krigara, get in a fighter and prepare to chase whatever leaves that bay. Wait for my command."

Krigara strode from the bridge.

Janwar stared at the Gathendien ship as a crack of light appeared along the bottom of the docking bay door.

Air and debris shot out as it rose.

"Their atmospheric shield must be down," he murmured. Had it been in place, it would've maintained proper atmosphere and pressure in the bay so crew members could continue to perform their duties as craft came and went.

Soval grunted. "I hope they evacuated the bay before—"

Several Gathendiens tumbled out into space, limbs flailing, reptilian tails flicking, and mouths opening in screams no one could hear in the vacuum of space.

None wore protective suits. All died.

Had Janwar not direly needed information, he would've cheered. As far as he was concerned, the only good Gathendien was a dead Gathendien.

A figure in a white protective suit was nearly sucked out after them but managed to grab hold of the edge of the bay's opening and jerked to a halt.

Janwar grunted. At least they'd found *someone* they could interrogate.

A small transport zoomed out of the bay, nearly dislodging the man who clung to the edge.

Janwar tapped the ship-wide comm button on his command chair. "Krigara, are you ready?"

"Almost there."

"Get your ass in the seat now. A transport just left the ship."

Curses carried over the line, accompanied by the thuds of boots hitting the deck at a brisk pace.

Janwar scrutinized the transport. It was Akseli in design and created more for fleeing enemies than for finding refuge in an emergency, so it would be faster than most transports. He didn't worry though. The *Tangata* could easily catch it, as could their fighter craft.

"What the *srul*?" Elchan muttered.

Janwar returned his gaze to the Gathendiens' docking bay.

The figure clinging to the bay's frame wore a helmet that hid his features and a baggy white suit that lacked any noticeable accommodation for the long tail every Gathendien sported.

"That's not a Gathendien," Elchan stated.

Janwar considered the figure thoughtfully. "Perhaps he lost his tail in an accident." The *grunarks were* prone to violence.

Drawing his knees almost to his chest, the figure in white shifted until his feet were braced on the edge of the bay. But he didn't make his way inside as they all expected. Instead, he looked out at the transport for a long moment, then pushed off. Hard.

"What the *drek* is he doing?"

"Are you *drekking* seeing this?"

Janwar ignored his friends' comments and focused on the figure.

Was he trying to catch up with his shipmates?

To what end? Even if he miraculously managed to utilize exactly the right speed and trajectory, it wasn't as though the shuttle could just open the hatch and let him in. That wasn't how transports worked. Once in space, the only way a shuttle could safely open its hatch was if a ship locked a docking tube to it that was capable of pressurization and—if they were smart— decontamination.

But the likelihood of the figure who currently cut through space with the speed of a *morilium* missile even coming close enough to the shuttle to—

"*Drek!*" Elchan blurted. "I think he's going to make it."

Janwar stared. *Vuan* if it didn't look like it. And yet... "He's going too fast to find a handhold."

Srok'a's face lit with excitement. "I'll wager fifty credits that he makes it."

"Done," Soval responded, leaning forward.

Bets began to fly as swiftly as the figure in white did.

"Ha!" Srok'a crowed as the figure grabbed hold of one of the transport's exterior ladder rungs and held on tight. "He did it!"

Those who bet against him all groaned.

Soval shook his head. "What does he intend to do now—cling to the exterior until the pilot finds a place to land?"

If so, the atmosphere of any habitable planet they sought to land upon would burn him up.

"Where exactly is the craft going?" Elchan asked, his expression baffled.

Janwar leaned back in his chair. "He's fleeing *us*. They know we're here."

"How?" Elchan countered. "I'm still seeing nothing that indicates our systems aren't fully functional. We're still cloaked. They *can't* know we're here."

Krigara's voice floated out of the bridge speakers. "I'm in the fighter. Do you want me to deploy?"

"Hold for a moment," Janwar murmured. He wanted to see what would happen next.

The figure in white crept along the exterior of the transport until he reached the front window. Tucking one arm in a handhold, he raised what looked like a *tronium* blaster in his other hand and fired.

Soval grunted. "He must be new."

All nodded. Every space-faring craft—large or small—constructed during the past two centuries bore windows made of indestructible *stovicun* crystal. If the *Kandovar* had indeed been destroyed, Janwar did not doubt that the dislodged windows still floated through space, wholly intact, sporting nary a crack.

When it became clear that the window would not break, the figure holstered his weapon and gave the occupants a gesture known throughout alliance-occupied space to be obscene.

Elchan laughed. "I don't think he appreciates being left behind."

Janwar battled amusement as the figure crept along the shuttle's exterior once more. "Any movement from the warship?"

Kova shook his head. "All is quiet there. Engines appear to be at full stop."

This was so odd. "Follow the transport." They'd piqued his curiosity now.

The transport began to swing back and forth in an attempt to shake off their furious shipmate. But the white figure clung tenaciously to its surface. Not far from the shuttle's front window, he again anchored himself to the shuttle with one hand and fired a continuous stream from his *tronium* blaster at the edge of the hatch.

Quiet fell once more as all watched, unable to guess the outcome.

"What's happening?" Krigara asked.

"The figure in white is trying to cut into the transport." Janwar nodded to Srok'a. "Send him the feed."

A moment later, his cousin let out a disbelieving laugh.

Elchan frowned. "He can't actually cut his way in, can he?"

"With a *tronium* blaster?" Janwar shook his head. "It might heat the metal enough to make those inside nervous, but it won't penetrate or puncture it."

"What are those things on his back?" Krigara muttered.

Two dark stripes Janwar had originally thought part of the suit's design moved back and forth as the figure was jostled. "Enhance visual."

The image of the transport grew and sharpened, as did that of the figure in white.

He frowned. "I think they're swords."

As though hearing him, the figure holstered his blaster and drew a long sword. He took a moment to reposition himself on the transport's surface, kneeling in such a way that both feet were wedged beneath a handrail. Angling the blade downward in front of him, he gripped the handle at the top, drew it back over his head, then plunged it down into the metal he'd just heated.

Janwar stared.

Again the man drew his sword up and drove it down into the metal.

"That *grunark* is *really* determined," Elchan said.

Too bad he wouldn't succeed. Janwar actually found himself rooting for the odd figure. Aside from rescuing Taelon, Lisa, and Abby, this was the most entertaining thing he'd witnessed in years.

But even heated, that metal wouldn't give. It was designed to withstand atmospheric entry and planetary temperatures that would instantly kill— "What the *drek?*" he blurted and leaned forward once more.

A little plume of atmosphere rose in front of the figure.

"Did he just pierce the hatch?" Soval asked, eyes wide.

"How is that possible?" Krigara blurted, watching the feed down in his fighter craft.

Janwar could only stare. "I don't know."

Again the sword rose and descended.

He actually saw it sink into the hatch's edge this time! No being Janwar knew of possessed the strength to accomplish that aside from the cyborgs the Akseli military had created.

Yet that was no cyborg. He knew it with absolute certainty. The Akseli had announced years ago that they'd decommissioned and destroyed all their biomechanical creations. The chances of encountering one on a Gathendien ship were nonexistent.

The plume of venting atmosphere grew.

Returning his sword to the sheath on his back with an ease that bespoke years of practice, the figure reached down and tugged at something.

Janwar gaped as the man wrenched the hatch open, exposing the cramped control room and the panicked Gathendien warriors inside.

None wore suits. Some bore weapons that venting atmosphere yanked out of their hands and deposited outside. All scrambled to hold on to something. One was sucked out into space, arms, legs, and tail waving. The figure in white reached in and yanked another out as easily as he would a helpless little *gravi* even though the Gathendien was big and bulky with muscle. Then he yanked out another and another, something that became easier as the cold and absence of breathable air slowed their struggles and weakened their hold.

A hush settled upon the bridge of the *Tangata* as all watched in stunned fascination.

His mission apparently complete, the figure in white sat back on his heels—toes still tucked in a handhold—rested his hands on his thighs, and lowered his head as though catching his breath.

Janwar had never seen anything like it. "Any movement in the warship?"

"None," Elchan said. "Only a few life forms remain. None are moving."

"And the ship is stationary," Kova added. "It's as if all engines have been shut off."

Janwar kept his gaze on the white figure.

"What do you want to do?" Kova asked.

He pondered it a moment. "Disable cloaking."

How would the figure in white react when an unidentified warship suddenly appeared beside him?

"Disabling cloaking."

Janwar knew the moment the figure saw them from the corner of his eye. His heaving chest stilled. His helmet rose. Then the faceplate turned their way, their massive ship reflected upon its surface.

A heartbeat passed. Then the figure threw up his hands in a gesture of exasperation Janwar had seen Lisa make a time or two while she blurted, "Are you kidding me?"

Vuan if it didn't make him smile and bite back a laugh.

Some of his crew didn't bother, their laughter filling the bridge.

"I'm starting to like this man," Soval declared, his deep voice full of mirth.

Janwar was, too. But he would still have to capture and interrogate him... along with the rest of the Gathendien crew.

The figure in white clambered inside the transport and disappeared from view.

Like the Gathendien warship, the transport now floated before them like a ghost ship. "He isn't going anywhere," Janwar decided after a minute or two. "Elchan, I want you to join Krigara in his fighter and board the Gathendien ship. We need to know if those life-form scans are accurate. Gear up in case they are. There may be a contagion of some sort."

Elchan left the bridge.

Janwar turned to the Rakessian brothers. "Srok'a, Kova, take a second fighter and accompany them."

Nodding, the two rose and departed.

If the scans were wrong and the ship was still heavily populated with soldiers, Janwar was confident the four would nevertheless be able to take out enough Gathendiens to commandeer the ship. They weren't the most feared pirates in the galaxy for no reason.

He and Soval waited quietly, dividing their attention between the transport and the warship.

Two sleek fighters raced toward the ugly Gathendien ship and boldly entered the docking bay.

Long minutes passed.

"Looks like someone disabled the atmospheric shield from inside the bay," Krigara commented.

Janwar frowned. "Is it still operational?" He needed live Gathendiens to question.

"Give me a minute." One minute stretched into several. "Got it," he said with a touch of triumph. "We're going in."

Mere seconds ticked past before curses erupted over the comm.

"I see why the one in white didn't want to be left behind," Krigara commented. "There are a *srul* of a lot of dead bodies here."

Janwar frowned. "How many?"

"Enough to make me think the life-form scan was accurate."

"Cause of death?"

"Battle," Krigara disclosed grimly. "This was no contagion."

"Stay alert." Janwar and his crew weren't the only pirates in the galaxy. Another party could've snuck aboard the last time the Gathendiens docked, intending to wrench control from them.

A quick search of the ship yielded more dead and several wounded. All of the latter were unconscious but would likely survive.

Yet the ship appeared to be free of hostile forces.

What had happened? Had there been a mutiny?

Janwar's gaze slid to the transport.

Had the figure in white been trying to *escape* the bloodbath, or had he *instigated* it?

"Elchan, lock down the bridge controls. Then I want you all to return to the *Tangata*."

"Yes, sir."

If one man had wrought that much damage, he wanted his entire crew back on board when they confronted him. That was a *srul* of an amazing feat. Gathendiens did *not* go down easily. Their thick reptilian hide was difficult to penetrate with a blade and could even withstand a few e-blasts. Throw in fear of the punishment their volatile emperor would mete out to any who failed in their missions and they became even harder to kill, most choosing to fight to the death rather than face his wrath.

Janwar studied the transport and detected not even a hint of movement inside it.

Once his men returned, he and Soval confirmed the *Tangata's* shields were still functioning at maximum efficiency then headed down to the docking bay, pausing only long enough to visit the armory.

Krigara, Elchan, Srok'a, and Kova exited two fighter craft and discarded their protective suits as Janwar and Soval entered the bay. Once everyone armed up with O-rifles and Bex-7 stun grenades, they retreated to the safe zone near the innermost wall. A small control station resided in front of it, boasting multiple consoles and data entry pads.

At the press of a button, an invisible shield rose up in front of them that could withstand the direct hit from a missile.

Beyond the open bay door, the transport floated placidly against a midnight backdrop that sparkled with distant stars.

Janwar glanced at Kova. "Bring the transport aboard."

Kova stepped up to one of the stations. "Locking acquisition beam now."

A beam of light shot forth from the wall behind them and streaked toward the idle transport. As soon as it touched the shuttle, the light spread like water until it engulfed the entire surface, effectively closing off the open hatch so the figure inside could not escape.

Not that the figure tried.

Janwar found himself hoping the man wasn't dead in there. He'd like to see the face of the one who had managed to conquer so many... and ask why he'd done it. Was he an assassin who had merely plowed through all the other Gathendiens to reach his intended target? Was he the sole survivor of a small pirate crew who had attempted to commandeer the ship? Was he perhaps someone seeking vengeance?

The Gathendiens had amassed an impressive list of enemies.

If the figure were any of the above, he might just be worth recruiting.

Guided by the acquisition beam, the mangled transport floated into the hangar and made a gentle descent to the deck. Magnetic clamps rose from the floor and locked onto the new arrival with a series of thunks.

The beam shut off.

"Seal the bay," Janwar murmured.

The large bay door began to lower, shutting off the view of space.

"If nothing else," Krigara murmured, "we've acquired another transport. Once we repair the hatch and rid it of the Gathendiens' stench, it'll make a nice addition to our fleet."

Janwar nodded absently.

The figure inside the transport opted not to make an appearance.

"Do you want a *ziyil*?" his cousin asked.

"Not yet." Raising his voice so the figure in white would be able to hear him, he called, "You may exit of your own accord, or we can force your hand. The choice is yours."

A faint sound reached their ears.

Soval arched his brows. "Was that a snort?"

Janwar would've answered in the affirmative, but the figure in white chose that moment to step into the open hatch. After pausing a moment to sweep the bay with what Janwar guessed was a very discerning gaze that missed nothing, the figure hopped down, landing nimbly on the deck.

He was smaller than Janwar had supposed. Clearly the baggy suit he wore had been made for someone larger.

The figure raised his wrist, drew back a flap, and consulted the screen embedded in the suit.

Was he confirming that the bay had a breathable atmosphere?

"No blasters or O-rifles," Krigara whispered. "His only weapons appear to be the swords."

The figure's helmet turned in their direction.

Had he heard Krigara? If so, his helmet must be amplifying sound because Janwar had barely heard his cousin, and he was standing right next to him.

Circumventing the shield, Janwar strode toward the newcomer. Krigara remained behind to man the controls should the figure choose to attack. The rest of the crew followed Janwar and fanned out behind him.

A heartbeat passed.

In a bafflingly fast blur of motion, the figure suddenly doffed his suit.

Someone sucked in a breath.

Janwar's eyes widened.

Or rather *her* suit. A slender woman garbed all in black now stood before them: black pants with many pockets, a form-fitting black shirt that hugged a narrow waist and full breasts, and heavy black boots that were similar to those he and his crew wore.

The fingers of both small hands now clutched the handles of long, gleaming swords.

Janwar stared. Her clothing was torn in several places. Her pale skin bore multiple gashes and splashes of red blood. Her long black hair shone beneath the bay's lights. And her face...

She was beautiful... even with a scowl creasing her forehead and her jaw jutting forward in defiance.

Judging by her appearance, she was a Lasaran, a Segonian, or an Earthling. Segonian women tended to be taller, often matching the men in height. And a Segonian soldier facing a possible enemy would've long since activated her camouflage. So he omitted that option. Her smaller build resembled that of a Lasaran woman. But a Lasaran wouldn't wear a shirt with sleeves short enough to bare her arms the way this woman did. Which left... Earthling?

Could they be so lucky? Could they have inadvertently stumbled upon one of the very beings they hoped to rescue?

Not that this woman *needed* rescuing, he thought with growing admiration.

She *did* remind him a little of Lisa in appearance.

Lisa was an Earthling. But her eyes were a soft brown. This woman's bore a bright amber glow that fascinated him.

Srul, everything about her fascinated him.

When he and his crew continued to stand there in what he hated to admit was dumbfounded silence, she arched a brow.

"Well, boys, are you friend or foe?" She spoke Earth English but with an accent Lisa had lacked. "If you're friend, I'm afraid I must take my leave of you. There are a few Gathendien bastards left that I need to slay before I steal their ship. And if you're foe..." She swung her swords in a showy display, then sent them a wicked smile. "Whose ass am I going to kick first?"

ACKNOWLEDGEMENTS

As always, I want to thank Crystal. I've said it before, and I'll say it again: You're amazing. I don't know what I'd do without you. Members of the Street Team and Books Group feel the same. I hope you know how much we all appreciate you.

I also want to send love, hugs, and a huge thank you to my fabulous Street Team. You all are *awesome*!! Your continued support means the world to me. Another big thank you goes to the members of my Dianne Duvall Books Group on Facebook. I have so much fun in there with you. And like my Street Team, I can always count on you to make me laugh and smile.

Thank you, Kirsten Potter, for giving the many characters that people my stories unique and entertaining voices that continue to delight listeners. It's such a joy to work with you.

And, of course, I want thank all of the wonderful readers who have picked up my books and audiobooks. You've made living my dream possible. Thank you for joining me on this exciting journey. I wish you all the best.

ABOUT THE AUTHOR

Dianne Duvall is the *New York Times* and *USA Today* Bestselling Author of the acclaimed **Immortal Guardians** paranormal romance series, the exciting new **Aldebarian Alliance** sci-fi romance series, and **The Gifted Ones** medieval and time-travel romance series. She is known for writing stories full of action that will keep you flipping pages well past your bedtime, strong heroes who adore strong heroines, lovable secondary characters, swoon-worthy romance, and humor that readers frequently complain makes them laugh out loud at inappropriate moments.

AudioFile Magazine chose *The Segonian* (Aldebarian Alliance Book 2) as one of the Best Audiobooks of 2021. *The Lasaran* (Aldebarian Alliance Book 1) was a #1 Audible Mover & Shaker. And Audible chose her Immortal Guardians audiobook *Awaken the Darkness* as one of the Top 5 Best Paranormal Romances of 2018.

Reviewers have called Dianne's books "fast-paced and humorous" (*Publishers Weekly*), "utterly addictive" (*RT Book Reviews*), "extraordinary" (*Long and Short Reviews*), and "wonderfully imaginative" (*The Romance Reviews*). Her audiobooks have been awarded AudioFile Earphone Awards for excellence. One was nominated for a prestigious Audie Award. And her books have twice been nominated for RT Reviewers' Choice Awards.

When she isn't writing, Dianne is active in the independent film industry and has even appeared on-screen, crawling out of a moonlit grave and wielding a machete like some of the psychotic vampires she creates in her books.

For the latest news on upcoming releases, contests, and more, please visit **www.dianneduvall.com**. You can also connect with Dianne online:

Subscribe to Dianne's Newsletter

Join the Dianne Duvall Books Group

Join Diann'e Street Team

Follow Dianne on BookBub

Dianne's Amazon Author Page

Dianne's Blog

Facebook

Instagram

Twitter

YouTube

Pinterest

Printed in Great Britain
by Amazon